SWORDS & CELL PHONES

TRACY A. BALL

Black Rose Writing | Texas

The author grants the final approval for this literary material.

First printing

This is a work of fiction. Names, characters, businesses, places, events, and
incidents are either the products of the author's imagination or used in a
fictitious manner. Any resemblance to actual persons, living or dead, or
actual events is purely coincidental.

ISBN: 978-1-68433-980-8
PUBLISHED BY BLACK ROSE WRITING
www.blackrosewriting.com

Printed in the United States of America
Suggested Retail Price (SRP) $21.95

Swords & Cell Phones is printed in Calluna

*As a planet-friendly publisher, Black Rose Writing does its best to eliminate
unnecessary waste to reduce paper usage and energy costs, while never
compromising the reading experience. As a result, the final word count vs. page
count may not meet common expectations.

For Matt and Kelly, who not only indulge my quests,
but often accompany me.

For Malakai and Octavia— the most magical beings in the world.

For Debi— for always being there, ready to catch me.

For Brian— the real "writer" in the family.

And for Mommie. Thank you for telling me a story.

THE RACES OF MAYADAL

Elves

Elves are a step away from Angels. They are almost pure and cannot function in an evil capacity. They are immortal as far as their life span. As a rule, they do not get sick, nor do they grow old. However, they can be mortally wounded.

Jodians

Jodians are a crossbreed of Elves and mankind. They do not live forever, but their life spans several thousand years. The blessing/curse of being a Jodian is they are influenced by their environment. In Mayadal, they are Elve-like, however, in Universe; they tend to become more humanized. When they are good they are angelically good, but being bad is easy.

Lephans

Lephans are essentially evil. They have the most knowledge and the least power. What they really want is power. Unfortunately, they are smart enough to get it. The Lephan life span is different in that they are both mortal and immortal. They do not automatically move on. If they have chosen the harder, more purifying lifestyle, death may come easier and there is a better chance of it being final. If they have not subdued their evil nature, a type of reincarnation can happen. Their evilness may hold them to this life until they reach a point where the evil destroys itself. No one knows exactly what level of good or bad is required for either result.

PRONUNCIATION KEY

*Books 1 & 2

Aezilden:	As – zole - din
Amadyius:	Ā- may- dee- us
Ayrorn:	Ā – ron
Aydin:	Ā- din
Balazze:	Buh- laze
Bedalamon:	bed- da – la - mon
Beridan:	Bar- ra- dan
Cinnge:	Singe
Christif:	Chris – tiff
Craizor:	Crāy - zär
Crystyl:	Cry – style
Darqueon:	Där –cone- nee- in
Dayown:	Day - own
Eyise:	Eye - ese
Eyrorn:	Eye - ron
Guafs:	Gwaffs
Hangel:	Hang- gell
Inaye:	In - ā
Jarkripi:	Järk –rip- pee

Jodian:	Joe- dee - in
Kelmaragin:	Kell – mär – again
Karloptini:	Kär- lope- ta- knee
Kildar:	Kill - där
Kiylonas:	Key – lone - us
Ledan:	Lee- dan
Lephans:	Lep - ponds
Loathel:	Low – thell
Mar`ek:	Mär - rick
Maldonus:	Mal-done-us
Mayadal:	My – uh – dale
Medrid:	Muh – drid
Monta`nae:	Mon - tuh – nay
Nagan:	Nag - gin
Narconess:	När- co - ness
Narlopami:	När- low- puh- me
Nijaj:	Nī - jah
Oclavia:	Oc – clave - via
Parrbrit:	Pär - brit
Queon:	Cony - on
Raegladun:	Ray – glad - done
Saeber:	Say - berr
Storr:	Store
Talazim:	Tal – luh –zim

Talive:	Tal – live
Tarrk:	Tärk
Tashnine:	Tash – nine
Telorena:	Tell – or – reen –a
Theokas:	Theo - cuss
Trill:	Trill
Tristole:	Trist - stole
Triune:	Try - oon
Twyla:	Twi - la
Vinneem:	Vin- neem
Walen:	Wale -len
Yaledemit:	Yail – duh - mitt
Zendelel:	Zen –dell - el

BASIC KELMARAGIN ALPHABET

uU	fF	K	L	O	Rp
a	b	c	d	e	f

v	X	aA	D	G	jJj
g	h	i	j	K	I

Z	p	I	s	bY	B
M	n	o	p	q	R

qV	h	Ee	N	Q	W
s	t	u	v	w	x

tT	dm
y	z

Note: There is no distinction between capital and lowercase letters.
The letter L is only written once in the Kalmaragin script when doubled.
i.e. full = RpEejJj

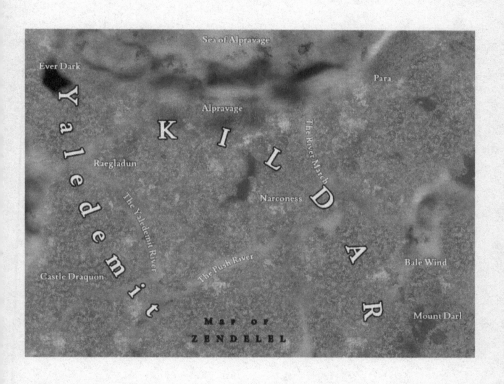

Sea of Alpravage

Ever Dark

Para

Y a l e d e m i t

Alpravage

K I L D A R

Raegladun

The River March

The Yaledemit River

Narconess

The Push River

Castle Draquon

Bale Wind

Mount Darl

MAP OF
ZENDELEL

*The Nephilim were on the earth in those days -and also afterwards- when the sons of God went to the daughters of men and had children by them. They were the heroes of old, men of renown. ~**Genesis 6:4***

*And it came to pass, when the children of men had multiplied that in those days were born to them beautiful and comely daughters. And the angels, the children of heaven saw and lusted after them, and said to one another: Come, let us choose us wives from among the children of men and beget us children. ~**The Book of Enoch***

Yearnings of her secret heart
Concealed within a sigh
No hand had ever touched it
Neither seen with eyes

Life within the modern world
Movement, sound, and action
Knew not what she needed
Gave no satisfaction

Upon the ancient hills he dwelled
The mystic woods he roamed
In a land outside of time
There he made his home

A thousand years, a million miles
A hundred days the same
He heard the yearning of her heart
He crossed them all, and came

PROLOGUE

MAYADAL

Lair. That is what they called it, a lair. It was the appropriate title, the only title, for any place he might abide, even a prison. Maldonus' lip curled with distaste as he scanned the book-lined wall, seeing volumes of technical journals and little else. He would know the how-to and what-for of every subject available. Yet there was nothing to engage his imagination, nothing to stimulate his mind. That was the real punishment.

He directed his sneer toward the windows, the cross rays of sunlight. Barred openings around him, above him, everywhere there was sunshine and much too much light. "Do they assume this will change my temperament?" he asked the air. "A silly thing to hope for. The wretched fools, how dare they cause this delay? No matter, they will suffer for this injustice." He hissed at the light. "But, the revenge must come first. No further interruption. No more infidels."

Reaching for a cooking journal, Maldonus dismissed the sun. Elegant as a king, he folded himself into a chair and opened the book. He smiled cruelly at a pasta dish on page eight. "Not that they can stop me," he told the eggplant-casserole on page nineteen. "Nothing can stop me." He paused over page twenty-six, interested in the drop-dead chocolate-mousse cake. "Not even death can stop me." He studied the ingredients.

***

One hundred eighty-four years later...

UNIVERSE

"Ahhhgggghhh—" Jalen sat up straight, holding his head, positive his brain had exploded. He couldn't move, couldn't call out. He could barely breathe. The clock by his bed glowed 2:12 a.m. He squinted against the glare and fell back onto the pillows. He muttered as blackness overtook him, "It sucks to be eighteen."

CHAPTER I

MAYADAL

Da, da, da da dadada, da, da, da da dadada... The theme song for *I Dream of Jeannie* buzzed in Medrid's head. *Buzzed.* He chuckled at his pun. What would make him happy would be to get rid of those idiotic notes. Now is not the time to be distracted. *Be.* Another one. *Ha.* He was tired. It was late, but the chamber remained bright, immaculate. Openings on three sides allowed the light and the alluring fragrance from the exotic plant life that existed in the second realm. *Da, da, da da dadada, da, da, da da dadada...* If only that stupid song would go away. He fluttered from his perch on the window ledge to a rafter. It would be harder to keep up with the goings-on below, but it was cooler—he would be less prone to napping. Although it was thousands of years old, the polished wood looked new. The architecture and décor of the building spoke of artistry beyond talent, skill, or ability. Heaven poured out her beauty, flooding Mayadal in angelic splendor. *Da, da, da da dadada—* No. No. He thought about putting his hands over his ears and humming a different tune. But he did not have hands...or ears.

"Unless you plan to sting someone, Medrid, you need not remain in your present state. My decision is set. I will call for fighters to assist you."

Talazim spoke to his mind.

Likewise, Medrid responded by sending his thoughts. *" Loathel and Trill. More will be unnecessary. At any rate, they are the ones I want."*

"Would you call those choices wise?"

"I do. We cannot accomplish this business without the expertise of the Elves. Talazim, there is none more capable than your son."

"It is so."

"We know Maldonus is seeking a Jodian, Who better for him to find than Trill?"

"There is none better. Why should we expect Trill to endure this trial?"

"Trill will do what he must. As with all things, his hardships will not interfere with his duty."

"It is so."

The black and yellow bee flexed his wings and flew. Spiraling downward, he weaved between the members of Kelmaragin's council.

The chamber doors opened. In answer to an unvoiced summons, two beings of magnificent wonder filled the space. Loathel, the Elven son of Talazim, stepped into the room. Beside him sauntered Trill, the Jodian Elite. They were a matched set. Their differences complemented one another and their similarities were too numerable to count. Together, they were the perfect war machine.

Like all the Elves of Kelmaragin, Loathel encompassed light. It radiated from his alabaster skin. His six-foot-six stalwart frame exuded power. Trill, amber-honey skinned, and not a full inch shorter was no less a commanding figure. Sleek as a panther, he was a dangerous predator. Loathel's elbow-length hair—so pale it was almost translucent—had a warrior's braid on each side, tied back after the fashion of Kelmaragin's fighters. Beneath his ponytail, the back hung free, cascading across his broad shoulders. Trill's hair, a deep ebon with whips of cinnamon, was almost the same length. On one side, his warrior's braid hung free. The other was collected with the rest of his silken mane into a tightly coiled braid.

Loathel scanned the room with eyes sharper than a bird of prey and so blue they seemed but a reflection of a clear sky. Even among his people, he was fair. Were it not for his sword, bow, steel arrows, and long knives, Loathel might have been mistaken for an angel. But his skillset aligned him closer to the god of war. He glided across the floor on soundless feet.

Trill's eyes were obsidian stones, penetrating the soul caught in his gaze, while they revealed nothing of the fiery volcano within. He carried a sword, bow, and steel arrows as well. Instead of long knives, the jeweled handle of a dagger protruded from his waistband. Dark power and heat rolled off him, dispelling any notion of the angelic.

"We have heard your summons and we answer." Loathel bowed in respect, first to his father, and then to the council members.

Trill duplicated his movements. "What service may we offer the Kelmaragin?"

Talazim inhaled, taking in the sweet freshness that wafted in from the gardens. "For six days we have held debate." He waved a hand to include the elders, eleven beside himself. Eight from the bright race and four from the next. "We ask our highest warriors to aid Medrid."

"Has Medrid become so advanced in years he requires assistance to carry out his mischief, Father?"

The bee buzzed past Loathel's ear.

"Hardly," Talazim answered.

"Mayhap," Trill said, "they need us to curb his ardor for troublemaking."

The bee made a pass around his head.

Even Talazim found the display amusing. "Your duties may include child care as we are sending him to Universe, his favored hotbed for trouble."

"The council approves of Medrid reclaiming the name of Merlin?" Loathel returned the conversation to its serious nature.

"Yes," Talazim said, "excepting Theokas, Ledan, and Beridan. I fear we will achieve no higher unity."

"Nay, we will not." Someone from the council spoke.

"Medrid is trustworthy," Talazim said to no one and everybody.

"Yea," Trill quietly confirmed.

"That and there is no other sensible choice." Medrid stood beneath the window at the far side of the room as if he had been standing among them the whole time. He lay his staff aside and walked to the discussion table with a confidant stride that made the walking stick superfluous. "Who knows Maldonus better than I?" Nudging his way between Loathel and Trill, he mumbled, "I ought to sting you both." Ignoring their snickers, he said, "Who knows better than I where he travels, whom he seeks, and what he intends?" He leaned his knuckles on the table, challenging. "Councilmen, in this generation, Christif has sired three children, one of whom is true Jodian. Maldonus travels to the fourth realm to seek his revenge. He will convert the child or kill him. He will not suffer any to inherit. This I know."

Talazim motioned him to silence. "This we have discussed for six days. There is no debate on Maldonus' intentions. Nor is there any here who would refuse Christif or any of his line protection."

"Seeing as you have no other ally to match Maldonus' abilities, you have no debate." Medrid focused on the three who would argue.

"Concern for you, Medrid, is why they hesitate," Talazim said.

"Bah." Medrid scratched his beard and relaxed his stance. "'Tis concern for what havoc l may seek to wreak on my own."

"Yea," Trill quietly confirmed. "There is that."

Nudging his way back between Loathel and Trill, Medrid said, "Our one advantage is Maldonus believes we remain unaware. That advantage is dwindling with every hour you spend in useless debate."

Someone from the council agreed. "You are right—"

"Of course l am," Medrid mumbled loud enough to be heard.

Talazim paid him no heed. "Our best course of action is for the mightiest warriors of the Kelmaragin to leave its shores." His eyes lit upon his son.

"l know not if we are the mightiest Father, but we do indeed go."

"Might or no, we will go," Trill said. "Maldonus' might is not in doubt, and we shall confront him."

"Humble speech, both of you. Confronting Maldonus or not, you are the mightiest. l am proud to speak it."

"Father—"

"Enough already," Medrid huffed. "It is good not to be arrogant but, you were not summoned because of your outstanding humility."

"Indeed," Talazim said. "Without your might, Medrid would have no need of your company."

Medrid walked away, pausing to retrieve his staff. "Do not presume to know my mind, Talazim. l have motives even you could not guess." An instant later, he was gone, having disappeared before their eyes.

Talazim stared at the vacant spot, determining if he was offended. Deciding against it, the council leader placed a hand upon the shoulder of each warrior. "May Triune, our Watcher, go with you, aid your cause, and speed you home."

"Thank you, sir." Trill stepped back. His body dissolved, becoming a fine mist. A flash of color, then he too was gone.

"Farewell, Father." Loathel hugged Talazim before moving back and doing the same.

CHAPTER II

UNIVERSE

Chris Lossman went for his morning run. The Spring Mills Community was a half-hour from his house, but he needed to be there twice a week when Winter and her mom got back from dropping the other kids off at school.

"Hi, Mr. Tom." Four-year-old Winter waved as she hopped out of her car seat.

"Hi, Miss Winter. Hi, Miss Megan." Chris knew their names years before Winter supplied him with the information. They accepted his bogus name at face value. He stopped to chat. "Did you eat breakfast?"

"Uh-huh," the child replied. "I had oatmeal with blueberries."

"Some oatmeal," Miss Megan said. "You didn't finish it."

Chris stooped to Winter's eye level. "You gotta listen to your mom and eat all your food, so you can run fast and beat me in a race."

"I will." Winter hopped, skipped, and ran in place to show her speed.

"Look at you. You will win." Having placed a positive thought in her head, he stood up.

"Thank you," Megan mouthed.

"My pleasure." He nodded. "I have to go practice now," he told Winter.

"By, Mr. Tom." She waved.

"Have a good day." He took off running again.

"You too," Megan called after him. She held Winter's hand, going into the house.

Chris' car was four blocks over. He needed to get home, cut the grass, and get ready for his kids.

***

Chris stopped the push mower. He released the safety bar, happy to hear the engine die. The day was too incredible to ignore. He studied the clear horizon, never tiring of the mountains framing the landscape. It was the primary reason he settled in West Virginia. For many, Charles Town was nowhere to speak of, but for him, it was close to heaven—close to home.

Home. The thought came to him again. It had returned more this past season than any time he could recall since his first years in exile.

Ahh, well. He reached down to restart the mower. As he did, a shadow fell across the grass. "What the—"

"Have you grown so lax, Master Christif, you detected not our approach?"

Recognition brought forth a broad grin. "In truth, Medrid, I have. In my defense, it has been many years since an approach of this type concerned me." Chris bowed before the wizard. "Even one as welcomed as yours."

Medrid extended his arms, and the two men embraced. "You may not find us so welcomed when you understand better our visit."

"Never. Nothing could remove my joy at seeing your faces." Christif embraced Loathel and Trill in turn. "Loathel, you are ever the likeness of your father. Trill, how pleasing it is to see my kin."

"As it is to look upon you," Loathel said. "But Medrid is correct. Save seeing you, our visit is not a pleasant one."

"Then come into my home. Let us be about this business and make this visit pleasant." Chris ushered them into his kitchen. "At least, we should get you indoors or I will have a time explaining you to my neighbors."

The back of a brown-gold braided head collected things from the opened refrigerator.

"Imani, honey, we have company."

Imani closed the door and mustered some graciousness. She was not fond of uninvited guests." Oh. Hello." Their appearances did not bode well for her naturally suspicious temperament. High boots, tunics, leather lacings, and cloaks; they look like a trio of pirates. She was already underwhelmed.

"This is... umm, Medrid or Merlin, if you prefer. And Loathel. And Trill."

She noticed the weapons and her wine-polished nails cut into her palm. "Are those real?"

"Real?" Loathel touched his sword. "Yes, they are real."

"When wielding sword, bow, or long knife, no one is more deadly than Loathel," Trill said, "Except myself."

"Trill, how amazing." Loathel poked his shoulder. "You appear awake, yet your words suggest you are locked in slumber."

The men laughed.

Imani did not. "Hunting is illegal within the city limits."

"Thank you for the information, Madame," Medrid said. "If I find myself among the hunted, I shall know where to come."

His comment made her pause. "I would rather not have those things in my house."

"Honey, it's okay, they're not here to hurt anyone."

"I need to talk to you, Christopher...in private."

"Time is short, my friend." Medrid laid his hat and staff aside.

Chris nodded. "Honey, please, give us a moment."

Her expression suggested he was out of his mind.

Chris 'eyes bounced from his wife to the visitors. Deciding it would be better to appease his wife, he led her into the living room.

"They can't be in here with those things." Imani crossed her arms.

"Imani—"

"Don't Imani me. The kids will be home any minute. I don't want Travon around that crap."

"What are you talking about? We live in West Virginia. He's around stuff like that all the time. Your dad keeps his hunting rifles on display."

"Locked in a cabinet, not on his hip. Daddy also has horses and goats. I don't allow them in my house either. I want those weapons gone. Who are those men, anyway? Why are they dressed like that? What do they want?"

"They are from my home. Trill is my kinsman."

"Kinsman? Do you mean relative? Christopher Lossman, you don't have any relatives. Are they from the orphanage? Am I supposed to believe they came all the way from Montana without so much as a call or a text? Why haven't I met any of them before? What do they want?"

"Sweetheart, please, I don't know what they want. Let me go talk to them. I'll explain everything to you when I'm done. Believe me, they wouldn't be here if it wasn't important." He kissed her forehead, then retreated into the kitchen, leaving her to stare bewildered at his retreating form.

***

"My apologies for the delay. I don't know if you listened but I have some explaining to do."

"Listen, humph. As if we had a choice. The inhabitants of the fourth realm speak so loudly, even the deafened should be able to hear every syllable exchanged. Really, Master Christif," Medrid *tsk*'d. "A Montana orphanage?"

"Was Montana necessary?" Loathel asked. "I thought people who did not fit in claimed to be from California."

"For me, yes. I did not wish to forget," Chris said.

"As if you could," Medrid mumbled.

Trill's face twisted, but he held his tongue.

"So, what is this unpleasant business? From your demeanor, one would assume Maldonus was up to no good."

They remained silent in the face of the truth.

"Maldonus has escaped?"

Three solemn nods confirmed Chris' suspicion. He leaned against the counter for support. "H-How can this be? I have been here for one hundred eighty-four years. I have not had contact with him once. Not once."

"We did not suppose you had, my friend. We came to assist, not accuse." Loathel's melodic voice sent waves of soothing throughout the room.

Chris took a deep, calming breath. "Thank you, Loathel. Long have I missed the miracle of Elven esprit."

"My peace shall rest upon you for as long as you have need of it."

"I do not understand. I am Maldonus' only safe channel. There is no other Jodian connected to me except Trill. Obviously, he did not choose that route."

"Obviously," was Trill's dry reply. "But you are wrong, my uncle. We have neglected forethought. It would seem you and I are no longer Maldonus' only channels."

"There is another? How can this be?"

"You have a son," Medrid said, "who is of age."

"Yes."

"He is true Jodian."

Chris 'face lit up and then fell. "I have cursed him with the connection."

"Do not regret things you cannot change." Again, Loathel filled the room with soothing warmth. "Things you had no control over."

The heaviness Chris felt lifted. "What has happened?"

"We don't know how Maldonus escaped," Medrid told him. "But seven days past, Trill felt a surge of power. The power was from you, but not you. We are reasonably sure Maldonus felt it also. We immediately went to his lair and found him gone."

"From me, but not me...Seven days ago, my son, Jalen, turned eighteen. I felt the power. I feel it each time one of my children comes of age. It does not make them true Jodian."

"Christif." Trill leaned forward. "You may feel the surge with each child. I do not. You are connected to all your children. From Mayadal, I am connected only to the one. He is a full Jodian being."

"It stands to reason," Medrid said, "if Trill is connected to your son and Maldonus is free, then Maldonus is also connected to him."

"Seven days ago, Jalen turned eighteen...what am I to do?"

"You will cease thinking this trouble belongs to you alone. I will protect my cousin with my life."

"As will I," Loathel said. "The protection of your son is the priority of us all."

"But what about—"

Medrid waved him off. "When it mattered most, you did not fail us. We shall not fail you."

"Thank you." Christif looked around the room, saying 'thank you ' again to Loathel and once more when his eyes met Trill's. "The question, then, is what are we to do?"

"You may start by introducing us to your family. They are coming."

They paused, trying to perceive what Loathel detected.

Chris broke the silence. "Either I need practice or the sounds of this world have confused you, Loathel. I can tell nothing."

"Indeed." Medrid put his hand up to his ear, straining to hear. "There is so much noise in the air I can barely separate the sounds."

Loathel chuckled.

A moment later Trill said, "There is nothing wrong with Loathel's senses. Three people related to you are approaching in a vehicle. They will arrive soon."

"There are four."

Again, they sat in silence, listening. A car pulled into the driveway.

Chris said, "I need practice."

When the fourth door slammed shut, Loathel beamed at Trill. "You are not the only one."

CHAPTER III

"Mommmm, Daaaddd, we're back!" Travon charged through the house, making the typical amount of noise for a ten-year-old. His orange and black Orioles' cap fell unnoticed from his head, revealing his fresh new haircut, as he headed for the kitchen.

Imani hurried down the steps to intercept him.

Travon burst through the kitchen door, stopping short at the sight of people. "Whoaaa. Wow, are those real?" Sparkling brown eyes, expanded to the size of silver dollars, saw nothing except the swords, knives, and bows. He stood between Loathel and Trill. "May I hold one?"

"Travon, where are your manners, and your greetings?"

"Sorry, Dad. Hi." All by themselves, his fingers reached out to trace the coils of the thin rope hanging from Loathel's waist. It was made of three colors that glimmered and fascinated him.

"Travon." Imani pushed through the kitchen door. "Get away from there." She pulled him to her. "Are you happy now, Christopher?"

"Mom?" A young man's voice penetrated the confusion. "Dad, what's up?"

Had he not had the same dark hair, eyes, and coloring as Christif, the visitors would have still known he was Jalen. But he did not hold their gazes. Behind him stood two women: one younger, about seventeen, the other older. She was closer to thirty.

Trill jumped to his feet in a flash of movement, nearly toppling his chair. He uttered forceful things in a strange language.

Loathel stood. His body was stiff, but his language was understandable, a clear warning. "Not the child."

Never taking his eyes off the door, Trill answered, "Nay, not the child."

The young one's almond-shaped sea-green eyes did a head to toe of every person unknown to her. "Look, it's the three Musketeers." Her gaze returned to Loathel every few seconds. *Hot like whoa.* To cover her gawking, she removed her headband, letting her hair fall forward into her face. It was thick but not bushy. The natural spirals grew strong and hung close to her waist. Like her eyes, her mane was a gift from her dad's genes, but her mom's resilience tamed it. Honor loved her hair. She took her time readjusting the headband—every inch of him needed inspecting.

The redhead beside her attacked her hair as well. With one hand, she pushed the firekissed locs behind her ear. Because of her head-tilt, the coils slipped free, and she repeated the action. Her mouth formed a silent *oh.* She stared at Trill and only Trill.

Medrid studied first Trill, then Loathel. "This is better than I anticipated."

Trill drew his sword, not heeding the gasps and frightened squeals echoing across the room. "What deviltry do you play at, old man?"

The wizard cackled. "Calm your mind, Trill, and then calm your body. I did nothing. I merely suspected."

Trill replaced his sword with trembling hands. He brought his arms up to better see the tremors.

"Can this be true?" Chris whispered.

"As we are witnessing the change, I would venture an affirmation." Medrid stroked his beard.

"What's wrong with him?" Honor pulled her gaze away from Loathel.

"Not to worry," the wizard said. "His body temperature is dropping. Note the ashy pallor." He pointed as if Trill's ashy pallor were an art exhibit. "Soon his blood will stop and the deathpain will begin."

They watched Trill struggle to breathe.

"Deathpains?" The redhead moved closer to Trill and bravely placed her hand on his arm. "I'm a nurse. Sit down. Let me get you a drink."

"Nay, Lady, do not yet move." Trill covered her fingers with his, marveling at her touch. Keeping hold of her hand, he slid back into his chair without looking away from her. Talking was painful, but his voice was hypnotic. "My eyes are now open. Never have I seen a more desirous and exquisite vision. Share-tell me your name, or must I know you only as lovely? Surely no tongue has uttered the expression that would be naught but a pale description of your beauty."

Her knees buckled. His voice. Those words. "I...I...uhh..." She pulled her hand back. "Annora," she mumbled. "My name is Annora." She backed up and did not stop until she bumped into the refrigerator.

***

Loathel remained standing. "What part have you played in my demise?" He fixed his lethal stare on Medrid.

"None, I'm sorry to say. None at all, except bringing you here. I wish I could take credit, but alas, I must settle for being a spectator. Although spectating is no small deed. Many will grieve to have missed such a sight. If there is any news that will be as welcomed as Trill coming into his fullness, then it is that Loathel has done the same. In the same moment, mind you. Such is a wonder." He banged his staff against the tile floor.

Loathel sat down, then jumped up again. "QxuUh viil aAqV RpEejJjpVqV hi zo?" (*What good is fullness to me?*) He swung around behind his chair, gripping the back so tightly it cracked.

The young girl shivered as if her spine had been caressed. "You know that's gibberish, right?"

"IB zo? HxaAqV aAqV uU fFuUL haAzo," said Trill. "aA kuUp plh vi hxBIEevx hxaAqV plQ!" (*Or me? This is a bad time. I cannot go through this now!*)

"That too." She frowned at Trill.

"Gentlemen, you will speak the evanescent tongue or not at all," Medrid said. "Not everyone speaks Mayadalian. Besides, Your complaints are pointless. There are still introductions to be made. Master Christif, if you please."

Chris took a deep breath. "Imani, you've already met. This is her sister, Annora." He indicated the woman pushing against the refrigerator. "Jalen, my eldest. My daughter..." He paused, wondering.

"Honor," Loathel supplied. "She was named for her aunt. No, Master Christif, there is no mistake." His eyes had become murky, but his face held its serenity.

Chris shook his head to clear it. "Travon, my youngest, most inquisitive child." He pointed to the ten-year-old.

While he talked, Honor tried to ease her way out of the room. The kitchen had a swinging door, but it wouldn't budge.

"You will stay, Honor."

She jumped, startled.

Even from across the room, Loathel's voice carried enough authority to halt her progress. "This concerns you."

"You would be so wrong if you think I care." Honor rolled her eyes. "So cringy. Dad, did you tell him my name?" *Stalker.*

"I knew what your name would be before you were born."

"Really? When you were what, two, oh psychic one?" *Cute or not, the boy is an idiot.* "Dad, can I go?"

"You will stay," Loathel repeated.

"Honey, you have to stay in here," Chris said.

She glared at him.

Loathel closed his eyes.

Chris went back to the introductions. "This is my nephew, Trill."

Trill labored with his breathing and did not acknowledge any of the people looking at him, except Annora. To her, he inclined his head and smiled as best he could under the circumstances, then returned to his pain.

"Nephew?" Annora found her voice.

"He's our cousin? Wow." Travon grinned at Trill's sword.

Honor pursed her lips.

"Nephew, Dad? How?" Jalen folded his arms across his chest.

"I will explain it all. There is a lot here to understand." Chris blinked back his emotions.

Loathel sent his comfort. Even in his present condition, the Elve filled the void.

"Loathel has been a friend to me for many years. Now, he is also family. No greater love has a man than I for him. I take immense pride in knowing he is the keeper of one of my greatest treasures." Chris made a formal bow to the Elve.

Loathel bowed slightly in return. "Do not place in my keeping what I cannot keep. Were it possible, I would do so with reverence. Your treasure is beyond value."

"Indeed," Chris said. "Do not be so hasty, my friend. If I know the way of it, you have less choice in the matter than anyone."

"As long as he has been around," Medrid interrupted, "he should know that by now."

Chris and Medrid were amused.

Loathel was not.

Trill sat in stony, dazed silence.

No one else understood the conversation.

Medrid addressed the room. "I grow weary of these introductions. Fortunately, they end with me. I am Merlintum Medrid. Merlin for short. Merlin the Magician."

"The real one?" Travon could barely breathe.

"Don't be stupid." Jalen shoved his brother.

"What's stupid about that?" Travon huffed. "How many Merlin the Magicians do you know?"

"None. They don't exist."

"I assure you, I do."

"Crin—gy. Heard enough. Got to go." Honor pushed against the door. It was still stuck.

"Yeah." Annora moved to follow her.

Trill's hand snaked out, viper-fast, to lock around Annora's wrist. His grip was firm, but his touch gentle. "Nay, Milady, I have need of your presence."

Annora's knees threatened to buckle again. His voice gave her a rush. He looked at her as if he thought she was gold, or God, or both. Her smile was without a named reason, but it was genuine.

Watching Trill touch her sister made Imani's nostrils flare. "Enough. Christopher, I want these people out of my house. I don't care who they are or what they want, they have to go." She reached out to slap Trill's hand away.

The air moved beneath her feet.

"Do not touch him." Chris sat her down, away from his nephew. "No one is going anywhere except into the living room, where we can all sit down. We don't have a lot of time and there are things you need to hear." His tone allowed no argument. He pushed the door. It swung open with ease. He held it while his children marched single file into the other room—Honor pausing long enough to see if anything had been blocking it. Ushering Imani out after the kids, he turned to Merlin. "How much longer?"

"'Tis nearly done. By the look of him, none too soon. As for Loathel, I am thankful he completed his transformation before you sent your daughter away."

"Loathel?" Chris studied the Elve with renewed wonder. "My apologies. You did not so much as blink. That fast, I forgot your need of her."

Loathel's face held its composure. The only telltale signs he had undergone anything were the deepening of his eyes and a single bead of sweat above his eyebrow.

"What happened?" Annora's nursing instincts kicked in again. She looked at the one called Loathel. Nothing was different, but he had changed in some way. If it were at all possible, he was more beautiful, radiating more light. He seemed somehow mightier and more ethereal than before. Her eyes drifted to the man at her side. She focused on him and was lost. Annora's breathing became erratic, while her heart skipped beats. In him, she saw tempestuous power, barely harnessed. Fathomless black eyes seared the core of her being. She could feel volcanic heat radiating from his touch. He flooded her with warmth, unlike anything she had ever experienced. She'd never felt more alluring, more alive, more wanted in her life.

Trill stood up then. She held her breath as he rose a foot above her, stately and alpine. His hair had come loose, cascading down his back in shimmering silkiness.

Annora's hand ached to touch it.

The tilt of his lips was devastating as he raised her palm to his thick mane.

With a will of their own, her fingers moved through the mass of softness. She sighed.

"It is finished."

Annora jumped, not expecting him to speak.

His timbre was a satiny caress with a virility that resonated through her soul. "tTlEe jJjuULt, uURo ztT RpEejJjpoqVqV. tTlEe xuUNO Klzo hl zo uUpl aA uUz plQ QxljJjo. aA qVxuUjJj fFo Qalhx tTlEe, RplB aA uUz tTlEeBqV." (*You, Lady, are my fullness. You have come to me and I am now whole. I shall be with you, for I am yours.*)

He wove his declaration around her heart, sealing her in a world so unreal she forgot herself. She felt lightheaded, drugged. The sounds he made were in another language, but she imagined she understood them. For a moment, she pretended he was claiming her. She gave herself to the fantasy, letting her mind feign he wanted her.

He added a feathery whisper, "QaAjJj tTlEe xuUno zo?" (*Will you have me?*)

Want!! her heart screamed. *Yes,* her voice echoed from within her mind. Her head bobbed up and down.

"It is done." Merlin shattered the dream world Annora had been wandering in.

She snapped back to the present, embarrassed by her loss of concentration. "Err..." She looked around for a clue to what the conversation was about.

Merlin moved toward the door. "Trill, kiss your bride but be quick about it, we have work to do."

"Huh?"

"Amazing. Simply amazing." Chris hugged them one at a time. "That you can know this joy is joy to me, Trill. Never did I expect to outlive my guilt. Annora, you have gained to husband the greatest among my people. I am proud to say what I know to be true."

"I'm sorry, I was spacing. What'd I miss?"

The occupants in the kitchen found her declaration amusing.

"No, my sweet, you were here." Trill put his arm around her.

His touch was a little too familiar for Annora's liking. She removed his arm, opting to forget where her hand had been moments before. "Here for what?"

He put it back. "Our joining."

She removed it. "Don't do that again. Our what?"

He settled for holding her hand. "Joining. The closest meaning I can match in the evanescent tongue would be...bond, wedding, to join, to become whole."

Annora found that amusing. "You are twisted." She pried his fingers loose and stepped away. "If you're well enough to tease, you must be okay. I'm leaving now."

"She knows not what she did." Loathel's unblinking eyes seemed to show humor.

"It does not matter." Merlin stroked his beard. "She cannot undo it."

"W-what did I do?"

Merlin said, "Knowing or unknowing, my dear, before witnesses, you have joined with Trill. The two of you are now one."

"CHRIS!"

Trill talked over her panic." I will show you." He turned her toward him. Incredibly, the scene replayed in her mind. Only now, she realized it was no daydream. She hadn't been pondering those things. He said those things. She heard herself answer yes aloud. The vision went away. Annora shut her eyes and tried to shake the images out of her head.

***

"What happened?" Honor led the others back into the kitchen.

Over Honor's shoulder, Imani inspected Annora for injuries.

Chris pulled her back. "It's okay, sweetheart. Annora is a little overwhelmed."

"Why?" She glared at Trill. "What did he do to my sister?"

"Marry her." Chris walked away.

"Dad?" Jalen said to his back.

"What kind of foolishness is this?" Imani followed him out.

"Come into the living room," they heard Chris say.

"How come we wasn't invited?" Travon asked.

"You weren't in here that long." Honor went toward Annora." I don't like your tricks, crazy-man. Get away from my aunt."

Loathel cut off her path. "Leave them. Our business lies in the other room."

"Who do you think you are?"

"I am Loathel of the Elvish people."

If he wanted to impress her, he had a ways to go.

"Look Lowell, the Elvis impersonator, move out of my way."

He did not.

She turned to her brother for reinforcements.

Jalen stepped forward and stopped. Loathel had done nothing more than stare at him, but Jalen recognized the possessive gaze of an aggressive territorial male.

That impressed Honor. Not only was Jalen not a coward, he was intelligent and rational. If he paused, it was for a good reason. She looked at Loathel, seeing blue steel and more reflected in his eyes. He was powerful and attractive, a dangerous combination. But she refused to let him affect her. It didn't mean anything. Still, she backed up a step.

He moved forward a step, a big step that put him inches from her.

"Don't you know anything about personal space?" She took another step backwards.

"No." He took another step forward.

Behind her, she heard people moving into the next room, and her bravado failed. The wall that was his chest loomed before her, shutting off her view of all else. She stepped back once more. "It's...it's not nice to get too close to people."

He moved in again.

"You are mistaken." He bent his head close to hers. "Sometimes it is very nice."

Honor wondered what it would be like to kiss him.

For a moment, the blue steel in his eyes became a blue storm: Dramatic. Charged with emotion. "Go into the other room, Honor. Now."

The color drained from her face. A fresh wash of new color replaced it. Her embarrassing thoughts made her angry. But she wasn't sure if she was angry because he made her want his kiss or if it because she didn't get what she wanted. Maybe it was because he wasn't struggling. Purely on reflex, her hand connected with the side of his face.

He didn't flinch, but those incredible eyes now held a look of complete surprise.

Honor was beyond surprised. She was horrified at her own behavior.

Ten seconds of a song blared at them from Honor's pocket, indicating she received a message. The interruption salvaged enough of her wounded ego to allow her to retreat with dignity. She let the ringtone play though for Loathel's benefit: "...it's so easy when you're evil..."

Loathel followed her out, concluding that, while she was not evil, she was decidedly not angelic. He chose to ignore Trill's chuckle.

***

Honor and Loathel's exit left Trill alone with Annora.

She was frightened.

To him, she was a hovering butterfly, ready to flutter away. "Before we join the others, would you do me the service of rebinding my hair?" His voice was pure euphony. He held out a small strip of leather, much like one would hold out a peace offering. She hesitated, but he was undaunted. "I can do it myself, but it would take longer and I am certain it would not be as neat."

Annora looked from his face to his outstretched hand and back again. He nodded when she accepted the band, then sat with his back to her. Her fingers quivered. He suppressed a smile at her intake of breath as she grasped his midnight locks.

She used a lot of energy attempting to braid fast. Halfway through the plait, she asked, "How did you do that?"

"How did I do what?"

"That...that thing to my mind. Where I remembered...where I saw what happened."

"I showed you what happened."

"Yes, how did you do it?"

"I shared my thoughts with you. At the time your thoughts were...elsewhere."

"How would you know that?" *Please don't let him know what I was thinking.*

"*I know what you were thinking. We are one. Your thoughts come to me.*"

"How did you do that?" She finished the braid and stood away from him.

Turning around to face her, Trill said, "I did nothing."

"You were talking in my head."

"You hear my thoughts. You may do that at will."

"I do what?"

"*Hear my thoughts.*"

"No, I don't."

"*If not, to whom are you speaking?*"

"Umm..."

"*Try it.*"

"Uhh...no." *He must be crazy. I'm not trying anything.*

"*I do not consider myself crazy.*"

"You heard that?"

"*Yea, as you hear me.*"

"I do not."

Masculine laughter flooded her mind and pushed her panic button.

Oh, please. No. Did he know I was fantasizing about him?" You can't possibly assume we're married."

"Nay, Milady. I do not assume." He stood up, taking both her hands in his. "Marriage, as you know it, is a weak comparison to the union we have."

Annora tried to pull away.

Trill would not let her move. "In your world, men and women spend time in one another's company to see if they wish to be together. If all things work well, marriage will result."

She bobbed her head slowly.

"In my world, it is the opposite. We do not search for someone to love." Again, she tried to pull away.

He held her fast. "We wait for Triune to select our mates for us. When he does, we are joined. That happened here. You and I are bound to each other. We will spend the rest of our lives getting to know one another and rejoicing in the choice made on our behalf."

"You are bound to someone you don't know, without one single date?"

"We know he will pick the right person. There is no reason to date."

"You sure picked the wrong person. I am not marrying you."

"Nay, Milady, you and I are more than married. We are joined, we are one." He placed his forehead against hers. *"You have already brought me more joy than I ever hoped to possess. My life is yours."* Releasing one of her hands but holding tight to the other, he led her out of the kitchen. *"Because we are joined, our minds share the same thoughts. There can be no deception between us. I know what you pondered."*

I can hear him, but I don't know what he's talking about.

"I am aware you fantasize about me. I feel happiness."

Annora stopped dead, petrified.

Trill pulled her forward.

CHAPTER IV

"I love you all very much," Chris said. "But until now there were things I could not share with you."

Imani's expression would haunt him.

"It was not because I didn't trust you, nor was I afraid you wouldn't understand. My silence was to ensure your safety."

"What are you, a secret agent?"

"No, Jalen, and spare me your sarcasm. This is hard enough as is."

"Sorry."

"I am Christif, Master of the Jodian people." It meant nothing to his family, but it was a relief for him to say it. "Along with the Elves and others like us, the Jodian reside on the shores of Mayadal, in the second realm. I have been in your world one hundred and eighty-four years."

"You're an alien." Honor didn't look up from her texting.

"And he is?" Imani pointed to Merlin.

"Another alien," Honor said.

"He is who he said he is. You have the privilege to be in the presence of Merlin the Magician. The same Merlin from your King Arthur legends."

His announcement received a snicker, a snort, and a couple of eye-rolls.

"Uh-huh, yeah, sure." Jalen also texted." Dad, I'm not buying it." He typed: **This is stupid af.**

"Are we on a secret game show?" Travon searched for hidden cameras.

Imani said, "This isn't funny, Christopher. I have had enough of this nonsense."

Annora and Trill walked in as the grandfather clock struck. An hour hadn't passed since she brought the kids home. "What is going on?"

Trill led her to the loveseat.

"Oh, Aunt Nora, it's all so deep and meaningful." Honor's fake-perky voice rang out from across the room. She sat in the window seat, responding to Jalen's message while ignoring the handsome Elve posted less than two feet away. "Dad's not half-white anymore. He's an alien from planet Smoking-something. Our cousin, Obi-Wan Glue-Man, who's attached to you, and his pal, the annoying Mr. Spock," she tugged on her ear and pointed to Loathel, "popped out of a rubber room. They went over the rainbow and found the Wizard of Oz over there. They dropped by to reminisce with Dad about the times they all hung out in Never-Never Land. Fun. Fun."

"You are being disrespectful, Honor," Chris said. "And offensive."

Big tears 😢

To her surprise, the objects of her scorn guffawed at her nonsense.

"Amusing, young lady, very amusing indeed. Such wit, I'll wager you will not be bored, Loathel."

"I have never been bored, Medrid."

Honor looked up, trying to puzzle out what her wit had to do with his boredom or lack thereof.

"I believe you, Dad." Travon crawled out from behind the sofa and gave Chris a hug. "I believe you too, Mr. Merlin."

"Why thank you. Your vote of confidence reveals more than you know." The boy came over and Merlin leaned down. "You may be the youngest and the smallest among us, but you shall do great deeds. You are wise."

"I am?"

"Indeed, I see in you a kindred spirit."

"You do?"

"No, you don't." For the second time, Imani pulled Travon away from the perceived threat. "Mr. Merlin, or whomever you wish to be, kindly refrain from putting asinine ideas into my son's head."

The room felt chilled.

"Madame," Merlin said. "You have held up these proceedings long enough. I will not tolerate your interference again."

There was something scary about him. The humans shrank back, unnerved. Annora leaned into Trill. He drew her closer, placing his arm around her shoulders. She accepted the protection he offered while purposely ignoring it.

Honor slid back against the window, bringing her knees to her chest. In two steps, Loathel planted himself in front of her, almost completely blocking her view. For some reason, she was grateful.

Imani took an involuntary step toward her husband. Jalen stopped trading impolite messages with Honor. He slid the phone in his pocket and stood up straight, away from the wall he had been leaning against. Travon stared at the wizard in awe.

"Who do you—"

"Imani, stop—" Chris 'warning came too late.

"SILENCE, WOMAN!" Merlin stretched out his staff. "I AM MERLINTUM, THE MEDRID!" Everything went dark. Jalen grabbed Travon. "THE LAST DRUID!" The room moved. The brothers were thrown off balance. They slid across the floor, landing in a heap against the wall. Honor pitched forward. Loathel caught and held her. He remained stable, unaffected by the shifting. So did Trill, who held Annora likewise. Chris had a more difficult time. Imani was the focus of Merlin's outburst. "DESCENDANT OF THE NEPHILIM!" A strong wind overtook them and lifted Imani off her feet. Chris held her, becoming her anchor while her body lay horizontal, hovering in the air, and her screams were ignored. "I HOLD SECRET KNOWLEDGE!" Objects caught in the windstorm flew around. Lamps, books, trophies, and knickknacks smashed into walls, each crash more deafening than the one before. "I AM A FORCE YOU CANNOT CONTAIN!" He appeared to grow and illuminate. The larger he became, the more light he disseminated. "I AM MERLIN, THE MAGICIAN!"

Then it stopped. The wind ceased. Everything airborne hit the floor with a resounding thud, including Imani. She landed on Chris, sending him to the floor as well. The room stilled. Daylight returned, and Merlin leaned against his staff, a tired old man.

"Forgive me, Madame. My greatest shortcoming is my quick anger."

Chris helped Imani to a chair.

Jalen and Travon untangled themselves.

"That was sooo cool, Mr. Merlin." Travon bounced up and down on his toes.

Jalen surveyed the wreckage with dismay.

"No, Master Travon," Merlin said. "I have not done a good thing. Wrecking a person's home out of irritation is not cool under any circumstance." He looked to the other son. "Master Jalen, mayhap you could be of service to your mother. A drink is what she most likely needs."

Jalen nodded and disappeared into the kitchen.

"I am so sorry." Annora scooted off Trill's lap without looking at him.

"You are sorry for seeking comfort?" Trill chuckled. "Should you not take what belongs to you?"

"So you say." She got up.

"So I know." He followed suit.

Across the room, Honor lifted her head from Loathel's chest. Deep sea-green eyes locked with sparkling blue ones. His arms were around her shoulders, hers were around his waist. She didn't recall how they got that way, but she wanted to stay there.

He tightened the embrace.

"Are they married or connected or whatever it is?" Annora pointed to the couple. "Are they joined too?"

The release was sudden. The turning away, quick. Honor went to her mother's side. Loathel began picking up debris.

Annora's question went unanswered.

Chris, Honor, and Annora tended to Imani while Loathel, Trill, Jalen, Travon, and Merlin restored order to the room.

"Why can't you zap it back like it was?"

"Once done, Master Travon, damage cannot easily be undone," Merlin said. "Quick fixes never hold a lesson. Besides, I think your mother would rather not have to see any more unusual displays at the moment."

"Whatever is going on, you are on our side, aren't you?" Jalen looked from Loathel to Trill to Merlin.

"Master Jalen," Trill said, "Medrid's temper tantrums are nothing much. They go as speedily as they come. He has never hurt anyone in anger and though it seemed so, he was never truly out of control."

"Do not let it trouble you or you will grow weary." Loathel collected pieces of a table lamp. "His outbursts are frequent and childlike. If you pay too much attention, it will encourage him."

"A child, you call me? Do you know how old I am?"

"Yes."

"There are two things you can be certain of, cousin. The one being: we will always be on your side." Jalen was at one end of the overturned desk. Trill stood opposite him. "And the other," together they lifted it," Medrid makes the biggest mess."

"Of which you can be sure you will have to help clean up." Loathel set the now restored lamp on top of the desk.

CHAPTER V

Chris's story did not seem far-fetched anymore.

Imani gripped the teacup to still her jittery fingers. "Why are you here now?"

"Let us begin again." Merlin was gentle. "Loathel, if you would."

Loathel filled the room with melodious tranquility. "Enoch has told you the right of it. 'And it came to pass,'" he quoted." 'When the children of men had multiplied that in those days were born to them beautiful and comely daughters. And the angels, the children of heaven, saw and lusted after them, and said to one another: Come, let us choose us wives from among the children of men and beget us children. 'For you, it is legend, the dawn of mythology. For us, it is history. Semjâzâ was their leader. Azâzêl followed. He taught men the ways of war and he overshadowed the maiden Savene. From their union, three sons were sired. The first child was Elve. He inherited Azâzêl's past. He was angelic in appearance and action, good in all things. Although he could not enter the Empyrean—heaven, he was the first of the Nephilim to return to purity. It is from him my people come." There was no pride in him, only truth.

"His next son, Jodian, was like Elve, but to a lesser degree, for he had taken after Savene. He was blessed with the mortality of men. Trill and Master Christif are from his line. They may enter Empyrean."

The newly reorganized living room was silent.

"An offspring from the line of his third son, Lephan, is why we have come. Lephan was his father's heir. His passion was turning the race of men from truth. He and almost all who came after are wholly evil."

"Triune showed mercy to the descendants of the fallen. He gave to them the land of Mayadal," Merlin said. "There, for all generations, the Council of Kelmaragin was set to be an authority over the line of Lephan. Many years ago, Maldonus, Lephan's heir, grew in power."

Only Loathel heard Honor's sharp intake of breath.

"Hey, isn't—"

"Shut up, you freaky little gnome," Honor talked over Travon. "Mr. Merlin is talking. Let him finish."

??? Jalen texted Honor.

Get your life, came the quick response back.

"He overthrew the council and placed in slavery the inhabitants of Mayadal. Only through many battles did the Elves and Jodians regain control."

"We would not have without the sacrifice of Christif," Trill said.

"Your own sacrifices are not forgotten," Chris answered.

Merlin tugged at his beard. "It was not an option to destroy Maldonus as befitted his crimes. But he could only be imprisoned for so long as Christif remained in your realm, we thought."

"Has this Maldonus escaped?" Imani asked anyone but Merlin. She flinched when he gave her the answer.

"He has."

"Will he come here?" Honor asked the floor. "Is that why you came here?"

"He will and it is, but that is not the only reason we have come."

"What else do we need to know?" Jalen said aloud. **What's going on?** He texted.

"Maldonus will come for me," Chris said. "He wishes me dead. More than that, he desires you, Jalen. Maldonus will come for you."

"Me?"

"Jalen?" Imani jumped up and threw her arms around her eldest child.

"What does he want with me?" Jalen reassured his mom with a hug.

"On your birthday, a truth was made known. One I had not considered before." Chris paused.

Trill finished." You are as your father and I are. You are true Jodian."

Jalen stood there, dumbfounded.

"Chris?" Imani choked out the name.

"What does that mean?" Annora whispered the question.

Honor averted her face and wiped her eyes.

"Is he like a superhero now?" Travon asked. "Can I be a Jodian when I grow up?"

Chris said, "We don't know yet, son."

I don't feel any different. How could they be so sure? Suppose I don't want to be a Jodian?

There was a soft chuckle in Jalen's head. *"As if you have a choice."*

Jalen's pupils dilated to three times their normal size.

The voice belonged to his new cousin. *"You need not be afraid. I disrupt your pondering to prove our words are accurate. Your father would know your mind but cannot perform the task himself."*

"I can read people's minds?"

"Not exactly. You may know the thoughts of those to whom you are connected."

"Oh, man, this is awesome. Can they know what I'm thinking?"

"If we could not, how would I know to answer a question in your head and not upon your tongue?"

A goofy grin spread across Jalen's face.

"I need not wonder about my son's joy, but I am concerned with my daughter." Chris turned to Loathel for an answer.

Honor tried to leave the room.

Loathel locked his hand around her wrist.

She attempted to jerk away.

His grip was light but immovable.

"Let me go," she ordered through clenched teeth.

"I cannot. Running away will cause needless delay." He imitated impatience.

"I am not running away. I don't feel like talking. I'm leaving. NOT RUNNING. SO MIND YOUR OWN BUSINESS!" Each phrase tumbled out, louder than the one before. Catching herself, she lowered the volume. "Get off of me." She tried twisting her arm free. "You are a bully." She rolled her tear-filled eyes, looking helplessly around the room.

"You are spoiled, but you need not fear," Loathel said. "Your participation was in ignorance. You were deceived."

He expected her to relax.

His expectation went unmet.

"How dare you presume to know anything about me? You pompous, arrogant..."

Groping for a stinging description, Honor did not notice Trill laughing, nor did she see Jalen deep in concentration.

Forehead wrinkled, eyes squinted, he focused on his sister. "She knows Maldonus. She's talked to him." Jalen flexed his muscles. "Yeah, baby. I'm it. I know."

"How in the hel-lo. How did you know?" Immediately Honor shifted her venomous stare to her little brother. "Did you tell him?"

"No." Travon hid behind Jalen. "I didn't tell you, did I, Jalen?"

"No." Jalen put his arm around Travon. "Tray didn't tell me. I know your mind. Yeah."

"Maldonus?" Chris stood in front of Honor. "What do you know of Maldonus?"

Loathel released Honor and stepped between them.

Chris took a deep breath, stepped back, and lowered his volume. "When did you speak to him?"

Doing something you shouldn't was one thing; getting caught was something else altogether.

"I...I..." From behind Loathel, she scowled at Jalen. *I don't know how you found out but 'IF' you can read my mind, then you should know I think you're a jerk. Wait for it, you traitor. Mom is so gonna find that gaming gear she told you not to buy.*

"You've always thought I was a jerk. I don't have to read your mind for that. It's not like I meant to blurt it out. I just found out I could do this, so I tried it, alright. Anyway, I got rid of the stupid gear."

Honor's jaw dropped.

"Do not lie to your sister." Loathel frowned at Jalen.

Jalen's jaw dropped.

"What's happening?" Imani rubbed her temples.

"Are they doing that head thing?" Annora asked Trill.

"Yea, they are," he said. "The young ones do not realize we are all a part of this conversation."

Jalen and Honor stared opened mouthed at Trill.

"I'm not." Annora shook her head.

"Only because you choose not to be. You have access."

"Never mind."

"I'm not in on anything," Imani said. "What is going on?"

"I don't know nothing either," Travon piped in. "All I know is, I didn't tell Jalen about Honor's spirit guide."

"Spirit guide?" Chris and Imani repeated in unison.

Imani shook her head. "Honor, you know better."

"She's been told a million times to stay away from that stuff," Chris said to Loathel. "What has she done?"

"Wait a minute." Honor stepped around Loathel. With one hand on her hip, she used the other to count issues between her parents. Addressing first one and then the other, she said, "You came from another realm or planet or something. You've had an indoor hurricane happen in your living room. Your eldest son is a mind-reading alien. Your sister is married to the nephew of your orphaned husband. You're on someone's hit list." She paused there, making sure she had their full regard. "And you can't find anything better to do than freak because I called the psychic hotline? Now, don't pop an artery, but I also joined the tennis team."

"Ohhhhh, she's a diplomat. She would set the Council of Kelmaragin on their ears, I'll wager." Merlin whooped and Trill joined in. The others seemed to relax.

Hmm. Honor's lips twitched. *I could get to like the old man, dress and all.*

"Artful dodger, you mean." To those who did not know him, Loathel looked serious.

"It takes one to know one is the saying," Merlin muttered.

"Twisting words does not answer the question."

The Lossmans sobered.

"Please, repeat that," Trill asked. "I am positive I misheard you."

Honor rolled her eyes and sighed. *Somebody that gorgeous has no business being annoying. If he would stand there and be quiet, I could drool over him in peace. But nooooo, he always has to open his big mouth and ruin everything.*

Loathel flashed her a radiant smile. He flooded her with such incredible warmth; she couldn't help but smile back. She took a small, almost unseen step, then another. Getting closer to him seemed to be all that mattered.

He reached for her again. This time, not a hold, but a caress. He slid his hand up her arm and twirled a thick strand of her hair around his finger.

It was an accident. Loathel had been monitoring Honor's thoughts from the moment he saw her. Something about her last musings stuck a note of pleasure. He was drawn to her but didn't realize the effect his smile would have on her, or the effect she would have on him. It felt so perfect. So right. It had to be...but it was not supposed to be. With a troubled heart, Loathel broke the contact and looked away.

Honor frowned at him. "Say it with me: Personal. Space. It's not hard." She back peddled away from him.

CHAPTER VI

Having run out of options, Honor told how she came to be associated with the name Maldonus. "It started a couple of months ago," she admitted. "I had a problem. It was a big one, at least to me, so I called."

"Why didn't you come to me?" Imani stiffened, affronted.

"I did, but I didn't like your answer. Yours either, Aunt Nora. I thought I needed outside help."

"What problem?"

"Mom, that is not the issue right now. Rest assured people, there will be no family powwows in which my personal business is the main topic."

"How about it if we get back to the main topic?" Chris said. "You, Maldonus. I want to know about that."

"Oh, yeah, right." Honor nodded. "Anyway, my psychic gave me the stupidest advice on the planet. I thought I was done with it. Then, one night about a week later, she called me. I can't get into trouble for that. I didn't tell her to call me. I didn't give her the number. It wasn't my fault."

Chris 'look indicated he disagreed.

"Anyway, she told me some stuff, some real stuff. When I asked her how she knew, she said we shared the same spirit guide and he wanted her to contact me. After that, we talked a good bit. She taught me how to prepare myself and how to tune into Maldonus. Tashnine, that's her name. We were related in another life or some weird crap like that."

Imani pursed her lips. "There is no other life."

Deciding against rolling her eyes at her mother, Honor kept talking. "Maldonus told us we were from the same source."

"You have spoken to him?" Merlin asked.

"Yeah, a couple of times. Do you want Tashnine's number?" She reached for her phone.

"We may be able to use this to our advantage. If she can contact him, it should be an easy thing for Trill or Loathel to locate him." Chris seemed to brighten at the thought.

"It is possible," Loathel said. "Her thoughts will have to be buffered. When she speaks to him, he cannot know her mind. We cannot risk him finding us too soon."

"Your wisdom never sleeps," Chris said.

"*What? You need an excuse.*" Trill wafted the thought to Loathel.

The Elve sent him a sensation of unease in response.

Trill grinned.

"You're gonna do what?" Honor's brow crinkled. "Do you mean like private number blocking? That's a given, but you can still hit star-six-seven if you like."

"We will also need to go through her memories," Trill spoke easy. To Loathel's mind, he said, *"Does that help?"*

"Whoa. No. I don't know what you're talking about, but whatever is in my head is my business. Formulate a new plan."

"Excellent idea, Trill." Merlin clapped his hands together.

"Uhh, hello. Look, I'm sorry and all. I didn't mean to cause any trouble. Feel free to use my phone," she waved it around, "but nobody is allowed in my head." She turned to Jalen. "You included, Spaceboy."

Imani huffed. "Will somebody please explain this head thing?"

"Jodians have the gift of sharing the heart of those who are close to us." Trill said.

"What does that have to do with reading minds?"

"To know the heart requires access to the mind. It works also in reverse. It is why we are usually only in the minds of those whose hearts we are also in; family, friends, people we are connected to." Trill's eyes lingered on Annora.

"I think Loathel can get into Honor's mind." Jalen was matter-of-fact about it. "They aren't related, are they?"

"Excuse me?" Honor scowled at Loathel. "What's that mean?"

Another wave of unease hit Trill. He grinned again. "Loathel suffers none of the shortcomings of our kind. He sees the mind and heart of every man. It was nothing for him to know the infamous gear remains in your room."

Jalen's snicker was guilty until a new thought came. "Dad, have you been monitoring our thoughts all these years?" His horrified expression was mirrored three times over.

"No." He had to talk over the displays of relief. "My capabilities are limited. I'm more human than Jodian. This is partially why I am in this realm. I no longer have that particular skill." If he was saddened, it did not show. "Trill and Loathel have remedied the situation. Between them, they are generously observing everyone's musing and broadcasting the information back to Medrid and myself. I am most informed, watch." He rubbed his hands together. "Ummm...Travon. We'll eat soon. Until then, you may have a few cookies to hold you over."

Travon looked up surprised. He didn't dwell on it but raced to the kitchen before Chris could change his mind. "And you, young man," Chris got serious. "March upstairs and retrieve that gear, or whatever it is. If your mother told you not to buy it, then it has no business in this house. Is that understood?"

"Yes, sir," Jalen mumbled.

Honor smirked the smirk of delicious revenge.

"You people know everything we think? Without telling us?" Imani's hazel eyes glowed angry. "Without our permission?"

"Honey, I know it's different and a little weird for you. Trust me; it's a good thing. It's a necessary function of my kind. You'll get used to it."

"I am not one of your kind. That's an invasion of privacy. My privacy. You can all stop it."

"How do you do it?" Honor asked. "I want to try."

"What a wonderful suggestion," Merlin said. "You are fast becoming one of my favorite people...dress and all. Loathel, send her a thought so she can get a feel for it."

"No."

"I don't want to know his thoughts."

Every male in the room knew she was lying.

"It would be so much easier if you helped her, Loathel."

The Elve seemed not to hear him.

"I said I don't want his help."

"My dear," Merlin said. "You cannot perform this operation except through Loathel."

"I'm sorry. I didn't hear you."

Merlin glared at Loathel.

At once, the three visitors stood and faced the front door.

"Someone approaches," Loathel said.

In unison, the warriors shimmered with color. They dissolved into a fine mist before disappearing altogether. The magician simply vanished.

"By nooo stretch of the imagination is that normal." Honor pointed to the spot where Loathel stood.

"We have to get the hell out of here," Annora said. "I don't know where they went, but I plan to be gone before they come back." She stood up.

The doorbell sounded.

Chris opened the door for Wesley and Vincent, Travon's friends.

"Hey, Mr. Lossman. Did Tray get back from the beach yet?" Wesley asked.

"Hi, boys. Yes, he did. Come in. I'll get him for you." He held the door open.

***

"Travon, Wesley and Vincent are here."

"They are?" Travon swallowed a mouthful of cookies and stood up. "Did they see Mr. Merlin? Can Trill and Loathel come out and show us how to use their bows?"

"Uh, no, son. They didn't see our guests and you can't tell them about them either."

"Why not?"

"It wouldn't be good. The more people who know about this, the more dangerous it becomes."

"But can't they see them?"

"Not at the moment."

This was beyond Travon's comprehension. He darted out of the kitchen in search of his new heroes.

Vincent and Wesley met him halfway across the floor.

"Hey, Tray."

"Hi, Tray."

"C'mon out."

"Get your glove."

Travon looked around the room. His countenance dropped." Hi, guys. Umm, I don't know if I can right now. Umm..." He tried to focus. "...our cousin is visiting. I-I want to see him."

"Aww, who cares about a stupid ol 'cousin?" Wesley shifted from one foot to the other.

"Yeah, you can see them anytime."

"My cousin and his friends are cool."

"C'mon, you were gone all week. Let's play some ball," Vincent wheedled.

"Yeah." Wesley punched him in the arm.

"Alright, but only for a little while. Dad, when they get here, will you make them stay until I get back?"

"Go play with your friends for a while. They'll wait for you. I promise."

Visibly relieved, Travon retrieved his glove. A moment later, he and his buddies were out the door.

***

Chris closed the door behind them. "Where is everybody?"

"Dad, they're girls. They did what they do best. They ran. All three of them. The general sentiment was an expressed resentment against people knowing what they're thinking." Jalen stretched lazily, full of amusement. "They were using words I didn't know they knew. Well, I knew Honor knew them, but not Mom and Aunt Nora."

Merlin, Loathel, and Trill reappeared.

"Where is everyone?" Merlin looked about.

"They left almost as fast as you did. Can I do that too?"

"Our leaving is neither gift nor skill, cousin. We merely stepped back into our realm to avoid being seen."

"Oh, is that all?"

Loathel noted his sarcasm and said, "You and your sister are alike."

"Except he is here where his sister is not," Merlin answered.

"Did they say where they were going?" Chris asked.

"Yeah, don't you guys know what happened?"

"We did not hold the contact when we left your world."

"So right now, I'm the man." Jalen pinched his shirt. "Without me, you wouldn't know anything."

"*Man,*" Trill said from inside Jalen's head. "*While you brag, Loathel has extracted the information.*"

"*Shall I share it on your behalf?*"

Jalen gave a small snort. "*Is there any way to turn it off if you don't want someone to know your thoughts?*"

"*Nay, you cannot.*"

"*No, such a thing has been done.*"

"*Unheard of.*"

"*Impossible.*"

He heard them together—full of negatives and not the least bit convincing. "Yeah, uh-huh. They went to Martinsburg. They think we can't find them at the Commons."

"It's just as well," Chris said. "They probably needed a break, and we need to make some plans. The five of us can do that better without distractions."

"Should I keep listening to their thoughts?"

"It is no longer necessary," Merlin said. "Contact has been re-established. If the warriors will allow it, you may continue for the practice. Soon you will learn the purpose of the ability. With it comes responsibility. It is not merely some cool thing Jodian and Elven boys do to annoy girls."

"Is the fun going to be sucked out of every new thing I learn?"

"Without a doubt."

CHAPTER VII

Imani and Annora trailed Honor to one of her favorite thinking spots: the sales rack.

"This is too weird." Honor shifted through tank tops and T-shirts. "I shouldn't have left the boys."

"The boys will be fine." Annora held up a soft, flowery dress.

Honor twisted her face, indicating a definite no. "Yeah, Mom. I doubt either of them would have come, anyway. Travon thinks they're amazing and Jalen thinks he's one of them. I like that one," she said of Annora's latest selection.

I don't care what they think. It's not safe there. I don't see anything in here. Let's go."

"Wait a second. Let me look over here."

Annora relieved Honor of the small collection of clothes she had accumulated. "It's not a matter of safety." She and Imani followed Honor around the rack. "Regardless of whatever is going on, Chris won't let anything happen to them."

"What is going on?" Imani asked.

Nobody had an answer.

"Ooohh... Look at this one." Honor held a daring pale-white blouse up for inspection.

Imani took it for her own inspection. "It's see-through." She hung it up.

"Mom, you're a lost cause." Honor picked it up again. "It gets worn over something. It kind of reminds me of his hair." She missed the funny looks she received.

Two stores, three drinks, and a plate of cheesy fries later, they still hadn't exhausted the topic. But the sunny day, the sidewalk table, and the normalcy around them worked against their fears.

"Do you suppose any of it could be real? Could Dad? I mean, none of this makes any sense."

Imani sighed. "I don't know what to think."

Two tables to the left, men loitered. They noticed the women and catcalled.

"What a shame," one hollered. "Y'all shouldn't be eating all by yourselves. You can come over here."

Imani positioned and repositioned her straw. "Why would any woman be attracted to that?"

"I didn't hear them." Annora concentrated on dislodging a few fries from the pile.

"Me either." Honor stole a particularly cheesy one from Annora's plate.

Imani focused on the food, too. "I can't believe we've been married for twenty-one years without me knowing any of this."

"I don't know why Chris would allow it unless he at least thought it was true. There is an awful lot we can't deny. We saw it happen. Get your own." Annora smacked Honor's hand away, thwarting a second theft. "I can't help but trust Trill."

Honor set her cup down with exaggerated force. "He looks like he jumped out of a Robin Hood movie. He thinks you're his wife, and you trust him?"

"I know it's weird, but I do. His explanation of this joining thing is, I don't know...romantic."

"Please enlighten us." Imani sneered. "The beauty of it all escapes me."

"I don't know, Mom. I can see the beauty in them. Trill and Loathel are both hot. Too bad he is such an idiot. But go ahead, Aunt Nora. How did Trill explain it?"

Annora took a deep breath. "It's kind of the opposite of what happens here. Instead of meeting somebody, dating, and then getting married, their deity-thingy picks the person for you. When it's the right one, something happens to you so you'll know it. After it happens, you get joined, or married, or whatever. It's supposed to be guaranteed and you spend the rest of your life dating and getting to know the person you're married to."

"That's romantic? Suppose the guy is a toad or a reject or something that doesn't click with you. Are you stuck with this person for life?"

"A toad, Honor?"

"They aren't, but they all can't look that good. Reject still stands."

"For them, it's a matter of trusting their god. They do. Also, don't forget whatever happens when they meet the person they think they should be with. Something happened—we saw it. That's got to mean something."

"To them, yes, but nothing happened to you." Imani picked at the salty wedges. "Normal men have reactions to women too." She thumbed at the rowdy guys at the other table. "You don't marry them because of it."

"Well..."

"Annora?"

"I don't know. I'm not sure, but I may have had some kind of reaction too. I was drawn to him from the beginning. It was more than his physical beauty, although granted, that was there. I was attracted to him as I have never been attracted to anyone else in my life."

"Tony Felton?"

"Not even Tony Felton."

"Whoa."

"Wow."

"Tony Felton didn't come close to the jolt I got from Trill. Then, of course, there was the dream."

"Dream, what dream?"

"I didn't tell you about the dream?"

"No."

"No. Out with the dream, Aunt Nora."

"Off and on for days, I have been having this weird sort of dream," Annora said. "This guy, I never saw him, but I heard him. I don't even know what he'd said, but it sounded like Trill saying his bondy-spell-thing. The voice in my dream was his. I dreamt about Trill. I don't know what that means, but it has to mean something."

"Oh, no." Honor paled.

"Honor?"

"What is it, sweetheart?"

"The other night, I dreamt I heard somebody talking. At first, I thought it was the guy from *The Lord of the Rings*—because I dream about him too—but it wasn't. I don't remember what he said, but he sounded hot. I thought it was something I ate." She shrugged. "I only dreamt it once, and I know I'm not joined to anybody." Honor grabbed the cheesiest fry she could find, but Annora's expression stopped her from eating it. "Aunt Nora?"

"Annora, what?"

Annora sucked in another deep breath. "Honor, honey, I don't know for sure but...but, I think you and Loathel *are* joined."

"WHAT?"

Heads turned. People whispered.

"Are you crazy?! Me, married to that...that...arrogant, egotistical, pompous, overbearing... He's white. He's whiter than Dad. He's whiter than white. He's paint. Me married to that...that...without my consent? Without my knowledge? He's swimming in privilege. No."

"Don't get mad," a man called out. "Come over here— "

Imani rolled her eyes at the interruption. "Where did you get an idea like that?"

"I didn't see anything, but they said he went through the change too," Annora said. "His sole interest has been in Honor—"

Honor cut in. "Caucasity."

"—He looks at her the way Trill looks at me—"

"Privilege."

"—Can you come up with another reason Chris would allow some man to talk to and touch Honor the way Loathel has done? Did you see how Loathel reacted when Chris got upset with her? Haven't you felt the electricity between them?"

She made sense. Too much sense.

"I am not married to anybody." Honor shoved the half-eaten plate of fries away. "I don't care what they say. I don't belong to that Elve-person, thingy, whatever he is. I don't."

"If it will make you feel better, sweetheart, I don't think he wants the joining thing any more than you do."

"What's that supposed to mean? Does he think he's too good for me or something? He ain't all that."

"No, no. He probably wasn't expecting it. He's thrown for a loop or something. That's why you two clash."

"No. We clash because he's a jerk."

"Can this be undone?"

"There's nothing to undo, Mom. I'm not married. When I get married, it won't be to him."

"I guess we'll have to go back and straighten this mess out." Imani finished her drink as if it were the last pleasure she'd ever have.

"Do you think we should?" Annora asked.

Honor was already on her feet. "Yeah, we have to go back. I have a thing or two to say to that stuck-up, pointy-eared fruitcake and the rest of those nuts as well."

CHAPTER VIII

"It is decided. I will take Jalen back to Mayadal," Merlin said.

"I get we have to split up, but I don't understand why I have to leave? No offense, Dad, but this Maldonus clown is your enemy. Shouldn't you be the one going into witness protection?"

"Mayadal is not witness protection, it is my home. You need training. You were thinking about the Marines, anyway. This will be harder, I guarantee it."

"Yeah, because an arrow is going to do more damage than an M27."

Chris didn't miss a beat. "In Loathel's hands, it can."

Jalen made an unbelieving face. "Can I take anything with me?"

"You may take what comforts please you, cousin. However, I do not think alphabets and numerals will avail you much."

Jalen opened his mouth to answer and then closed it. He stood up. "You people are going to train me. Hmmm. I guess I better go pack."

***

Screeching tires and slamming car doors announced the girls' return. No one was startled by Honor's outburst. "Are we joined?" She stomped across the floor, stopping too close to Loathel. One hand went to her hip and with the other, she used her finger to thump him in the chest. "Did you do something to me?"

"No."

"No?"

Merlin and Trill exchanged glances.

Loathel was stoic. "I have spoken no vow to you. I have engineered no wrongdoing."

There was an awkward pause.

"Must you continue to poke at me?"

"Oh." Stiffly, she removed her hand. "Sorry, I thought…"

"I know what you thought."

Trill spoke to his mind. *"You are playing a tricky game."*

"Am I to be blamed for her lack of persistence?"

"You shall be blamed for much when she realizes what you've done."

"I have spoken no vow."

"As if it matters."

"She is a child and an evanescent. It is not my will to join with her."

"As if it matters."

Although conversations flowed around the room, Annora's eyes darted from Trill to Loathel and back.

"Soon you will be caught," Trill said. *"My lady is collecting her nerve. When she does, she will know what I know."*

"You know too much." Loathel's concentration turned outward. He stood up, drawing his sword. Senses honed by years of practice and wisdom with no parallel held no doubt when he said, "He is coming."

Trill was by his side. Likewise, he held his weapon ready. "Christif, the women. Medrid, gather Jalen and Tra—" he stopped mid-sentence. Travon was not within the safety of the house. A dark oppression filled the air with a rancid heaviness that made it difficult to breathe. Upstairs, there was a scream and then the lifeless thud of something hitting the floor. Next, Chris went to his knees, holding his head.

Imani and Merlin came to his aid.

Trill scaled the steps in search of Jalen.

As suddenly as it appeared, the presence was gone. It left a chilling stillness in its wake. No one moved or talked until Trill descended with Jalen in his arms. A flurry of motion had them surrounding the sofa where Trill laid him. "He is shocked but unharmed."

By now, Chris could stand up. He held his head and leaned on his wife for support.

The Elven voice, usually filled with ataraxia, now conveyed raw anguish. "Travon has been taken."

"Taken," Chris repeated. "No."

"Where's my baby? What happened to my baby?" Imani rushed to Loathel, her eyes pleading with him for some measure of comfort.

"He is yet living, Madame. If it were not so, your menfolk would know this by now."

She turned first to Chris, then Trill, and received a double affirmation before allowing herself to exhale. In that decisive moment, she gave her trust to the strangers who invaded her home. "What are we to do now?"

"Our plans have been for naught." Merlin paced. "We no longer have the time to get Jalen and Christif separated. Nor can we ignore Travon's plight while we get the rest of you to safety. We must act quickly or it will be too late to act at all." He leaned over the sofa. "Jalen, can you hear me? Are you all right, boy?"

"Yeah. I think...I think so. What happened?" With assistance, he sat up. "One second I'm packing, and the next, my head exploded." His breathing became easier as his strength returned. "I thought I had electrocuted myself. I don't remember anything else. You can keep this Jodian crap. I don't want it."

"Do not worry. Learning to protect your mind is simple. You will not be affected so once you master the ability."

"I still don't want it."

Annora and Honor huddled together.

"*Trill?*"

"*In all things, I am at your service, Milady.*"

The thrill of his voice swept through her.

"*I don't want to get anyone's hopes up, but could you could talk to Travon? Make sure he's okay, you know. Tell him not to panic. Is something like that possible?*"

"*Intelligence and beauty, what more could a man ask than to remain in your company?*"

She buried her face in her hands. This was not the time to blush. Her cheeks needed to realize that.

Trill's timbre reverberated throughout the room. "The wisdom of Annora dictates we should seek to speak with Travon. He may require comfort."

Chris nodded at his sister-in-law. Imani and Honor looked at her, puzzled.

"This you cannot do straightforward, Trill," Merlin said. "I am almost certain Maldonus is unaware of your nearness. We must keep him unlearned for as long as possible."

"I will speak to the child."

"No, Loathel. Your services are needed elsewhere. The harder task falls to you. Trill will see to Travon's comfort through Jalen."

"Me? What's wrong with Tray? Where is he?"

"Maldonus has come," Merlin told him. "That was the reason for your pain. He has taken Travon. You will need to use your newly acquired skill to contact your brother. Trill will be with you. He will direct and protect you."

"Okay. Umm, if this is a matter of passing thoughts, why do I need protection?"

He received no reply. Instead, Merlin returned his focus to Loathel. "You will scan Maldonus' mind if you can. We may be able to see what he is up to. You will have to do it quickly and remain undetected. I am uncertain if we can accomplish it from here, but I daresay you are the only one with ability enough to try."

Loathel nodded.

"Undetected?" Chris said, "I have never heard of such a thing. Who has tried it?"

"More than likely, Balazze. Eyise, without a doubt." Merlin named beings the Mayadalians were familiar with. "Aydin has perfected the technique. He is unstoppable. My worry lies in the distance. No one in my awareness has ever achieved an unknown range. However, my mind is if it can be thought, it can be accomplished."

"So call the Aydin person," Jalen suggested.

Chris talked over him. "How do you suppose Loathel get in?"

"Through the one who was already given access to Maldonus' thoughts." As Merlin talked, all eyes gravitated to Honor.

"Oh no. We've been over this already." Honor backed up. "Nobody's getting into my head. Formulate another plan."

"We do not have the time. Your brother needs us now." Of all the arguments Merlin could have used, he chose the one that had the largest effect.

Her arms plopped against her sides. "This is going to help Tray?"

Loathel came toward her. "This may be the only way we can reach him. At any rate, we can only attempt it if we work together. For his sake, we must try." When he was next to her, he extended his hand. "Armistice, Mistress." He smiled that smile again. The one she had no defense against. The one she couldn't help responding to.

Of their own accord, her fingers drifted, the tips coming to rest in his outstretched palm. Her rich brown skin enclosed in his pale porcelain grasp was hypnotizing. She let him lead her to the couch. Seated beside Jalen, Honor searched Loathel's face. "A truce?"

"Yes, Miss. For however brief the time, I assure you I will count it among the happiest of my life."

The warmth of his sincerity so affected her, the fact that he hadn't spoken aloud did not register. His eyes once again became a blue storm: passionate, emotion-filled.

Wow. At that moment, he could do no wrong.

At that moment, Loathel could do no more than stare at Honor, bewitched. His resolve was fast melting. He would need to get through this and put her back on the defensive. If he didn't, he would be lost.

Putting it in perspective helped him regain control. He went down on one knee before her. With work on his mind this time, he fastened his eyes to hers. "When you speak to him, tell him you need his help. Something happened to your brother. You turn to him for wisdom."

"Okay."

"Do not mention who is with you. Do not focus upon us."

Oh yeah, right. You, in front of my face, so hot you should be illegal, but I'm not supposed to think about it? Uh-huh, sure, I'll get right on that.

"You will have to get on that. It is necessary."

From forehead to neck, Honor shaded over, embarrassed. She squeezed her eyes shut. If she couldn't see her family, they couldn't see her.

"The things in your mind are being shared with no one. Even your brother is denied access."

Honor teetered between thinking and speaking.

"Either will work. If you leave it in your mind, it will remain private."

"Why aren't you denied access?"

"Because...I am an Elve."

She didn't have time to dwell on it; Merlin was talking to her now.

"Before we begin, you must understand, my dear, what you have done is a harmful thing. A proclivity you undoubtedly inherited." He ignored the flat look he received from Chris. "Nevertheless, since the damage cannot be undone, we must use it to our advantage. You will engage him in conversation. Perhaps distracted, he won't notice our communication with Travon, or Loathel observing his thoughts. Once we are done, you must never seek to reach him again. Having the faculty to know another's thoughts is one thing. It serves a specific purpose. Taking unto yourself that which is unknown is dangerous. Heart and mind go hand in hand. If you give one to anything, the other will follow. Under the guise of a spirit guide, you were being deceived by something extremely evil."

"She comprehends, Medrid."

"Of course she comprehends." Merlin dismissed Loathel's undisguised warning. Still, he was gentler when next he spoke to her. "All will be well, child. Do your best and all will be well."

"Now, my boy," He turned to Jalen. "You must heed what Trill tells you and nothing else. Do not, under any circumstance, let yourself become distracted."

"I'll try."

"That is all anyone can ask."

"Why do I feel our children are going to be in danger?" Imani leaned into Chris.

"They're not in danger, no immediate danger in any case," he said. "It may be a little difficult because it's new to them. This isn't normal stuff."

"You think you have to tell me that?"

Everyone sat down to await the outcome.

Merlin said, "Honor, you will begin. Jalen, stand ready."

Honor tensed, panicky. "Tashnine helps me. I've never done it by myself. What do I do?"

Loathel submerged the entire room in an ocean of tranquility. His melodic sonority was in Honor's head, filling her with serenity. *"I will be with you. Call him."*

CHAPTER IX

Speaking the words she had been taught, Honor centered her thoughts on Maldonus. "Olm-lem as-hi she Bo, olm-lem as-hi she Bo, Mal-do-nus, olm-lem as-hi she Bo, Mal-do-nus, olm-lem as-hi she Bo, hear me, olm-lem as-hi she Bo, Mal-do-nus..." She repeated the chant until the room faded away. Her mind caught a swirl of sounds and sensations without thought.

Her parents and aunt looked on nervous.

She stopped chanting and went into a rigid trance, not knowing what took place around her. She did not hear Merlin tell Jalen to begin.

"There is an unease in your spirit. Why have you awakened me, my child?"

She knew it was Maldonus, yet the voice had somehow changed. Before, it was hypnotic and harmonious; what she heard now was dry and crackling, the vowels and consonants scraping her eardrums. She would have recoiled if not for the peace coming to her. *"I-I need your help."*

"You are stronger. Good. Why do you turn to me for aid?"

"Because y-you are wise and...and this is something I need your spiritual guidance for."

***

"Tray, buddy, it's me, Jalen. Don't move or say anything. I can hear your thoughts."

No response; only sobbing.

"Travon, I know you can hear me. It's not your imagination. This is Jalen."

Still nothing.

"Remember our friends? Our cousin? Did you forget I can do this?"

"Jalen?"

"Hey, buddy. Don't move or talk out loud."

"Am I thinking this or is it really you?"

"I'm here, shh..."

***

Loathel sent Trill a warning: Maldonus' eye was on Travon.

Unease washed over Maldonus. He looked at Travon but could not detect anything unusual. Satisfied the problem was not with his hostage, he returned his attention to Honor. *"Why would I help you? More importantly, how will you help me?"*

"I don't know. Help you do what?"

"That remains to be seen. I am sure you will be of great use to me if you wish it. Is that what you wish?"

Loathel silenced her yes. **"Do not acknowledge my voice. You are not to answer his question. He seeks to bend your will to his. Instead, repeat every word as I say it. Yes, I wish to be of great use. It is in my heart to aid the cause you are involved in."**

"Yeah. I want to be of use. Ummm...great use. I want to, I mean, it is in my heart to aid the cause...ummm...aid the cause you are involved in. Yeah."

"Very well. Now, my child, how may I help you?"

***

"Don't worry, buddy, we're coming to get you. What I need you to do is rethink everything that happened."

***

"My litt—"

"Do not say little." As Loathel received information, he instructed Honor. **"Do not mention you have more than one brother."**

She took a deep breath. *"My brother is missing. The police can't find him. Can you tell me what I should do or where we should look? Would you know if he's okay?"*

"I know all things. Why do you seek this information from me?"

"Ummm..."

"When your brother disappeared, you felt his presence. You knew he came to aid you."

"When he disappeared, I felt you near me. I knew you were coming to help."

***

Maldonus closed his eyes, savoring the power he wielded over Christif's children. As he focused on himself, Loathel slipped into his thoughts.

***

"Trill says for you not to mention anybody but Mom, Dad, Honor, or Aunt Nora."

"Why?"

"Maldonus doesn't know your thoughts. He doesn't know we're coming. Trill says he might try to scare you, but he won't hurt you as long as you don't tell him anything."

***

"Your brother is no longer of this world. His life's blood has left him."

Honor's shock was so terrible her whole body shook.

"The doer of this foul deed was none other than your father."

"My father? Daddy was—"

The end of her sentence was cut off, but Maldonus failed to notice. *"You will find the truth with Tashnine. She can reveal his guilt. You must go to her. Tashnine will tell you what is to be done."* He left her.

***

Given a signal from Loathel, Trill's last message to Travon was he was not alone. They would be there, soon. Contact was broken as Maldonus' rasping laughter touched Travon's ears.

***

Honor became aware of the room around her. She sobbed. Loathel gathered her into his arms. He rocked and soothed her, uttering soft Elvish sounds.

"It's not true Honor, you know this. In your heart, you know it is not true. Jalen has spoken to Travon. He is unharmed."

"Why...w-would he...he say that...t-to to me?" She buried her head in his chest.

"Evil enjoys the pain of others. He sows malice and despair and naught else ever."

"Are you s-sure?"

Her voice echoed her fright. He let his repose seep into her soul, calming the heartbreakingly beautiful sound. "Your brother is not dead."

Despite Loathel's words, Imani cried.

"Why did you let her think such a thing?" Christif reached for the tissues while he vented at Loathel. "You were with her. You should have protected her from grief." He gave the box to Imani.

"And spark Maldonus' curiosity as to why such devastating news affected her not? I found it worth a few moments of reparable sadness for your daughter not to provoke the trouble Maldonus would cause were she not believable to him. Would you rather he lie about Travon's demise for pleasure or make it an actuality out of spite?" Loathel's voice never changed in octave or tone, yet the rebuke was palpable.

"I understand your reasoning. My reaction was hasty."

"You need not question my judgment where she is concerned." It sounded like a suggestion...almost.

***

Once Honor regained her composure, Trill shared the information they gathered. Loathel fed him all that was in his mind then closed himself off, sitting alone, brooding in silence.

"His knowledge of Christif's activities runs deep. He has been following your line for generations," Trill said. "We would not have guessed all he has planned. He is gathering Queons, enough for an army. They await him in Zendelel. He seeks to use them and the Kildar to overthrow first Mayadal, then Universe. He desires to open the gates of

Bedalamon. The evil this world knows is but a shadow of what will come if he succeeds."

Imani asked, "What does this have to do with Chris? Why has he taken our son?"

"Because, Madame, alone, Maldonus cannot do all he wishes. He requires the strength of Master Christif. He knows the same power resides in your son. His plan is daring but miscalculated."

"How so?" Chris and Merlin asked, in unison.

"He has taken the wrong son. He does not know you sired two boys. Maldonus had no awareness of Travon; he came for Jalen. He perceived in the boy the blood of our line. Cloaked as you, he lured Travon away. He thinks he has captured the one he pursued. He does not realize in Universe, if Travon is indeed true Jodian, it will not develop for some years yet."

"What will happen when he figures out his mistake?" Annora asked.

"Let us pray we have Travon back before then."

"There is much to do and we've not much time to do it." Merlin stood up. "Make ready, people. Take only what is essential for a week's travel. Be quick. We depart within the hour."

"A week?" Imani panicked. "We need to get to Tray a lot sooner than next week."

"The realms beyond Universe are not subject to the confines of Universe, Madame. Where we travel is beyond your comprehension of time." Realizing it was not enough information to get the Lossmans moving, he continued, "I set an estimate to keep you from overburdening yourselves. But time means nothing."

"It means something to me. My child is missing."

"My goal is days and hours. Maldonus seeks permanence."

That was enough to motivate them—everyone except Loathel.

"I'm not taking much." Answering a question no one asked, Honor plopped down close to him. "What's wrong with you?"

His eyes were a blue-black, reflecting a sorrow born of deep suffering. "I cannot speak of it. The wound is yet fresh."

"No idea what you are talking about. But, seeing as our truce isn't over yet, I'll wait." She pulled out her phone and clicked on a game. "When you get ready, you can tell me all about it. Who knows, you might even make sense."

Even with his burden, Loathel smiled.

Overhearing their conversation, Jalen went to Merlin. "Do you know what happened to him?"

"I do indeed, Master Jalen. Loathel's race is the farthest from corruption. Yet, it is not without a price. As high and far as his might and beauty may go, to an equal degree, so does his sorrow sink. He is in a hard place. No one in this room could have done what he did and lived. Many of his own kind could not." He paused to admire the Elve. "He has touched the heart of unequivocal evil. His mind has been flooded with unimaginable filth. Now, he must get rid of it before it becomes a poison to him."

CHAPTER X

Outfitted with as much equipment and food as their backpacks could hold, to the undiscerning eye, the Lossman family and friends were going camping.

"We need a moving body of water. What would be nearest here?" Merlin asked.

"Harpers Ferry. It's not far and being that it is already night, we won't cause a scene," Chris said. "This is still somewhat of a bedroom community."

Honor rolled her eyes. "What are we supposed to do, march down 340 single file?"

"What's wrong with the SUV?"

"Mom, you are talking about eight people. Some of them big and wearing funny-looking clothes. Plus all this stuff. You think we're all going to fit? Good luck with that. Tell me how it works out for you." Still, she followed the group, following her parents to the garage.

"Can't we zip-zip, like you guys did when Vincent and Wesley were here?" Jalen snapped his fingers.

"Zip-zip?" Merlin mimicked him. "What is a zip-zip?"

"You know, when you left and came back."

"I can assure you I have never zip-zipped in my life. If we were to do such an undignified act as zipping, how share-tell would you accomplish it?"

"That's what you're here for, isn't it?"

"Triune forbid, I have no higher purpose than to teach you how to zip."

Annora broke up their word game. "Why do we need a body of water?"

They loaded the SUV while Merlin explained. "To get to Maldonus, we must travel to Zendelel, located in the third realm. Trill, Loathel, and I can do this with ease. If the rest of you are to accompany us, we must open a gateway for you. Doing so requires the current of a river or large stream. The water creates the force we need to open the gate." His mind seemed to wander. "Regrettable act."

"What?"

"The gate," he said. "Oh, the mystery of it all. So many extraordinary abilities. There is not a race in existence that is not gifted with something. Traveling between the realms is a thing many know how to do. But it is knowledge better left untested. A skill that should not have been sharpened. To the ruination of many, they followed not the rules. Then the foolish one discovered a way to open the gates, making it easier for them to do what they wished rather than what they ought."

"I told you it wouldn't fit." Honor snickered at Trill and Loathel unloading half of their equipment, and Chris and Jalen rearranging the rest. "Why is it wrong to travel through the realms?"

"One reason," Loathel said from behind her, "is the psychic hotline. Those summoners invite criminals into your land."

Honor gave him a hard look. Their truce was winding down fast.

"Why would anyone do something they know they shouldn't?" Jalen claimed his seat. "If Elves and Jodians are so great, they should know better."

"It happens all the time," Merlin said. "Where we live, it is called life."

Annora passed the last backpack to Trill. "Who was the one who figured out how to open the gates?"

"That foolish individual was me." It was a simple statement. "Too much knowledge is my curse." The wizard climbed into the front passenger seat. "Miss Honor had the right of it. We cannot all fit. Unless you can procure another means of getting there, some of you will have to wait."

"We'll take two cars," Imani said.

"Honey, I don't think that's the best idea."

"Why not?"

"We don't know how long we'll be gone," Chris explained. He tapped the hood of the SUV. "This could end up impounded. One would-be abandoned vehicle is fine, but it will raise some questions having two cars, side by side belonging to the same family. The last thing we need is curiosity."

She pointed to the space beyond. "Travon is out there. I want to get him, not play taxi."

"It's five minutes, Imani."

From his seat behind the driver, Jalen shot Honor a quick text. **5 mins? He lettin me drive?**

From six feet away, she sent her answer. **Better than her. Get there faster walkin.**

"Fine," Imani snapped. "I'll wait."

Annora elected to wait with her. Trill waited with Annora.

"I'll wait too," Honor said.

"It would be better to have a seasoned warrior on either end." Merlin adjusted his robes for better comfort.

The men looked at Honor.

"What?"

Loathel held the door open.

"Do I look like a seasoned warrior to you? I'm staying with the rest of the girls."

"Honor, get in the car." Chris' fatherly authority carried from the driver's side. It lasted only until Loathel's displeasure reached him. "Please."

The 'please' made her move. She slid in next to Jalen, who appeared as surprised as she was. Loathel came right behind, filling his space and part of hers. His presence made it too difficult to think, much less figure out why it was necessary for her to ride to Harpers Ferry squished between him and her brother.

"Christopher." The full scale of Imani's mood echoed in the calling of her husband's name. She came to his car door and spoke low. "I don't trust him."

Chris added to her delusion the conversation was private by whispering, "Loathel is the best chance we have of getting Travon back." He slid in behind the wheel.

"I'm grateful he's helping us. I am. But that has nothing to do with Honor." He shut the door, and she leaned in to kiss him. "I don't want those two together. Why does she need to go?"

"Sorry sweetheart, you don't have any choice in the matter. She goes where he goes."

"Excus—"

"Loathel is our son-in-law. We'll have to get used to it." He backed out of the driveway, leaving her staring opened mouthed after him.

"What'd he say?" Jalen turned to Honor.

"Who?" Honor looked up from her phone.

***

Imani crossed over to Annora. "He said Loathel was our son-in-law."

"He lied. I knew it, they are joined." Annora put her hand on her hip in an Honor-like fashion.

"Elves do not lie. It is not in Loathel to do such a thing." Trill returned to the house with Annora and Imani on his heels.

"He told her they weren't joined."

"How do you get un-joined?"

"He never told her that." Trill cocked a brow at the woman connected to him. Addressing her sister, he said, "It cannot be undone."

"Oh yes it can," Imani said. "I'm not being cliché when I say we have a lawyer, you know."

"I admit, Loathel is better with animals than I. I have no experience with lawyers. Is your pet free-roaming or is there someone to care for it while we are away?"

"You know what? I have some calls to make. Annora, I'm going to let you two...umm, talk."

"Thanks, Imani."

***

"Well."

"Well, Milady."

"Well, what?"

"You have questions."

"No, I don't. Well, actually, I do."

"I am aware."

"You are not."

Trill grinned. "You have questions."

To keep from looking at Trill, Annora made a full circuit of the living room. All the books were back on the shelves. All the pictures were back on the walls. The room seemed as if nothing had happened. It was weird. "I don't get it. Loathel told Honor they weren't joined."

"He did not."

"I was there," she said over her shoulder. "I heard him."

"You did not." Trill hadn't moved, but Annora felt him very close to her.

"Are you saying I didn't hear what I know I heard?"

"He never told Honor they were not joined. You may revisit the conversation if you wish."

"No, thank you. I remember the conversation well enough."

"*If you think he said they are not joined, you do not remember it at all.*"

She felt him chuckle. "*How about this? I'll stay out of your head and you stay out of mine. Okay?*"

"*Nay, pretty lady. What you suggest is impossible.*"

"*Not only is it possible, that is the way it is going to be. I don't want you to know my thoughts. I most certainly don't want to know yours.*"

"*Might I inquire why you are examining them if you do not wish to know what they are?*"

She had not realized she was doing it. "You made me do that."

"*Nay, Milady. I do not use compulsion. You are responding in a way that is natural and welcomed.*"

"I don't want to do this." Annora thought about running up the steps. "I don't want to be connected." There were beds up there to hide under. "I am not your prisoner." She took a step.

That fast, he was beside her. "*Do not be frightened.*"

She turned, but he was there too. She couldn't get away. Yet, somehow, she felt comforted. She sensed his distress; she caused it.

"*I know a lot has happened to you in a brief time. It is the same for me, but trust. If you cannot trust me yet, then place your trust in destiny.*

Whatever the circumstance, fate knows what it is doing even when we do not."

"*I don't care about fate. I don't want to be your prisoner.*"

"*Is there anything as sweet as you?*" The awe he expressed was unnerving. "*You are not a prisoner. If it will help, I will explain the purpose of mind sharing.* I will vocalize it if that would put you more at ease."

He was so...so...something. He made her feel...he just was. She breathed deeply. "Yes. Please explain it to me. Out loud."

"As you wish."

Catching her hand, he led her to the window seat. "The males of my people are born not fully functional. We go through life half-asleep. The part of us that carries emotion does not awaken until we meet the one who brings us into our fullness. That took place when first we met. No one but the female destined to do so can awaken it. We rarely have occurrences of intimacy outside of joinings. Until we meet the one we are to love, there is no desire in us. There is no emotion."

"None?"

"We know family bonds. We know loyalty. We accept and give comfort, but we do not have true emotions. We know what is good and what is not, yet the males of my kind cannot tell a happy day from a melancholy one. We do things that are right or wrong, but we do not do what we feel because we feel nothing until we come into our fullness."

"What's the change like?"

"My heart stopped, then began to beat in a new way. It changed to match the rhythm of yours. My blood is synchronized to yours. We live and breathe as one now."

"We do what?" Annora crinkled her forehead, confused and displeased about it.

"In your wedding vows, does it not proclaim: The two shall become one?"

"Yeaahh. And?"

"We have one heart, one mind. We are joined."

"We are not joined. I didn't join anything. Okay, let's say everything is the way you claim. What's it mean? Why do you need to know my thoughts? Why do we need to have the same heartbeat? What's the point?"

"It is my onus to see to your happiness. I am a filter for you. Every communication that comes to you must first go through me. If it contains poison, I will dispel it. It will not reach you."

"Come again?"

"It is my task to see that your mind is protected. Before any thought or word can reach your consciousness, I determine if it is fit for you to receive." He said it as if it were a good idea.

"That is too ridiculous. You must be out of your mind."

"*Only when I am in yours.*"

"Stop that." Her dimple ruined any serious effect. "This is too weird."

"Recall your time at the place you hid...the Commons. How many expletives did you receive?"

"I got you now. You can't go anywhere without somebody, somewhere being rude. In fact," Annora strummed her fingers on his thigh. "There were some guys. Wait a minute, I'll tell you what they said. Ummm, wait a minute. They pissed Imani off, umm..." *Come on Annora, think. There has to be something.*

"*There will be nothing. Guarding your mind is a duty I shall not forsake.*"

"I am so not liking this. What about my thoughts?" She realized what she was doing and pulled her hand back.

"I do not control your thought process. I have jurisdiction concerning only what you say."

"You have what?"

"It is for me to determine which thoughts you give voice to."

"Are you implying you can shut me up whenever you feel like it?"

It was his turn to be reluctant. "Yea."

"You must be on drugs. That is the mos—" Nothing else came out. She tried to talk but could not. Her voice box was gone. Her horror-filled eyes widened. A second later, all was normal. "Oh, hell."

"Do not be alarmed, Annora. I vow I will never silence you without reason. If you should utter something that might bring harm or regret perhaps, but not for sport. Neither can I stop your thoughts from reaching me. This gift is not intended for my merriment."

"You get to play God with my head, and you call it a gift?"

"I am given authority over your voice, yes, but in truth, I am the servant. You are the master of our destiny." He brushed the back of his hand along her cheek. "My heart can only function as you direct."

Her distress became wonder as she listened.

"As I have said, Milady, until we receive our fullness, we are without emotion. I have emotion now, yet it is a fickle thing. I can do nothing save see to your happiness and protection. If I wish to feel joy, you must be joyful. If you are saddened, I can feel only sorrow. When you are angry, I must act on behalf of that anger. I may be entertained or burdened, and things can affect me, but it comes to me only through you. I can decide what is right or wrong, but I can only know joy or peace when they reside in you."

Annora's mouth dropped into a perfect O—the sound she would have made had she been able.

"*I did not do that.*"

She giggled despite herself.

"If it makes you happy for us to climb a mountain, it will make little difference if I wish to climb a mountain or not. I will only be content when you are content, so I will climb and see you safely to the top."

She still didn't like it, but it was better than him being in charge of everything.

"I have the same control over that as you have over me governing your voice." His eyes lingered on her lips. "We are joined. One heart. One mind. Together we work or together we suffer. Either way, the two shall be one."

Annora swallowed hard, feeling his desire and her own. "This is too much. I can't believe it." *Why am I not more upset? Why did he have to be so handsome I can't think straight?* "Uh-oh. You know what I'm thinking, don't you?"

"Yea, I do."

She laughed, hard. "It's too late to be embarrassed. This is too weird." She laughed harder, rich and throaty.

His expression colored with elation, and he laughed with her.

She laughed with him.

They passed the feeling back and forth, and between them, acceptance was conceived.

CHAPTER XI

Merlin, Jalen, Honor, and Loathel waited while Chris went back for the others. Famous for its Civil War ghosts, Harpers Ferry resembled a ghost town at night. Merlin wandered, reading plaques and signs, learning the town's history. Jalen found a bench and took a nap. At the outlook beside the train tracks, Honor leaned against the rail near Loathel. For a while, they absorbed the peace.

Three minutes was enough peace for Honor. She pulled out her phone and punched keys.

Loathel watched her fingers and the phone with interest.

She felt his stare and glanced up once. "Do you want to know what this is for?"

"I do." Anything to hear her voice.

"It's called a cell phone. This device lets me talk to people in other places." She handed it to him.

He studied it briefly, then gave it back. "It has no capacity to think."

"It doesn't need to think. I do the thinking. It sends my thoughts to other people."

"Much like the mind sharing of my kind."

"Sorta, only less intrusive. Your kind should consider investing."

"My kind possesses the capacity to think."

Honor shoved the phone into her pocket.

Loathel brooded while Honor turned to private thoughts that weren't private.

A few minutes later, he said, "You come here often."

"Yeah, I love this place. Whenever I have stuff on my mind that shopping can't fix, I come down here. There's something restorative about it. Helps me to get my balance. Do you have any places like this where you live?"

"My home is filled with wonder. We could not survive without it."

"Are you being arrogant?"

"I am being truthful."

She huffed.

He wanted her happy. For one tiny moment, he gave in. "I did not mean to imply your world is without beauty. This realm has tremendous awe and majesty. Where we stand is not the least of them." He felt the lessening of her irritation. He liked it.

"Tell me about your home."

"Mayadal is the twin of paradise. Together, the islands make up the second realm. My home is in Aezilden, between the three rivers. The waters there are said to flow from Empyrean and nothing can make them impure. The trees grow to heights so tall the tops are lost from view." His voice became like music. "The leaves change depending upon the weather. When it is warm, they soak up the sun and become a fiery gold. When it becomes cool, the leaves turn silver."

"Ooh, that sounds beautiful."

"The only sight more becoming is the third color they take on. When it is neither hot nor cold, when everything about the day is perfect, it is unforgettable. So magnificent, you could sit and gaze upon them in wonder for hours without tiring. There is nothing in the world, yours or mine, to surpass the beauty they hold when they are that color."

"Let me guess, it's your favorite." She smiled.

He liked her smile. "It is."

"You didn't mention what color they turn."

"The beauty of my world is at its peak when they take on the color of your eyes."

Honor looked at him and could not look away. He gazed at her, enchanted. Her breath caught. *To him, it may only be a comparison to trees, but that is the most romantic thing I have ever heard in my life.* "Wow. You know, you can be charming when you want to be."

"And you are breathtaking whether you wish to be or not." He hadn't meant to say it aloud, but she was soft and dangerous and he couldn't defend himself. His pledge was coming. He knew it. "Unfortunately, you ruin it with your mockery. It is unbecoming."

It took Honor a full minute to respond. "I take it back. You can't be charming when you want to be. You can only be charming by mistake." She turned away, stung. "Look, you don't like me and I don't like you. Why don't we stay away from each other? Our little truce is over, so go away, you...you annoying little fairytale reject."

There was an unmistakable sadness in him. "You are wrong."

"I said go away. Shoo." She waved him off.

Loathel looked across the water, unmoving.

If he's not going to leave, I'm not going to leave. She folded her arms and turned her back to him.

They pretended to ignore one another. Out of sheer stubbornness, they stayed that way until the SUV returned.

***

"All right, Christopher," Imani said as soon as they pulled out of the driveway. "Why did you let your daughter get joined? How can it be undone? Honor doesn't even know it. He lied to her."

"I couldn't stop it. I wouldn't have, anyway. Honor couldn't do any better than Loathel. I am honored his fullness comes through her."

"Excuse me? His what came through her? This is nonsense. I want it put to an end. Why did he lie to her?"

"Honey, you ask too many questions at once. What do you want me to answer?"

"All of them."

Chris sighed as the traffic light went from yellow to red seconds before he got to it. "Fullness is a way of saying it's guaranteed they were made for each other. You can't put an end to it. You can't change it, sweetheart. You'll have to accept it."

"No, I don't. You keep skipping the part about why he lied. You knew he was lying. Why did you let him deceive her?"

Chris stared at the light, disgruntled. "To tell you the truth, it's a mystery to me. I heard what he said. I'm positive they're joined, and I know he didn't lie to her."

"That doesn't make sense."

"Finally."

"Excuse me?"

"The light," he mumbled, smashing the gas.

"Well?"

"Well, what?"

"You know good and well what. They're joined, but he said they weren't, and it wasn't a lie. That doesn't make sense."

"I know. Nevertheless, it's the truth."

"How can you be so sure?"

"When a couple is joined, it cannot be hidden. Whether Loathel admits it or not, they are joined."

"So he li—"

"No, sweetheart, he did not lie. He can joke around as well as anybody, but he is not capable of lying. I realize it sounds crazy. Believe me, they are joined, and he didn't lie. Maybe Trill can shed some light on this for us." He adjusted his rearview mirror so he could see the occupants behind him.

Trill sat close to Annora, whispering something that made her giggle.

"Nice try, nephew. I know you couldn't miss this conversation if you wanted to."

"I want to." He never took his eyes off Annora.

"You could solve this mystery for us."

"Mayhap you should seek Loathel for your answers. I do not consider it my place to reveal his motives." A devilish smirk tickled the corner of his mouth. "Of course, I am not the only one here who knows Loathel's motives. Annora does not yet owe him the allegiance I do."

"What are you talking about? I don't know anything about it." She pushed her hair out of her face. It fell back again.

"If you wanted to know, it is but a small matter for you to look." He pushed her hair out of her face.

"Uh-uh. I'm not looking at anything in your head. You can wipe that smirk off your face. I'm not doing it."

"Ah, well, if you do not wish to be of service to your sister and your poor unsuspecting niece, that is your choice. Although, it is indeed a small thing; a thing you have done once or twice already."

"Annora, what do you know?" Imani turned in her seat.

"You are a manipulator." Annora shook her finger at Trill. "You want me in your head. You like it or something,"

"More than anything, Milady."

Annora gave an exaggerated sigh, bit her bottom lip, and focused. It was super easy. In a few minutes, she had all the information she needed. She stopped when she got to the part where Trill contemplated her beauty and didn't care if she knew. "Stop making me blush." She covered her face with her hands.

"Nay." He pulled her fingers away.

Chris cleared his throat. "Annora, can you tell us anything?"

"Yes, I can. He never answered her question."

"Yes, he did."

"No, Imani, he didn't. Honor asked him if they were joined *and* if he did anything to her. He answered the second question."

"Ha." Chris sniggered but stopped when he noticed Imani's scowl. "Honey, it's done. We can't undo it and I don't recommend interfering." He pulled up where he had parked before. "Irritating Medrid is one thing. You didn't have any idea of what he's capable of. Now you know there is more going on here than you can possibly understand. Leave Loathel alone."

Imani rolled her eyes at the reminder.

***

Honor released her tight stance the moment the SUV stopped.

Loathel moved the exact moment Honor did.

***

Before they got out, Trill sent Annora a message. *"You may wish to warn your sister: If she tells Honor anything it is because Loathel allows it. Honor can receive nothing he does not hear first."*

"Oh boy, this is too complicated. Hey, stop making me forget: I don't want to do that."

He grinned. *"Nay."*

She concentrated on her sister. "Imani, honey, be careful."

"What do you mean?" Imani walked toward her daughter and the Elve who followed.

Annora whispered in a rush of syllables, "He'll-hear-what-you-say-before-she-does. If-he-doesn't-like-it, she-won't-hear-it."

"What?"

"He-can. It's-weird-but-true. Trill-did-it-to-me." She shut up as Honor approached.

"Honor, honey, there's—"

"Did you say something, Mom?" Honor stepped past her, then backed up.

"Uuhhh...nooo...no, I was...I wanted...you to come help unload." She pointed behind her.

"I was." Honor hunched her shoulders. She climbed in, making her way toward the back.

Tongue-tied, Imani watched Honor disappear. When she turned around again, Loathel stood in front of her.

Smirking, his soul-piercing eyes, bright even in the darkness, silently implied he had done what she thought he had done.

She went to the back of the SUV, fast.

Trill's laughter drifted to him. *"You would have her believe you stopped Honor's hearing?"*

"Her error is her own."

"Do not forget, she has a lawyer."

The Elve unsheathed his long knives and examined the blades, unconcerned. *"Do they bleed?"*

***

"Da, da, da da dadada da, da, da da dadada..." Merlin returned from somewhere in a pleasant mood.

"Nice of you to help us." Jalen thumbed at the unloaded equipment. "Where were you?"

"Let us hope nosiness is not one of your stronger attributes. If you must know, I was in the church. The one on the hill up there." He pointed. "It's charming inside. The Crucifix is quite stirring."

"What were you doing in a church?"

"It appears nosiness *is* one of your stronger attributes. Pity. Since I was not gone long enough to have attended service—I go on Christmas—I was talking to the priest and this is where your interrogation ends, kibitzer."

"You talked to a priest?"

"He has a story to tell."

"What's that?" Jalen pointed to the small leather pouch Merlin held.

Merlin's hand disappeared into the folds of his robe, emerging again empty.

"What's what?"

CHAPTER XII

Merlin touched his staff to the water's surface. Back and forth, he disturbed the river, chanting in an ancient language. Gently, while maintaining the movement, he lifted the staff above the current. As he did, a firefly flicker of light appeared. With each rotation, the light grew until before them, hovering over the water, was a dazzling brightness. He stepped back to view his handiwork.

The wing-footed Elve darted through and disappeared. Before anyone could react, Trill lifted Honor by the waist and handed her through the light. She didn't have time to be scared. The instant she went in, she came out the other side. In unison, Trill let go and Loathel caught hold of her, pulling her down beside him. Honor looked about her, mouth agape. Loathel returned his focus to the light, ready to catch the next person.

Trill lifted Imani through. Christif went next, followed by Jalen. Once Merlin was on the other side, Trill surprised Annora by picking her up. Holding her to him, he cleared the opening in a single bound.

***

The sensation was without comparison. The senses were at once exulted and confused. The darkness and river that lay before them was now a hillside soaking up the midday sun. To the untrained eye, Zendelel could have been an undiscovered paradise. There were grass, wildflowers, and trees, but no sign of modern civilization. No roads, no cars, no buildings; there was nothing to suggest a world similar to what the newcomers called home. It held a virginal beauty that was both familiar and altogether new.

"That's a no." Annora backed away from Trill the moment her feet touched the ground. "I don't get picked up. I don't get carried...through...lights."

He arched a cocky eyebrow at her: Purely dominating. Purely male.

Loathel chuckled.

"My body does not belong in...your...arms." She frowned at her lame wording.

He added a cocky grin: Purely dominating. Purely male.

She turned away.

Trill's chuckle mingled with Loathel's. Then they got serious. A notable silence engulfed them. The land held its breath in anticipation.

"Accepting I have not been here in almost two centuries," Chris said, "we are some distance from Alpravage."

"A safe distance from Alpravage," Merlin said. "It would be foolish to appear moments behind Maldonus. He is watching. He is waiting. We cannot risk him finding us before we are ready to be found."

"I have to readjust my thinking," Chris said by way of explanation. His family was too busy exploring to care.

While those new to Zendelel took in the majesty, Merlin, Loathel, and Trill scanned the area for signs of trouble. It was not long in coming. A spot in the distance caught the eagle eyes of the Elve. "Kildar border patrol, we have to move."

The group set off, hoping to take cover in the closest woods. They walked a distance with no one talking, stopping only long enough to determine if they were being followed. They were. The patrol closed in.

Trill sought Loathel's counsel. "Can you tell how many?"

The Elve stood atop a boulder, looking back at the path they had taken. "Eighteen, no more than twenty."

"How long before they overtake us?"

"Within the hour. What do you suggest?"

"I say we take our rest and wait for them."

Merlin sat down on a large rock. "It's about time. I don't know why we didn't do that before." He gave disapproving looks to Trill and Loathel. "I wonder if either of you understand why you are with me."

Loathel jumped off the formation he had been standing on. As soon as he did, Honor climbed up. "I don't see anything." She squinted. "Is something actually after us? Or are you more delusional than I thought?"

She leaned too far forward to maintain her balance and would have tumbled headfirst into some sort of thorn bush had it not been for the quick hands of the tall, pale object of her disdain.

He set her down, laughed at her clumsiness, then dismissed her. "We are with you, Medrid, because you had some foreknowledge of the fullness of Trill and the downfall of me. By bringing us, you get to witness the spectacle firsthand."

"There is that," the wizard answered. "It had also occurred to me, as a bonus, you may possess some skill in combat. If nothing else, you look scary."

"Medrid," Trill said. "We are under your leadership. If that was your mind, you should have spoken sooner." He pointed to the people with them. "They are not used to this. What were you thinking?"

"What I am thinking is never a question to me. I do wonder why it is now that you choose to make a stand?" His eyes twinkled with mischief. Not waiting for Trill to answer and turning instead to Annora, he said, "My dear, you are to be commended. We have come this far without bloodshed only because you could go this far. If you did not require rest, we would still be moving. I would ask you to have a care for an old man. Loathel is the only one able to keep up with Trill, and you are the only one who can make him stop."

Christif and Jalen supplied some good-natured heckling. For different, embarrassing reasons, Annora and Trill looked away. However, Annora got some enjoyment from his discomfort. *Payback.* He lifted the thought from her mind. Her pleasure was alright with him. He was not used to having feelings. He certainly was not prepared to have them laughed at, but he took it in stride. "For that," he said to Merlin, "When next she tires, I shall carry her." He winked at Annora. "You need not count on stopping until I tire."

"Then I needn't count on stopping at all. You do not possess the wit to know when you are tired. But enough, we need a plan."

Becoming serious again, they removed their backpacks. Loathel tossed Christif his sword and dashed off.

No, he didn't abandon us. Honor studied his exit. "Did he leave?"

"Why not ask him?"

"Like, how am I supposed to do that? Chicken Little doesn't have a phone." Cousin or not, being Loathel's friend made Trill irritating too.

"I do not abandon. You remain within my sight."

Honor jumped and twirled around. She looked to the left and to the right, baffled.

Annora recognized the look. "He's in your head. You forgot he could do that."

Her forehead crinkled. Ever since Harpers Ferry, most of her thoughts had been about him. *"Have you been in my head? Do you know what I have been thinking?"*

"An enemy approaches. Do you assume I have no busier work than to monitor your thoughts?"

"Ooohhh!" Honor stamped her foot.

Trill came over to the women. He pulled out his dirk and was momentarily confused when they recoiled. "Annora, I would rather give this to you, but I do not believe you yet have the heart to use it." He turned to Honor. "You would use it gladly, but 'twould be upon the wrong enemy. We have need of Loathel; I dare not trust it to your hands." He offered it to Imani. "Because you are without your lawyer, it is best for you to have it for this first battle. You possess a multitude of frustration. It could serve you well if the border patrol gets too close." Imani took the dagger. "Here is a purposeful opportunity for you to protect your sister and daughter." He bowed to the ladies, knowing they couldn't tell if he paid them compliments or insults. "Stay close to Medrid." Turning away, he let them wonder. "Master Jalen, we have but a short time. Find the largest stick you can. Help guard the women."

"Stick? Women?" Jalen snorted. "What are they, damsels in distress? Why can't I have a real weapon?"

"You do not know how to use a real weapon. Worry not, you will learn soon enough. Besides, there are no more. Find a stick." Trill walked away, stopping when Jalen began to talk.

"You have a sword and a bow."

"Yea, I do. Find a stick." Trill tried to walk away again.

Jalen followed him. "You could give me one of those."

"If you give him a weapon, he will injure himself." Loathel wafted the thought to him.

"Agreed." To Jalen, Trill said, "I have need of them. A good warrior can make anything into a weapon. Find a stick." He took a few more steps, turned on his heel, and squared off with his still following cousin. "What?"

"You're a good warrior. You use the stick. Let me hold the sword."

"Let you hold the...who would make better use of it, you or me?"

"That's not the point."

"Oh? Share-tell, what is the point?"

"It doesn't matter what you fight with, you're good. But for me to have to use a stick with all these real weapons around, that's not cool."

"I see. Strip the experienced warrior so the inexperienced boy can look cool. That is the most important issue here." Trill massaged his temple; it throbbed. Annoyance was not an emotion he cared for. "Are all the under-men of your realm like this?"

"Yes, give in."

Trill pointed to the trees. "Stick. Now."

"But—"

"Now."

He took a few dejected steps, then stopped near his father. "Hey, Dad."

"Jalen, did you hear what Trill said? Your first lesson as a warrior will be to learn to listen to those who are in charge."

"But, Dad—"

"Go."

He moved off, then stopped again. "Hey, Mom—"

"GO!"

"GO!"

Chris yelled at the exact moment Trill bellowed. Jalen went away mumbling something about surround-sound.

CHAPTER XIII

From a distance, the band of riders was intimidating. At close range, they were hideous. They were unlike anything the humans had seen before. Brownish, hairy, rotted faces with protruding warthog-like tusks. Their eyes sunk into their sockets, giving the illusion of hollow cavities. There were exactly eighteen in all.

Trill stood in the center of the path, leaning on his bow.

The crass voice of the lead rider reached their ears. "You have trespassed on lands unfriendly. What is your business?"

"We go about our way, causing no trouble, seeking no harm or interference from anyone."

"You may not have been seeking it, stranger, but you have found it. State your business and be quick about it."

A second rider said, "They are of warm blood, three are females."

The leader looked over the group, becoming mindful of the women.

Trill brought the attention back to himself. "Do not ask questions for which you will regret knowing the answer. Leave us and we will inconvenience you not. You have the word of Trill, Jodian of Mayadal."

"Trill." The name echoed throughout the group. It was a name with celebrated deeds attached, known to many, few without fear.

"Am I given to understand that I am in the presence of Trill, second son of Crystyl, Jodian Master of Mayadal?"

"Your understanding has not failed you."

"You are reputed to be a notable warrior. I must admit, to look at you, I am unimpressed."

"I will not state my business, but be assured, impressing you is not it."

The leader emitted a cackle of false enjoyment. He motioned to his troop. "Capture the females, kill the rest." He angled his mount aside. Some of the creatures moved forward; others dismounted.

A rider fell from his horse, a steel arrow piercing his neck. A second howled and topped over, an arrow protruding from his chest. Confusion ensued.

Confident none of the riders would escape Loathel, Trill dropped his bow and unsheathed his sword. He walked toward the leader.

Three of the ghouls shifted to intercept him. The first one died before he could raise his weapon. Trill engaged the second and the third in a flurry of calculated movements. He dispatched them both. Two more took their place, two more died within minutes. One other came after Trill. His fate matched the five before him.

Having killed all on horseback except the leader, Loathel next aimed for the ones on foot. Chris also joined the fray. For not having battled in over a century, he held his own against his attacker. Jalen stood ready with a big stick, although he did not fight. No Kildar came near. All had died by blade or bow. Chris drove his sword home and looked around. There was a litter of bodies everywhere.

Trill pointed his sword at the leader, the only one left of his entire band. "By blade or bow? You may choose the weapon of your death, for it is coming to you."

"I would not choose to be the target of your archers. A group so cowardly, they wait in ambush instead of doing battle with honor."

"I know your kind for what they are. You have proven to be more foolish than most, to speak ill of the Elve who has an arrow aimed at your heart. If you choose the sword, so be it, but let me correct you. You name a host of archers where there is only one. One more brave than the legends of him depict."

While Trill talked, Loathel changed positions, centering the rider between himself and the Jodian.

The rider gaped at his dead in wonder. "This damage was done by no other than Loathel of Aezilden."

"Indeed."

"I would not look upon the repulsive sight of the Bright Elve. I will fight you. When you are bested, I will be granted safe conduct from this place."

Trill stepped back so he might dismount. "The same safe conduct you granted us. You will die, evil one, whether by sword or bow remains your choice."

"Then I shall at least take you with me." He lifted his leg, putting his body on one side of the horse, and then he yanked the reins, using the beast as a shield. The horse completed four long strides before his rider fell off, dead. An arrow pierced his heart from behind.

"You almost missed." Trill said to the air on his left.

Three arrows flew past him; each embedded into the ground several feet further than the last, and all were a good distance in front of the fallen rider.

"Show-off." Trill wiped his blade on the cadaver nearest to him before re-sheathing it.

Loathel walked out of the trees. He recovered his arrows from the bodies he felled and his display. Chris returned Loathel's sword to him and claimed one whose former owner could no longer brandish it.

The women remained where they had been throughout the fight: still and speechless. Epic battles of movie proportion required cameras and actors and choreography, not three men barely exerting themselves. Trill wiping his blade, Chris wiping his brow, and Loathel collecting his arrows were the only proof they participated.

Merlin used his staff to push himself off the boulder he had been sitting on since they stopped. "Now you understand my lack of patience. Running. From the Kildar, no less. Bah. One could have fought them with the same result."

A triplicate of disbelieving stares prompted him to say, "It is truth I tell you. In all the realms of existence, there are seven Elites. You gaze upon two of them." He huffed. "They train against more adversaries than that. They dragged it out to impress you girls, I'll wager."

Jalen tossed his stick down. "Trill, you dissed me, man."

Trill's raised eyebrow was his answer.

"You didn't use your bow."

"There was no need."

"You could have given it to me, instead of me using a stick."

"Did you use the stick?"

"Luckily, I didn't have to."

"You judge this to be the result of luck?" The older cousin looked around. "Loathel, our young protégée has informed me of your lack of skill. According to him, the result of this fight was a matter of luck."

"Mayhap, if l aimed next at him, his feeling would change." Loathel positioned an arrow in his bow and drew the string back.

"Hey, don't point that thing at me." Jalen rolled his eyes. "That's not what l said."

The warriors laughed. Trill said to him, "There are plenty of swords now. Choose one that is not too heavy. l will teach you to wield it."

"For real?"

"Yea."

"YES!" Jalen forgot everything else as he searched for the perfect sword.

"Hurry, ladies, we've got to go." Christif picked up his backpack.

"Nay, Master Christif," Merlin said. "We cannot leave before these bodies are disposed of. It requires the assistance of everyone."

Imani found her voice. "Are we supposed to bury them?"

"No, Madame. Burn them."

"l don't recall that," Chris mused.

"l doubt you had need before."

Rather than respond, Chris asked a different question. "Won't a fire draw attention?"

"It may, but there is great folly in leaving them as they are."

"Why?" Jalen strapped on a sheath and narrowed his choice down to four swords. He swung them like baseball bats.

"Unless we destroy them, they will be on our trail and none too happy with us, l can assure you." Merlin shook out his robes.

"What are you talking about? They're dead."

"Killing them is only half the task, destroying them is the other."

Trill and Loathel added to the mound of bodies they had made. Christif and Merlin went to help them.

"I'm sorry," Honor said. "l don't understand. Killing, destroying," she weighed the air with her hands, "kind of like the same thing, isn't it?"

Merlin was serious when he turned back to them. "They are dead now, but unless we destroy their shells, they will be back."

"Eww."

"We could finish the task sooner if everyone helped," Trill called out.

Having found the perfect sword, Jalen discarded the others. He picked up the legs of the nearest Kildar guard.

"Uhh, no." Honor recoiled. "Sorry. I don't do icky, yuck, or gross."

Imani shrunk back. "I'm not touching those things."

"Count me out." Annora waved them away.

"What pleases you," Loathel told them. "But if we do not get it done in time..." He let the sentence die for effect.

"What pleases me?" Honor said. "I say we start walking. When you kill them the next time, do it in a pile."

Loathel turned away...and laughed.

Together, the reluctant females dragged one dead body at a time for a total of one. By then, the task was completed. Loathel selected eight horses and freed the rest.

Imani returned Trill's dagger.

"Thank you." He tucked it into his waistband. "There are weapons aplenty if you ladies desire one."

"Do we have to carry them?" Honor asked.

"Yea. Your weapon stays on your person at all times."

"Then...no." Honor shook her head. "I'd use it on the wrong enemy, anyway."

"I don't have the heart to use it." Annora shrugged.

"I'm good. Even without my lawyer," Imani said over her shoulder.

"Y'all salty," Jalen called out.

Trill cut his eyes to Loathel. They were in unfamiliar territory.

As the others mounted and prepared to ride, Merlin pointed his staff toward the heap. "Rhaba ik dejaka." A blaze ignited. They rode away from the burning bodies and the battle scene.

CHAPTER XIV

The gentle hum of rushing water preceded the sight of an unpolluted river. The River March was wide and winding, reflecting an indigo sky. They stopped near it and those of the earth were grateful. The afternoon was giving way to evening, but according to their inner clocks, it was the wee hours of the morning.

Loathel and Trill set off to hunt, leaving the others to make camp. Christif, Imani, and Jalen erected tents while Annora and Honor arranged sleeping bags. Merlin filled a pot with water to boil. Once everything was ready, Jalen fell asleep fast. Christif, preoccupied, and seeming to need space, collected firewood. The others let him be. Merlin started the fire, and the girls clustered around it, discussing the day's events.

"Did you see them fight?" Honor whipped out her phone, checked her messages, and holstered it in a manner that would make a gunslinger proud. "We actually saw dead people-things."

"How could you miss it?" Imani asked. "They killed them all. Dead."

"This might seem cruel," Annora said, "especially coming from a nurse, but I'm glad they're dead. I would be petrified if they were following us. I don't want to know what would have happened if..." she interrupted her comment with a shudder.

The others agreed.

Imani said, "Eighteen. They took on eighteen. It was like something out of a movie."

"Better than a movie."

"Yeah," Honor said. "When guys fight like that in movies, it's always so phony. No one man could be that legit. He didn't have a hair out of place."

Imani and Annora exchanged a look.

"I don't get into movies like that. Guys slugging it out isn't my thing. Although, I have to admit," Annora shook her head, "wow. Those things were gross, and I hate dead stuff, more now than ever, but they were impressive."

"I can't even deny that one." Imani threw a stray branch into the flame.

"That is because they were not slugging it out." Merlin sprinkled herbs of some sort into his water. So far, nothing else was in it. "They did what they are trained to do. Fighting for them is a necessity. They are warriors. It is their right, their responsibility. Integrity demands it of them."

"They did a good job, whatever the reason." Honor removed her headband so she could play with her hair. "You too, Dad. I was impressed with you."

The others echoed her sentiments.

Christif dropped an armload of firewood, thanked them, and set off to collect more.

"Mr. Merlin," Imani got his attention. "You called Trill and Loathel Elites. What does that mean?"

Merlin stirred his pot. "It is their warrior's rank. As they train, the best fighters become Champions. The best Champions become Masters."

"You guys call Daddy a Master," Honor said.

"Christif is a Master." Merlin nodded. "One of the best. I name Jalen an honorary Master because I have no doubt he will earn the title early on."

"But you don't call Trill a Master." Annora asked, "Why not?"

Merlin continued his explanation. "From Masters, the Majestic emerge. There are nine Jodian warriors so titled."

"You don't call Trill a Majestic, either." Annora wanted her suspicions confirmed.

"An Elite is the highest warrior-ranking in the second realm. Six elves have achieved it. Trill is the only Jodian to extend that far."

They understood how powerfully dangerous the warriors were.

"Whoa," Honor said.

"Wow." Imani added her thoughts to Honor's.

Annora whistled. She didn't have any words. She could feel Trill's pleasure at her non-response.

After a moment, Honor spoke again. "I have a question, Aunt Nora."

"What?"

"What happens now for you and Trill? Are you married? Is this like a honeymoon—which, by the way, strikes me as pathetic—or haven't you thought that far ahead yet?"

"No, I have not. Nor do I intend to. I don't know about this connection thing, but I am not married."

"*For certain, you are not married. I have told you, we are more.*"

"Stop it!" She startled everyone around her.

"Knock it off, Aunt Nora," Jalen turned over.

"I'm sorry," she said. "He's in my head again."

"*I am always in your head.*"

Annora ignored the masculine laughter tickling her inner ear.

"My dear," Merlin said, "that he is able to be—as you say— in your head, should give you some indication the things he has explained are true."

"Yes! That's it." Annora jumped up and dusted her jeans.

"Aunt Nora." Jalen buried his head beneath his pillow.

"Sorry." Her dancing around did not give the impression she was sorry at all. "I got it, I got it," she sang.

"Got what?" The other girls wanted to know.

"Give me a minute." She held up a finger. "I've got you now," she told the trees above her head. "I don't want anyone to know my thoughts. It would make me happy to keep them to myself."

Chris dropped another armload of firewood. This time he stayed to watch.

Imani and Honor stared at each other, puzzled.

Merlin clapped his hands. "This should be good."

"*I cannot stop myself from receiving.*"

"You're okay. It's the other one I don't want clued in."

"*Loathel is not monitoring your thoughts.*"

"But he could. We don't want to tempt him."

"*As you wish, Milady.*"

"You may not warn him or I won't be happy."

"*You understand.*"

"*I do.*"

"*Does this mean you accept what I have said? Will you believe we are indeed joined?*"

"I didn't say all that."

"You know how it works. If you act upon my claim your happiness is above all else to me, you must accept the reasons why."

"If this doesn't work, we'll know you are mistaken."

"Am I to be blamed for feminine insanity?"

"Yes." Now Annora was ready. She rubbed her hands together. "We're going to play charades."

"Charades?" Imani repeated.

"Where did that come from?" Honor stopped her hair game. Her aunt required her full concentration.

"You forget; he can block her hearing."

"Oh." She let out a frustrated breath and chewed on her bottom lip.

"Why don't you write it down?"

"Oh. Thank you," Annora smiled into the air. While everyone watched, she went through her backpack frenzied, searching until she found a notepad. She scribbled the message and held it up to Honor to read.

Loathel IS joined to you. He dodged your question. You have to be direct to get the truth out of him!

Honor screamed.

Imani snatched the note and read the message herself.

Jalen sat up.

Honor pointed at him. "If you open your mouth, E.T., I swear, I will shove that new sword down your throat!"

Jalen raised his hands in silent surrender.

New resentment at Loathel surged through Honor. "You Peter Pan wannabe! Where are you? I'm going to kill you! How dare you? Don't come back! Do not show your face around me ever again! Do you hear me? I know you can hear me!" She stomped in a circle, shaking off the hands of those who tried to console her.

The warriors were close to camp when Annora thought up her scheme. Loathel walked out of the trees behind Honor on soundless feet. "For certain, I can hear you. The entire forest can hear you. It would be better if you stopped screaming."

He was too relaxed for her liking. She swung at him.

With electric quick reflexes, he caught her wrist in a gentle grip of steel. "Don't. You could break your hand."

She snatched her arm away, his speed robbing her of thought. "You...you...the total caucasity! You are beyond white with your presumption! How dare you! You...you...I can't think of anything vile enough to describe you. You... you..."

"There is another matter I must attend to. After which, I will show you reason. That should give you time enough to invent some entertaining insults." He had the nerve to grin. "I anticipate hearing what you will declare. Only your best will do for this occasion."

His audacity left her speechless.

Loathel walked over to Trill. In a flash, he had his sword drawn, the tip touching the Jodian's throat.

Trill's hand was on his own slightly raised sword. He said nothing but gave a curious glance to his friend, not seeing friendship reflected in Loathel's hard gaze.

There were shouts from those around them. The air was thick with layers of unease disseminating from Loathel. Jalen leapt to his feet, but no one else dared to move for fear the Elve would cause the Jodian harm.

Merlin added more herbs to his water.

Loathel stood statue still, a menacing figure. "Mayhap you should have warned your woman. There are consequences to meddling in the affairs of others."

"I'm sorry." Annora stepped forward. "It's my fault. He did it for me. You know that. It's my fault." Her hands shook.

Loathel answered without turning from Trill. "Indeed, it is. Do you not yet realize when your happiness is based upon your desires alone, he who is sworn to protect you, because he can do no other, will pay for your selfishness?"

"Hey, I'm new at this. I didn't know he would have to suffer because of me. I should have. I wasn't thinking. I'm sorry. Please, please, let him go. It won't happen again." She smacked at her tears. "This is too much."

"No, you were not thinking." The oppression evaporated. Loathel re-sheathed his blade and assessed Annora. "Fortunately, it was concern for your niece that governed your actions. The concern I appreciate. Because of her age, I will yield to you and your sister a small amount of interference. Nonetheless, I warn you both, 'tis no small boon. Tread lightly, ladies."

He bowed to the sisters, piercing them with his ever-blue stare, then focused on Trill. "Did I nick you?" He looked to see if there was a mark on his friend's neck. "For a moment, I was afraid I had cut you."

"The point of a blade rested against my jugular, yet you were afraid?" Trill was irked. Annora's tears were the source. He made his thoughts known to the Elve.

Loathel answered with delight. "Do not be such an innocent. You should have known better than to move."

"Reaching for my sword when under attack is a habit for me." He stooped to pull feathers from a large bird they had downed. Loathel reached to assist, but Trill said, "Do you not have a second matter to which you need to attend?"

"Thanks to you, I do."

"You would have to address it sooner or later."

"My preference was later." The Elve returned to Honor.

She, like the rest of her family, stood frozen in their spots, wondering if they were safe.

Merlin sampled his herb-water.

"Come, we will speak in private." He held out his hand.

Honor took a step back. "I don't think so."

"Yes."

"No."

"Yes."

"No."

"If you wish for answers to your questions, I will supply them."

"I don't have any questions."

Clear blue eyes reflected amusement.

"None for you anyway," she amended.

"Honor, please come with me."

"No, I'm not going anywhere with you."

"The hour grows late; I am weary."

"Listen to me, Lowell. Aside from the fact that you are a deranged, unbalanced crackpot who tried to kill his friend, you are also creepy and weird. You couldn't make me spend one minute in your company." She crossed her arms, full of attitude. "Why don't you go back to the North Pole or the Keebler Cracker Tree or wherever it is you Elves hang out and leave me alone?"

"Couldn't make you?" Before she knew what happened, he scooped her up and walked off.

"Put me down, you disproportioned fairy!" She kicked her feet and beat at his chest.

He held her easily, ignoring her and the looks he received from the others.

Christif stopped Imani in mid-stride. "Do not interfere."

Merlin mumbled, "He called me a child. Humph. Temper-tantrum indeed."

Even above Honor's noise, Loathel heard him. "At least I do not smash lamps or move furniture, Medrid."

CHAPTER XV

Annora and Imani stared at Loathel's retreating form.

"Christopher, can't you do something? He carried your daughter off like a caveman."

"'Fraid not, Hon. Even if I could, I wouldn't. This is great, isn't it?" He asked the fellows.

"Highly entertaining," Merlin said. "He better enjoy having the upper hand while he can. He has met his match in that one, I'll wager. They're like fire and ice."

Brown-gold braids whipped around as hazel eyes that were missing their warmth pinned Christif where he stood. "Great? Did I hear you say, 'Great?' You think it *great* to see some madman kidnap your daughter?"

"He's not a madman. You ladies have to understand: you cannot interfere. Honor belongs to Loathel now. She is his responsibility. We have no part in it."

"Shouldn't she have a part in it?" Annora asked. "Women stopped being property a long time ago."

"That depends on where you are." Trill washed his hands.

"They aren't property where we come from." Annora told herself she wouldn't look at him. She did anyway.

"We are not where you come from, now are we?" With a heart-melting tilt of his lips, he added, "I did not mean it to sound cold. He belongs to her as well."

"You people seem to forget," Imani said. "None of this was her choice. She didn't choose him. She didn't choose to belong to him or with him. She wasn't given a choice."

"No, she was not. Neither was he. The choice, Madame, did not come from either of them. That is the folly, which gives your world infidelity and divorce. Your daughter is saved from that. The volition was Triune's, the one you name God. When he chooses, there can be no mistake." Holding out his hand to Annora, Trill said, "Will you walk with me, Milady? I would see your anger spent ere this hour has passed."

It never occurred to her to refuse. Placing her hand in his, she let him lead her away from the camp in the direction opposite of that taken by the determined Elve and his hostile captive.

Trill stopped beside a fallen tree. He removed his cloak, spread it across the rough bark, and beckoned for her to sit.

That small gesture of consideration drained the anger out of Annora. Normal men didn't behave that way; at least, not the ones who came from Earth.

"Tell me, my sweet, why are you displeased with me?"

"You're the mind reader, you tell me." It was hard to stay mad, but she gave it her best effort.

"You are angry because you think I should have told you what would happen." He took her left hand in his. "You are angry because you think your actions almost caused me injury." He did the same with her right hand. "You are angry because you think Loathel and I planned it to frighten you." He looked deep into her wide wood-burnt eyes, his obsidian gaze a liquid flame.

Annora fought for her frown but lost it anyway. Her reactions were no longer subject to her will. "I didn't mean for you to actually read my mind. I guess now that you have, there's no point in us talking."

"I beg to differ." That smooth as moonlight voice whispered temptation in her ears. "You have but to search my mind to know I had no foreknowledge Loathel would react the way he did." He kissed one hand. "I do not hold you accountable. Your actions did not cause me injury. Any damage that may have come to me would have been because of Loathel and no other." He kissed her other hand. "We planned nothing, although Loathel had time to think upon it. He is in Honor's mind as I am in yours. Also, the moment my thoughts were closed to him, he instinctively knew to draw from Medrid. You did nothing unknown to him."

"I should have figured." Annora's relief mingled with an awareness of his touch. "It didn't seem like you were afraid."

"I had no fear."

"Why not? Does he do that often?"

"He has never done that before. It was unexpected but understandable."

"Understandable? Someone putting a gigantic knife to your throat is understandable?"

"It has been noted, for a while following the process of coming into one's fullness, the male can be unpredictable. He has a whole range of emotions to learn. Being more advanced, I am certain Loathel had more control than I would in his place."

"You must be joking."

"Nay. The beginning of a joining is crucial. It is the foundation for the rest of their lives. In the coming together of the she and the he, there is no room for the input of others, no matter how well-intentioned."

"Why didn't you tell me that?"

"Would you have believed me? Should I have given up a chance to have you admit what your heart has already accepted as truth?" He brushed his lips across her knuckles again. "I will keep you to your understanding. You know I hold your happiness above all else. You will no longer deny what you know to be true. You will accept and acknowledge our joining."

"I don't know about that." It was hard to function with him standing so near. Sunshine touched the strands of cinnamon shot through his ebon hair. She wanted to feel it again.

"Yea, you do." The sound was silk. He placed her fingers on his braid. "I look forward to having you re-bind it when you are done." Then he closed his eyes, content with her administrations.

She let her fingers touch here and there, marveling at the feel. "Understandable or...or...not, I—...uhh... would think you'd have still... have still been afraid."

"Afraid of what?" Clutching the palm he held to his chest, he leaned forward, resting his forehead against hers. The braid came loose, and she almost didn't hear him finish. "If Loathel wanted me dead, then dead I would most assuredly be."

***

Trill had more confidence in Loathel than Loathel had in himself. In his arms was a fighting she-cat. Discerning her mind as he did, he did not relish the thought of putting her down. He found a clearing within sight of the river and eased her to her feet. He steeled himself for the vocal tirade he knew was coming. He expected her to become violent and was poised to catch her when she ran.

He got none of it. The moment her feet touched the ground, Honor went completely still. Instead of the outright display of rage he knew she was feeling, her face reflected boredom, almost.

"Now we will talk."

Her countenance never changed. She thought about the TV shows she was missing. Seconds became minutes with neither moving nor speaking.

Loathel scowled.

Honor responded by listing in her head all the songs she had ever heard in her entire life.

Loathel was match enough for her stubbornness. It was her need that moved him. He could tell she was tired of standing there, so he tried again. "Why do you ignore me? I admit preference for your outburst over your silence."

She attempted to spell to herself all the colors backwards.

Loathel admired her. She was the most willful mortal he had ever known. But he'd had enough. "We shall not leave this place until we have an understanding. Thanks to your aunt, against my will, the thing that is between you and me must take priority. If you wish to prolong this confrontation, you will delay the aid Travon needs." He moved to the water's edge.

Honor ran in what she hoped was the right direction back to camp. Loathel caught and returned her to her original spot. As soon as he released her, she took off again, this time running in the opposite direction. Loathel was none too gentle when he deposited her a second time. Four times she tried to get away. Four times he caught her. By now, it was getting silly. They struggled not to laugh.

"The only direction you have not flown is across the water. Perhaps Elves cannot swim."

It was a dare.

Honor was an excellent swimmer.

She kicked off her shoes and socks. After putting her phone in her hiking boot, she tiptoed to the edge and tested the water with her toe.

Loathel removed his cloak but not his shoes.

Honor raised an eyebrow at him, but withheld comment. The next instant, she darted through the water, intent on getting deep enough to dive.

He gave her a six-step head start before charging in and scooping her up. He made a U-turn and came back to their starting point. This time, he sat her on a large rock. Honor noticed he was mostly dry. To confirm her thoughts, Loathel lifted one foot to show her that the bottom of his boots was the only thing to have been submerged.

She forgot her vow of silence. "How did you do that?"

"Elves are light-footed."

"Can I see it again?"

"You would have me cross over so you may have an advantage when next you run."

"I didn't think of that."

"Yet."

"I want to see you go across the water. I won't run away."

Wherever the tension went, they were happy to have it gone.

"If I have your promise, Mistress, I shall be at your beck and call." He bowed low. At her nod, he left her side. Setting a brisk pace, he took several strides across the water and back again without sinking.

"Wow."

"It is no great feat," he said. "It is something Elves do."

"Walk on water?"

"Walk lightly. We are close to nature. It is not in us to upset the balance."

"Call it what you will. Only Jesus could do that."

"Nay, Mistress. Did he not bid one of his followers to do the same?"

"Yeah, but that was through him. Yours is different."

He could not help the swelling of masculine pride at her response. "There is a contrary side to it."

"What's that?"

"I do not swim well."

"Right."

"I do not jest. I have little reason to practice."

"That's funny. I guess you don't have to swim through it if you can walk across it."

"Mayhap, you will teach me someday."

Sapphire and sea green glittered at each other.

"Mayhap, I will."

He placed his cloak around her shoulders, covering her completely. "You got wet," he teased, pleased to hear her bubbly giggle.

The moment passed, but the serenity remained. They looked across the water into the blooming abundance of evening. For a long while, they said nothing, not wanting to break the spell.

Honor bit her lip. She didn't want to mess up the moment, but she wanted to know. Loathel touched her hand. It made her brave. "Will you please explain this to me?"

"I wished only that you would ask." With words made of music, Loathel told her everything. Concluding with, "Coming into my fullness is the greatest occurrence of my existence. I would like nothing so much as to claim you and shout it from the treetops. I am blessed of all: Elves, Jodians, and Humans. Of all existence, you alone have no equal."

He stirred her to tears.

"Such wonder is not without its price." His intonation changed to one filled with lamentation. "Because I am as I am, I am unfit to be graced with one such as you."

"That's not true." She brushed her hair back, talking away from him. "I doubt I'm good enough for you."

He heard her anyway.

"Not that I buy this stuff anyhow."

She filled him with joy he couldn't contain. "You would not easily adapt to the Elven way of life, nor would I wish to live as the evanescent do. Besides, the end is too bitter a thought to bear."

"What end?"

"Elves are not allowed Empyrean. If we are joined, you may be denied the gift of mortality. To be with me may sentence you to sempiternity parted from your family. You may end up outside the first realm." He was serious. "For the evanescent, eternity outside of heaven is hell."

She took a while, rethinking the enormity of the situation.

He gave her all the time she needed.

"So, you're saying, according to your customs, we should be together. But because we come from two different worlds, not only will we not click, I could get locked out of heaven? That doesn't seem like a good deal to me."

"It is not for you. As the one who should be pledged to you, I can do naught but see to your happiness. Being joined to me would bring you bitterness and grief. Those things I cannot do. I will not do. I would rather bear your hatred now before we grow in love."

"I don't hate you. I tried, but it didn't work." His gentleness made it easy for her to tell the truth. "I don't think you need to worry. I wouldn't have fallen in love with you, anyway."

"Yes, you would."

"Arrogant, aren't we?"

"Only me."

"You got that right." She made a show of pulling her hair out and pushing it behind her again. "You know what? You aren't my type."

"Yes, I am."

His sincerity made her giggle. "Pretty sure of yourself, aren't you, Lowell?"

"I am sure of the ancient laws. We would not have evoked the joining if we were not to love. Lowell? Why Lowell?"

"Why not? I like Lowell and you could use a little humbling." After a pause, she asked, "Why would God put us together if it can't work?"

"I have been pondering that question since the first moment I saw you."

Somewhere a bird called out. The rosy purple-and-orange sky languidly dipped behind the trees, only shadows of its reflection touching the water here and there. Now talking, then silent. Loathel and Honor lingered. Having concluded they would not be a couple, there was no reason for them to remain at odds.

While they spoke of causal and curious things, barriers fell, and resolve melted. In the echoing of laughter, the lingering of eyes, the brush of fingertips against a shoulder, a deeper communication passed between them. Now silent, then talking. Their words they were able to control, but their bodies were betrayers, confessing desires not yet examined, divulging emotions not yet investigated. Beneath the decorum, negotiations for transformation were taking place between his heart and hers.

Somewhere a bird called out and was answered. The sun moved on to brighten other parts of the world, taking the orange and rose with it, but leaving the purple to welcome the fullness of night. During that greeting, Loathel and Honor made their way back to camp. The battle that brought them away was little less than a memory. Fully evident was the deep attraction each felt toward the other.

CHAPTER XVI

Jalen was asleep again, and the others were eating when Honor and Loathel returned. If anyone thought the new companionship strange, they did not mention it. Only Imani seemed on edge.

They talked, discussing where they were going and what they would do once they arrived. Loathel checked on Travon—an easy task for him. The boy was in a dungeon, frightened but unharmed. From Travon's memories, they recognized the outer structure of Alpravage, the long-standing stronghold of Azâzêl, of ages past. No enemy of the fallen lord had ever entered the fortress of Alpravage and returned to describe it. Even so, they did not consider the possibility of not rescuing Travon.

Merlin entertained them with an explanation of the world, as understood by the inhabitants of Mayadal. "There are five realms," he said, "Empyrean being the first and the highest. The twin islands of Mayadal and Paradise make up the second. Next, is this one, Zendelel—the land of sleep and Purgatory. Your home is in the fourth realm, called Universe. The fifth and final realm contains the most woebegone place in existence. The prison of Bedalamon, known in your language as Hell."

"Wow, I can't believe there's so much we don't know."

"I can." Loathel's light jest earned him Honor's elbow in his ribcage.

Questions about the various places they had seen and the adventures they had kept them talking for a while. At length, Merlin made his exit. "Except for Jalen, everyone seems to have a mind full of ideas. This means I must retire. I need to be well-rested. For whatever it is you meditate on, I may wish to exploit it for my own purposes." He sounded serious, which made it even more humorous.

A short while later, Loathel stood up. Feigning exasperation, he said to Honor, "Are you not wise enough to know when you are tired? Do you need to be told to go to sleep?"

"Me?" she shot back. "You are wiped out, sitting there worried you're going to miss something."

"If you would go to sleep, mayhap I could. As it is, I am afraid you'll get into mischief if I do not have my eye upon you."

"Sorry, Lowell, you're so exhausted, you're delusional. Mischief making is your department." She waved her fingers, signaling he should pull her to her feet.

He did.

"Good night, all."

The others said their goodnights. Honor and Loathel had a pushing match as they headed toward the beds. Honor stopped next to her tent, waiting to see if Loathel would choose a bedroll close enough for her to talk with him.

"I will always be close enough for you to talk to." He did not pick out a sleeping bag. Rather, he moved to a large tree.

Honor watched him climb out of sight. "What are you doing?"

"*Going to sleep, same as you.*"

"*In a tree?*"

"*I like trees.*"

"You are going to sleep in a tree?"

"*Tonight, I shall.*"

"Silly me. I thought you couldn't get any stranger. May I ask why?"

"*I want to rest, and I am sure you snore.*"

"I wouldn't recommend coming down anytime soon, cat boy."

"*Would you like to come up?*"

"*Nope. I'll stay where I am, thank you. There are sleeping bags in case you want to try normalcy.*"

"*It is normal for Elves to sleep in trees.*"

Honor snuggled under her blanket. "*All the same, be careful turning over, Tarzan. I can't imagine that being the best way to wake up.*"

"*Tarzan, he was good.*"

"*Yeah, I like the Tarzan stories.*"

"*I was not referring to the legends. I meant Tarzan was a good man.*"

"You know what? I won't dare to wonder what you're implying. Good night...Lowell."

"Does it have to be Lowell?"

"Yes, it does."

"There will be no end to Trill's teasing."

"All the more reason to keep it."

"Spoiled. You really are...good night."

Her smile floated up to mingle with his. A warm feeling surrounded her. Honor knew it came from Loathel and she basked in it.

***

"I guess they've settled their differences." Chris stretched and yawned.

"I don't like it," Imani said.

"I think it will be fine." Annora hoped it would be fine.

Amusement tilted the corner of Trill's mouth.

Annora felt it. "What?"

"It is nothing."

"Yes, it is. You know something, don't you?"

"I do not wish to know anything."

"But you do. What is it?"

"They are deceived."

"What?" Imani leaned forward.

Chris yawned again.

"What do you mean?" Annora was cautious. Trill didn't seem bothered, but what did she know?

"They believe they are ill-fated. They do not think a bond will develop between them, so they are free to be friends." He placed a reassuring hand on hers. "This will only deepen the bonds they do not admit they share."

"Maybe they're right," Imani said.

She was the only one who thought so.

Having no more to add, Trill stood up. "You should get some sleep, Master Christif. The second watch will be here before long." Speaking to Annora, he said, "You need sleep as well, Milady."

"I was thinking the same thing."

"I know."

Chris and Imani said their goodnights and retired to their tent.

"What about you? You have to be exhausted."

"It is not my time to rest yet. The first watch falls to me."

"That's not fair." She counted on her fingers. "You fight, you hunt, and now you have to stay awake. Why can't someone else take the first watch? You've done enough for one day."

His teeth were even and white. His smile was deep. "Loathel has done the same things."

"Loathel is sleeping now, as should you be. Anyway, there are other people here. We're not helpless. We can do stuff."

"They will get their turn."

"I said we."

"I said they."

She wanted to be indignant, but he made her giddy inside. "For the sake of argument, why can't *they* take a turn now?"

"It is most dangerous during the first and third watches of the night."

"Why?"

"An attacker who is smart will be aggressive when his victims are most weary; when they first settle and have not yet taken much rest. Or he will wait until they are locked in slumber and least expecting."

"Thus the first and third watches."

"Loathel does me the service of taking the third watch tonight. It is the harder of the two."

"What you're hinting at is you having the first watch should not irritate me."

"Nay, you should not be upset. Though, I admit, I am delighted you are."

He thrilled her. "I'll keep watch with you."

The flames dancing in his pupils had nothing to do with the campfire. "Nay, Milady. I am honored you would wish to keep me company. But it would not be wise for you to do so."

"Why not?"

"You would render me a poor watchman. My mind would stay focused upon you and naught else."

"Stoppp."

"Stop what?"

"Stop saying stuff like that. You embarrass me."

"Why would the truth spoken in earnest embarrass you?"

"Because..." Her grin was pure radiance.

"To bed with you, lady. I would not see your loveliness marred by lack of sleep. Although I doubt anything could affect it."

"Trill..." She covered her cheeks.

The obsidian blaze in his eyes said that was the reaction he wanted.

"Good night," Annora said. "Be careful."

"Sleep well, Milady."

Annora went to her tent with new emotion. Thanks to him, she wouldn't be able to concentrate on anything but him. She couldn't pretend she didn't like it.

Twenty minutes later, she was close to drifting off when she heard a voice in her head. *"Aunt Nora..."*

That was different. Only Trill spoke to her that way.

"Aunt Nora..."

"Honor?"

"I did it!"

"Did what?"

"I can talk in people's heads, too."

"Well, good, I guess."

"It must be because I'm half-Jodian."

"What are you talking about?"

"Mr. Merlin said Loathel had to help me. He's asleep and I'm doing it so I must have this ability."

"It could be because you are joined."

"We're not joined."

"Honey, you have to know there's something between you two."

"No, there isn't. He's great and really hot. Really hot. Fire. But it's not like you and whatever is happening with Trill. What is happening with you and Trill? Is he going to be my uncle or are you going to be my cousin?"

"You sound like Travon."

"I hope he's okay."

"He is, sweetie. We'll get him back." Annora sighed. *"We have to. Hey, have you been practicing this mind thing?"*

"I started a little while ago."

"Could you reach anybody else?"

"Oh, yeah."

"Who?"

"Loathel."

"Honey, I thin—"

"Know what he was thinking?"

"Is this something he's going to want me to know?"

"He was thinking about me."

"You're surprised?"

"Me. He was thinking about me."

"He probably thinks about you quite a bit."

"He was rethinking our conversation by the river."

"Okay."

"He likes my eyes."

"Your eyes are beautiful. And he's attracted to you."

"No, he's not."

"Is it safe to say you are attracted to him?"

"You think? Who in their right mind wouldn't be? You're attracted to Trill, aren't you?"

"You think? But I'm not pretending it's nothing. I may not know what it is, but I know it's something."

"What do you guess it is?"

"Logic tells me it's chemistry."

"But?"

"But in my heart, I believe him. I don't know why, but I do."

"What are you going to do about it?"

"Nothing."

"Nothing?"

"Wait and see. Enjoy it while it lasts. What about you?"

"What about me? I hope we can get close, but I won't let my heart get all mixed up and confused."

"What about Loathel?"

"What about him?"

"His heart? You said he was thinking about you."

"And? I was thinking about him, too. That's how I got into his head. It doesn't mean anything."

"You were focusing on him because you think he's hot."

"Facts."

"Honey, that means something."

"Yeah, it means I have incredibility good taste in my choice of crushes, and if anything, so does he."

"Why are you so confident there could be nothing between you two?"

"Because..."

"Because?" When Honor remained silent, Annora probed. "Because why, Honor?"

"Because that's not how things work. We all want to hit the lottery. But how often does the big win happen to regular people?"

"Not very, but it happens."

"Not to me."

"It could."

"If Mom heard you, she wouldn't be happy."

"Why not?"

"The last thing she wants is for me to be infatuated with Loathel."

"She told you that?"

"Not exactly."

"You talked to her?"

"Not exactly."

"Honor."

"I was practicing."

***

"Loathel, is this doing anything to you?"

"It is like two bees buzzing around in my brain. I do not enjoy girl talk when I am tired, even if the things they say are pleasant."

"Should we remind them we are not excluded?" Trill wondered.

"I do not believe the news would be welcomed."

"Perhaps not, but if they don't settle down, I may go insane. I am not used to nonstop chattering in my head, especially when the chatterboxes should be asleep."

Loathel said, "We could silence them."

"I know that would not be welcomed."

"I would welcome it most gratefully."

"As would I. Unfortunately, I told Annora I would not do that without reason."

"This is a reason."

"Not a good one."

"In gaining fullness, you have lost wisdom."

"An easy thing to do when females are involved. And you're one to judge."

"Do you mean Honor?"

"Who else, Lowell?"

"I exercise great wisdom in my choice to speak no vow."

"We shall see."

***

"What the hel-lo?"

Annora sat up. "Honor, what is it?"

Honor doubled checked her phone. "I hear Loathel talking."

"Okay?"

"He's in the tree."

"Why is he in a tree?"

"Because he's weird. That's not my point."

"What's your point?"

"Who is he talking to in a tree? Squirrels?"

"Oh my."

"What?"

"He's talking to Trill."

"Trill's in a tree?"

"No, he's still by the fire, but I can hear him talking."

"Oh. That makes me feel better."

"Not me. If we can hear them, I bet they can hear us."

"No!"

"Yes."

"They probably don't realize we're awake."

"They will if we keep talking."

"I'm shutting up. Good night."

"Good idea. Good night, sweetheart."

***

Twin sighs of relief escaped from the Elve and the Jodian.

"Why did we not consider that?"

"Because we are too worn down from late night girl conversation to consider anything." Loathel stretched and shifted positions on his branch. *"I will enjoy the silence while I can."*

"As will I. Good night, Loathel."

"Be at peace, my friend."

The silence lasted about two minutes.

"Aunt Nora...Aunt Nora..." Assuming Annora was already asleep, Honor turned over. Her question could wait until morning.

"I only vowed not to keep her from speaking."

"I vowed nothing."

Feeling justified, Loathel fell asleep, and Trill enjoyed the quiet stillness of the first watch.

CHAPTER XVII

Dawn had not yet arrived when the camp began to buzz with activity. They ate, packed, and moved out with speed and efficiency. Traveling and camping over the next few days kept them in the same pattern. During the hours of rest, Trill was true to his promise. Jalen received lessons in swordsmanship and did little else but practice.

Annora spent the time getting to know Trill. She peppered him with questions to which he supplied endless answers. Frequently they went off by themselves, walking, talking, and learning of one another.

Honor and Loathel behaved as if they had known each other forever. They played like children, sharing a daily never-ending game. Often, Loathel would steal some item in Honor's possession because he could. She'd chase him to no avail, then attempt turnabout.

No one understood Honor's captivation with tying Loathel's hair to hers. But she did this every evening as a ritual. While Loathel entertained himself with her phone—a thing that fascinated him—she would twist and braid, adding clips and bands until they were connected by a mass of tangles. Afterwards, she would sit in awe, watching him work to remove each one. Her explanation for this bizarre procedure was, "Because he's so dumb, he lets me do it." Secretly, it was her excuse to sit near him, touch him, and get lost in those brilliant blue, crystalline orbs known as his eyes.

Secretly, her motives were no secret.

Christif became increasingly uneasy. So far, his time in Zendelel gained him a newfound short temper. Normally, he was a man of patience with an outgoing personality; now he seldom spoke and when he did, it was curt. Concern for Travon was voted the most likely cause. Only Merlin showed signs of skepticism.

***

Jalen, Honor, and Loathel had a merry war with some nuts they gathered for that purpose. For the moment, Loathel and Honor double-teamed Jalen. He sought refuge on the safe side of the wizard. "So...uhh...how much longer 'til we get to this Alpravage?" He feigned interest.

Honor's miss-aimed acorn sailed straight at Merlin's head. Her hand flew to her opened mouth, embarrassed and then amazed when Merlin vanished a split second before contact. The nut bounced off Jalen's shoulder, making him yelp in surprise. Merlin reappeared a moment later, picking up the conversation as if he'd never been gone. "We are not going to Alpravage. At least, not straight away."

"Sorry," Honor called out.

"Where are we going?" Imani nudged her mount forward.

"Not to worry. Not even Loathel could hit—ouch!" Merlin grunted, a nut missile thumping him in the back. "Show-off," he muttered.

"Mr. Merlin," Imani persisted.

"Madame, we journey first to Raegladun, the home of Gale and his people."

"No."

The word was loud and authoritative, bringing attention to the speaker.

"Is there a problem, Master Christif?"

"Neither I nor any member of my family will set foot in Raegladun." Chris stopped his horse.

So did Merlin. "Like it or not, Raegladun is our destination."

The others brought their mounts to a halt.

"We need to change our plans, Medrid. Now."

"There is no need to fear Gale or his people unless you have something to hide," Merlin challenged.

"I hide nothing, especially my contempt for Raegladun. I will not subject my family to that evil."

"Again, those who do no wrong have nothing to fear. Also, I would remind you, Master Christif, this expedition needs but one leader and you are not him."

"I am the head of my family. I decide where we will go."

"As head of your family, your concern would be better spent upon your younger son. He has need of you, yet you waste time in useless debate. We will proceed to Raegladun." Merlin set his charger in motion.

Trill beckoned for Annora to follow him. They nudged their steeds into action. Honor was staring at her father when Loathel caught hold of her reins. He pulled her horse along as he set out to join the others. Honor's energy went into maintaining her balance. Only Jalen and Imani remained. They looked at each other, uncertain. Riding on while ignoring Chris' wishes felt weird, but this side of him was a new thing.

Chris took no thought for them but sat unmoving, following the path of the riders until they were out of sight.

"Uhh, Dad." Jalen shifted in his saddle. "Shouldn't we catch up now?"

"I will not go where they go."

"Okay, what are we supposed to do?" Imani pulled her braids into a ponytail. "Travon..."

"We can get to Travon without going to Raegladun."

"Can we get to Travon without them?" Jalen asked. "I don't think so."

Neither did Chris.

"What are we supposed to do?" Imani repeated her question. "Why don't you want to go there? Do you know how to get to Travon? What about Annora and Honor?"

"There is no end to the evil that resides in Raegladun. It is poison to all who come within its borders. I will not risk any of you going there."

Jalen shook his head. "I don't think Mr. Merlin would do something unnecessary."

"Haven't you read the King Author stories? He is every bit as unpredictable and dangerous as the legends tell. You can never be sure of his motives. His kind is untrustworthy, every single one of them." He spoke more to himself now. "I won't be forced."

"What about my baby? Suppose they won't help get Travon back?"

"Don't worry, once Medrid realizes my mind is unbent, they will return."

"I hope so." Imani looked around despondently. She noticed an acorn in the grass and wondered if Honor had dropped it.

Chris dismounted. "We may as well get some rest. Merlin will have to run off his anger before he turns back." He walked over to help his wife down and crushed the nut.

***

The moving party made good time, covering a great distance before stopping at a stream to water and rest the horses.

"Why did you take my reins?" Honor said as soon as she dismounted. Both hands on her hips, she tapped her foot, waiting for the Elve to respond.

"To be certain you and I were in the same place." He bent down to splash water on his face.

"What am I, an idiot? You people brought me here and you ain't getting rid of me until you take me back home. I love them all, even Jalen, but they are as helpless as I am. Wandering around lost won't help Tray one bit." She let out a puff of breath, blowing off his insinuation she wouldn't have followed on her own.

"Truly?"

"Somebody needs to work on his mind-reading skills. Like I think you're going to let something happen to them, anyway. So what's the deal here? Why didn't they come with us?"

Annora asked Trill the same questions.

"Your sister and Jalen remain with Christif. He determines to change Medrid's mind." He spread a blanket for her to sit on while he tended to their horses.

She conceded that battle and let him work.

"A fool he is for it. I will not allow his folly to dictate our fate." The wizard used unnecessary force to unbridle his mount. "We will rest here and give them a chance to meet us, but I warn you, we will be hard-pressed to make up the time he has caused us to lose."

Honor accepted the canteen Loathel offered her. When she had taken a long drink, she thanked him and gave it back, uncaring that he knew she was thirsty. "Why is Dad so against this place, this Ray-ga-somebody?"

"Raegladun," Loathel corrected.

"Whatever." Seeing that Loathel still held the canteen available, she took it back.

"Maybe he's worried something might happen to one of us." Annora sat, legs crossed, searching a supply bag for a snack. She set the multipack of fruit cups beside her—they were next—and opened a box of peanut butter crackers.

"It is not concern that compels him," Merlin said. "I am afraid it is the opposite."

Loathel unsaddled Honor's horse. "Zendelel is the most complex of all the realms. Known to us as the land of sleep because its inhabitants are the products of dreams."

"Does that mean nothing here is real?" Honor plopped down next to her aunt. She claimed the crackers and helped herself to a fruit cup.

"Nay, everything here is real." Loathel moved to his own mount. "Your kind is full of strange thoughts, ideas, emotions. If they are healthy, they bring good things into existence. Even if they are not, things come to be because of them. When the evanescent pass out of the fourth realm and on to Empyrean or Bedalamon they do not take these things with them. Some remain in Universe, others collect here."

"This place is full of nightmares," Annora tossed out her theory as she fished through the bag again and found the trail mix and a granola bar. She tossed the supply bag in the center for the others to reach.

"Mostly," Loathel said. "The people of Raegladun are neither friend nor foe. Medrid believes they may have some helpful information. If nothing else, it is the safest passage into Maldonus' territory and our best chance to come undetected."

"If technically they aren't enemies, why is Daddy worried about them?"

"The Rae live for one purpose." Trill sat beside Annora and helped himself to her snacks. "Eternal discord. They are masters of mendacity." He smiled at her frown at his audacity.

"That doesn't sound good." Honor opened her fruit cup and popped an apple slice into her mouth.

Annora grabbed the supply bag again and renewed her search. "Do we want to trust people who live for lying?" She discovered a full package of sandwich cookies.

"When faced with truth, they become truth, for they cannot change it." Loathel relieved Annora of a fruit cup and the cookies, unmindful of her irritation. "But if you go before them bearing any deceit, they will know it."

"They will feed upon it, using it to the utter ruin of the person who lies from either his lips or in his heart," Trill said.

"It's still not clicking for me." Honor finished her fruit and side-eyed the cookies. Loathel gave her the package and helped himself to her peanut butter crackers.

"Master Christif is not concerned for our welfare. He has secrets he does not wish to share." Merlin stood in front of Annora, rocking on the balls of his feet.

Resigned, she offered him a fruit cup, dug into the supply bag, and gave him the first thing her fingers touched—a bag of pretzels.

"Why thank you, dear heart." He moved off to the side.

Once everyone had something, they passed the junk food around and rewarded Annora with some of everything.

Merlin shared his thoughts. "Christif is afraid staying in the house of Gale may bring about his downfall."

"Downfall?" the girls echoed.

"I do not wish him ill, but if my suspicions are accurate, he may be right."

Loathel and Trill exchanged glances. Merlin's suspicions usually became fact.

"You people are big on privacy invasion. I'm with Daddy. I don't want to go anywhere that may mean I end up hurt or dead because I don't want people to know my business. I'm not going."

Loathel asked her, "Are your secrets more important than Travon?"

"No, but that's not the point."

"That is precisely the point. Every person is required to make sacrifices on behalf of another. It is rarely a pleasant thing we are called to do, yet is there a greater cause than the young one?"

"What will happen to us?" Annora found a bag for the trash; it would help fuel the nighttime fire.

"There is naught that will befall you, Milady," Trill said. "You and Honor are in no jeopardy."

"We're not? How come?"

"There is but one way to stand against the power of the Rae. They can only use those thoughts that are dark or hidden. Once revealed, they cannot be twisted. The key in overcoming the Rae is removing the power from negative thoughts. You cannot control what comes to you. But what you confess cannot harm you."

"And we're safe, how?" Honor moved her hands, indicating Trill should continue.

"You are fortunate not to have secret thoughts, good or otherwise."

"Lucky us," Annora muttered.

"I have secrets thoughts." Honor stared into the faces of three disbelieving people and an amused Elve. "I do. I have thoughts so secret, sometimes I don't know what I'm talking about. Wait, that didn't come out right." She cleared her throat. "What I mean is, he can get in my head," she pointed to Loathel, "but he doesn't know everything."

No one said anything; neither did they change their expressions. She dropped the subject.

"For you ladies," Trill said, "there is the subject of your memories."

"Are you saying you don't have access to them?"

"I have access, Milady. I thought you would prefer to permit me to share them. I wait upon you."

Why is it, every time he opens his mouth, I melt?

"Because you, in a liquefied state, is most pleasing. I desire nothing more than to have you thus."

Her expression told the world they spoke intimately. Loathel, Honor, and Merlin diverted their attention.

"Hey, what about my mother and the rest of you?" Honor poked Loathel. "Your thoughts aren't all that big of a secret either, you know."

"Loathel and Trill have you ladies as well as each other to keep them accountable," Merlin said. "Besides, they're practically immune. I have little concern for either of them in this matter. I'll wager Jalen will be alright as well. He's too young to have done much, anyway. The only real trouble could come from Christif and myself, of course." He hunched his shoulders and gave his beard a scratch.

"You are always a potential troublemaker." Trill fed Annora a bite of his stolen granola bar.

Merlin hunched his shoulders again. "It's a talent."

"And my mother?"

"What is to become of your mother," the wizard said to Honor, "is the dilemma your father faces."

CHAPTER XVIII

Easy riding and a stop for a real lunch brought no sign of Christif, Imani, or Jalen. The five remounted and trudged on. They left Honor's backpack with a day's supply of food, expecting the three to find it. The traveling was slower and they stopped more often. Nevertheless, by the time they made camp for the night, the others had not caught up.

***

When it became apparent Merlin was not going to reconsider, Chris had a dilemma. Raegladun was not an option. His pride fought against following Merlin's trail, but he did not know where else to go. It had been years since he was last n Zendelel; its routes were beyond his memory. He did not know who was friend or who was now foe. He could not get Travon, nor could he go home. In the end, they indirectly followed the path taken by the five.

***

The rich orange and black emblem of the Orioles—the family baseball team—blazoned on Honor's backpack stood out like the beacon it was meant to be. Finding it full of food thrilled Imani and Jalen. They were tired and hungry; catching up to the others was a great idea.

Or not.

"You dare taunt me, Medrid!" Chris snatched the backpack from Imani's prodding fingers. "Never again will you humiliate me." He hurled the knapsack, food and all, into the stream.

Chris' spite, Imani's incredulity, and the food floating away were enough for Jalen. *"Trill? Loathel?"*

"We are here, Jalen."

"It is past time you exercised wisdom."

"You guys could have called me, you know."

"Called to you for what?" The Elve teased. *"Directions?"*

"To see if we were okay."

"We know you are well."

"You've been keeping tabs on us?" The thought was comforting.

"Yea, we have. What has happened, cousin?"

"Dad. Something's not right with him."

"Besides having you hours from where you ought to be, what more is amiss?"

"He threw the food you left us into the river. He thinks Mr. Merlin is out to get him. I doubt he knows where he's going. I tried to see his thoughts but I couldn't—"

He was interrupted by both. *"You could not?"*

"No. I've done it before, but now I can't. That's why I'm worried. At first, I thought he was overreacting. Now, I'm wondering if it's more than that. Something weird is going on with him."

"Jalen, this is serious. You have to catch up to us, with or without my uncle. Do you understand?"

"Yes."

Likewise, Loathel's playfulness ended. *"From where you are, travel along the Push River until you reach the waterfall. Once there, head west, away from it. Keep the mountains always on your right. Ride hard, you need to be here ere this night has passed."*

Jalen swallowed. *"By myself?"*

"If your parents will come, they will be welcomed," Trill said. *"You cannot help your father or your brother from where you sit."*

"Always, we will be with you," Loathel promised.

"Okay." Jalen refocused on his parents. "We need to get moving that way." He pointed.

"Did you hear anything I said?"

"Nope. Wasn't listening."

"We're going to camp here tonight. Stay with your mother, I'll find some food."

"No."

"What did you say?"

"I said no, Dad."

"We can't both hunt, son. I didn't think you cared for it."

"We wouldn't need to hunt if you hadn't thrown the food in the river. Honor is going to be heated, by the way. We're not staying. At least, I'm not."

"You know less about this place than I do. What are you going to do, run off to who knows where? Why?"

"I know where I'm going. If you're smart, you'll follow me."

"Jalen? Chris?" Imani looked from one man to the other. "Is this place doing something to you? Something is not right here."

"It's okay, Mom. I got directions."

"You got..." Chris understood. His jaw dropped. "You've been speaking to those traitors. Is inciting Honor and Annora against me not enough? Now they plot to steal my son as well. Devil take them all. I will not allow it. Do you hear? I will not allow it."

"Christopher, you're frightening me." Imani stepped back away from him.

The next second he was poised, a changed person. "I'm sorry, that was never my intention." He held out his hand.

Imani let him envelop her in his embrace.

Jalen was not convinced. He didn't trust the conversation.

"I apologize to you as well, Jalen. I am consumed with anger that Merlin would deliberately place our family in jeopardy. Don't run off half-cocked, son. We need to rest and then we'll decide what to do."

The words sounded reasonable to Jalen, but they didn't ring true.

"*He may believe it,*" Trill's voice came to him. "*What he is saying is not accurate. Darkness covers his mind. You cannot linger.*"

"Dad, if you're telling us the truth, we need to get with Mr. Merlin. Aunt Nora and Honor have not turned against you. Neither has anyone else. You don't have any idea why he thinks going to this place will help Tray. If nothing else, we need to plan something as a family. We can't do that with half of us here and the other half there. I'm leaving."

"He's right, Christopher. This is about Travon. I don't care where we have to go; I mean to get my child back." Imani climbed on her horse and looked down at her husband.

"Fine." From his tone, they knew it was far from fine.

***

"Will you walk with me, Mistress?"

Having felt his burden, Honor went willingly. "I don't like it when you're not happy. What's the problem?"

"There are things you should know, but I fear you will not wish to hear them."

"Why do I need to know them?"

"Soon it will be known to you anyway. It is better to be prepared."

"How do you know I'm going to find out something?"

"The information is known to me." He moved a low-hanging branch aside.

"So?" She ducked under his arm.

"Anything known to me will become known to you."

"Make sense, please."

"Honor, you may know my thoughts as I know yours."

"I know."

"Nay, you believe we can communicate with one another and sometimes share ideas. That is a small portion of it. Nothing in your mind is secret to me. I am there permanently." He paused, wishing he did not have to say more. "All I think is knowledge available to you."

"All?"

"All."

"ALL?!"

"All."

He kept her from stumbling over a root.

"Why didn't you tell me this before?"

"There was no need, nor did you ask."

"What else don't I know?"

"Plenty."

"Hmph."

He kept her from stumbling again.

"Get a grip, girl," she told herself. "Was that the big news?"

They came to the edge of a clearing. He leaned against an ancient knurled Yellowwood tree. "Nay, the big news is your father. When he arrives, he will need to confess things difficult to hear. If he chooses the path without wisdom, what he keeps hidden will come to life before you. Either way, you will be better able to accept were you not surprised."

"If you already know about it, why wouldn't he confess?"

"What I know matters not to him. I am not the one he wrongs. He does not wish your family to know what he has done to your mother or your cousin. Because he cannot undo those deeds, he desires to keep them buried."

"I can understand that, I guess."

"Being responsible for your actions is the better choice."

"What did he do to Mom and Trill, I wonder?"

"Come, sit by me. I will tell you. I need to tell you. Until I do, there will be no peace within me."

She caressed his cheek, wishing she could remove the pained expression from his angelic visage.

He covered her hand with his, holding it there a moment longer. Not letting go of her fingers, he sat with his back against the Yellowwood, pulling her down to sit between his legs, resting her head on his chest. He enfolded them both in his elven cloak and nuzzled her dark spiral curls, taking her scent deep into his lungs.

"Mmmm." She snuggled against him.

The musical sound of his voice caressed her ears as he began his tale. "Many generations ago your father and Maldonus were friends."

Honor shifted to look up at him in disbelief.

"At the time there were some Lephans who seemed to have lost their love of evil. They lulled us into a false comfort, weakening our resolve. Master Christif, like many, was deceived."

She settled back against his chest.

"Over time, Maldonus held notable sway over your dad. He persuaded Christif to go places and do things that, with better judgment, he would never have done. Ages before, Medrid had discovered the gates. Numerous times Christif and Maldonus traveled to the fourth realm, although the will of Triune is against it. Together they affected the lives of many. It is believed the time in your world affected Christif also." He paused allowing his mind to return to the season of Christif's fall. "Jodians adapt to their surroundings. In Mayadal, they are virtuous and noble. On Earth, they take the nature of men. Christif got lost in the ways of the evanescent. He desired and took many women."

"Daddy? Are you sure?"

"I am. The repercussions are not yet ended. Trill's destiny is forever changed because of him."

Honor felt his grief. She rubbed his arm soothingly.

"Trill was a mirror child."

"A what?"

"He was a twin."

"Oh. Cool. Wait, was?"

"His brother, Yaunt, dwells in the first realm."

"Aww, that's sad. What happened?"

"Yaunt and Trill were so close, they could hardly ever be found apart. They shared an intimacy unique even for mirror children and a special playmate. Her name was Montanae."

"Was? Did she die too?"

"Nay, she lives on, but not as her former self. We do not speak of her now."

"Oh."

"They were always together. It was presumed, when the boys were old enough, Montanae would bring one of them into their fullness. Days before they were to come of age, Christif returned from his travels for a visit. He looked upon Montanae, who had grown beautiful in his absence, and lusted for her. With Maldonus' urging, and because deceit was a part of him, Christif was able to make everyone believe he came into his own fullness at the sight of her. In truth, pure fullness was lost to him when he accepted the ways of the evanescent, but we did not know it at the time.

"Montanae was given into Christif's care. Yaunt and Trill were heartbroken. They did not mind her belonging with one of them; there was no jealousy between the boys. But it did not seem right for Christif to have her, for she was already a part of them both. Although she felt nothing, Montanae went to your father gladly. To her, Master Christif was exciting and more appealing than her childhood friends.

"Christif kept his pretense going for a few seasons until his interest in Montanae waned. Afterwards, he disregarded her and pursued Telorena, an Elven maiden."

"Daddy, *my* daddy?" Honor shook her head, her hair dancing under Loathel's chin.

"Maldonus chose this time to reveal his true motives. He betrayed Christif by telling Montanae what he had done. Trill and Yaunt felt her distress and came to her aid. She told them what she learned. Because she was hurt, she demanded vengeance. Blinded with outrage, Yaunt agreed to do her bidding at once. Trill wanted to question Maldonus first. He was among the few who never fully trusted any member of Lephan's line, save one. Not willing to wait, Yaunt and Montanae set off after Christif while Trill searched for Maldonus.

"As it were, they found him with Telorena. Telorena knew he was bound to Montanae. She wanted no part in his deception. Her refusal angered Christif. He overwhelmed her and was attempting to force his might upon her when they arrived. Yaunt challenged him for the honor of both women. Telorena lay broken and dying from his brutality, yet instead of getting help, Montanae stayed to watch them fight. She was determined to have her revenge. Fear for her safety colored Yaunt's judgment.

"Feeling his brother's struggle, Trill left his search for Maldonus to come to Yaunt's aid. He was a short distance away when Christif slew Yaunt. Christif did not mean to kill his nephew. But it could not be undone. As the reality of his actions came to him, he panicked. He realized Montanae alone witnessed his crimes. Trill appeared just as Christif's sword pierced Montanae's breast. Christif was dazed and no doubt tired from his assault on Telorena and his fight with Yaunt. Blind pain governed Trill. Within moments, he disarmed his uncle. Christif and Trill faced each other unmoving. Christif awaited his death blow while Trill regained control of himself. He could not look at the mirror image of his father and hold his hatred.

"Montanae's groan caught his ear. Once he realized she at least was not dead, he dropped his sword, giving her his full attention. By regulating her heartbeat, Trill slowed the bleeding and saved her life. This is how I found them. Many of us loved Yaunt and felt his struggle. I was nearest, though not near enough to have prevented those tragedies."

"Loathel, you can't possibly think any of that was your fault."

"I do not blame myself. I am sorry it happened. The loss of Yaunt is a deep wound for me, more so for his brother. Trill never returned to himself. It was as if he died also." Loathel hugged her tight, refusing to examine why that little gesture gave him such satisfaction. "You cannot know the change Annora has brought about in him. Trill would not tell of what took place. He would not let us share his memories. With the help of Triune and the strength of the Elves, Telorena lived. It is through her we learned.

"When Montanae recovered, she was a changed person, her thoughts twisted. She was angry at Yaunt's death, but not because her friend was gone. His dying robbed her of her retaliation. The way Trill saved her life indicated he was the one fated to be with her. She did not welcome this news and would not so long as he allowed his uncle to live."

"That ungrateful...never mind." She pressed her ear into his chest, enamored with his thunderous heartbeat.

"Precisely. You will find none in Mayadal who disagree. Trill chose to leave Christif's fate in the hands of the Council of Kelmaragin. Because of this, Montanae went to Maldonus' lair and secretly joined with him. Days later, she returned claiming she had not been herself. Pretending to reconsider, she sought to join with Trill. Trill felt it his duty to place Montanae under his protection and lift the disgrace Christif brought upon his family's honor. A Jodian such as he could do no less." Again, he hugged her, needing the contact. "At Montanae's request, Trill agreed to speak his vow in ceremony. Claiming her publicly would have returned her to her former status. As it were, while we gathered and awaited her arrival, she was assisting a band of renegade Lephans in destroying our homes and most of our weapons. They overran the Civic. Aezilden was invaded and Kelmaragin overthrown. War began that night. Many were enslaved or killed because of the evilness of Maldonus and the hatred of Montanae."

"Don't forget Daddy. He had a little to do with it too."

"Yes, he did. I can tell you he has paid a large price for his indulgence."

"He was punished?"

"Yes. The council sentenced him to the prison of Bedalamon but the war spared him. Instead he fought bravely, risking his life time and again to help others and to subdue the Lephans. He blamed himself and made it his responsibility to see Mayadal liberated."

"That part sounds good." One hand on his chest and the other on his thigh, subconsciously, she beat a rhythm, echoing his heart.

Her soft touch made his heart race. "Despite his earthly flaws, Christif became good again."

"So then what happened?"

"Maldonus."

"I'm beginning to hate that name. What did he do this time?"

"He is smarter by far than most everyone. Montanae had been his target all along. By urging Christif to join with her and then joining with her himself, Maldonus established a connection between Christif and himself."

"Whoa, like us—umm, like Aunt Nora and Trill?"

"Yes, a connection like...theirs."

"That is bizarre."

"That is smart. Christif is a powerful warrior. He was a renowned leader, coming from a line of Masters. Who better to have under your will?"

"Under his...is Daddy his slave?"

"Maldonus has authority over your father's mind."

"Why not the other way around?"

"Montanae. Her will gives leverage. Christif is enslaved to her and her will is now enslaved to Maldonus. The three are so entwined, Christif could not remain in the same realm with them and not do their bidding."

"Is that what the big deal is with Jalen? Because he's Daddy's little Jodian, he may be connected to Maldonus."

"There is no doubt, Jalen is connected. Maldonus was unable to use Master Christif as he desired. He will try with your brother, but he cannot risk them combining their strength and overpowering him. It almost happened before; he will not allow it again. He must kill your father first."

"How did it happen before? Did Montanae help Daddy?"

"Nay. There is another who is also connected. His will dominates Maldonus."

"Where is he? Let's get him."

"We have. He is—"

"Trill," they said together.

"I should have known. Why only him?"

"Twins are a double blessing; they receive a double portion. Yaunt and Trill's capabilities were always twice that of other Jodians in their range.

When Yaunt passed into the first realm, his strength transferred to his brother. There is no Jodian or lesser being of equal puissance. Were he not made of good, even the Elves would have a difficult time stopping Trill."

"Wow. Why doesn't he get rid of Maldonus?"

"He would have; in fact, he almost did once."

"But?"

"But 'twould have been a grave mistake. I am grieved to dwell upon what would have been lost had Trill not called hold in those final seconds." He stroked her hair.

"A mistake not to be rid of Maldonus? I'm gonna need a little bit of convincing."

"Lephan is the least of the children of Azâzêl, but what he lacks in ability he makes up in knowledge. They are driven by the need to know. Consequently, they know much. Maldonus possesses vast knowledge and the power that comes with it. Capturing him is no small task."

"But you did."

"Against his struggles, Trill was able to shut down his faculties long enough for me to put an end to him. Only a moment before my release, Trill called hold. Almost too late, he learned how deep Maldonus had bound Christif. In a freakish ritual when they were friends, he convinced your dad to eat his flesh and drink his blood. To do this is an evil beyond imagination. It is twisted truth."

"And gross beyond belief. Eww. That's cannibalism. Why?"

"Maldonus secretly purposed to harness Jodian strength to combine with his own. In this way, he could defeat the Elven gifts and conquer first Mayadal, then Universe. Maldonus wanted Christif to become an extension of himself. He wanted control and he achieved it. Trill learned the instant before Maldonus' death, your father is bound to that monster in mind and body. Unless the bonds can be broken before Maldonus dies, Christif will be no more. Because of what he has done, if he dies connected to Maldonus, he cannot enter the first realm."

"Whoa."

"We must keep Maldonus alive or Christif's life will be forfeit. All the while, as long as Maldonus breathes, he will seek to destroy us all."

"Can it be reversed?"

"Mayhap. But any attempt to sever the connection could end Christif's life. We would have only the one opportunity. If we were wrong, his hope would be lost."

"Loathel, this is...beyond crazy."

"Your father risks much by keeping secrets."

"My father risks much, period."

"Yes, but you knowing and not hating him will go a long way in helping him to make the right choice."

"For a change."

"Can you be nice for a change?"

"Doubtful. You mentioned my mother. What did he do to her?"

"It is not so much what he has done. It is what she will know."

"This sounds like it's going to be good...in the worst possible way."

"Christif has been banished to the fourth realm for almost two hundred years."

"Yeah, I heard that. He's well preserved."

"He has not been alone all this time."

"Meaning?"

"Your mother is his seventh wife."

"Do what?"

"One died early, one he divorced; they were childless. The others he stayed with long enough to have grandchildren. At least thirty years in each marriage."

"Insane. I kinda understand he's going to outlive everybody, but he should want us to know this now. What about his kids and grandkids? Does he ever see them? Man, we've probably got relatives all over the place."

"You do. Unfortunately, he has made another error in judgment."

"There's a surprise."

"He and others like him—"

"There are others like him?"

"Earth has quite a few Jodians."

"This time last week I might not have believed it. At least it explains the dress code."

"Your dress code defies explanation."

"Touché, Lowell, you're learning. Now, knock it off and tell me the rest."

"As you wish, Mistress. If you want me to continue, do not interrupt." He pulled her closer, indulging in the feel of her against him. She was a perfect fit.

"Mmmm." She sank into him. "Get used to it."

"Where was I, hmmm...somebody's prattle made me lose my thought."

"You did not. 'He and others like him,' pick it up there."

"He and others like him...what?"

"He and others like him will know a certain Elve got pinched if he doesn't get on with this story." She sniffed, caught his scent, and sniffed again. "You smell like," one more big sniff, "I don't know, but we've been here for days and you still smell good. You better hurry up and talk. I can't concentrate."

Loathel had the same problem. Holding her was the only luxury he would allow himself. That small action was as addicting as it was gratifying. With effort, he returned his thoughts to the subject. "Your father has done much to further the tenet of psychic ability."

"He has?"

"He conversed with relatives and friends as the voice of their begone. Because of him and others doing similar things, the psychic industry has prospered."

"And he got mad at me. I wonder if Tashnine and I are related."

"You are."

"You're kidding."

"Her great grandmother is your sister."

"Okay, my mind can't grasp that one."

"Because of their Jodian blood and Christif's visits, his second family became involved in psychic activity, more with each generation. They have allowed many beings access to your world."

"Whoa."

"We were not aware of it, but it is through them Maldonus was able to maintain a connection to your father. He could not control Christif but he could watch and wait for an opportunity such as the one Jalen's birthday presented him."

"Did my dad do anything right?"

"Many, the best of which was having you."

He could feel her smile.

"I'm not getting why he wouldn't want us—Mom at least—to know this stuff. It's all in the past. He should know she would try to understand. I would have some serious problems, but Mom would understand."

Loathel did not respond.

Honor turned to face him. "What won't she understand?"

"Would you understand if your husband told you he manipulated you from infancy? He handpicked you as a babe, directed your thoughts to the things he wanted you to learn and know? Painted your dreams so your desires could be found in him?"

"What?"

"Would you understand if he told you, your replacement has been born and he has for the past few seasons been bending her mind to his will?"

"Uhhhhgh."

"Would you understand, Honor, if you found out he has already selected the last day of your life with him?"

"Would you please tell me something good? Otherwise, I'm going to throw up."

CHAPTER XIX

Trill paced the perimeter of their encampment. He worried over Jalen's assessment of Christif. Where was his uncle getting the strength to shield his thoughts? What did he mask? To avoid Bedalamon, Christif pledged an oath not to conceal the workings of his mind. It was hard enough serving as protector to his brother's murderer, knowing the face that took Yaunt's life was identical to the one that gave it. He did not need the fool backsliding into rebellion. He could not be expected to stand idle a second time. There was too much at risk. Trill would not allow harm to befall them; nothing would hurt Annora.

As if he called to her, Annora appeared at his side. "Is there something I can do to help?"

Immediately, thoughts of all else left his head. "Allow me the privilege of feasting upon your loveliness and my needs will be met."

"You sure are easy to please." She slid her hand into his.

Trill's breath caught. She had given him a signal; his time had arrived. "I long for one thing only."

Their eyes met: hers curious, his intense. He made his thoughts known to her: his desire, and his intention.

Her wood-burnt eyes widened, and her heart raced. The idea of kissing him had been in her mind more than she dared admit. When? If? When?

In answer to her wayward thoughts, Trill pulled her to him and embraced her. He seemed to draw out time, giving her an opportunity to stop him if it were not her desire.

Her breathing came fast and erratic. A burning knot of fire coiled in the pit of her stomach, giving birth to butterflies. There was no resistance in her. Annora could not stop him from doing what she desperately wanted him to do.

He bent his head, never taking his eyes from hers, holding her mesmerized. Their lips touched. Passion kindled, white-hot and blinding. His mouth was gentle but firm, hers soft and pliant.

As he deepened the kiss, all other realities faded from Annora's awareness. He filled time and space. The hardened muscles undulating beneath his tunic. The zesty clean scent of him permeating her skin, etching itself into her memory. She came to absolute oneness with Trill. Total control and complete mercy blended into the most exquisite of sensations. His unadulterated maleness incited the core of her femininity, beckoned to her longing, called her home.

The volcano within Trill bubbled into a hard, fast boil. It threatened to erupt, incinerate him where he stood. A kaleidoscope of emotions singed his veins with liquid heat. He dreamt of this moment for more years than he could count. At first, an obscure hope, quiet before he came to Universe. Each day since finding her, his longing grew more potent until finally, it became a dangerous need he could barely contain. Now she had given it to him. It was more than he could take in, utterly immense in its grandeur: all the waiting, all the wanting, all...so worth it. She was an enchantress, far beyond the lowly likes of him. Yet she gave herself to him, had been made for him, only him.

He could feel her desire and was heady with the knowledge someone, *she*, would want him. His gratitude spilled over. She made him strong and humble. He never knew anything could be so tantalizing, so enticing; he would never be able to get enough. He needed to; he had to draw the very life from her. He had to; he needed to give her his in return.

Long did they keep the moment. For the duration, there was only the coming together of the she and the he. The two became one. The kiss should have ended, but Trill continued to tug and nibble on her deliciously bruised lips. He could not help himself. With substantial effort, he pulled back a hair's breadth, trembling. "Thank you, Milady," he whispered.

A single tear slid down Annora's face. Reverence for this moment, for this man, consumed her. Something awakened within her. It was now alive and growing. For the span of that kiss, she felt pure, untainted love. She knew with him, through him, she would feel it again. *Did he feel it too?*

"Yea, Lady. Yea, I do."

For the first time, she was happy he knew her thoughts. His kiss left her speechless.

***

The warning came to Loathel where he and Honor sat in compatible silence. He hated disturbing that. "Honor, we need to get back to camp."

"Already?"

"There is danger drawing near."

"Lions and tigers and bears, oh my." She made herself get up and allowed him to lead her back.

***

Merlin met them at the edge of the encampment. "I was about to search you out. I did not know if you were too distracted to notice."

"I noticed."

"I didn't notice anything." Honor looked left and right. She held her hands out, palms up. "What am I not noticing?"

"Where is Trill?" Merlin asked.

"Where is Annora?" The Elve answered.

"They are both here." Trill came from the opposite direction, holding Annora's hand.

"They are moving closer, stalking us," Loathel said.

The girls spoke in unison. Annora asked, "Who?" Honor asked, "What?"

"We have to go after the others." Merlin studied the horizon.

"We cannot leave the women," Trill countered.

"They will not make it without our aid."

Loathel and Trill spoke to one another in Mayadalian. Each had a decision to make. As usual, they agreed. Simultaneously, they looked at Merlin. He waved them off. "Yes, yes, of course, I will stay. Hurry. There isn't much time."

Having learned the hard way, when their men spoke in Mayadalian, they also thought in Mayadalian. The women went back to the basics.

Honor grabbed Loathel's sleeve. "Yo...enlightenment?"

"Trill, what is it?" Likewise, Annora touched Trill's arm.

The sight of her chewing on her lip made him stop. He wished he could do it.

"We will gather your family," Loathel said.

Trill tore his eyes away. "Medrid will remain here to guard you."

Merlin walked around the campsite, making a large circle with his staff. The women followed the warriors to their horses.

"Guard us against what?" Honor took in Loathel's countenance. "On second thought, don't tell me. You don't look like you want to tell me. If you don't want to tell me, I don't want to know."

"What's out there?" Annora asked. "Not the burnt-dead-guy thingies."

"Nay." Trill kissed her forehead before mounting his stallion. "Werewolves."

"Too much information." Honor glared at her aunt. "Sometimes it's more than we need to know."

Loathel tugged her hair before swinging up onto his charger. "I realize it will be difficult for you, but try to behave while I am away."

"Try not to be gone too long." She touched his thigh, unable to give a true voice to her emotions.

Loathel understood them anyway and covered her hand with his own. "As you wish, Mistress." He filled her being with the warmth of springtime.

In a flurry of dust and hoof beats, Trill and Loathel rode off. Merlin completed his circle and called Annora and Honor to the center, motioning for them to sit by the fire. With upraised arms, he began reciting a chant. Smoke came from the ground, rising from the circle, giving off an eerie gray light. When it reached more than twelve feet high, Merlin was silent. He lowered his arms, looking around at his work. Satisfied, he sat across from his charges. "For good or ill 'tis done now."

"Good or ill," Annora repeated. "What's that mean?"

"It will serve its purpose for a while," he said. "The trouble is it will attract the werewolves, though they cannot get through." He leaned forward, stirring a pan of something he had been making before the interruption. "They will gather and wait. By the time the shield dissolves, and I assure you it will, the blasted things will have us surrounded." He studied the forlorn faces before him. "There is little hope of our warriors getting back in time to help us."

"Because you asked," Honor shook her head, "I get more information than I want."

132   TRACY A. BALL

"Da, da, da da dadada..." Merlin returned to stirring. "What's worse," he jumped back to the present, "if they make it back in time, they will have to fight their way through." He reached for the pan's handle, muttering to himself, "Of course, being tired and possibly injured, attempting it would be suicide." He raised the pan, ignoring their horrified expressions. "Anyone hungry?"

CHAPTER XX

The gathering oppression was thick, making Loathel and Trill loathe having to ride away. They pushed hard, fighting against it, and the desire to return to their women.

***

Jalen put his phone to sleep. He didn't care about the game he was playing. He hadn't cared for the last half hour. He stared at the landscape, ignored its beauty, and wondered what he should do. *"Trill... Loathel...Mr. Merlin...somebody..."*

"What is it, cousin?"

"I don't know. I think I...feel something."

"You sense something?"

"I feel something weird following us."

"Rapidly do your senses grow, Jalen. It is most impressive."

Loathel's compliment was troubling. *"Am I right?"*

"Your perception has not failed you, young one," Trill replied.

"Great. Now what are we supposed to do?"

"Keep to your course, we are coming for you," Loathel said. *"Have you informed your father?"*

"No. I didn't want to worry anybody when I wasn't sure. What's following us?"

Trill did not hesitate. *"Werewolves."*

"Werewolves? Did you say werewolves?"

"I did."

"You must be joking."

"This danger is no matter for jest, I assure you. Warn your parents. Under no circumstance are you to stop. There are many. For your family's sake, you must outrun them."

Jalen reached for his father's mind. *"Dad...Dad?"*

Christif considered not answering. It could be important. However, if he replied, the boy might realize his skills had returned. If the others happened to be in Jalen's mind, they would know. He could pretend Jalen was holding the contact, or he could wait for Jalen to address him verbally.

"I am un-fooled, Master Christif. Answer your son."

Loathel had given the command in such a way Christif dared not disobey. *"What is it, Jalen?"*

"Werewolves."

Christif turned in his seat, straining to find them. They were not visible, but once he focused, he could discern their presence. He wondered at Jalen's ability. It was amazing for one as inexperienced as he to be so acute. *"Pick up the pace but do not alarm your mother."* He called out to the riders, *"Loathel, my friend, are their numbers known to you?"*

"I wonder at the value of being called friend by you. Nine run with you. More gather beyond your daughter and still others are drawing near." Every syllable was bejeweled with irritation.

"I thank you for coming for us."

"I desire not your appreciation but your remembrance. Your disobedience has brought your family into danger and left your daughter unprotected."

"The blame is mine and I accept it, though my folly is not without reason."

Trill broke his silence. *"Only the evanescent believe folly needs nothing more than a good excuse."*

***

The pace was tiring. Imani reined her horse in, letting him fall behind. Chris and Jalen slowed down, keeping her between them. The animals pulled at their harnesses, eager to be away.

"Honey, we've got to keep riding."

"Mom, we can't stop now."

"Yes, we can. Why the rush? The horses need a break and so do I."

"Not now, we gotta move fast." Chris nudged his horse forward, expecting her to follow his lead.

Imani came to a complete stop instead. "I need to—"

Double voices called out a warning in their heads. Chris circled back. A large black shape leapt through the air, intent on Imani's unprotected side. Jaws wide, sharp fangs exposed, gleaming with saliva, anticipating its kill.

Jalen acted on instinct. Lightspeed were his reflexes. He unsheathed his sword with one hand and shoved his mother down with the other. He swiped over her head and was rewarded with a pained yelp before the thing fell to the dirt. He took no moment to wonder at his feat; another creature had come. He hacked down at it. His father was there, also swinging his sword. His mother screamed and kicked at something but appeared unharmed. The horses reared in terror of the wild beasts snapping and biting at them. It was impossible to control the horses and fight the wolves, but they didn't give up.

One animal of great size and strength locked its jaws on Imani's horse's throat, bringing it to its knees. A steel arrow sank deep into the thing's chest, killing it at once. In its struggle to regain its footing, the horse unseated Imani. She fell hard onto the ground. Teeth cut deep into her shoulder, tearing the flesh. She would have fought, but the thing backed away. She sat up, coming face to snout with another animal; then it fell over, dead.

Trill and Loathel advanced onto the scene. They fired arrows with intent and accuracy, even from a distance in the dark. All was silent when they rode up. Seven massive wolves lay dead, four with arrows protruding from their bodies.

Chris came to Imani's aid. He pressed his palm against her shoulder to stop the flow of blood. Her horse lay dying beside the fallen wolves. Nearby, they heard a wolf howling, calling to his brothers.

The Mayadalians dismounted. With amazing speed, Trill removed Imani's bedroll and backpack. He handed them up to Jalen. Loathel collected the arrows and with one shot, put the wounded horse down. By the time Chris remounted behind his wife, the warriors were ready to ride out.

They kept a steady pace, not willing to stop again until the circle of gray smoke became visible. Reining their horses in, they could see many dark creatures gathered and waiting.

"To move closer will alert them of our presence," Loathel warned. "We may be too close as is."

"What's that thing?" Jalen pointed to the smoke.

"A wall of protection, Medrid's handiwork. The others are safe for now, but we have to get to them before the smoke disappears." After his explanation, Trill shut off his thoughts from everyone but Loathel. Conferring privately, they formed a plan. Once agreed, he spoke again. "Wait here until you receive a signal. As soon as we give it, race for the wall. The others will be waiting."

Loathel added, "You will only have this one chance. If you do not make it in, we will not be able to come to you. Do you understand?"

Jalen nodded, but he didn't understand at all.

"I can aid you in this," Christif offered.

"Nay, my uncle. Your wife has need of you." Trill set his horse in motion the exact second Loathel did. They rode toward the wall of smoke.

The Lossmans watched their companions charge through overgrowth and underbrush, into danger. Immediately, several large wolfish beasts set upon them. They galloped away from the camp, drawing the animals behind them.

"*NOW! RIDE! DO NOT STOP!*" Loathel sent the message as soon as they were far enough away to give them running room. He and Trill split up, hoping to confuse the demon hounds.

Chris and Jalen spurred their mounts into motion. With eyes fixed on the wall, they kicked up dirt and dust, riding as hard and as fast as they could. It almost wasn't enough. The noise and smell of overworked, sweating horses reached the werewolves, and they were pursued. Chris and Imani passed through with Jalen a pace behind. The deadly jump of the nearest wolf was thwarted by Merlin's barrier.

The champions pulled the pack away from camp. They circled back, needing to get to safety before their animals were overtaken. They knew it was a gamble: winded horses, innumerable beasts. One of them making it in would be a miracle; both of them being so fortunate was inconceivable.

Travon reached out with uncertainty. It had been hours since he last felt anyone's presence. Maldonus told him terrible things: his father sold him, Chris killed his other family members, and he would remain a prisoner forever unless he answered the Lephan's questions. Maldonus' Queons tortured him; not physically, but he was hurting all the same. They chained him to some dead thing. They would not let him sit or lay for extended periods. The shackles around his wrists and ankles were too tight; they cut into his skin. *"Hello..."* His voice shook with fright.

Trill recognized his need. *"Master Travon, why are you yet awake at this hour?"* He put effort into projecting lightheartedness, though he was currently racing death.

"Trill, is that you?"

"Indeed, it is."

"Are you on watch duty?"

"Of sorts."

"I'm glad you were the one to hear me."

"Why is that?"

"'Cause I'm kind of scared. I didn't want nobody to laugh at me."

"No one would laugh. You have every right to be afraid."

"Maybe, but they don't know how bad this place is. Sometimes Jalen and Honor are dumb."

"I am glad you have reached for me. What has frightened you, my cousin?" He let Travon talk. It cost him precious concentration, but he would not shut off when he knew the child needed him.

***

Less than two hundred yards from the wall of protection, Loathel's horse toppled over, pulled down by the mighty beast. Only his agility allowed him to leap clear of the falling stallion. The Elve somersaulted over the horde of wolves devouring his steed. He hit the ground in a roll, coming up with a long knife in each hand. He dashed toward the wall while stabbing and slicing the vicious, snarling creatures. A few steps from the smoke, Loathel turned and made his stand, fighting off the werewolves, refusing to go in.

***

Having to ride, fight, and converse in a manner soothing to a child was close to unrealizable. Trill's success at it was amazing. Even greater was his lack of despair over his ever-rising obstacles. He felt the crippling jolt. Too many times did the creatures bite into his horse's legs. The horse limped, no longer able to run. Trill jumped onto a low-hanging tree branch, listening as Travon told him about his game card collection. The limb snapped. The first animal sank its teeth into him, and he slew it while asking the boy which cards were his favorite and why. The Jodian backed into the tree, fighting and killing as many of the wolves as he could. The rest ate at him, too numerous to control.

***

Loathel remained on the outside of the protection, too aware of its virtues. No enemy could get in. On the inside of such a ring, until the smoke dissolved, no ally could get out. His arms were tired, his horse lay dead; the Elve was helpless to come to Trill's aid. Without aid, the Jodian would not last. He locked his mind with Trill's, and it came to him, what he needed to do. One step backward and he was safe inside the wall of smoke. The others crowed to him as he rushed to Annora.

She was nursing a panic attack. She was not fully aware of what was happening, but she knew it was not good. Trill was in tremendous pain and too occupied to communicate with her. She tried to go to him but could not get out of the circle. No one else felt what she was feeling. No one else understood the mortal danger he was in.

Loathel opened wide her fears. "There is but one chance to save him. The task falls to you." Sounds of shock, surprise, and sadness came from the others. Annora let her tears spill. "I will help you. His time grows short."

"What do I do?" She smacked at her eyes, waiting on the Elve.

"Travon is currently connected to Trill. You may reach him upon that path. Take the conversation. Trill will not leave him, but he will not live unless he does. He cannot free himself without cutting the boy off. If you are with Travon, he will be released to do what he must, if he is able."

"How–how do I-I do it?"

"Focus and call to him. Be cheerful, Travon is unaware of what is happening. Trill does not mean for him to know."

Annora nodded. *"Tray, sweetheart..."*

"Aunt Nora?"

"What, you think Trill is the only one who wants to talk to you?"

"I didn't know you could do this. Are you a Jodian too?"

Secured that the boy was not alone, Trill spoke to Annora. *"Thank you, Milady. I am certain, in the short time I have been with you, I have known love."* Then he was gone.

Annora felt a void in her mind where his presence had been. She went numb, her heart refusing to believe what her brain told her.

A voice penetrated her thoughts. Instead of the Jodian invasion, it was the urging of the Elve she heard. *"Talk to Travon. He has been injured and has need of you."*

With a heavy heart and happiness she did not feel, Annora kept Travon's company for as long as she could. Everyone talked to him, including Imani. If there was any doubt for Merlin or Loathel concerning Christif's regained capabilities, Imani being able to communicate with her son telepathically dispelled it. Not long after, Travon drifted off to sleep, content his family was safe and had not forgotten him. Only then would they let themselves grieve.

Annora had by now given up any attempt at bravery. She curled up in her sleeping bag, weeping. Although she had not known Trill long and wasn't at ease with their bond, the pain of separation and the forfeiture of his comfort was more than she could bear. Imani and Honor stayed with her. They didn't talk. There was nothing to say.

Merlin, Christif, and Jalen watched the wall. They took turns traveling the inner perimeter, checking areas for thinning smoke. Loathel appeared to be in deep meditation. He hadn't spoken since his aid to Annora. The others deemed it best to leave him alone. Honor cast him tentative glances. She wanted to go to him but felt it wrong to leave her aunt.

"Nay, Mistress, do not come to me. A display between us would remind her of her suffering. It is right for you stay with her. When it is appropriate, we will make up for the time lost." His words carried a promise.

Honor clung to it.

CHAPTER XXI

Jalen jerked awake, his head staticky and unclear. He looked around, wondering when he fell asleep. All about him, the encampment was silent. Everyone was sleeping except the Elve. Loathel stood at the wall, gazing out between a two-foot section that was smoke-free and widening. Memory flooded back to the teen. He rose to his feet, grabbing his sword in the process.

"There is no need for panic." Loathel did not turn around. "Dawn has brought about our salvation."

Jalen stood beside him. Birds flew, squirrels scurried, the woods went about its business. There were numerous dead wolves scattered around, but none living. He whistled low, relieved.

"Remain close to Medrid. Follow his instructions precisely, regardless of what your father says. It may be difficult for you, but you must choose Medrid's counsel. Christif is not to be trusted."

"Excuse me?"

"His mind and will are not his own."

"Whoa, umm, won't you be here?"

"Tell your sister I will return as soon as I am able."

"Loathel?"

"As soon as I am able." Loathel's form shimmered then disappeared, leaving Jalen to wonder. Having nothing else to do, he took up the guard position vacated by the Elve.

A short while later, a refreshed and buoyant Merlin joined him. "Good morning, young master. Quite an adventure so far, wouldn't you agree?"

"I don't want any more adventure."

"Nonsense. The adventure is yours, whether you will it or no." He untangled his whiskers.

"Loathel is gone."

The magician sobered. "Yea, he could do no other."

Jalen wanted to ask why Loathel left them. Stirrings from other members of the party stalled his question.

"Are they gone?" Christif came over.

Jalen inspected his father for signs of crazy.

Merlin made room. "They are, indeed. However, the worst of our troubles have not yet arrived."

"Meaning?" Honor jumped into the conversation. Her eyes darted left and right, searching for Loathel.

"Meaning, my dear, we are not in danger of being eaten at the moment, but we are prisoners where we stand. I fear our captors are none too pleased with us."

"Prisoners? Captors? What am I missing? Where is Lowell?" Honor reached for him mentally but felt only a void. Anxiety crept into her expression. "WHERE IS HE?" she boomed, startling her mother awake.

Imani sat up, massaging the soreness out of her shoulder. Merlin cleansed and treated her wound as soon as she arrived. Now, a few hours later, all that remained was a mark and the stiffness.

Near her, daylight recalled Annora's pain. She struggled to her feet and staggered toward an open section of the wall.

Swift movements that belied his age brought Merlin to her side. He pulled her back. "No. You cannot leave."

"I have to find him. I can't...not go. He could be...hurt."

"Nay, Madame. He is beyond our help."

"NO! Don't tell me that! I don't want to hear that!"

"It is my desire to give you some measure of comfort, but I cannot. We can do nothing for Trill. He is beyond us now."

His statement held such a note of finality; Annora was not alone in her crying. They all mourned. Trill had given up his life for Travon and them. His honor and their grief were without bounds. In the tearful silence that followed, Annora let Imani comfort her.

Wiping her face, Honor returned to her subject. "Mr. Merlin, where is Loathel? Why can't he hear me?"

"He was here when I got up," said Jalen. "He told me to tell you he'd be back."

"Be back from where?"

"No idea."

"Why can't I talk to him? Why didn't he tell somebody where he was going? If he's seeing to—" she stopped and started again. "I'm half-Jodian, I should still be able to talk to him." She tapped her forehead.

Merlin did not answer her. He was concentrating on something. "They have arrived."

"Who?" Jalen and Honor spoke together.

"The werewolves." Merlin began prosaically but quickly reached a level of high agitation when Jalen drew his sword. "Put that thing away! Do you wish to get yourself killed?"

The boy followed instructions though not without reservations. "What are we supposed to do, stand here?"

"You had better do that and nothing else."

Brother and sister eyeballed one another. To their surprise, they heard approaching footsteps accompanied by voices. Soon several men came into view. There were at least thirty bare chested, burly men. At first glance, they looked to be wearing pieces of clothing made from fur. But a closer inspection revealed they weren't wearing anything; they were partly covered with fur. Each held more than one weapon in his possession. Within minutes knives, swords, axes, and spears surrounded the encampment.

"Friend or foe?" Christif whispered.

"Foe. Definitely foe." Merlin frowned at the intruders.

"Who are they?" Jalen matched his father's tone.

"They are who I said they are. Now be still."

They watched a man come forward. He was as tall as Loathel or Trill, but more rugged than graceful. He had compelling eyes. One gray and the other gold, with a glassy animal-like glow. Sweat glistened across his muscular chest and arms. Honor crinkled her nose against the scent of wet dog.

The newcomer sneered. "I am pleased you had the wisdom not to run. The only true wisdom you have shown. Why are you here?"

"We merely pass through. Had we known the place we stopped, we would not have lingered." Merlin kept his eyes downcast.

"Your lack of knowledge has killed many. For this, you will compensate."

The combination of what he said and how he said it pushed Annora into a seething rage. She flew at the unknown man, hitting, kicking, and beating at whatever body part she connected with. "You killed him! You killed him! For no reason, you just killed him!" Fists and feet and red locs spewed anger and heartache and black pain. "You killed him! You did it!" Each blow was meant to transfer her hurt to him.

He did not flinch. The stranger watched her attacking him with repulsed interest but made no move to stop her assault.

Chris and Jalen rushed forward, peeling her off her would-be victim. Annora collapsed into Imani and Honor, her mind turning into itself, retreating from her pain.

"Has she an ailment? Does injuring herself against me serve a purpose?" The dark warrior wiped at his skin and hair as if he had been soiled.

"Yeah," Christif snorted. "You killed the man she loved. What do you expect?"

"I expect her to control herself. The only murder we will discuss is the reckless slaughter of my people. Your losses are unimportant."

The Lossmans protested until his lethal stare prompted Merlin to order them all to silence.

Christif ignored the warning. "Your people were killed because they attacked us. They earned it."

"Christif," Merlin hissed.

Angry growls rippled around the camp. Some of the wolfmen moved forward, stalking the travelers now huddled together behind Merlin. The man, obviously their leader, raised his hand and received instant silence. "Taking a meal is now a crime punishable by death? From whence do you come, barbaric one?" He arched an eyebrow at Chris.

"I come from many places. Killing and having dinner are separate matters."

"You don't resemble the grazing type. Share your ideas with the cow when next you dine on steak. Wherever your journey began, you are not from here. Were I in your homeland, I would not choose your meals. You are the trespasser. Do not make judgments upon ours."

Chris looked away, dismissing him.

Gold and gray glittered at Merlin. "Is he your alpha? Are you all so inane? If so, it is little wonder you show no wisdom in your decisions."

"He does not lead us," Merlin said. "Furthermore, I request anything he says henceforth be for his condemnation alone." He ignored Christif's indignation.

The wolfman tapped his chest. "There is intelligent life here. I am relieved to find it. It shall be as you dictate. You are no doubt the wizard."

"I am."

"Why did you not keep your people inside your lighted refuge?" The question was a reprimand.

"Some of my people, not wishing to be led by me, followed at a slower pace."

"I need not guess of whom you speak. Where are the murderers? Surely they," he pointed to Chris and Jalen, "are not responsible for the damage my people suffered."

"Our warriors are with us no more."

"Valiant souls." This time he touched his chest in salute. "I would have enjoyed meeting them. No matter." He blinked and the sentiment was gone. "They would have died anyway."

Merlin did not look him in the eye. "You were there?"

"I was for a time, though not for hunger, at least not hunger for food. This is the reason I have chosen not to kill you outright. I am known as Dayown. I have come to collect what I have claimed."

"We have naught belonging to you."

"I beg to differ. She belongs to me." He aimed the tip of his finger at Imani.

"Excuse me?" Imani drew back.

"Sorry to disappoint you," Chris scoffed, "but she's my wife."

"Was your wife. She carries my mark, she is mine."

"I'm not giving you my wife." Chris positioned himself in front of her.

"You are alive because I haven't gotten around to slaughtering you. If you attempt to resist my purpose, I will delay no longer. Do not fool yourself into believing I require your permission. You have no means to stop me." Jeweled eyes moved from Chris' face to the brown-gold braids peeking from behind him. "Come to me, female."

Chris' hand stayed her.

The easy cock of Dayown's head motivated four of his spear-carrying soldiers. They touched their spears, two each to Jalen and Chris' chests.

"Stand there if you wish them dead. I leave it to you." Dayown made a slight bow in Imani's direction. "Pity," he mocked when her shaky legs brought her forward. "I did hope you wanted to be rid of the stupid one. By what are you called?"

"I–Imani," she stammered.

His answer was a satisfied grunt. Dayown yanked the shirt away from her shoulder to inspect the bite mark.

She recoiled from his touch, from him.

Contrary to becoming offended, Dayown snorted. He addressed his companions. "There's a reaction I don't get...ever." For their added amusement, he said to Imani, "I have been told I am not unpleasant. I look forward to finding out if you know better or if you will change your mind." He leaned in, not quite whispering, "I think 'twill be the latter." Then he was back to business. "Before we leave, it is important you understand, Imani, you control the kismet of your friends. The length of their lifespan depends on you." He held out his palm.

As nervous as she was, Imani did not hesitate to place her hand in his.

Dayown grunted, pleased.

"Get your filthy hands off of my wife!"

"Except him," the wolflord said. "He will bring about his own destruction. Possibly before this hour has ended. That is what I hope." He led Imani away, pausing to give orders over his shoulder. "Some of you see to our fallen brothers. The rest of you help them along by relieving them of their weapons. Begin with the wizard's staff."

Medrid gripped his staff with both hands. "Once I was young and spry, but those days are no more. I require the assistance of my walking stick. You would not deny me that, would you?"

"No, no, I would not." Dayown continued walking. "Nor would I be so foolish as to overlook the hazard you present. There are few things more dangerous than the weapon in the hand of one who knows how to wield it. If you need a stick, the wood is full of them. Help yourself."

146   TRACY A. BALL

CHAPTER XXII

"ZuUtT hxo souUKo qXaAKX KlZOqV RpBlZ hBaAEepO fFO tTlEeBqV."
(*May the peace which comes from Triune, be yours.*)

The Elvish healing chant pierced the darkness. He could make out some words, but he could not grasp what was happening. Cool water touched his parched lips. He drank and with effort, opened his eyes. Trill's first sight was the angelic face of the Elve.

Loathel's expression was grim, yet his presence bespoke of hope. He did not stop his mantra to talk but filled Trill with soothing warmth. He worked to ease the Jodian's pain, anointing him with liberal amounts of oil from the rare but potent Talive-root.

Trill marveled he was not dead. When he transferred himself back to Mayadal, it was the last of his strength. He lost consciousness before he arrived. It was a miracle Loathel found him. But if Loathel was here, only Medrid stood between the Lossmans and harm. Trill struggled to sit up.

"Nay, my friend." Loathel pushed him back. "They are safe for now. Medrid is more than able."

Trill yielded to the Elve's wisdom. He could not help them; he could not help himself. If Loathel would risk coming to his aid, he would not interrupt that effort. His mind reached for Annora and felt nothing. He remembered his coming to Mayadal meant breaking contact with her. He thought of breaching Mayadal's law. His intentions would be good, not like the Lephans or Queons, who followed not the rules but their own desires. Despite his need, he resisted the urge.

"Your choice is difficult, but right. All who ignore the law believe their circumstance warrant it. Few are correct in their assessment. It is the same for me."

He nodded. It was a small but painful movement. Neither added what they both knew: Trill had not yet survived. Was it fair to offer Annora hope he did not fully possess? She was on his mind when he lost consciousness again.

***

As soon as he arrived in Mayadal, Loathel called to his father. Talazim was their foremost healer. If Trill were to recover, he would need Talazim's aid. Talazim came with several of his people to assist. They brought the Jodian back to Aezilden so Talazim could work.

The leaders of Mayadal gathered. They were amazed to learn the Jodian had come into his fullness. The island united in prayer and kept vigil. Trill had lived so long without hope, it was not right this should happen when he was so newly joined.

Later, Talazim and Loathel spent time alone. The son told his father things that required privacy.

"We did know well enough if Christif and Maldonus were together, the evil one would have control." Talazim walked through the gardens of his home beside his son. Sounds and scents carried on the night wind. They drank it in, breathing in the air and all its richness, never denying themselves the beauty that was their subsistence.

"I am sorry we chose Universe. He is more human than Jodian, polluted beyond redemption," Loathel said. "I dislike being in the company of such pride."

"Bestow upon him the same patience you bestow upon the mortals of Earth. They do not know the harm they bring."

"Father, how can we aid him when he is without humility?"

"How can you not? He suffers from a disease. One of his own making, to be sure, but he suffers all the same. To turn our backs on him is to lose our humility. We cannot do that. We will not do that." The dark cloud hovering in Talazim's voice dispersed. "I noticed you have omitted one detail. One important detail." Inhaling deeply, he waited.

"Which is?"

He quirked an eyebrow at Loathel's feigned ignorance. "Oh, come now, think you I, Talazim, of the Elvish People, founder of Aezilden, Kelmaragin Council leader, holder of secret knowledge, would look upon my son and not know he has come into his fullness? Fear for Trill may have kept the others from seeing it, but it is not something to be hidden, especially from one who has wished for it for as long as I. I would hear all about she who owns your heart. She has achieved the dream of countless maidens. You have waited many ages for your fullness. You should be most eager to share your joy."

"If all I felt was joy, I would have shared it the moment it happened. For me, the joy is bittersweet. If I cannot still the love growing within me, I shall be doomed."

Talazim paused beside a kiylonas bush. The plant provided the nutrients for Elven esprite. Snapping a few leaves, he released its soothing fragrance into the air around them. "These are grievous remarks. Elucidate, their meaning bodes ill."

"I refuse the joining. I will speak no vow."

"You may attempt it. Be warned, it will not have the effect you wish. This is not something in your control. It does not go away simply because you refuse your responsibility. Why would you not accept Triune's offering? Do you have reason to believe she is not the one?"

The kiylonas had an effect. Loathel's tension uncoiled. "My belief is she would have been the one. I will have no other." He snapped a few more leaves. "My eyes have been opened. I have seen beauty to surpass all that was ever thought lovely." An image of Honor filled his senses. "Her skin is softer than this petal." He touched a creamy tava blossom. "A flawless brown. My hand trembles to touch it." He struggled to explain. There were no words quite good enough. "Posh is a paltry imitation of her hair. It is dark like the deepest night. It shimmers and beckons to me as she moves. When she speaks," he grinned, "the moments I am not overcome with jollity, I am humbled. Every utterance from her honeyed mouth comes to me in a whispered caress. Her eyes, oh her eyes...they are the color of the trees of Aezilden when the day is perfect. She is perfect. There is naught I would not do to have myself reflected in her eyes. I desire nothing more than to see myself thus."

Talazim laughed. "You speak like one who has come into his fullness. Besotted dolt. Spellbound fool, spouting poems and sonnets, it is always the same. Have you had enough?" He indicated the kiylonas. At Loathel's nod, he resumed their stroll. "Who is this enchantress beyond compare?"

Loathel fell in step beside him. "Her name is Honor."

"Fitting. Where did you find this treasure?"

"She is Master Christif's daughter."

"I see."

"I do not think you do. She is his daughter, an evanescent."

"Ah, now we come to the heart of the matter."

"Yes, the heart. It is madness for me to be joined to someone not of our realm."

"Trill is joined to an evanescent."

"Trill is Jodian. He can choose to pass into the first realm. I do not possess that gift."

"Immortality is seen by some as a gift. Is that now so bad for you?"

"It is when it keeps me from the one with whom I am supposed to spend eternity."

Talazim remained silent.

"How can I be joined to someone whose destiny lies elsewhere?"

"It has become comprehensible to me. I understand your sadness, but have faith, my son. We cannot see or know all that is to be. Why not accept the gift and enjoy the time given to you?"

"Father, her life is a fleeting thing, no more than a breath of infinity. The sweetest of wines she is to me. Am I to be content with but a sip? A memory before my thirst is quenched even a little. Nay, I shall not awaken a hunger only she can satisfy. A hunger with no relief once she is gone."

"Son, she is Jodian."

"Half Jodian."

"Half Jodian may be all that is necessary. Here, her life would be considerably longer. Christif's blood may enable her to live as long as other Jodians do, which is long enough."

"Or being joined to me may give her Elven immortality."

"It is quite possible. You should be hopeful, yet I detect bitterness."

"Yea, bitterness. Harsh bitterness I should find myself the gist of Triune's merriment. How can I claim to love her if it is because of me she loses her time in Empyrean?"

CHAPTER XXIII

The prisoners marched silently.

"*Mr. Merlin. Mr. Merlin, can you hear me?*"

Merlin did not look in Honor's direction.

"*Dad...Dad? Mr. Merlin?*" She switched her attention from one to the other.

Jalen noticed her distress. "*Are you okay?*"

She turned to him but did not answer.

"*Honor, can you hear me?*"

"*Jalen, can you hear me? Why won't you answer me?*"

"*Honor!*"

Together, they realized the other was striving to communicate. Together, they realized the other could not hear. Simultaneously and without detection, they reached for their cell phones.

Can u hear me?

No. Can u hear me?

I cant hear anybody. ???

Idk. Let me try. "*Umm, Mr. Merlin... Dad...Mr. Merlin!*"

"*Yes, my boy?*"

Jalen let out a breath of relief. For a moment, he thought the problem was him. "*There's something wrong with my sister. We can't hear each other.*"

"*Of course you can't. Loathel isn't here.*"

"*Okay?*"

"Women do not have that particular ability. Her communication is through Loathel. You would not be able to breach the barriers I am positive he has erected by now. Excessively private, he is."

"Oh. She won't like that."

"Like it or not, that is the way of it."

"How come he never told her?"

"My guess would be, she never asked him. We must inform her. The way she is squinting, I am afraid she is going to sprain her eyebrows."

U cant do the head thing w/o L. Jalen shut his phone down on her response. He didn't feel like reading profanity.

"Sir Dayown," Merlin called out. "Might I request a small break?"

"We have only gone a few miles. You have not tired already?"

"I am without my staff." The wizard dragged his left leg.

"You are a poor pretender," Dayown said over his shoulder. "But I am entertained."

Merlin returned to his normal walk. "I was thinking of the women."

"You were not." Dayown stopped. "We will take a brief rest, very brief. If my men catch up and call me a sluggard, I shall be forced to kill you. Couldn't stand the embarrassment, you know."

"I understand. I would not expect less from you."

Dayown nodded, jovially saying to Imani, "I am quite serious."

She didn't answer; she didn't have to. No one doubted him.

Merlin removed his hat and rubbed the back of his hand across his forehead. "Are we permitted to confer amongst ourselves?"

"By all means. Mayhap for sport, you could attempt to escape and we'll see how long it takes to catch you."

"Allow me to mull it over. I will get back to you as soon as I am able."

They seemed more like gentlemen jesting at a social gathering than a prisoner and his enemy.

Five of the six travelers sat close together with their guards scattered about. Dayown led Imani to a rocky cluster. He lowered himself to the ground near her feet. "You need not have fear. You are safe. As I am sure you have questions, this would be the time to ask of me what you will."

Imani gave him a look that said she wasn't feeling safe at all.

Dayown's two-toned eyes bore into her, yet he did not speak again.

She watched him watching her and trembled.

He continued to wait for her.

She waited on...she didn't know what, but whatever it was, it wasn't coming. The strain became too much. "W-why?" Her voice quivered, making the question sound cracked. Annora was the soft-spoken sister. Imani had always been loud and clear with whatever was on her mind. But she couldn't make out her thoughts, much less share them.

"If I am to understand your inquiry, you will have to use more words." Amusement played around his mouth.

She cleared her throat. "Why can't I sit with my family?"

"There now. That wasn't hard, was it? You remain secluded for many reasons. The largest is your wizard."

"I don't understand."

"I do not doubt his abilities. If there is a way to escape, he is aware of it. However, if he were going to leave any of you behind, he would have already done thus. I cannot suffer you all to be within his reach. Also, you and I cannot get acquainted if you are busy planning your flight."

"What do we have to talk about?"

He sniffed the air. "Oh, I don't know. We could begin to become accustomed to one another. If you survive this night, you will be my mate."

***

"Where are they taking us?"

"What do they want with Mom?"

"Why doesn't my head thing work without Loathel?"

"Shouldn't we try something before the rest of them catch up?"

"What are we going to do?"

"Am I the only one who can't hear anything?"

Only Annora remained silent.

Merlin shook his head and frowned. "If all the evanescent were so foolish, your kind would have died out ages ago. Voice nothing you do not wish to become common knowledge. These wolfhound people can hear a footfall a half-mile away." He gave them time to absorb the information. "They are taking us where they will. Since our only choice is to go where we are led, the destination is of little consequence. Two will have to trust. Without the aid of our warriors, speech unspoken is not possible. Your mother appears to be the only reason you remain alive. I can tell you, now more than ever, I regret disorganizing her living room. Like all bad choices, it could come back to haunt me."

Merlin painted a grave picture, yet he did not seem concerned. That gave them a measure of hope. Soon Dayown set them in motion again. In the deliberate noise of their rising, Merlin mumbled, "Those who can communicate should not have to be told to do so."

"Don't look at me," Honor said. "I tried. Blame the dumb Elve. He is in big trouble. I'm serious." She was so mad she forgot to be frightened. "I don't have these problems with my phone. As long as it's charged, it works. It doesn't need a pointy-eared attachment."

"*Do you have a plan, Medrid?*"

"*I plan for you to open your wife's thoughts to me. If you can help it, do not inform her of your presence. I doubt she can divide her attention. We wouldn't want Dayown to suspect. And you will need to check upon your brother, Master Jalen.*"

"*Jalen?*"

"*All your gifts have not yet returned, Master Christif, if you detected not your son's presence.*"

Christif did not comment.

"*What should I tell him?*" Jalen asked.

"*Tell him naught that will cause him worry. Of Trill and Loathel say nothing. If you cannot help it, suggest we wait upon them.*"

"*Okay, I'll try.*"

"*That is all anyone can ask. Christif, your wife...*"

"*Medrid, I don't think—*"

"*I did not ask you to think. You will do what I command or you will die.*"

There was a long silence while Chris pondered his options. Soon, Imani's thoughts wafted to the wizard.

***

Hours later, they came to the foot of a mountain. Here and there, scattered along the base, were several cave openings. They took the prisoners into a long, dark, twisting corridor. Pitch black was all around them, but the wolfmen had no problem navigating the passage. They shoved the hostages through the darkness until it opened into a cavern deep within the center of the mountain. The area was extensive, with many tunnels and byways leading off from it. Here, there were touches attached to the walls and several fires tended by wolf people who delighted in the return of the soldiers.

Dayown held out his hand, speaking to his captives as if they were guests. "Narconess. Welcome to the Hollow Hills."

"My lord, how good you are." A young lady skipped over. "There will be no need to hunt this eve; such is the feast we shall have with these." She grabbed Imani's arm.

A low growl rumbled in Dayown's throat. She released Imani as if she'd been burned.

"Touch her again and I shall reward you with death." There was no emotion in his voice, but his words held more than a threat.

The girl lowered her head. "Yes, Lord Dayown. I did not know."

"How could you know? You are simpleminded, Occlava. Anyone with sense would have waited to see what I would do. Tell me, what knowledge would I gain if I allow my visitors to be eaten ere the visit commences?" Dismissing the girl, he gave orders. "See to them. I want them protected for now."

The warriors led Imani in one direction and the five in another. Up levels and further back into the mountain until they arrived at a section of cells that proved to be no more than barred holes in the wall. Their captors forced Annora and Merlin into the first one and Honor and Jalen into the last, with Christif alone between them.

The guard holding Honor did not release her arm. He yanked her back against him. Burying his nose in her hair, he sniffed through the strands. "I will claim you," he said. "You please me."

Honor twisted, trying to break free. Her struggles made him laugh.

"What makes you confident you will have her?" said another of the jailers. "It is my desire to claim her." He yanked Honor from the first guard's grasp.

The first guard grabbed her back. "She is in my possession. She will be mine."

"You have no entitlement."

"I say I do."

Being caught in the tug-of-war gave Honor some momentum. She pulled out of their distracted grips and set off in a heated dash, not knowing or caring where she went. Footsteps fell close behind.

One guard began to contort.

"HONOR! HALT! DO NOT RUN!"

...It's so easy when you're evil...

Merlin's yell and the song blaring from Honor's pocket stopped everybody in mid-stride. The changing guard snapped back into human form. He seized and dragged her back the short distance she had run.

"No witchcraft, you stupid girl." A forceful slap sent her to the ground, making her cry out.

Jalen ran forward. Rough hands compelled him back, shoving him against the wall.

"She is but a child and new to this realm," Merlin pleaded through his bars. "If you can show pity, I beg you, do so now. If not, I pray you to have a care for your master's orders."

The guard paused midway through his second swing. With as much force as he could muster, he thrust Honor into the cell. She fell hard across the dirt floor. Once more, Jalen charged forward, halted by the slamming of the cell door. The bolt slid home and their captors moved away, forgetting them altogether.

***

In Aezilden, within the house of Talazim, out of a deep and much-needed sleep, Loathel awoke.

***

Jalen helped Honor to her feet. They looked about the cell, seeing a small airshaft and nothing else. No lights or windows, the walls and floor were bare. Parallel to the back wall, a tiny stream of water flowed into and out of each cell before disappearing somewhere in the mountain. They were in the damp, drafty darkness, with nothing for comfort but each other.

"Honor, are you alright?" Annora called out her first communication since their capture.

"Yeah, I'm okay." She wrapped her arms about herself to ward off the chill and memory.

"Mistress Honor," Merlin said. "I apologize for what you've endured. I note your deed as one of true valor. Unlearned, mind you, but true valor, nonetheless."

"Unlearned? If I am unlearned, magic-man, whose fault is that? What kind of idiot would bring us here and not tell us what to do?"

"I am partially guilty of the former and completely innocent of the latter. Guilty no more than Loathel or Christif. As for the idiotic action of bringing you here, the credit goes to King Dayown, not me. It was my intention to take you to Raegladun. I gave you instruction regarding that place."

Honor snickered, despite her raw mood. "Yeah, well, instruct me now."

"There is not much instruction to impart at this point, except to implore the use of common sense. Listen, I tell you all, these that hold us are dogs. Sometimes they possess the looks and rationale of men. Do not be fooled. Even when they don't seem it, they are always dogs: dangerous, evil."

"Like the hounds of hell."

"Master Jalen, they are the hounds of hell," the wizard said. "If you know anything about canines of any breed, you will remember not to run unless you wish to be pursued. Moreover, to them, the chase and the hunt are the same. What they hunt, they eat. They cannot help themselves. Within a few paces, those men chasing Honor would have become vicious, snarling wolves. In that form, they cannot reason. They would not recognize her. To them, she would have become prey. You saw them. Our one hope lies in not doing anything to invoke the change from man to beast."

The reminder made Annora weep. Merlin gathered her close, giving her what comfort he could.

"Will they change tonight?" Jalen peeped through the bars.

"I imagine they change every night." He handed Annora a handkerchief produced from the folds of his robe.

"What are we going to do?" Christif said from between them. "I don't want to be here when they come back."

"I do not understand why not. This is the safest place to be, I'll wager. I suspect we are here for our protection, as much as imprisonment. We may not get out, but as wolves, they cannot get in. I find that comforting to know."

Honor checked her message.

"Who called?"

"Kourtney."

"Are you going to tell her she saved your life?"

"Yeah, Jalen. There's a conversation." She put her phone to her ear. "Hey, Kourt. Ever hear of Zendelel? Didn't think so. I'm in jail. Waiting to become dog food. How are you?" She put her phone away. "I'll text her later."

"Hey," Jalen said. "I have an idea. Mr. Merlin, why don't you zip back to Mayadal and bring back five or six hundred of Loathel's cousins? We could be done here, in and out of Alpravage, and back home in an hour."

"Jalen, you're a genius." Honor high-fived him. "I'm sick of this place, anyway."

"Practicing to be a dictator, are you?"

"What's that mean?"

"You have ignored the fact that we are the trespassers, and have wronged Dayown, according to his laws. You would send forth countless numbers to sacrifice their lives as if they were mere game pieces created for your purposes alone. War is our last resort, not a first thought. You would have me join forces with Maldonus, initiating the bloodshed of which he is so fond. Large-scale fighting leads to large-scale death. I will take no part in the fulfillment of his dreams. Besides," Merlin said after a pause, "there are places in Zendelel where zipping, to use your phraseology, is not possible. Narconess is one such location."

"He could have said that in the first place," Honor muttered only loud enough for Jalen to hear.

Christif changed the subject. "Medrid, do you know what Dayown wants with my wife?"

"Yes, don't you? Are you not present when you share her thoughts with me?"

"I know her mind, but it makes no sense to me. She is in a pleasant place, well treated. They are preparing her for something, although she knows not what. What must she survive this night? Why does he want her? She belongs with me."

"King Dayown's desires are his chief concern, Christif. He believes Imani to be his mate. This night will prove it."

"Why don't I like the way that sounds?" Jalen asked.

"If it is confirmed she is not his mate, it would bode ill for her, I am afraid."

"Maybe she will be," Honor said, remembering the conversation she had with Loathel before the wolves. "It is possible, isn't it, Mr. Merlin?"

"I daresay anything is possible, child, but it is a large thing to hope for."

"What do you mean?" Christif focused on his daughter as best he could without being able to see her. "Honor, why would you think something like that is possible? She already has a husband."

That his pride took precedence over Imani's predicament was obvious and annoying. "You're the expert, Dad. If you can do it, why can't she?" Because she was who she was and her mood was as it was, Honor said, "If you can have seven wives—at least, that's all we know about—why can't Mom have two husbands? It's not as if she has a choice, now or then. But don't worry. It could fit with your plans. Mom and Dayown can babysit number eight for you until she grows up."

Merlin erupted in a fit of hysterics, hardly able to control himself. "You are brutal, merciless, and too much fun for someone my age." He slapped his thigh and cackled. "Have a care, I beg you. If I die of merriment, it will be upon your head."

Honor giggled, unable to help herself.

"Do you think they would babysit for him?"

"Why not? They might give her a stepbrother. Or a puppy. Or a stepbrother who is a puppy."

Their amusement had the wizard holding his sides, and the teenager doubled over.

Chris stomped to the back of his cell.

"Honor, what are you talking about?"

"Trust me, Jalen," she said between gasps, "you don't want to know. The first time you hear it, it's so not funny." Then she laughed some more.

"Not now, Honor," Chris said.

Merlin laughed harder.

Jalen wondered what he was missing.

Annora didn't care.

CHAPTER XXIV

It functioned as a bedroom, spacious and neat. One wall boasted a fireplace centered between a massive wooden rack of weapons and two large trunks. The bed against the opposite wall had several blankets made from rich fur. Multitudes of candles lent their glow to the illusion of cozy. Two large openings served as windows. Instead of glass, animal skins pulled tight across them against night and bad weather. A rug, a small table, and two crudely made but comfortable chairs sat before the fire. The room had no other furnishings but held a homey feel. Except the walls were stone, the floor was stone covered with hard-packed dirt, and Imani knew she was in a wolf's den.

She was in the care of three women, one of whom was Occlava. Imani shifted under the girl's scrutiny.

"See to her bath and coverings, I will stay with her." The young Occlava held some authority. The other two did her bidding while she and Imani studied one another. The girl was close to Jalen's age, a year or two older, perhaps. Her wide eyes, twice colored, were dissimilar shades of green. They created an interesting contrast to her dark skin and wild brown hair.

"What will you do to me...if you remain?" Occlava's nose twitched; she sniffed the air.

"Why would I do anything to you?" Imani pressed her arms close to her body, assuming she smelled.

"I would retaliate were I you."

"Retaliate for what? What position am I in to retaliate for something?"

"Are you dimwitted? Do you understand what has happened to you?"

"My family and I are being held hostage."

"I know naught of your family, but you are dimwitted if being the subject of Dayown's attention is anything other than spectacular to you. You have the opportunity to become the alpha. You would be our queen. You would be Lord Dayown's mate. Dayown."

"I'm sure it's an honor, but I am not, nor do I wish to be Dayown's mate. I have a mate already."

"Do not trouble yourself. Dayown will kill him."

"I don't want him killed; he's my husband."

"You don't? Do you want Dayown to share?"

"No, I don't want him to share. I want him to find some other mate and leave me alone."

"You are odd."

"I don't know how things work here, but in my world, you can't murder a man because you want his wife."

"Here, you want Dayown to want you. Nothing else matters. If he is willing to kill for you, what could be better?" She shrugged. "It's all speculation, anyway."

"Why? What's going to happen to me?"

"Maybe nothing, maybe everything," Occlava sniffed again, catching a whiff of fright. "You cannot change this eve. There is no purpose in worrying over it."

"I'd like to know all the same."

"King Dayown will have to tell you. I have learned my lesson. I only wondered if you were planning to retaliate. Your bath is here."

***

Dayown made his way down the corridor. Tristole, his brother and second-in-command, fell into step beside him. "Have you gathered them all or does the hunt continue?"

"They are all here."

"I noted not any seasoned warriors. Yestereve there were at least two."

"Some of us fed well."

"On horse meat, not human."

Dayown stopped to stare at Tristole a moment. Being the younger brother, Tristole carried favor with Dayown. For this reason, the king chose not to reprimand him for his tone. "They are gone. If someone brought them down and did not satisfy his hunger, I am not responsible. Neither will I hunt what no longer exists."

"If they are not dead, they could come back."

"If that is our fortune, we will eat them later. Do you have a reason for pestering me?"

Their footfalls made no sound on the cave floors.

"Not usually, but this eve I do. What is to be done with the females?"

"Do you want one?"

"Everybody wants one."

"I am not asking everybody."

"Yes, I do."

"I have marked the one I have chosen. You may take your pick. The third can be shared by all."

"I will not choose one."

"Shall I choose for you?"

"No, I will not partake."

"You said you wanted one."

"I want one, but I do not need one. I do not feel up to the challenge such a female would present. I wonder if it is a good thing for you."

"A good thing for me? It would be a bad thing if I were not to have her."

"Do you have some purpose for her?"

"No, she is useless."

"Why keep her?"

"I want her."

"Selfish and wasteful."

"Am I supposed to be another way?"

"No...wise, maybe."

"Wise, as in demanding you leave my presence?"

"Wise, as in not wasting your energy on something you do not need."

"She may end up serving some purpose. Besides, this conversation is premature. If she does not survive, what will it matter?"

"I concur. If you allow it, I will be at your side."

"Thank you, Tristole. Have you hope she will pass?"

"No. I have hope she will be delicious when she fails."

"So do I. Either way, it will be a good night."

CHAPTER XXV

Imani bathed and changed into a shimmering gray dress made of some soft material she could not identify. She washed her own clothes and laid them by the fire. She planned to change again before she left; she didn't doubt she was leaving. Next, she made a careful inspection of the rack of weapons.

Most were objects she couldn't lift. She did, however, come across a few minor items of interest. One was a case containing a lady's ring. The plain band supported a raised rectangular plate with an intricate design engraved on it. Wondering why such a treasure should be considered a weapon, Imani took a closer look. To her surprise, with the slightest touch, the plate flipped open and released a tiny blade. "Seriously?"

Holding the ring between her thumb and forefinger, she flung her hand out. "*En garde*, Barbie." She was close to the rack and should have bumped it. But the tiny knife sliced right through. Not believing it, Imani tried again. It cut through the wood with ease. Becoming bolder, she turned to the fireplace and touched the blade's tip to the stone. It sunk into the rock like Jell-O. "Okay, I'm convinced." She flipped the top down. "Sorry, Chris." She removed her wedding band and put it into the case, hoping no one would notice. The new ring was big, but not too big. She slid the plate around to the inside of her hand.

Returning to her inspection, she came across a giant nail and pocketed it on a whim. Scanning the next shelf, she didn't hear him approach, didn't know how long he stood there, and nearly had heart failure when she caught sight of Dayown leaning against the stone archway.

"Find anything of value?"

Imani raised a hand to steady her racing heart. She turned, willing herself to face his bared canines.

"I do not mind inquisitiveness, but tell me, what interests have you in weaponry?" He came toward her in smooth strides.

She swallowed her desire to run.

"You look lovely, my pet." He assessed her. "That is no revelation to me." He offered her his hand. "Your dinner will arrive soon. We will talk while you eat."

Not seeing an alternative, she placed her fingers in his. He pulled her close, too close. While he breathed her in, he reached into her pocket, extracting the nail.

She remained silent.

"After tomorrow you own all I have, the bitinesaw included." He held it out to her.

"Sorry. That's not an offering I trust." She tried to pull away.

He would not allow it. "Consider it a token of my esteem."

She forced her fingers to curl around the bitinesaw.

"I must warn you, it is dangerous, but it will not aid you against my purpose." He held her gaze a moment longer before leading her to a chair and placing himself in the other. "There was no time for preparation, but I hope you will find the room to your liking."

Having the spike in her pocket was comforting. "The room is fine. Where is my family?"

"They are safe for now. Tell me about them."

Imani wondered how to answer. The first rule of warfare was not to give information. However, she was positive the rule-makers had not considered Dayown. "Chris, my husband—"

"I do not wish to hear about him. Speak of another."

"My son is here."

"Ahh, a son. Good. Good."

"So glad you approve."

"I do. By what is this son called?"

"Jalen, he is my eldest."

"He is close to manhood. I may look forward to training him myself." The thought seemed to please Dayown. "You have this one son?"

"No, I have two sons and one daughter. She is here also. Her name is Honor."

"Young one. Full hair."

"Yes, the other girl is my sister, Annora."

"It is my understanding your daughter is brave. Already several have expressed a desire to claim her."

Hearing the news made Imani glad Loathel was 'joined' to Honor. Between elves and werewolves, elves were her magical beings of choice. If Loathel were alive, Honor had the best chance of escaping. If all they said was true, he would not abandon her daughter.

Dayown understood her silence to be approval. "I am encouraged if this pleases you."

"What pleases me concerning claims on Honor is of little consequence." An image of Loathel carrying her out of camp came to mind. "Honor can be quite a handful."

"Some of my men have already learned this. Even so, I can tell she brings you much joy. She will be a good choice for my brother, Tristole. You said you have two sons. Where is the other?"

Tension washed the mirth out of Imani.

Dayown leaned forward, feeling it. "What misdeed has befallen your second son?"

Hope sprang to life within Imani. Maybe if he understood, he would show mercy and let them go. "In case you didn't know, we are not from this...this realm."

"I am aware."

"My younger son is a prisoner. We are trying to get him back. He's just a little boy, only ten years old. That monster kidnapped him. You can't keep us here. We have to get to my son." Unshed tears threatened to spill.

"Who has done this thing?"

"Somebody called Maldonus."

"Maldonus is returned?"

"You know him?"

"I do. I have been to Alpravage, but there is no kinship between the heir of Azâzêl and myself. His Queons are the mortal enemy of my kind. If caught unaware, they will hunt and feed upon us. That is when they are not cowering in fear."

"Why cower if they're the hunters?

"They are not always the hunters. We also hunt and feed upon them." He stopped speaking when a server arrived. She placed a tray laden with food and drinks on the table between them, bowed low, and retreated.

"I hope it is to your liking." Dayown poured two glasses of wine.

"It looks wonderful," Imani said. Sipping the wine, she studied the meal. "What is it?"

"You may trust me. It is your dinner, fashioned after the nourishment your kind consume." To shatter her disbelief, he inspected the foodstuff. "It appears to be venison, roasted." He pointed. "Carrots, potatoes, wild berries, and spiced apples, warmed. Over here is bread with butter and this..." he lifted his glass to sample its contents, "is the finest wine we have stored. I pronounce it a feast fit for a king. A good thing too, since I am king; nothing less will do. May I serve you?"

"Please." The food smelled delicious, and she was famished. Five or six bites in, she noticed he made no move to prepare anything for himself. "Aren't you going to eat?"

"Later. For now, I am content to be in your company."

"Is it you don't eat cooked food?"

"I eat it often."

"You do?"

"Mmm-hmm, what form I am in when I get hungry determines what I eat."

"Oh." She filled her fork. "If you and Maldonus don't get along, why do you go to Alpravage?"

"We make covenants, promising our people will not take one another's lives. We also break those covenants. Unlike the Queons, my people have no accountability. After all, what pledge or bond can you expect to hold a wolf to?"

"I can see why that might be difficult."

"I can see you've turned this conversation. I am to ask you the questions."

Imani contemplated her half-empty wineglass. The room was warm, her vision fuzzy. "This wine must be going to my head." She gave her braids a shake and found the motion amusing.

"It should, my pet. It is drugged."

"Is it?" Imani tried to keep a straight face. "I should have had a bigger glass." She finished the contents and held the goblet up for a refill. Dayown obliged her. After a healthy gulp, she slurred, "Vhy?"

"So you would not have fear."

"I don habe vear, I gotts a itch." She proceeded to scratch her back. "Does you habe fleas?"

"I do not believe so." Charmed, the wolflord watched her struggle. "Would you like me to assist?"

"Uh-huh." She swirled around, offering him her back.

His fingertips touched here and there, rubbing the irritation away. Not wanting to stop, Dayown's scratching became a gentle massage.

Imani rested her head on the back of her chair. She could not think of anything but the strong hands stroking her back and shoulders.

***

"You evil, demon-bred dog! I will slay you for this treachery. How dare you pollute her!" In the dark of his cell, Christif was more animal than human.

"Christif, calm yourself."

"Calm myself? Calm myself. Medrid, he takes advantage of my wife. If I cannot save her, I will die in the effort."

"Wonderful." Merlin stroked his beard. "But making an ass of yourself is not how to get your objective met. If they slay you for the noise, how then will you help her?"

Christif slid to the floor, head in his hands, sobbing.

"Christif, listen to me," Merlin said. "You rightly fear for her life, yet you worry at what her survival will mean. Know this: in my heart, I believe she will be spared. However, it will not be because she is Dayown's mate. Admittedly, Honor and I teased, but I do not believe it can be thus."

"How can you be so sure?"

"It is not the way of nature. What you did is done. She is your wife. She belongs with you, and you with her. Until death do you part is the law of Universe."

"We are not in Universe."

"That matters not. She is bound to Universe; bound to you. This is a test of Dayown's desire, not Imani's destiny. No matter how much he may want her, her heart is in your keeping."

"That may cost her life."

"No, Master Christif. Her life is at the mercy of Dayown's greed. On that account, we must pray it runs deep."

"What about what I have done?"

"What about it? Confession, repentance, and atonement—preferably before we meet the Rae—make the crooked lines straight."

Christif wiped his nose on his sleeve. "You make everything sound easy, Medrid."

"It is easy. Knowing a thing is no wizard's feat. Knowledge can always be found. Answers are simple. The doing is where the difficulty lies."

***

Dayown nuzzled Imani's hair and skin, lost in the wonder of her loveliness. When her shifting and muttering ceased, he glanced at her face. The wine and his touch put her to sleep.

It was time.

He scooped her up and then hesitated. He was attracted to the female, but wondered if it was enough? The ritual could wait. He resettled them in his chair, her on his lap. He licked her, grooming her shoulder. She snored. He wondered if prolonging his time in her presence would help bind her to him. He did not care, but it was something to do.

CHAPTER XXVI

Loathel stood by Trill's bed, praying. "Be at peace, my friend. Although it is difficult, Triune's will is always best. I do not begrudge you the gift of passing into the first realm, but I would forever mourn my loss. Were my way to prevail, I would keep your companionship throughout my days with no thought of what you would miss. Even in my sorrow, glad am I, this is not the way of it. I take comfort in the knowledge, should you pass into the first realm, my loss would be wondrous gain for many. None more than Yaunt, who must by now be out of patience waiting upon you." He put his hand on Trill's shoulder. "I leave you with this promise: Your Annora will live under my protection until she comes to you. I will hold you to the same oath with Honor. When she reaches the first realm, you must see to her in my place. You know I have love. Love for her. Love for you. Be at peace, my friend." Struggling against the desire to remain until Trill either recovered or passed on, Loathel turned away.

Talazim was waiting. "Days in karloptini yet you depart without a full night's sleep. Is it wise to return to Zendelel in such a state? How much use will you be if you do not reclaim your strength?"

"More than I can be if I remain here."

"You worry overmuch. They are in Medrid's care. What could be safer?"

"My care. I know Medrid will do his best, but there is trouble. I can feel it."

The tilt of Talazim's head was graceful. "You can feel it from here? Have you become so mighty you perform impossible feats? Tell me, Loathel, exactly what can you feel?"

"Honor."

A father's amusement gave way to amazement. "Honor? Is this so?"

"It is, indeed. She is somewhere she does not wish to be. Someone has brought pain upon her. I can do no other than go to her."

"Have you spoken to her?" Talazim frowned.

"Nay, Father, I have not. Still, I know the truth of it, although I know not how."

The Elven king was thoughtful. "Your bond with this girl is more unique than you know."

"The bond is nothi—"

"The bond is enough to bring you to her side no matter how great the distance."

***

"All right, this is weird."

"What's weird?" Jalen went from the back of the cell to the wall Honor sat against. He leaned over her to see what she held. "Your phone. Ohhooo. Maybe I'll get one just like it." He walked away.

"You're an idiot." She didn't bother to look up. "I'm talking about Kourtney calling me."

"Yeah, I know. I was there."

"And you're still an idiot. Which is why I don't bother talking to you." She shifted her position. "Kourtney's call was from the night we left. I told her to meet me at Harpers Ferry. She called to see where I was."

"Why did you tell her that?"

"The reason I refer to you as an idiot is because you live up to the name." Honor shook her head. "I wanted her to get a look at Loathel. But that isn't the point."

"You have a point?" Jalen rattled the bars once and strutted to the back of the cell.

Honor exaggerated her sigh. "My point, Dufus, is why didn't I get it before? It's like time is moving slow or weird or something. For as long as we've been here, I still haven't lost a single bar on my battery." She clicked on the internet and clicked off again. "Not that it matters. Not that the person I want to talk to is available." She shut the phone down and brushed her hair out of her face. She quit playing with it hours ago and now it annoyed her. *Where is that Elve?* she wondered for the hundredth time since she awoke that morning. She'd been through a spectrum of emotions, from concern, to fear, to anger several times over. Now she was edging toward despair. It had been a while since they had dinner. No one came after that. All about them had grown eerily quiet. She woke up her phone to check the time: 12:34. She didn't know what that meant in Zendelel. Her mother's fate was unknown and a source of tremendous worry. Their only hope lay with the missing Loathel. With each passing hour, that hope dwindled.

"Jalen, knock it off."

He ignored her. He checked the bars again in case one was loose. Annora's sobs echoed. Merlin and Christif were silent.

From nowhere came a sense of peace. After so much turmoil, the feeling was wonderful. It occurred to her Mr. Merlin and her dad were silent because they were asleep or contemplating escape—good idea, either way. She shut her eyes. Jalen passed by again and she reopened them to stare holes into his back. "I'm going to get Mr. Merlin to come up with a Prozac-potion for you."

Jalen juggled the bars.

Enough is enough. If I stick my foot out, he'll trip and knock himself unconscious. Ahh, the quiet... She stretched her foot out, intending to move it at the last second.

Without breaking stride, Jalen made a wide path around her outstretched leg.

She clicked her tongue.

"If I'm getting on your nerves, too bad. Next time I'll step on you."

"Why don't you sit yourself down somewhere and leave me alone?"

"I can't. I can't sit here doing nothing while Mom is...I don't know where Mom is. This is frustrating."

"You should try to get as much rest as possible. If we do get out of here, being worn out won't help."

"Yeah, I know. I...HONOR!"

"What?"

"We're not talking."

"Normally, no. Since you are the only other person in this cell, I had to lower my standards."

"You cretin. Up 'til now, we were doing the head thing."

"We were?" Honor jumped to her feet.

"Is it...?"

"Has to be." She waved him off. She had things to do. *"Loathel."*

A wind-chime lullaby whispered through her mind. *"The lady recalls. It is time you turned your thoughts unto mine. Intentionally tripping your brother, you are ever the brat."*

The dim cell brightened with her smile. *"That's nothing compared to what I'm going to do to you. Where are you?"*

"En route to you, Mistress, where else?"

Her heart did an erratic flip, making it hard to remember why she was angry. *"Where else? How am I supposed to know where else? It's not like I had any information. Where'd you go? How come this head thing only works when you're around? Huh? You didn't say goodbye."* Her mood dipped with the last sentence.

The Elve was immediately aware. *"A hundred years will pass ere I have restored one lost hour of this day. Still, it was just a day and one too long away from your company for my liking. Forgive me. Had I another choice, I would have taken it and rejoiced."*

Honor came close to swooning.

"I hope your goofy grin is because of Loathel. You look stupid af," Jalen said.

She silenced him with another wave of her hand. *"We're prisoners in...umm...I can't remember the name, the empty hills or something."*

"Narconess. It means The Hollow Hills."

"Yeah, that's it. Can you help us?"

"I am coming there."

"Lowell."

"Yes?"

"Thank you."

"It is my onus to be of aid to...your family. I will be where you are soon. It would help me if I had the benefit of your memories. Will you permit me to share them?"

"Sure," she said, wondering if it was a good idea. After all, her primary activity had been thinking about him.

"It is."

"It is what?"

"It is a good idea. A very good idea."

CHAPTER XXVII

For Honor, the minutes dragged on slower than before. Sleep was out of the question. She traded mindsets with Jalen. He settled down, comforted to know Loathel was coming to their aid. Now Honor was antsy. Unable to hold her composure, she shuffled around, exercised, and checked the bars every few minutes.

"Please tell me I wasn't that bad." Jalen watched Honor pace.

"You were worse."

"Much worse," Merlin called out from his niche. "Da, da, da da dadada..."

"Hey, I thought you were on my side," Jalen yelled over Honor's giggling.

"I am on Loathel's side. He is the only one who could be of any use to me at the moment. Da, da, da da dadada, da, da..."

"What is that song? You hum it all the time," Jalen asked.

"'I Dream of—' blasted '—Jeannie.' Can't get the silly thing out of my head."

"It's an old sitcom." Annora surprised them with a moment of focus. "About a genie and an astronaut."

"If you haven't seen it," Merlin said, "now is an opportunity for you to put those pocket devises to use. Turn up the volume. Perhaps if I hear the notes, they will leave me."

Honor sent Jalen a text. **You asked. You watch. Wake me when its over.**

The Elve ran at a breakneck pace, covering a vast distance in a short time.

The full moon shone down, illuminating the motionless figure. A cool breeze sifted through the thin material of her gown, making her shiver, awakening her. Imani tried to blink through the fuzz. She didn't have a notion where she was or how she came to be lying on a mat in the center of a ring with her hands tied. She fingered the collar around her neck; it held her chained to a stake. Someone covered her with a blanket. She pushed it aside. "What happened?" she questioned herself. "How did I get here?"

Imani did the first thing that came to mind. *"Chris...does this work? Can anyone hear me?"*

"I am with you, honey. I have been waiting only for you to awaken."

"Oh, thank heaven. I'm scared. I don't know what's going on. Is everybody okay?"

"I'm here too, Mom," Jalen cut in. *"We're all fine."*

"So am I," Honor said. *"This is the first time I've been able to do this all day. Do you want to know why? I'll tell you why. Because Loathel is on his way."*

"Sweetheart, I have never heard better news. As a matter of...fact...oh...my..." Her scream reached them all.

Coming toward Imani was the biggest wolf she had ever seen. His eyes, one gray, one gold, fixed on her. Two more wolves followed. Now they understood. If there were a bond between Dayown and Imani, it would have to be strong enough for him to recognize her in his current state. It would have to be strong enough for him to protect her from the other wolves and himself.

Loathel crept through the entrance of Narconess. Most of the wolf-people were hunting. Most. The darkness did not hinder his Elven vision. Neither did the winding passage slow him. Keen Elven ears alerted him before he reached the great cavern that animals were about. Mothers nursing pups, others—injured or old—lying near the warm stones of old fires. He advanced stealthily along the wall, seeming no more than a ripple of air or light sweeping across the shadowy jagged rocks. Periodically, one or another of the animals would raise its head as if sensing some curiosity or danger, but the Elve slipped past their sharp hearing and acute sense of smell.

In wolven form, Dayown's people could not climb the rope ladders. They kept everything of human interest or value on the upper levels to ensure the safety of anything an animal might destroy.

Loathel knew what he was after would be up there. He scurried up the nearest ladder with monkey-like agility.

**

Imani silently pleaded for the wolfking to recognize her. Not willing to count on it, she forced her tied hands into her pocket and clutched the bitinsaw. Dayown said it would not aid her. She would see about that.

He stopped a few yards in front of her. A low growl hummed through him. The two other wolves paced behind him.

Merlin spoke to her via Christif. *"Madame, I realize this will be difficult, but I pray you accept my counsel. Try to relax as much as you are able. It may go better if you do not present a threat to them. Do not look them in the eye and try not to make any sudden movements. Gentleness may succeed where aggression will surely fail."*

It was Chris' turn to attack the bars. "I can't stand by and let this happen. We've got to get out of here! Medrid, can't you do something?"

"I am capable of doing many things, Master Christif. Opening locks without my staff is not among them. Think you Imani would be in this position if there were aught I could do to aid her from here? Think you I am unwilling to help? I will credit it to your distress this time. Nonetheless, you would do well to remember I am indeed capable of many things."

"They would be easier accomplished with this, I'm sure." His staff slid through the bars.

Annora jumped, surprised.

"I wondered if you would ever find it."

"You are welcome, Medrid." Loathel handed Christif his sword, then stepped away unconcerned.

"You know I am thankful." Merlin aimed the staff at the lock. It popped open. Annora followed him out. "Did time permit, I would sing twenty songs of your astonishing deeds." He did the same to the lock on Christif's cell. The return of his staff did wonders for his mood.

"I am grateful we are hurried." Loathel stopped before the last cell. "Honor."

"Lowell."

They stared at one another, desiring what they saw. The cell door opened and Jalen walked past, relieving the Elve of his weapon. Loathel did not acknowledge him. Honor stood rooted where she was, unable to move under the intensity of his gaze. Mesmerized by her, Loathel could not as much as blink.

They were contemplating the same thing: What to do about this? The desire was there. Honor longed to run and jump into his arms; he ached to crush her to him. Loathel wanted to taste the softness of her lips; she needed to feel the firmness of his mouth moving over hers. They both yearned to give in to their desires, yet they hesitated. These were the meditations of lovers, not friends. Still, they desired. Knowing the thoughts of the other fanned those flames.

Jalen called out over his shoulder as the others moved away, "Kiss her and speed it up. We have things to do, you know."

"My sentiments exactly," Merlin said.

Honor lowered her lashes and made herself walk past the handsome Elve. He caught her hand and held it. This was not what either of them wanted, but it was enough. Hand in hand, they followed the others.

The travelers came to a cross-section of corridors. Torches lined the walls, illuminating the passage they were in and the one across from it. A third walkway burned less bright. The last was completely dark.

The Elve and the wizard conferred.

"We do not have much time, and we cannot risk becoming lost in these tunnels," Merlin said.

"This is the way you came in," Loathel indicated the brightest path, "but we cannot return by that route. The main hall is not empty."

"My wife, I need to get to my wife," Christif urged.

"The air moving in this direction suggests a nearby exit." Loathel pointed to the semi-dark passage. "But we will not find Imani there."

The six made their way down the dark corridor.

Merlin waved his hand over his staff. Small streams of light emitted from his fingertips to illumine the end. The tiny glow gave off enough light for him to see directly in front of him. Christif, Jalen, and Annora stumbled along behind, trying to keep as close as possible to Merlin without tripping. Loathel walked as easily as he would have in bright daylight. Still holding his hand, Honor followed his lead and did not so much as kick a pebble.

CHAPTER XXVIII

Imani attempted to relax her breathing. She lowered her eyes. The only thing left to do was pray. She threw herself into the task.

One of the smaller wolves grew restless. He took a bold step forward.

Imani did not move.

Dayown did.

He snarled, placing his body between her and the animal. Whether it was recognition or assertion of his authority over the meal was anyone's guess.

From nowhere, an airborne knife sailed end over end. It struck the third beast, making him yelp in startled pain. A second knife found its mark, killing him. Then there was movement all around. Shadowy figures separated from the darkness and surrounded the ring. The two wolves stepped about, confused. They growled and bared their fangs but could not escape. Something was holding them in a frenzied trance.

Eight beings came closer, encircling Imani and the animals. Four she recognized as the same creatures they fought when they arrived in Zendelel. She had never seen anything like the other four. Whether it was the darkness or her dismay, she could not make out any real features. What she saw were burned-boned skeletons, their bodies glistened and encased a gel-like substance. Three tiny laser-like dots appeared to be eyes.

It was more like seeing the outline of something instead of an actual thing. She could almost see through them. They glided across the ground and carried the stench of decay.

One blew a whistle of some sort. Imani couldn't hear it but it affected the werewolves. They behaved as if they were suffering and could not move away from it.

Another of the things spoke. A serpent's tongue issued from where a mouth should have been. "A mossst forrrtunate cirrrcumssstance," he hissed. "The Dayown's flesssh will be sssatisssfying."

"We mussst eat now, beforrre the othersss arrrive," the third of the gruesome beings said.

"No. We mussst wait. They mussst sssee we have taken Dayown."

"I don't care what you Queons do with those mongrels. We want her," a Kildar told them. "She was with those who attacked our company."

Imani's sharp intake of breath drew their attention.

"I see you remember me. No, I did not pass from this realm. Saving rains doused the fire your mighty Trill set before we all burned. We, Kildar, have been everywhere seeking you out. It is our task to bring you to justice. Where are the rest?"

A Queon leaned over to retrieve his knife from the fallen wolf. "Firssst we feassst." The next instant, he was down on all fours, gorging on his kill.

His action kindled the cravings of the other Queons. They crowded the dead animal, forgetting all else. Even the one blowing the silent whistle left his duty for the fresh meat. The moment the noise ceased, the wolves attacked. Two of the Queons never had a chance.

"Get the female," the Kildar leader called out to his companions. He unsheathed his sword. "I'll deal with the dogs."

Dayown backed away from the Kildar. He let loose an ear-piercing howl, a call to his people.

The Kildar laughed. "Where do you think you are going?"

Imani stretched and swung the bitinesaw with all her might. The motion caused the tool to extend twice its length, a double-edged razor. The guard fell forward, his arm severed, his sword tip nicking Dayown's foreleg as he fell. King Dayown's jaws locked on his throat before he hit the ground.

Imani swung in the direction of the next closest Kildar.

The six exited the tunnel into the ring. Loathel's arrows dispatched the three remaining Kildar guards. Chris and Jalen ran forward, swords drawn. The wolves ran. Free of the animals, the Queons turned their attention to the newcomers. Rage and adrenaline were on the side of the Lossmans. Both demons died quickly.

Annora and Honor scurried to Imani's side. They untied her ropes. Honor tugged on the chain a few times. "Guys, help."

"I've got something." Imani's tone was mild for a woman experiencing her ordeal. She pulled off the ring and freed the blade before giving it to Annora. "Be careful. Don't go too deep, that thing could kill me."

"What do you want me to do with this?" Annora eyed the tiny knife.

"Hurry, they are coming." Loathel joined the women.

"Who?" Christif asked, "The wolves or the Queons?"

Loathel took the ringblade from Annora. He sliced through the collar. "Both."

He helped Imani to her feet. They heard noises. The Queons had arrived. The travelers made a circle. Loathel, Christif, and Jalen held their swords. Merlin aimed his staff. Imani held the bitinesaw poised. Annora and Honor stood ready with a long knife each. Still, they were outnumbered by a lot.

Almost on the heels of the Queons came the werewolves, led by Dayown himself. They attacked the demon's heels and higher.

Taking advantage of the distraction, Merlin shared his plan. "RUN!"

They moved as fast as they could toward the trees and a clear getaway, only to come up short at the sight of a second Kildar border patrol. Attracted by the clamor, they came to investigate. The patrol rode down hard on the seven, herding them back into the fiasco, forcing them to separate.

The commotion combined with the scent of blood and wolves was too much for the Kildar horses. Rearing and sidestepping, they would not join the fray. Before long, controlling their mounts and keeping the wolfhounds at bay took precedence over the escapees.

Chris swung his blade wildly but expertly, striking demon and demon-dog alike. Beside him, Imani did considerable damage with both the ringblade and the bitinesaw. What she lacked in finesse, she made up for in determination. They hacked their way to the base of the mountain and climbed too high for the wolves. The Queon had no interest in them and the Kildar were too busy to follow.

Merlin and Jalen made it back into the tunnel. Once inside, Merlin lit the way.

"Is this smart?" Jalen asked as they ran.

"I don't have time to decide. I am going on the hope every werewolf in Zendelel is out there. If not, we couldn't do anything more stupid." They backtracked to the cross-section, this time choosing the semi-dark passage.

Loathel kept close to Honor and Annora. Together, they fought for their freedom, doubling back toward the trees. Violently accurate, Loathel murdered everything having the misfortune of being in their path.

Annora and Honor helped to keep the numbers manageable. Surprisingly, if only to themselves, they were battle-ready. After one accurately placed jab with Loathel's blade, Honor considered her feat. Responding to movement behind her—movement she hadn't been aware of—she concluded somehow the Elve was doing it. *He had to be.* She deftly switched the longknife from her right hand to her left, lashed out, and was rewarded with a pained yelp from something else she didn't know was there. *Wow, I'm better than Jalen.*

Loathel, standing in front of her, switched his sword from his left hand to his right and back again six times over, arcing and swirling, in a blaze of movement that left four Queons, three Kildar, and a wolf dead.

"*Okay. So you're better than Jalen.*"

"*I should hope.*" He stabbed something over her head.

After that, they were both too busy to hold the conversation.

***

It wasn't long before the sounds of battle faded. When he felt they had run a safe distance, Loathel let them rest while he reached for the others. "*Jalen, are you safe? Well? Is anyone with you?*"

"*I'm both for the moment. Medrid is here.*" Jalen did not see Merlin smile at his use of the wizard's elven moniker. "*What about you?*"

"*I am well, as are your sister and aunt.*"

"*So are your mother and I,*" Christif joined in. "*We're coming around Narconess. Where is everybody?*"

"*We have gained several miles on you, I think. Jalen and I benefited by going through Narconess. What of you, Loathel? What route have you taken?*"

"*The original route we set upon.*"

"*Show-off. How foolish of me to ask.*"

"*So, what's the plan?*" Jalen asked.

"*It is not safe for any of us to linger,*" Merlin said, "*not even to wait for one another. It is best we come together at Raegladun.*"

"*Raegladun?*"

"*Christif, this separation, the werewolves, the loss of our supplies, horses, time, and not to mention, Trill, can be traced back to our last conversation concerning Raegladun. What else do you wish to risk?*"

A streak of lightning split the sky. Thunder rolled through the clouds. The women looked upward, wondering if a storm was approaching. The men knew Merlin was in a foul mood.

"*I did not wish this trouble upon us. I sought to avoid problems.*"

"*Then do so now,*" came the hypnotic tones of the Elve. "*Resisting Raegladun would bring death to your wife and Bedalamon to you. Travon deserves better.*"

CHAPTER XXIX

Each group walked as fast and far as they could before giving in to weariness. The deep of night began to crack. Gray fingers clawed at the sky, scratching at the dawn. A few stars shined cold before snapping out, casualties in the battle lost. They didn't complain, but the women struggled to continue. "We shall sleep here." He stopped beside a large tree.

Honor plopped down at its base. "It's about time. I can't go one more step."

"You will have to," he said. "Climbing is necessary."

"Climbing?"

"Climbing?"

He pointed up.

"How are we supposed to get up there?" Annora followed the line of his finger.

"Formulate another plan." Honor folded her arms. "I'm not doing that."

"Should they decide to hunt us," Loathel said, "There is no escape. Wolves cannot climb. If they come in human form, or the Kildar, or the Queon, your best hope lies with me. I shall be in this tree. Out of reach. Asleep." He swung himself onto a low branch and scrambled out of sight.

"Lowell!"

"Loathel!"

He landed on the ground in front of them. With expressionless features, he removed the thin gold, silver, and green woven Elven rope from his waistband. "Annora, tie this around your waist." He gave the rope to her. Turning to Honor, he said, "Attempt to behave yourself while I see to your aunt." Again, he swung himself up through the branches. "Hold on to the rope and brace your feet against the trunk." He hauled Annora out of sight so quick it looked as if she were running up the side of the tree.

A few minutes later, Loathel dropped to the ground beside Honor.

"Wow. You are fast."

"Tree climbing is not a difficult task."

"So you say."

"I do." He stepped in close and tied the rope around her middle. He did not move away when he finished but let his hands rest on her waist.

She lifted her eyes to connect with his.

A tidal wave of emotion surged through him, passing through to her. A rush of passion kindled within her before returning to consume him.

"*aARp aA uUz hl fFoLuUzpoL, jljoh zo uUh jljouUqUt huUGo gplQjljoLvo lRp tTIEe QaAhx zo,*" he whispered. (*If l am to be damned, let me at least take knowledge of you with me*).

"Please," she replied.

He drew her to him. His muscled arms were silken rocks under her palms. She would have pondered the feel of them if the power in his gaze allowed her the freedom to do anything but sigh.

He captured her sigh while it was still warm upon her lips, drinking it in. He took into himself her essence. She yielded to him all and innocently offered more. For all he took, he replaced with himself and she could not get enough. Together they ascended, erupting into spiraling fragments of light and fire only to mesh again, an entanglement of him and her, no longer separate and different. Now together. Now one.

Hearts raced, breathing became erratic, yet they did not stop. The moment held them as they held each other, not willing to let go. Desire turned into hunger too great to ignore. They became wild trying to sate it. Somewhere, deep in the unexamined places, the young lovers shared the same fear: this would be their only time, their only chance. They fought to hold on until it was more than a moment, would become more than a memory. They fought until knowledge of the other burned in their souls.

Only because they had no more breath to give or take did the kiss end. The strong Elven Prince looked at the powerful young woman in awe. Never in the four thousand, six hundred twenty-eight years of his life had he ever beheld a sight more enthralling. "I would beg your forgiveness were I not unsorry. To promise it will not happen yet again is a lofty goal. One l have no desire to attain, though I know I must try." Unable to stop himself, he kissed her once more. "If you will not hold my weakness against me, I will attempt to do better." Releasing her, he moved to the tree and slipped out of sight.

Honor stood there, bewildered. She heard him mention something about 'doing better.' She touched her lips with the tips of her fingers. For the life of her, she couldn't think of one thing that could be *better* than what he had done.

***

More than sixty feet off the ground, Annora sat on a thick limb, hugging the trunk as tightly as she could. Loathel stood near her, pulling Honor up to join them. He took her hand and brought her to her feet next to him.

Honor made inarticulate sounds.

"Do we have to be *this* high?" Annora translated for her.

"There is no place safer."

Staring straight down in petrifaction, Honor said, "Unless we fall." She tightened her death grip on Loathel's arm.

"These branches are thick, strong. They will not bend or break and are wide enough to lie upon. That should give you confidence." He helped Honor get to the place where the limb connected to the trunk.

"Unless we fall."

"I don't think I can't sleep up here," Annora said. "I'm too afraid to move."

"I will aid you if you allow it."

"Yeah, if you've got some trick to hold me still and take my mind off of the height."

"I can do both." They watched as he skipped across the branches with ease. He gave Annora his rope. "Tie it around your waist again."

"Yes—I mean, are you sending me back down?"

"Nay, you will remain within my sight. Lie down." When she had done what he asked, he bound her to the branch, comfortable but secure. Lastly, he made a cover for her with his cloak. "I will hold this end of the rope. You will not fall."

"I hope you got another rope for me." Honor studied her aunt's makeshift bed. "Otherwise, Aunt Nora, you're going to have to move over."

"I do not have another rope." Loathel jumped, landing lightly before her. "But you need not be concerned." He sat down where she stood. Reaching for her hand, he pulled her down to rest between his outstretched legs. "My arms will be the rope to hold you." He drew her back against his chest, enveloping her in his stalwart embrace. The warmth from his body heated her against the cool air. She snuggled closer, as he filled her mind and Annora's with tranquility, flooding them with peace. Within minutes, both women were out and he was in a state of karloptini- the watchful sleep. His body rested, but his mind and senses remained alert.

***

Before Imani opened her eyes, she knew he was there. She could feel his presence. She lifted her eyelids to see the towering wolflord, armed, standing over her and her still sleeping husband.

"A weakling for a protector you have, lady. Were it my desire, neither of you would be alive to see the beginning of this day."

Chris awoke, startled by the resonating echo in Dayown's voice. "Why aren't you dead?"

"Because there are none in possession of the skill to slay me. I could ask the same of you, but I am aware of the answer. You are not dead because I let you live, for now."

Imani talked over Chris. "Why are you here? Are you taking me back?"

"I am here for various reasons. Where I take you is still undetermined. I have examined the battle scene. There is evidence to prove you acted on our behalf, mine particularly. I am grateful."

"You saved him?" Chris pointed.

"Indeed," Dayown said. "She did so in such a manner, I could hardly be angry about the borrowing of my things."

"You gave me the bitinesaw."

"Not the ringblade. 'Tis a family heirloom of great importance. This is not an equated trade." He held up her wedding band.

Chris jumped to his feet. "What's he doing with that?"

"She left it in her room."

"You took off your wedding ring?"

"I had to."

"It was good she did." Dayown stepped forward. "Had she not, her life would have been forfeited."

Chris kept quiet.

Imani took off Dayown's ring and held it out to him.

"Nay, Lady. While I am in your company, you may keep it. I certainly have no intention of letting you wear this." He made a disgusted face at her band.

That was all the quiet Chris could keep. "What do you mean, you have no intention? You came without your little army. She is my wife, do you understand? Mine. You have no claim on her. Get it? This is your warning, dog-man. I will not tolerate your games anymore. Another word about my wife and you will feel the edge of my sword."

"When first we met, I wanted you dead. I should have followed my initial instinct. It is always correct. You have no choice but to tolerate any action I execute. I have been here a few hours. My men are not far away. You are alive only because I was too lazy to lift..." He scanned his many instruments of war, "any of them. But I am rested now. If you are weary of this realm, step forward and I shall send you to the next." His cocky, nonchalant statement held a note of sincerity.

The tension crackled in the air.

Imani stepped between them. "Stop it. Both of you."

Chris stood down.

Satisfied the Jodian would not meet his challenge, Dayown continued talking to Imani. "As I am in your debt, I make an offer of my services to aid your cause."

"I'm amazed at your nerve," Chris said. "We don't want your help."

"I was not speaking to you."

"Imani will tell you the same." He turned to his wife.

"Pray she does not."

"Services for what?" Imani placed a reassuring hand on Chris' arm. "What do you want from me?"

She received a radiant show of teeth for an answer. "We have unfinished business, you and me. Although, I admit I cannot yet be certain, I believe you are still alive because you belong to me."

"I don't belong to anybody. I'm still alive because you were interrupted."

"'Tis possible. However, I should have been feeding when the Queons and Kildar arrived."

"I'm not a Happy Meal, you know."

"No one is happy to become a meal, but there are worse purposes than sustaining life. At any rate, I make you an offer. Because of your valor, I will lead you to Alpravage and assist in the return of your second son."

"You will?" Imani's hand dropped to her side.

"I will. I would spare your life no matter how much you tempt me," he told Chris.

"Do not expect me to offer the same to you."

"Why?" Imani asked. "Why would you do that?"

"Because I owe you something. It distresses me to know a son of yours is in need. I now have business at Alpravage. Why not take the journey together?"

Chris stepped forward. "What would you gain from this union?"

"I will take the greatest of pleasure in foiling whatever plans Maldonus may have. I would see your son returned and you gone from my lands."

"That's it?"

"It is."

"No Raegladun," Chris mumbled. He relaxed.

Imani was not so trusting. "Returned and gone from your lands. Me as well?"

"No."

"No?" Chris repeated. "What is this madness you speak?"

"I speak no madness. What I offer is to help you get your son. Get him and go with my blessing. That has naught to do with her whom I have claimed." To Imani, he said, "My interest is in you, not your family. They may go or they may feed many. It will matter more to you than me. What I offer you is an opportunity to rescue your son—something you cannot accomplish without my assistance—and time to learn of me. If you refuse, I take you back, devour your husband and forget your child exists. One of the greater attributes of my people is our lack of conscience. You have earned the offer, but either way suits me."

CHAPTER XXX

Merlin and Jalen walked for three uneventful days. Having no more excitement than avoiding a pair of Guafs, Merlin used the time to teach Jalen about his ancestry and the skills he would acquire. In addition to sword fighting, Jalen also began strengthening the muscles in his mind.

Jalen got to know Medrid, as he now called him. He learned the wizard had several names and was the subject of many stories. For miles, he entertained the boy with tales of his misadventures, as he referred to them.

"I had quite a time of it when I was experimenting with dimensions and proportions, I'll tell you." They shared some ripened fruit Jalen could not identify but ate anyway.

"What happened?"

"'I Dream of Jeannie,' that is what."

"That again? I don't get it."

"I had managed size-reduction and was concentrating on enlargement. I was frustrated when I came up with the bright idea of decreasing myself. That way, it would become a necessity to find a solution. Well, I ended up sleeping in a bottle for safety's sake. I own several cats, you see. My brother thought—"

"You have a brother?"

"Of sorts. Anyway, my brother thought it would be fun to seal me in, without my staff, mind you. Let's say he wanted to show me off. He took me into your realm, where I became lost in Arabia for I don't know how long. By the time I was found again, I had learned the secret to expansion." He leaned forward, saying in hushed tones, "It's in the smoke."

Returning to his normal volume, Merlin continued, "I was so grateful to the young man who found me, I allowed him to benefit from my abilities three times. At first, the stories were wonderful." His eyes took on an animated glow. "I was big, and powerful, and dangerous...and now...what have they done to me? Now, I am remembered as a half-dressed girl, of incorrect nationality, who muddles everything for the sake of humor."

"You're, 'I Dream of—'"

"And we won't discuss that Yeti nonsense. Humph. I will be the first to admit, I had been in the wilderness for quite some time without a haircut or a bath, but I was alone. I had important things to do," he added to himself. "I can understand a person becoming startled, seeing someone they couldn't rightly recognize. I am sure I seemed a monster. But I ask you," He stopped where he stood, lifting his robes as he spoke. "DO I HAVE BIG FEET?" The indignant wizard stuck his foot out for better inspection.

Jalen almost choked on his fruit, but he suppressed his wit and shook his head.

"Bigfoot, indeed." Merlin slammed his foot down. He stomped the first few paces of their continued walk.

Before sunset, they came within sight of Raegladun. For all intents, it looked like a small village, picturesque with its houses large and small, stately and well-manicured. No sign of trouble. Jalen didn't know why he felt ill at ease.

"We need to stop here, my boy." Medrid found a comfortable rock.

"Why? We're this close. The others could be there by now."

"Loathel, without a doubt. Your father's decision remains to be seen. We wouldn't make it there tonight, anyway. Besides, we have things to discuss, you and I."

"We have been talking for days. What's left?"

"Much. Tell me, young Master Lossman, what do you feel?"

"Impatient."

"I am sure. Your kind always is. Now concentrate. What do you feel?"

Unease. But that wasn't all. Jalen felt a drumming in his heart, could almost hear it. Something was there, searching. He recalled things he would rather have left forgotten. Things he should not have said or done. Things he had gotten away with. Little things nobody knew. He would have liked to have kept it that way and had no idea why they were coming to him now.

Merlin interrupted his thoughts. "The poison is in the negative. The only preventive is to get it out."

"Get what out?"

"The Rae feed on our imperfections. They seek to make the dark places darker. That discomfort you feel are your deceptions gaining life. They'll haunt you for the rest of your days, which could prove to be short-lived indeed if those sins are grave."

"I'm not going in there."

"Nonsense."

"I know I'm not perfect. I don't need reminders of my mistakes."

"Who would? Which is why you have to take the time to get it out. Me, too. You can at least be grateful you have not committed a tenth of the misdeeds I have since last I was here."

"So I've got to—"

"Confess, same as me."

"Confess."

"Do not think it such an ordeal. I promise you, I am no judge and frankly, your manipulations interest me not. It is a process. They can touch nothing that has come to the light. Confess and be at peace. Do not confess and they will follow and feed on you forever."

"And you won't hold it against me?"

"I won't remember it."

"And you'll confess too?"

"I will confess first if it will make you feel better."

"And that's it."

"Mmm-hmm. Loathel will take care of the rest."

"What rest?"

"He will scan our minds. We wouldn't want any new thoughts to feed the darkness."

Jalen was silent.

"What is it?"

"The Rae feeding on our thoughts, the werewolves feeding on us, is there any place around here where we aren't a part of some bizarre food chain?"

"Not likely in Zendelel. You evanescent take your fill of evil. Everything comes full circle. Here, those evils take their fill of you."

CHAPTER XXXI

Creepy. The Rae were creepy. They seemed fully materialized specters. Although they could change their appearance, they resembled an army of small hairless women. They had wide unblinking eyes, and square jaws. They talked little, and they were never cheery. Blank, expressionless, haunted, haunting faces. They saw more than should be seen. They lingered, remaining out of reach, yet close enough for you to feel their hunger.

Annora sat by the edge of a stream, staring across the distance. The air was balmy. All around her was beauty, like a dawn meadow or something from a picture book. She saw none of it. In the quietness, she gave in to her grief, allowing it to consume her. Her grief was all she had left of Trill. She clung to it, replaying the 'what ifs,' punishing herself for the unknown conclusions. *What if he survived? No one came to his aid. What if she had forbidden him to ride out? He would still be here. What if he was alive somewhere? He was better off away from them, from her. What if he would have never come into her world? She would never have known how lost she would be without him.* It was pointless to hope. Merlin or Loathel would have known if he were alive. She would have known. But the hope was there, warring with guilt and the insurmountable sadness of uncertainty.

Not far from her position stood two of the Rae. Ever present, ever searching, they could see her soul. It should have been ripe with dead spots. But she was untouchable to them. Something covered the holes. Even in sorrow, she had no dark places they could detect. Instead of feasting, they became subject to her will. Her needs were met as soon as she felt a desire. The Rae could only do her bidding and wait.

It was the same for Honor. The Rae shadowed her nights, ever watchful, ever waiting. Loathel alone was left in peace. They could not be near him long, lest he filled them with his radiance and their essence receded. Gale, the Rae King, would have refused Loathel's admittance, but the Rae are slaves to purity.

Loathel and Honor kept an eye on Annora but gave her space to sort through her sorrow. They also used the time to break every restriction one or the other of them placed on their *not real* romance. In the day and a half before Merlin and Jalen joined them, the young lovers spent every waking moment together.

Raegladun was charming, or so it appeared. Loathel and Honor walked about, and he explained, "Much of what you see is not there."

"What do you mean?"

"It is an illusion."

Honor looked about. Everything seemed real. "An illusion?"

"Yes, Mistress. Meant to make you feel safe, lessen your awareness. Where there is trouble, people are alert. It is when all is quiet evil thoughts come to mind."

"Those sneaky little creepy shadow things. I wonder what it looks like."

"Do not. It would scare you."

"Can you see the real Raegladun?"

"I can."

"So while I'm looking at gorgeous homes and scenic gardens, you see something else altogether?"

"I do."

She waved a hand in front of his face. "Can you see me?"

He smiled. "I can."

"Wow, that's awesome."

"That I cannot be fooled into believing there is splendor here?"

"Yes, but you know, it's kind of sad too."

"Why sad?"

"Because you are an Elve, you see nothing but ugliness while I get the good stuff."

"I share your thoughts. As you process them, I experience the wonder you see."

For once, Honor was glad he had access to her mind.

"Also, I did not say I see only ugliness. I see beauty, true beauty. Radiance far beyond these mere illusions. Loveliness surpassing reality. I see a reflection of the perfect."

Honor looked into his thoughts and found he was speaking of her. Her breath caught. *Dream. Come. True. He always says the right thing.*

"The truth is easy for me." He answered her musing, making her eyes light up with joy. "Yes, I will kiss you."

"I wasn't thinking about kissing."

"I was." He reached for her, then stopped. "My moment has passed."

"No, it hasn't." She leaned into him.

"Your brother and Medrid have arrived. Jalen's fears are birthing a multitude of unkind thoughts. If I do not go to them soon, the Rae will never leave him."

"Jalen is my brother, my older brother. His discomfort brings me endless pleasure," Honor teased as she fell into step beside him.

"Jalen is smart. He could find a way to share his discomfort with you."

"Well, now, that's what you're here for, Lowell, to protect me from my big brother."

"Based upon your memories, your brother may need protection from you."

"Whatever are you talking about?" It was hard to project innocence when he brought her pranks to mind.

"Do not play naïve with me. Were not the love unconditional betwixt you two, I would feel honor-bound to turn you across my knee as a favor to him."

"*Would you please?*" Jalen joined the conversation.

"*Regardless of what he says, the Elve is on my side. Unless you want to take one of these tag-a-long robot ghosts thingies home as a pet, I suggest you be very nice to me.*"

"*Uggh. No. I can't think of anything bad enough to describe these things.*"

The Rae scattered at Loathel's approach. "Calling curses down upon the Rae will increase the number following in your wake."

"They're going to follow me around?" Jalen made a face.

"Night and day unless Loathel is with you," Honor said.

"You have got to be kidding."

"Nope."

"Lowell, buddy, I might have to be your shadow for the duration."

"If you want assistance, that name will not earn it for you."

"It works for Honor."

"Everything works for Honor." Honor smirked.

A pretty young girl with long hair and mature curves greeted them. She favored Jalen with a brilliant smile. "I am Twyla, your servant."

Jalen's jaw dropped. Her seductiveness made him salivate. "Mine?" He pointed to himself.

She nodded. "Follow me. I will show you where you may rest. I will see to your comfort."

"Yeah." Jalen took a step toward her.

Loathel stayed him. "Nay." The Elve stepped in front of the girl.

Twyla shielded her face from Loathel's radiance.

"Hey—"

"Jalen, all here is not as it looks," Merlin said.

Loathel spoke to the girl. "None of your tricks. He is under my protection. They are all under my protection."

Twyla covered her ears. "Do not speak to me. I beg you, do not speak to me."

"Reveal yourself, then be gone, or you shall hear it endlessly."

"Yes, yes, Bright Elve, Twyla will not come near." She bowed and stepped back. "No more mischief." The fantasy disappeared; Twyla revealed herself. Instead of the voluptuous beauty, another member of the Rae society stood before them: ugly, depressing, without light.

It went away without urging.

Honor took a picture, immortalizing Jalen's forlorn expression. "Don't take this the wrong way, Jay, but think about it. Big, tall, strong, gorgeous Elve dude standing here, and she doesn't look. Come on. How real can she be?"

CHAPTER XXXII

Christif, Imani, and Dayown moved across country away from Raegladun. It was an uneasy companionship. By day, the men expressed open hostility toward one another, like lovesick rams competing for Imani's attention. Nighttime was different. Before sunset Dayown removed his weapons and made them available, should there be a need. Afterwards, he tied a rope about his neck and secured himself to a tree. He believed Imani was too gentle to make the knots tight, and Chris would use the opportunity to strangle him.

Sleep was difficult the first few nights. It was hard to rest with a wolf staring at them. Gradually, Dayown became less vicious and somewhat friendly in his wolven state. They kept him tied up, but soon it felt like having a pet.

Each day brought them closer to Alpravage. Each day Christif's personality altered a little more. He told Imani the others were aware of their change in plans. He pretended to be in contact with Merlin or Loathel, telling her all was well, and it was wise for them to move ahead. According to Master Christif, Raegladun was time wasted. Medrid learned nothing, and they hastened to catch up.

When the three entered Maldonus' territory, there was a noticeable shift in the Jodian. He spoke less. He stopped troubling himself with Dayown's advances toward Imani. He encouraged his wife to be more tolerant of the wolfking. It left him free from concern for her wellbeing.

Merlin questioned Gale about Alpravage and the activity therein. He learned the location of such things as horses, boats, arms, and military strength. He collected an abundance of intel in a matter of hours.

Eager to move on, the five planned to depart from Raegladun as soon as they were able. They received horses and supplies. Anything they needed, the Rae produced. They wanted the Bright Elve and his companions gone from their midst.

The night before their departure, Jalen voiced his concern. "What about Mom and Dad? Shouldn't they be here by now?"

"They should be," Merlin said, "but they have chosen a most foolish path."

"Are they alright?" Annora's heart sank. She braced for yet another tragedy.

"If you mean do they live? The answer is yes." Merlin supplied her with a handkerchief. "My wisdom tells me they are moving toward Alpravage without us."

"No," Jalen said. "That's crazy af."

"And stupid. Loathel, can you reach them?" For Honor, it was basic.

"Nay, Mistress, your father has closed his thoughts to us. The distance is too great for me to penetrate his barrier. The morning after our escape from Narconess is the last I connected with him. They had been joined by King Dayown."

"Dayown?"

"Yea. I do not believe he wished them harm. That is when Christif shielded his mind. Were he in trouble, he would have called to me."

"Why would Chris shield his mind?" Annora chewed her bottom lip.

"Christif would go to great lengths to keep his secrets hidden." Merlin hung his head. "His folly grows ever bigger."

"I don't get it. This isn't Dad at all," Jalen said. "Is it, Honor?"

"You are right," Merlin said. "It is not your dad. He of all people should know the consequences of willful disobedience."

"What is he getting himself into now?" Having some knowledge of his history, Honor expected anything.

"Your father is no match for the power of Lephan's heir." Loathel took over the conversation. "In his unprotected state, the closer he gets to Alpravage, the easier it becomes for Maldonus to take possession of him. I pray I am incorrect, but I presume Maldonus has full access to Christif's mind by now, full authority over his will."

There was a moment of silence as they digested Loathel's implication.

"What will happen to Mom?"

"I do not know, Master Jalen. I do not know."

***

Sleep eluded them that night. A general unease for the outcome of this ordeal and the Lossmans' future weighed upon them all. Loathel sent out waves of tranquility, but the peace was short-lived because of the wailing of the Rae. The discomfort the Elve caused them was so tremendous he had to cease. Compassion for the lowly creatures led him to a quick decision, bringing him to Honor and Annora's chamber door.

As a compromise, he gave no aid to Merlin or Jalen, and in this way, he lessened the distance his balm traveled. He did, however, cocoon Honor and Annora in veils of restful repose. He did not take his promise to Trill lightly, nor was there anything more important to him than Honor's comfort.

The current troubles combined with Loathel's peace rendered Annora oblivious to the shifting in the atmosphere. She was unaware of the presence occupying her being long before he found her room.

***

Loathel stood as Trill rounded the corner, coming into view. When they embraced, it was impossible to tell who was more elated.

"Trill!"

"Loathel, my forever friend!"

"Death had defeated you, yet in the final moments, it is you who has cheated death and robbed him of his victory."

"Indeed, but I did not fight the darkness alone. I would have passed into the first realm had you not barred the way. Were I an Elve, I would not own enough years to repay the devotion you have rendered unto me. I am most humbly and extremely glad to be perpetually in your debt."

"I did what you would have done were our places exchanged."

"Never doubt it."

"Does my father know you are here?"

"What can escape the eye of Talazim?"

Loathel chuckled. "What I mean is: are you here with his permission?"

"Think you he would have granted it if I had asked?"

"I can be sure he would not."

"So was I. That is why I did not seek his consent."

"I became aware of your presence only moments before I saw your face. How long have you been in this realm?"

"I arrived only moments ago. I had no knowledge of where fate would lead you. My purpose was to come to the last known destination and begin my search from here. It is my good fortune you remain still."

"It is the good fortune of us all, none more than Annora. These many days have been difficult for her."

"Less difficult than they would have been without your attendance. Another thing for which I am in your debt."

"Your presence is the gratitude I require. Will you wake her?"

"Nay. Seeing me will be a shock. It is best she remain asleep to be better prepared for it on the morrow."

The men sat in the hall talking. Loathel told Trill of all that took place since the werewolf attack: Master Christif's downfall, the plans they made, Annora's struggles, and his feelings for Honor. Before dawn, they dozed a little, wanting to be refreshed and ready to move on.

CHAPTER XXXIII

A happiness Annora hadn't recognized was within her. The world felt brighter before she opened her eyes. She felt like singing. She wanted to dance about the room and jump with joy. The sensations were annoying.

She did not want happiness. She did not want good feelings. She recalled her misery but her dimples were stubborn. She thought of Trill and snickered. "Enough." She threw back the covers and got up. "Honor, honey, wake up. I'm in trouble." Her attempt to be serious made her giggle.

"What?" Honor asked through a one-eyed yawn.

"I'm cursed." Annora grinned at her.

Honor sat up straight. "Cursed? What are you talking about? What's so funny?"

"I don't know." Annora took a few calming breaths to no avail. "I'm happy." Her lips twitched and her ribs felt like they were going to burst.

"Ooookaaay, why?"

"Don't know." She did a slow turn about the room, partly to look for some clue to her predicament, partly because she felt like spinning. "It's not like I want to be happy. I can't make it stop."

Now that Honor was more awake, Annora's mood was contagious. She was happy, too. "What's wrong with feeling better?"

Annora spun in another circle, a little faster this time. "Everything. I don't want to feel better. This is horrible." She didn't feel like it was horrible. "I'm never going to get over him. I don't want to get over him." She spun some more. "Somebody cursed me. Someone made me happy on purpose." After she made herself dizzy, she plopped across Honor's bed. "This has got to stop."

"Aunt Nora, you can feel better and not be over him. Nobody put a happy spell on you. Stop feeling guilty about feeling good. Trill would want you happy."

"I don't want me happy. I want me miserable." She paused for a moment, taking a much-needed deep breath. "What kind of conversation is this? Who talks about not wanting to be happy? Who invented the happy spell?"

"You. Do you have any idea why you're happy?"

"Yeah, I've lost my mind."

"Besides that."

"I've conjured him."

"Who?"

"Trill," Annora whispered the sacred name. "I've tricked myself into believing he's with me again." She went off into a daze.

"Aunt Nora—"

"That's fine for dreams, but I can't walk around behaving like he's actually here."

"Aunt Nora—"

"I am not having hallucinations or schizophrenia—"

"Aunt Nora. Maybe you didn't conjure him."

"What?" For the first time, she was able to be serious.

"I felt the same way when we were in that Narca place, when Loathel came back, remember?"

Annora allowed the thought to play in her mind for a moment. "Uh-uh, I conjured him. Let's get dressed and find your boyfriend or Merlin. One of them needs to un-hex me. My face hurts from smiling."

***

The girls prepared for the day with Annora singing and humming. When all was ready, they went to meet the others. Annora opened the door, speaking to Honor over her shoulder as she did. "For the first time in forever, I'm starving." She walked out of the room without seeing the six-foot-five Jodian standing in front of her. She bumped into his chest and thought she had walked into a wall. His arms crushed her to him. Recognition came, and she screamed. Happiness, fear, disbelief, and hope merged to shock her senses. Her mind reeled, her emotions exploded, and she lost the ability to function.

Through it all, Trill held her.

This can't be real. I've gone off the deep end.

"Nay, Milady, I am no vision," Trill spoke to her mind. *"Be at peace, my love, and receive me, for I have need of you."*

She looked up into the familiar obsidian gaze, praying she was not hallucinating.

Behind her, Honor proved it was no mirage. "Trill. Wow, you're alive."

"Indeed, I am, cousin. It is good to look upon you." To Annora, he said, "Shall I convince you I am real?" Without waiting for an answer, he captured her mouth with his in an all too consuming, all too real kiss that left her without a doubt why she was happy.

Loathel took Honor by the hand and led her away. "We will give them time to become reacquainted. The separation has been difficult for them both. The challenge ahead will be harder. An hour for themselves is the least they have earned."

***

Maldonus watched Christif's movement. The Jodian was careless. His time in Universe had left him weak. Maldonus took Christif's will a little at a time to be sure his effort went undetected. With his son almost broken and Trill nowhere near, Christif was at his mercy. The Grand Lephan was unstoppable, his revenge almost complete.

Maldonus called his soldiers in, making it easy for the unsuspecting trio to get to Alpravage. He gave his attention to his plans for Master Christif. As his prey moved closer, Maldonus became absorbed. The other movement toward his fortress went unnoticed.

***

Jalen saddled his horse. The lack of restful sleep didn't keep him from wanting to be gone. Near him, Merlin was likewise engaged, but more jovial than usual. "What's up, Medrid? If I didn't know better, I'd think you were happier than I am to get away from here."

"Huh? What? Happy? Oh yes, yes, why wouldn't I be happy? This is wonderful, absolutely wonderful."

"Your horse?"

"My hor— What are you babbling about?"

"Me? You're the one with the wonderful horse."

Merlin shook his head. "You speak as if...no, wait...I refuse to believe...tell me you are aware."

"Aware of what?"

"Aware of what? Are you not true Jodian?"

"How should I know? Until we met you, I didn't even know what a Jodian was."

"Any idea where your aunt is? Or your sister?"

"Honor is with Loathel. No-brainer. I guess Aunt Nora is sleeping in." He tightened the straps.

"Lackwit. When you get around to it, use your skills. They might come in handy someday."

"Use my skills for what, Sasquatch?"

"For finding out what the rest of us already know."

Jalen stopped what he was doing and focused his energy on...he wasn't sure on what.

"*Good morrow, my cousin. I wondered if I would procure a greeting from you.*"

"Whoa." Jalen shook his head to clear it.

"*Yea, I have returned. Your skill ever-increases.*"

"*Who would notice? The imbecile forgets he has them.*" Merlin's fondness for Jalen was obvious.

"*Trill, is that you?*"

"*Indeed it is.*"

"*Last night I dreamt you were back. Wait, that was no dream, was it?*"

"*Lackwit. I know three-year-olds who can tell the difference between a dream and someone entering one's awareness.*"

"*Is there any way to get him out of my awareness?*"

"*No, although many have tried. It is the common goal of Jodians everywhere.*"

"*Do not forget the Elves, my friend,*" Loathel's voice came to them. "*Long have we desired to be unaware of Medrid. Should you figure out a method, Jalen, let me know. We could become wealthy selling the knowledge."*

"You guys better leave Mr. Merlin alone." Honor joined the conversation. *"Mr. Merlin, can't you turn them into toads or something?"*

"Good morning, my dear. I'm glad at least one of you is smart enough to choose the correct side. It is only because of you they aren't hopping around searching for flies as we speak."

"Don't let me stop you. I love to read a great mind at work."

Annora had been silent throughout the exchange. Now she shared her thoughts. *"You know, this is weird. We're in three different places, having one conversation without electronics. That's not supposed to happen."*

"Pretty awesome stuff, isn't it, Aunt Nora?" Jalen asked.

Annora thought about Trill. Life without him, all this *stuff,* and how it affected her. *"Oh yeah, this is definitely awesome."* She meant it. Her doubts were gone. This was her life. She accepted it and wanted to strengthen the bonds she and the Jodian already had.

Shielding her thoughts from all but himself, Trill told her, "It will be thus, Milady. We will spend the rest of our days making it thus. Your desire reflects my own."

CHAPTER XXXIV

It was a jolly party riding away from Raegladun. The bleak future facing them did not disturb their heightened spirits. Trill was back; nothing was impossible. Annora rode light in her seat. Her mind and body soared with her spirit. She peppered Trill with questions concerning his health and whereabouts. It amazed them to discover Trill was the only known survivor of a werewolf attack. A few bites could kill a person; he was mauled. Thanks to Talazim, only the scars remained. Scars, Annora felt, added to his appeal.

Trill told them of Loathel's deeds, explaining the impossibility of what he accomplished. "When we trek together, we begin from the same origin. Our minds merge and we know where we're going. If we travel separately, we are still aware of the other's starting point and ending destination. That is not what happened. Loathel was not with me when I left. He did not know where to look. I did not know where I was and was unable to call for help. Mayadal is a large island. With only a general idea from whence I began, Loathel tracked, found, and saved me."

"Do not exult me," Loathel said. "Is there anyone here who would not have done the same?"

"Come on, Lowell. Is there anyone here who could have done the same?"

"Could it be we've finally found a flaw in the line of Elve?" Merlin raised his eyebrows in mock wonderment. "Tell me, Loathel, is it you, or are all your people so thick-skulled when performing a task, you forget to consider if what you are doing is possible?"

"Who has time for details, Medrid?"

It felt good to laugh, yet the seriousness of the mission loomed. Trill reached for Travon as soon as they were away from Raegladun. He became a shadow in the child's mind. *"Could it be my young cousin no longer has any thought for me?"*

"Trill?"

"Yea, young Master Travon, it has been many days since last we spoke. I desire your companionship."

"Where have you been? Were you sick?"

"I was. I have since regained my health."

"I knew that was it. They didn't tell me, but I knew."

"You knew because you hold the highest intelligence. I hope you will not hold it against anyone. They did not wish for you to worry."

"As long as you're alright. Jalen said nobody could talk to me for a few days because of where you guys were. He said somebody might notice and tell."

"We have left the area and will be with you soon."

"I'm glad. It didn't take me as long to get here."

"No, I do not suppose it did. I trust you will also forgive us the delay."

"It's okay, as long as you're coming. It's not so bad here. I'm in a cool room, with lots of toys and stuff. I get all kinds of food. Some of it I've never had before, but it's good. I have some friends and no more scary stuff. Lord Maldonus is nice now. He made me a chocolate cake. All by himself. It was better than Mom's, but don't tell her. He said Dad would be here today. I didn't ask about anybody else, but I think it might be okay to let him know to expect more guests. How come Dad will be here first? Where's Mom? Why aren't you all together?"

Aware of the danger, Trill didn't speak. Instead, he enlisted Annora's help.

"Travon, sweetheart, listen carefully. They are attempting to trick you. Enjoy the food and whatever they give you, but don't be fooled. You have been smart, keeping everything to yourself. Don't stop. No matter what they do, don't tell them anything. Okay?"

"Okay. How come you're talking to me? Is Trill mad? Did I do something wrong?"

"Oh, no, no, sweetie. You didn't do anything wrong. We're being careful is all. If they find out someone can reach you, we want them to think it's only Honor or me."

"Oh. I won't tell. I promise."

"I'm not worried. You're awesome."

A knock on Travon's door interrupted them. *"Aunt Nora, I gotta go. Dad's coming."*

***

Imani was bewildered. No matter how many times Dayown said it, she would not believe Chris abandoned her. But he was gone. He left before she awoke. That was hours ago, and there was still no sign of him. Dayown offered to track him for her, but his heart wasn't in it. He didn't care where Christif was and hoped he never came back.

Imani worried about him. Did something happen? Did he get captured? Where was he? Dayown served as their guide and supplied them with food. It was unlikely he was scouting or hunting.

"My pet, it is folly to linger. He is gone. We must accept our good fortunes as they come." Dayown stretched, then resumed his reclined position against a tree.

"Good fortune? My husband is missing." Imani stopped pacing long enough to look at him for signs of insanity.

"What could be better?"

"I cannot believe you said that."

"Believe it."

"I'm worried. This is my husband, okay? You may not like him, but I happen to love him. That doesn't change because you want it to. Biting me won't change my feelings."

"Ahh, you are wrong. Marking you changed everything. I want you; I shall have you. Nothing else matters, especially not Chris."

"The man is missing. Aren't you concerned at all?"

"No."

She walked away, only to turn back again. "Do you have a heart?"

"Yes."

"You don't act like it."

"Not having a conscience gives me a different perspective than your kind."

"I thought you were being impudent. You can't be serious."

"I assure you, I am." Making himself get up, Dayown retrieved his possessions as he talked. "In my world, there are two things of importance: loyalty and my desires." He secured his knives. "My entire being is centered around those two issues." Next came his halberd and tomahawks. "My people live for those two things alone." Finally, he fastened his sword around his hips.

Imani watched with detached, horrified fascination. The man was a walking arsenal.

He went on, unmindful of her scrutiny. "Your husband does not fall into either category. I cannot make myself have a care for him. Nothing would cause me to lose serenity over his disappearance. I cannot remember when I've felt happier."

"I'm sorry, Dayown, but that is wrong. No compassion, no consideration for a fellow human being—"

"I am not a human being." He moved toward her.

She took a step back, turning away from his overwhelming presence. "Even dogs have...have..."

"Loyalty." He put a hand on her shoulder. "Dogs have loyalty. I have loyalty, Imani."

She stiffened against his touch.

"Loyalty to you is the only reason I put up with him. If you desire it, I will locate the imbecile. Because I knew it would make you happy, I've ignored the hunger pains I get whenever he opens his stupid mouth. I will protect the idiot from the danger he invites upon himself—for you. I have loyalty. Parts of me are human-like, but I am a werewolf. You would do well to remember that."

She stepped away from him; the intimacy was more than she could bear. "I'm human. All human. How could you think we should be a couple?"

He snorted at her resistance, not in the least discouraged. "I do not think we should be a couple. I am more absolute. You belong to me. There is a difference."

"I'm going to be sick."

"I did not pronounce it a bad difference. I want a mate, a human mate. I have chosen you. You will benefit from the union, I assure you. Once you get used to it, I'm positive you will be happy."

"Don't wolves mate for life?"

"They do."

"So do humans. You got the wrong girl. I'm taken."

"If humans mated for life, half of the beings in this realm would not exist."

"I'm mated for life. How's that?"

"My list of reasons for wanting him gone ever increases."

"You are not nice."

"No, I am not. It is unnecessary as long as I remain loyal. You need not be concerned, I will make you happy."

"You are doing a sorry job of it so far."

"You are not happy because your husband is missing. Your sadness is his fault, not mine."

Imani wanted to argue but couldn't. Between the two men, Dayown had given her far less trouble than Chris. Dayown had been more attentive, more considerate, and more concerned for her wellbeing. Chris barely talked to her. Often he would brood, excluding her from his thoughts and feelings. Sometimes it was as if he had forgotten she was there. Dayown hadn't left her alone. Her comfort seemed to be his utmost interest.

He held out his hand to her. "Come, my pet. It's time to go."

Chris' behavior troubled her. His disappearance was more than she could take. Nevertheless, she clung to one thought: She was Mrs. Christopher Lossman. She had loyalties, too, and hers were not in question.

With nothing else to do, Imani accepted the extended hand and let him lead her.

CHAPTER XXXV

The riders rode hard, fast, sharing the same sense of urgency. As a unit, they moved, with Merlin in the center, the vanguard, leading them into the mouth of evil; an evil he could only hope to defeat. Of all the deeds credited to him, he knew this would be among the biggest. It could be his last.

Next to him rode Jalen. A better right hand could not be found. The young man had become a soldier. His natural abilities were coming to the forefront. Already, he held a stature like his teachers. There had been no mistake: Jalen Lossman was true Jodian.

To Merlin's left was Honor, and Annora flanked Jalen. Each woman was named in truth and destined for greatness. They were not there because they needed safekeeping; they were necessary. They were the hope. They were the heart.

At the far ends were the protectors. Again, there were two. Trill's stallion kept pace with Annora's horse. Because of her, he defeated death. Because of her, he was able. By her side, he was born to be. By her side, he would remain. To him, it was simple.

For Loathel, the end of the quest would be bittersweet. He kept close to Honor, often reaching for her hand, touching her. He gathered the memories he would need to sustain him throughout the eternity he would have to spend without her.

While they rode, they told Jalen and Annora about Maldonus and Christif. The conversation brought them into a clearer focus as to the importance of defeating the enemy.

***

Merlin halted the travelers. They had come to the center of Kildar, Maldonus' territory. Alpravage loomed before them from menacing heights, casting cryptic shadows across the land. It was built into the mountain upon which it set. The precipitous cliff protecting its backside dropped several hundred yards to meet giant daggered rocks jutting out from the roaring, silent sea.

On the remaining three sides of Alpravage, the land lay still. The fullness of the forest thinned, gradually losing life until the timber nearest the fortress was nothing more than a withered, rotten testimony of the decay found therein. All traces of pleasantness had been beaten from the ground, leaving it hard and angry. No grass, vegetation, or life of any kind. The air was heated and weighty. The smell of blood and death assaulted their nostrils and scratched at their throats, making it difficult to breathe. The lack of beauty anywhere warned of an abysmal level of malfeasance. From beneath the earth to above the clouds, everything boded ill. An eerie hush blew across the peaceless land.

"I guess we're here. What are we supposed to do now?" Jalen asked no one in particular.

"This place looks exactly the way I expected." Honor surveyed their surroundings and made a face.

"Honor, how could anybody picture something so...so...depressing?" Annora suppressed a shudder. She gave her horse a reassuring pat for comfort.

"I don't know, maybe because of my contact with Maldonus."

Merlin snapped his fingers. "You, my dear, have supplied the answer."

"I did? Answer to what?"

"How we are going to get in. 'Til now I had no idea." His fingers worked their way through his whiskers.

"How did I do that?"

"You shall lead us."

"Mr. Merlin, don't take this the wrong way, but the fact is, you *have* to be getting up there in years. I'm not sure your mind is as sharp as you hope it is. Formulate another plan. I'm not leading us anywhere." Honor held up her hands, attempting to halt his reasoning.

"I thought you were on my side."

"I was when your craziness was directed at Jalen. Me leading? No. Uh-uh. I'm not sure I'm going."

"What do you propose?" Loathel asked.

"Nothing," Honor said, "because I ain't doing it."

"Maldonus will be aware of something," Merlin explained. "If we manipulate what he receives, mayhap we can hide our assets."

Trill considered the possibilities. "Do you deem it will be enough?"

"No, it won't be enough. It won't be anything. You told me not to contact him anymore."

Merlin talked over her. "We can only hope he is overconfident and does not probe too deep."

"Listen to me, people. Aunt Nora, help."

"Aren't the women supposed to be left behind? You know, watching from a safe distance, that sort of chauvinistic-thing you people do here."

"Yeah." Honor pointed to her aunt. "What she said. Safe. Chauvinist. I'm a woman for a reason."

"There is no safe distance in Zendelel, especially near Alpravage." Trill addressed his beloved, "There is naught that would make me willing to leave you unprotected."

Merlin spoiled the moment. "Besides, we need you, both of you. By now, Maldonus has over a hundred Queons, not to mention those blasted Kildar. We'd be terribly outnumbered without you."

"You're terribly outnumbered regardless," Annora said.

"Of course we are, but that is not the point. The point is to get the most out of the numbers we have."

"You have a plan."

"It is so, Master Jalen, it is so."

"Do I have to contact Maldonus?" Honor whined.

"No, no. Do not think it." Merlin gave her a reassuring pat. "He will contact you."

"Go me." She rolled her eyes.

Loathel reached over and surprised Honor by plucking her from her horse. He settled her in front of him, wrapped his arms around her, and filled her mind with serenity. "Your unease crushes me. Know you not by now I will be with you?"

His open display affected her as much as his tranquility did. She closed her eyes and breathed him in. *Please, God, keep us like this forever. Make the world go away. Just him and me and these incredible arms.*

"Holding you would be fine for a thousand years or so, but if we are requesting forever, I should like some other things as well."

Honor's eyes popped open. She turned and saw her reflection in his. The heated smile touching his lips inspired a like reaction from her. Where he held her, flames licked at her skin, burning her with his desire. It was a desire that mirrored her own.

Unable to stop himself, he placed a downy soft kiss on her forehead. "Behave." Once again Honor found herself lifted from one horse to the other as Loathel returned her to her mount. "You are a distraction."

"Me?"

"I bet she does it on purpose," Jalen said.

"I am sure of it," Loathel told him. *"At least I hope so."* The last part was for her alone.

"What is this plan?" Annora brought them back to the subject.

"The plan is simple," Merlin spoke to the group. "We cannot hide our presence, so we must disguise it. Annora and Honor will be the bait, so to speak." Twin looks of disgust prompted him to add, "Oh, do not worry over it. I'm riding with you. If we are fortunate, they will not kill us right away."

"That is so not a good plan." Honor turned to Annora. "The man is cracked, I'm telling you."

"It is the best we can do under the circumstances."

"What does that have to do with me leading something?"

"Once he knows you are here, he will seek your mind to ascertain our purpose. Hopefully, the visual and intention we provide will distract him and our real motives go undetected."

"What are they going to do," Annora nodded toward the others, "sneak up from behind?"

"They will sneak up from in front."

"Huh?"

"Our warriors will be there protecting us...theoretically."

"I'm missing something," Jalen announced.

"Master Jalen, you are about to have your first wish made reality. We are going to teach you how to zip."

CHAPTER XXXVI

Imani was not deceived; Dayown was leading her away from Alpravage. She bided her time, memorizing as much of the scenery as possible. "Shouldn't we be there soon?" she asked when they halted for the evening.

"Soon." Dayown echoed, unconcerned.

She played with a piece of firewood, watching as he secured himself for the night. "Is it tight?"

"Tight enough, why?"

"Satisfying my curiosity." She stood up, walked behind him, and tested the knot.

"Are you frightened?"

"Yes."

"Why now?"

"I wasn't alone before."

"I am with you."

"You are what I am afraid of." She ran her fingers through his hair, not enticingly, but with an interest in the texture.

"My sweet pet." He closed his eyes, enjoying the administration. "You have nothing to fear from me. If I were going to do you harm, it would have befallen you by now. You have my loyalty. What more could you ask for?"

"My family, you sorry son-of-a-bitch." Imani grabbed a fistful of hair and yanked.

Out of the corner of his eye, he could see the tip of the ringblade she held close to his temple.

"I don't think you should move."

Dayown didn't. "Allowing you to keep my ringblade was an unwise decision."

"I'm not so stupid I don't recognize backtracking. You betrayed my trust and you've lied to me. You serve yourself and that is the extent of your loyalty."

"What I do is for the best."

"Your best, you mean. What I do is for my child. My instincts tell me to kill you and be done with it, but that's too much like something you would do. I'm sparing your life, wolfman. When you get free, go home and leave me alone. The next time you and I meet, you will have to kill me. If you don't, I won't spare you again."

"Why would you want to kill me? Have I not been good to you?"

"I don't want to kill you." She let go of his hair. "But I will. I would kill anyone who tries to keep me from my son. Do us both a favor and go home, Dayown." Imani clubbed him with the firewood. Dayown's world went black. She watched as the unconscious man became an unconscious beast and was grateful. It would be morning before he knew what happened. She searched his belongings until she found her wedding band. She intended to leave his ringblade but on second thought, decided she needed it more than he. She gathered their remaining food and ran, too afraid of what she had done to be afraid of anything else.

***

Maldonus sat on his throne, king of depravity. He possessed the same flowing hair and muscled physique as the other occupants of the second realm. Strong and handsome, he was beautiful, except for his eyes. His eyes were hard and unfeeling with a calculated coldness that did not understand mercy. His hands were smooth, sharp nails at the end of long fingers with darkened tips. Unlike other Lephans, his sorcery was not connected to an object. The totality of Lephan's spirit could not be channeled through a staff or wand. His body was the medium by which the spirit generated power and manipulated the elements. If not for his bloodlust, there would be no need for the gold-handled sword that hung at his side. He was as great as he perceived himself to be. In his mind, none could withstand him. He was the Grand Lephan, Azâzêl's heir. He would conquer Mayadal, crush Earth, and open the gates of Bedalamon. Christif bent to his will. Cristif's son would follow. He was unstoppable.

According to the reports, Merlin's meddling had come to naught. He would not get to the boy in time. By bringing Christif to Zendelel, Merlin had given him to Maldonus. Best of all, thanks to the werewolves, Trill passed into the first realm. The only potential threat to him was the elusive Bright Elve. Loathel could be a problem for certain, yet Maldonus was confident without Trill, even an Elve as strong as Loathel would not defeat him. Now, the backward magician led the remainder of Christif's family to his door. Who more appropriate to pay for his years in captivity? Lastly, he would do what he determined from the start. He would remove the disgrace that was Merlin. These thoughts filled the evil one with such jocund malice he sent for his prisoners.

Christif was brought before Maldonus, a mindless puppet: eyes glazed, and expression blank.

"Christif, why have you come?"

"I do the will of my master."

"Good, good. I will bring your son before you. You will command him to do the will of your master."

"I will."

Lord Maldonus grunted in satisfaction. Besides reestablishing the rule of Azâzêl, he had a hundred and eighty-four years' worth of personal revenge to extract. He was eager to get to it.

***

Maldonus sipped wine from an intricately designed glass, watching the father and son reunite.

"Daddy!" Travon threw himself into Chris. "Dad."

Hearing his child brought Chris total clarity. "Travon!" He hugged the boy tight. "Are you alright?"

"I'm good. Where's Mom?"

Confusion overcame Chris. He had no idea where Imani was. He didn't know where he was or how he got there. He searched the room, his eyes halting when they came to Maldonus. "You! What have you done? Where is my wife, my family?"

"Greetings, Christif, master warrior." He sat his glass down next to a plate of assorted bread and cheese. "It has been quite some time since we last looked upon one another. Tell me, are you happy to see me?"

"Are you mad? You must be to wonder such a thing, Maldonus."

"Your manners are lacking. Henceforth, you will refer to me as Lord Maldonus."

"To hell with—Ahhughhh..." A hard, fast pain shot through Chris, bringing him to his knees.

"I am the master here. Any decisions regarding hell will be mine." He waved his hand, and the discomfort abated.

When he could stand again, Christif rose. "What do you mean to do?"

"Are you requesting an itinerary, or do you merely wish to know how long you have left to live?" He found a type of cheese to his liking and bit into it.

"I am concerned for my son, Maldonus."

"Lord Maldonus."

"Lord Maldonus."

"No need to worry. Travon is in much less danger than you are. He is, of course, a much better person than you are. He's smarter, too." Maldonus mock-saluted Travon and reached for a piece of bread. "The little fox has not compromised himself. He is to be commended. To his credit, he has given away nothing thus far. Perhaps he doesn't know a damned thing. You were always one for keeping secrets."

Christif stood in front of Travon. "You have me, Lord Maldonus. Let my son go."

"Am I to bow to your will? By whose authority do you issue orders to me?"

"I am placing myself at your mercy, Lord Maldonus." Christif went down on his knees. "I am begging you to let my son go. Your anger is at me. Take it out on me. He has not wronged you. He is just a child. Please."

"As gratifying as this degrading display is, you need not continue. It has no effect upon me. What is this 'place yourself at my mercy?' Where do you think you are? You wish me to let him go. Where is he to go? Am I to turn an innocent child out, leave him in the wilderness to fend for himself? It is not as if he has any family left. Well, he won't by the time I am through.

What kind of father are you? You'd rather have him die alone out there as opposed to the warm, nurturing environment we'll provide for him here. Could it be you find the company unsuitable? At one time, it was the company you preferred above all else."

Christif stood up. "I made a mistake, lots of mistakes."

"Ahh, yes, you have indeed. Alas, all things come due. You have done much, Master Christif. Now, it is time for you to purchase those things you have squandered. You received many benefits because of me. I require payment."

"I have suffered because of you. Many have suffered."

"A bonus. What did you think I offered? Pleasure aside, I am who I am. My kind are servants. We can do no other than bring hell to all who seek it. You sought it in earnest. You are fortunate I aided your cause. After all, I am the best of my kind."

"It is as you said. My choices brought me to this place but not his." Christif pointed to Travon. "He has nothing to do with this. He has done nothing to earn your attention."

"You are right. It is so. The only person he has to thank for his circumstance is you. Did you take him into account when we started that cult? Oh, how they worshipped you. What about the time we gave those girls opium? They were fun to watch. They were about the same age as your daughter, I recall. Surely, they should have made you ruminate about the future of your own children. Then again, some people consider nothing beyond themselves and the pleasure they may take from the moment."

He reached for his nearby glass and held it up. "The future be dammed is my motto and I mean it. Travon, have I shocked you? Do not waste your time on such a silly emotion. The things your father has done would not be looked at favorably by some. However, his deeds are marvelous. Worthy of all my attention. I assure you, under my influence, you will grow to greater heights. You shall be heir to all your father began. You will receive what he turned from. You will administer his judgment."

"No, I will not!"

Maldonus finished his wine.

"I love my daddy. I don't care about that stuff. I'm not following you."

"My dear boy, you already are. When you give your emotions free rein, you give them to me. At any rate, you will not have a choice in the matter. Thank your daddy."

Christif placed a comforting arm around Travon. "What do you mean to do to him?"

"I mean to have him kill you."

"No, I won't!"

A servant came in. He stood beside Maldonus' throne. "My lord, intruders are approaching."

"Yes, you will," Maldonus said. "You see, your father is going to do away with you. The only way to save yourself is to slay him." He gave his attention to the messenger, ignoring their horrified expressions.

CHAPTER XXXVII

Da, da, da da dadada da, da, da da dadada...

Annora, Honor, and Merlin set out across the plains of Alpravage. The girls were afraid but confident. They trusted Merlin's judgment and had tremendous faith in their men.

Da, da, da da dadada da, da, da da dadada...

Merlin had the best understanding of the situation and the capabilities of all involved, and he was downright petrified. His plan was full of holes. The chances of it failing were excellent. The power they were going up against was worse than he let on. He felt his petrifaction was justified.

Da, da, da da dadada da, da, da da dadada...

***

The warriors watched from the trees, merged with the riders and waiting for the signal to proceed.

***

Lord Maldonus did a quick mental sweep of his kingdom. Merlin, Loathel, and Trill. How could this be? "Take the boy. Tie him up somewhere for now."

Two of his foot soldiers held Christif while another peeled Travon from his grasp and dragged him away. They passed a second messenger as he entered.

"My Lord, we have identified the intruders. It is the magician and two of the women the border patrol have been seeking."

"Women? The presence of women is not what comes to me."

The messenger bowed low. "Forgive me, lord, it is no disguise. Women are approaching."

"I am the deceiver and therefore I am above deceit. I will witness this approach myself. If these females are to come before me, I will know the why of it." He left his throne, intent on investigating, but stopped short, remembering his other prisoner. "Christif, I need not ask who these women are. But they cannot save you. The men hiding behind them will perish as well, all because of you." With a backward wave of his hand, Maldonus reduced the Jodian master to a lifeless puppet with no will of his own.

***

From the highest tower at Alpravage, Maldonus looked down at the approaching riders. This was a puzzle indeed. He saw them and knew them for who they were, yet he could not deny the presence he felt. He tuned into the mental path he had communicated with Honor on before. *"Why have you come?"*

Honor heard him as if he rode beside her. She looked around, not knowing what to do.

*"**Answer him as if you do not know to whom you speak.**"* Loathel's Elven esprit was at its finest. She could feel his caress against her skin.

"What was that? Who's there?"

"Do you not know me, child? When it is I who cares for you more than any other?"

*"**Now you cannot be sure. You are wondering if it is your father or me.**"*

Honor didn't understand those instructions at all. She hesitated, not wanting to say anything because she wasn't sure who would hear.

*"**He will only receive what I allow. We wish him a different perception.**"*

Honor still didn't get it. She decided it was best to do what she was told. *"Is that you, Loathel...Daddy?"*

"It is I...Christif." Immediately, the voice changed to match her father's. "Where is Loathel?"

"Daddy!"

It may sound like your father; in truth, it is not. Tell him you think I am...with Trill. Reveal to him, Trill left Zendelel, mayhap passed into the first realm.

"My child, why do you not answer your father? Have I not taught you proper respect?"

"Who does he think he is?"

"The Grand Lephan. Answer with meekness."

"I'm sorry, Daddy. It's...you know...thoughts of Loathel bring to mind certain memories. I miss him."

"He is not with you?"

"No. He's...he's with Trill." She'd have to ask Loathel about that. He was good at being misleading without telling a lie.

"Where are they?"

"Daddy, you know that much. The werewolves attacked Trill. Has anyone ever survived?"

"I did not have to help you at all. You are Machiavellian in your own right." Again, the Elve caressed her senses.

"And you believe Loathel has joined him?"

"I know Loathel is with him, otherwise he would be here with me." Loathel gave her a question to ask. "Daddy, why do I feel your presence in more than one place?"

Maldonus paused. He, too, felt Christif in two separate locations. The second a little different, a little stronger. To this, he had no answer. No doubt, some trickery of Merlin's. Now he understood what was going on. "Tell me, my daughter, the other female with you—"

"Aunt Nora?"

"Yes, Aunt Nora. Was she mated to Trill?"

"That's a crude way to put it. It's called—"

"Do not tell him of Trill's joining to Annora."

"Repeat yourself. Your words did not come to me."

"I said, mating sounds harsh but yes, they were together before he got attacked."

"She reeks of him as you do the son of Talazim." Maldonus sneered. "Why have you come?"

"You follow his footsteps."

"Why have we done any of this? We're following you."

"I am pleased. I shall be here waiting for your arrival." Having learned all he needed to know, the Grand Lephan broke communication.

*"**As in all things, you were perfect.**"* Loathel's compliment exhilarated Honor down to her toes. He communicated what transpired to the other members of the party.

"Well done, dear heart," Merlin added his appreciation. "Any success we have will be largely due to you."

Honor didn't know what the exchange was about, much less why it mattered. But she was happy they were happy with whatever she did.

While Honor held Maldonus' attention, the warriors slipped into and out of the second realm. Less than a minute later, they stood on the parapet of Alpravage. Jalen beamed as if he'd won a prize. "That was awesome af. Now, what do we do?"

"Our plan," Trill said, "is to find your father and brother, destroy as many of this army as possible, face Maldonus, reunite with the others, escape this place, and locate your mother."

"Are any of those things actually possible?" Jalen grabbed his phone and wrote a text.

"They are all possible," Loathel said.

"Why do I feel like there's a 'but' in there?" Jalen didn't look up. He finished his message and closed the window.

"Because you are growing wise, cousin. Those things are possible because we have no choice *but* to make them possible."

CHAPTER XXXVIII

Loathel, Trill, and Jalen moved along the wall, trying not to draw attention to themselves. Ahead of them, five unsuspecting Kildar gathered at the top of the stairs. Trill and Loathel readied their bows. Four were dead before the fifth could register from what direction the attack came. He saw Loathel the second before the Elve's steel arrow inserted itself between his eyes. They collected the arrows and journeyed down the steps as fast as they could, needing to do as much damage as possible before they were discovered.

Midway down, they encountered two more Kildar ascending. Trill's sword made quick work of dispatching them both. Down the spiraling staircase, the three continued. They came out on the next level. No one was about, so they rested and planned their course of action.

"We've not much time," Loathel told them. "Medrid and the girls are nearing the halfway mark."

"Jalen," Trill said. "Connect with your father, but do not reveal your presence. I will locate your brother." He found Travon locked in a room somewhere toward the center of the castle, a few levels below them. Travon was frightened, but Trill could not risk comforting the boy. *"Milady, I am in need of your service."*

"What is it, Trill?" Annora asked, anxious.

"Do not worry so, I am in no danger."

"What a strange statement. You are currently somewhere in the stronghold of unimaginable evil and you feel safe."

"I am in no danger at the present. My plea is for our nephew. Travon is in distress. Would you do me the service of speaking to him? It would not be wise for me to attempt it from this proximity."

Despite the seriousness of the situation, his use of the word 'our' thrilled her. *"You are so sweet. Yes, I'll talk to him."* At once, she went about her task.

"I do not believe the last two Kildar think you are sweet." Loathel reminded Trill his thoughts were not private.

"Only because they do not know me so well, Lowell." Trill felt Annora's thrill and was thrilled.

"When they come back at nightfall, they will be more attentive."

"If we are still here by nightfall, the Kildar will be the least of our problems."

"There is a least problem?" Jalen said. "You mean there is actually something not as bad as all the rest of it?"

"Are you and Honor twins?" Loathel asked.

Christif was further down in the dungeons. He had no comprehension of the world around him, no memory of what had taken place. There was a presence with him, but Jalen couldn't determine who or what it was without establishing contact. His dad was in a bad way, but they had to get to Travon first.

Movement in the stairwell came to them.

"This way," Loathel called for them to follow him down a long corridor. The three ducked into a draped alcove where they waited for the danger to pass. Six Queons glided by, oblivious to all but the summons from their lord.

"Beheading them is best," Trill whispered to Jalen.

Taking on two apiece, all six Queons lay decapitated in a matter of minutes.

Onward they charged, slaying everything having the ill luck to encounter them. Around every corner, there seemed to be Kildar and/or Queons. For the warriors, the fighting was never-ending. But the only chance they stood against Maldonus' army was to cut them down a few at a time.

**

"They have gotten halfway," Loathel said.

They felt Travon's presence in the passage.

"We must not linger," the Elve said. "The merging will not conceal us for much longer. Soon he will realize we are here."

"Well then, let's not waste time." Trill raised his sword and kicked in the nearest door.

Travon sat, tied to a bedpost, staring wide-eyed at the broken door and his three towering rescuers. "Hey, guys! That was sooo cool."

Loathel and Trill checked the room while Jalen went to his side. "Hey Tray, buddy." With a flick of his wrist, Jalen sliced through the ropes, freeing his little brother.

Travon was full of amazement. That his brother could cut a rope was beyond his comprehension. "Whoa. Is that yours?"

"Of course it's mine. What, no hug?"

Travon threw himself into his brother's outstretched arms. Trill and Loathel also received embraces of remembrance and gratitude.

Loathel went down on one knee before Travon. "Master Travon, we have to make the best use of our time. Will you permit me to share your memories?"

"Uh-huh, you can do whatever you want."

The Bright Elve smiled his thanks and focused on the child. A moment later, he stood up, making the information available to the others. "They are approaching."

They bolted through the doorway so as not to become trapped. Loathel led the way, followed by Jalen, then Travon, with Trill protecting them from the rear. Evidence of earlier battles had been detected. An armed garrison searched for the culprits. The retreating warriors were spotted and an alarm raised.

They ran blindly, having no choice but to rely on instinct. The bonds Trill and Loathel shared with Annora and Honor were the only guide they had. They trusted it without question. Alpravage was vast and complex, a labyrinth of passages and tunnels, meant to confuse and delay potential foes. Their only hope of getting out lay in their connection to their fullness.

The garrison following them knew the design of the fortress. They separated into two bands: One following close behind and the other splitting off to take another route. They converged on the warriors from both directions.

With no other recourse open to them, the three surrounded Travon and made their stand. With one hand, Jalen drew his sword; with the other, he reached for his phone and hit the button to send.

CHAPTER XXXIX

Merlin halted his horse and waited for the others to do the same. "Ladies, we have a choice to make."

Honor and Annora felt ill at ease but refrained from contacting and/or distracting either Trill or Loathel.

"What's happening?" Honor asked.

"They have Travon." Joyous outbursts and sighs of relief were short-lived. "However, they are locked in life-or-death combat."

"What can we do? I am not losing Trill again."

"We cannot wait here, as Maldonus is already aware of our presence. But if we venture further, our fighters may not get to us in time. In all likelihood, we will be captured."

They waited for him to finish, both positive there was more.

"If we turn back, even if they are successful in this fight, they will not find their way out. You ladies are the light which leads them."

"And?" Honor prompted.

"And if we go nearer, Maldonus will know they are there."

"And?" Annora urged.

"And because they are fighting for their lives, they cannot rescue Christif. There is no time to wait and see. Maldonus means to see him dead before this hour has passed. It is my suspicion Lephan's heir is too occupied torturing Master Christif to notice the others are betwixt his eyebrows. It is fortunate for our fighters, but grievous for Christif. A circumstance that will not last; either way, I am afraid."

Now he was done.

Looking from Merlin to Annora to Alpravage, Honor heaved a deep sigh. "If we keep going, we're going to get caught and blow their cover, probably getting us all killed."

Annora said, "If we stop or go back, we're never going to see any of them again. Is that correct?"

"That about sums it up," Merlin told them. "The choice falls to you. Which is it to be?"

Annora looked at Honor. Honor looked at Annora. It was not a decision either felt capable of making.

"*I would see you far from this place were I able to send you. That is my desire.*"Trill's voice reached Annora in a gentle whisper.

"*Go. Leave while you are able. I beg you, grant me the peace of knowing you at least remain unharmed.*"Loathel's melodic phonation filled Honor with warmth.

...It's so easy when you're evil...

In the silence of indecision, the chiming cords of Honor's phone signaled a text message. A mechanical reaction prompted her to view it. Her heart stopped beating when she read the name Jalen teasingly called her as a child:

DisHonor. Whatever happns, 1 luv U.
Don't forget it. Pass it on. Thx.

Honor gave Annora the phone so she could wipe her eyes.

Annora read the message and gave Merlin the phone so she could wipe her eyes. While Merlin read—not understanding it in the least—Annora looked at Honor. Honor looked at Annora. The decision was made. They were in agreement and walking away wasn't it. As one, they kicked their horses into motion. Merlin was hard-pressed to keep up.

Loathel called out to the others, "I do not think communicating with them was wise."

"Mayhap not," Trill said, "but it leaves us no choice but to claim victory...and swiftly." They fought with renewed strength where before hope was dwindling.

Being in a narrow corridor with no place to run was to their advantage. There was not enough room for the troops to advance at once. The growing number of bodies lessened the space further.

Standing in the ragged torchlight, Travon felt helpless. Around him, the battle raged and he could do nothing but stand out of the way while his family fought to save his life. Beside him, a large Kildar guard pressed Jalen into the wall. "I remember you, weakling. You had a stick. Mayhap you should have kept it. Your sword isn't doing you any good. Did you drag me over to the fire? Were you hoping I would burn? I'm going to make you pay."

Travon heard enough. He extended his hand to the torch above him. In a flash, flames engulfed his brother's attacker. "Whoa. Cool!" he said to no one in particular. He was so captivated by the Kildar burning, the enormity of his actions never registered. He turned to set someone else on fire.

The burning Kildar did his part, too. He thrashed about, bumping into other Kildar, falling over dead bodies, setting them ablaze as well. The fighting stopped. Smoke filled the corridor. Blinding, choking fumes consumed them while the passage became an inferno. In the panic and chaos, the four infidels were forgotten.

"RUN!" Trill shouted. The others followed him, running hard, striving not to become trapped. Jalen and Loathel were hindered by Travon. He was so enamored with his wonder torch, he kept trying to find something else to set fire.

Finally, Jalen took it from him. "You did good, but that's enough. Move."

Through several twisting halls and long corridors, they ran an erratic pattern no unlearned individual would be capable of following. They bypassed turns that would have taken them deeper into the fortress. With only a few skirmishes, they came to the ground level where the main hall and the gatehouse were located. Here, they stopped to catch their breath.

"No time to do both," Loathel answered an unspoken question.

Jalen lay on the floor, doubled over with his tongue hanging out. He marveled Loathel could hold a normal conversation as if he hadn't run a marathon with the rest of them.

"We have to separate." Trill, although taking deep breaths, recovered fast enough to impress his cousin. "You and Jalen get Travon out, get to the others."

"I will protect her. I will find you," Loathel promised.

"I am confident on both accounts." Trill bowed to his companion. He spared an affectionate glance for Jalen and Travon, then made a mad dash down the hall and out of sight.

"Wh...wh...where's he...go...go...ing?" Travon panted.

"To delay Maldonus. Come, we must move."

"Where...are...we...go...ing?"

"To get your family."

"Now?" Jalen was still on the floor. All the strength he had gained was gone with the pronouncement of that one word.

Loathel granted him twenty seconds. "We are grateful for your astuteness, Master Travon. Were it not for you, our lives may have been forfeit."

"Do you want me to get another torch? I can burn something else if you want."

Loathel walked away. "Not in this moment. Our chief concern is getting your lazy brother in motion."

Travon pushed himself away from the wall.

"Hey, wait up," Jalen called out, not moving.

"Can I have another torch?" Travon asked.

"*The last time you did not keep up, werewolves were the result.*"

Sudden energy came to Jalen.

"Can I have a sword or something?"

"I am certain you will at some point." Loathel led them around a corner.

"Can I have a sword and a torch?" Travon imagined the great deeds he would do with his trusty sword and reliable wonder torch.

Jalen wondered at Travon's new addiction to fire.

Loathel's senses told him the fire Travon started had not been extinguished. More than likely, the guards had perished, and it burned out of control. He wondered how long they had before it would spread beyond the one floor.

"Maybe I can have two torches..."

234   TRACY A. BALL

CHAPTER XL

An armed patrol waited for the travelers. Merlin slowed his trotting horse down. "Steady now, steady," he warned. "We are being watched."

"How come 1 knew that?" Honor asked.

"Too much TV," Annora said.

"And nobody's here to help us." Honor stated the obvious.

"No, my dear. I am afraid we are on our own."

"What do we do?" Annora whispered.

"We will not have to do anything," the wizard said. "Remember to utilize my thoughts."

The ambushing patrol surrounded them. "Stupid, stupid humans. Did you assume your trespassing would go unnoticed?"

"On the contrary, 1 hoped we would be treated as expected guests."

The leader drew his sword and placed the point at Merlin's throat. "Biting remarks will only hasten your imminent death."

"In my line of work, imminent death is a constant. 1 am a wizard. Take us in or 1 shall call lightning down upon you all." For effect, there was a distant roll of thunder.

He lowered his sword, and entire band moved back.

"That's better. Now we can proceed. We have urgent business with your overlord."

The leader guided them toward the gates of Alpravage.

"*Fortunately for us, there is a general lack of common sense. It would have been quite impossible to call anything with my throat slit.*"

"*Mr. Merlin, does anything ever bother you?*" Annora asked.

"Does being bothered solve problems? There has to be some benefit of old age. If I hadn't conquered my feelings by now, there would be no hope for any of you."

***

Honor couldn't withhold the secret smile that came to her during their last few paces to the gate. It prompted the curiosity of the nearest rider. "Do you think on me, my beauty? I see hunger reflected in your eyes. I know you are wishing for a male."

"Think on you? Ha! Oh yeah, like you matter. What you see reflected in my eyes is A) nothing to do with you and B) none of your business. If you knew who I was thinking about, you would run. So get out of my face, I don't have time for you." Honor waved him off and nudged her horse away. Part of her marveled at her bravado. The other part couldn't believe herself. *What am I doing? This isn't school. Man, my mouth gets me into more trouble.* She was positive her outburst was going to come back on her.

The look she received from Annora didn't help. Merlin, on the other hand, struggled to contain his mirth. He tried to imitate the way Honor flicked her wrist. The Kildar was indignant. The other riders enjoyed their companion's embarrassment, incensing him further. They stopped to wait for the gatekeeper.

The insulted Kildar retaliated. He reached for Honor's reins, pulling her nearer to himself. "Come here, you short-lived parvenu. I will have the name of this fearsome male." He seized her arm. "You are going to be my slave. I'd like to thank him for the gift." When she showed no signs of alarm, he taunted further. "Maybe I'll find out right now if you're worth it." He leaned in as if he would kiss her.

"Tell him."

Honor proudly did as she was told. "My thoughts are for Loathel of the Elven People."

"Loathel." The guard's stricken look satisfied Honor immensely. "Loathel?" he repeated, wanting to be sure. It was his last word before the first of the great archer's arrows whizzed past his face, tearing off his lips. On reflex, the ghoul turned to see his attacker. The next arrow made a hole in the back of his neck, having gone straight through his mouth. A third arrow embedded itself in his chest and he fell over dead.

More deathsticks followed the first. More soldiers went down. The rest of them drew their swords and searched the area for the bandit. One Kildar snatched Annora back against him, using her as a shield. In answer to that threat, Loathel placed an arrow directly through his ear, deep enough for the tip to emerge from the center of the other ear.

The gatekeeper had long been slain, and the portcullis was closed to them. The remaining patrol abandoned their prisoners and rode away from the attack. When they were gone, the gate rose high enough that Annora, Honor, and Merlin slipped in.

The brothers deserted their position at the winch to greet the newcomers. Travon was showered with kisses. Loathel climbed down from his vantage point.

"Lowell!" Honor threw herself into his arms. Her eagerness consumed him, making him forget his purpose for a moment.

"Where is Trill?" Annora glanced around, noticing the bodies of the slain Kildar and the headless Queons scattered about but not her Jodian warrior.

"He is unharmed," Loathel said. "Do not let that be your fear."

She exhaled, letting go of her chief concern.

"He has gone to face Maldonus."

"I thought as much," Merlin said. "It is too soon."

"He attempts only to delay him. Christif's time is almost at its end."

"Then we must hurry. It will be no good for Trill to hold him if we are not there to do our part."

"What are we waiting for? Let's go." Annora started toward the fortress.

"I am sorry, dear heart." Merlin was gentle but firm. "You ladies must not enter."

"Excuse me?" Oh, they were entering. Annora was unhappy with the holdup. "Trill is in there. I'm going in."

"If you wish for Trill to return, you will wait here," Loathel said.

"You forget." Merlin paced back and forth in front of them. "Once inside those evil walls, none escape. If we gain success, getting out will become a large desire. Jalen and I have to rely upon Loathel and Trill to find the way. You two guide them. If either of you goes in, the warrior bound to you will be lost. Although I did not realize it at first, you are the most important part of this mission." Feeling he had made himself clear, Merlin turned to Travon. "Master Travon, would you please stand there, next to your womenfolk?"

Travon did as he was told.

"But..." Annora understood. Still, Trill was in danger. She wasn't going to stand by and do nothing.

"Annora." Even in the courtyard of Alpravage, the euphonious tones of the Elve were felt. "You know his heart. If we are to win, you will have to be in the safest place possible. Otherwise, you put him at a disadvantage. You know his mind. Many have been the times when he would have been justified to act differently than he did. Always, he chooses what is right rather than what he wants. Trill would never place his desire before his duty. The best reflection of your love for him is mirroring the standard he has set."

"Yeah, yeah, yeah. Can you guys go now before I change my mind?"

"That will not be possible." Merlin aimed his staff. "Plikea boc nihuve sotah." Too quick for anyone to react, the ground beneath Annora, Honor, and Travon turned white and began to move. A clear white light rose around them, connecting above their heads. Then the ground stilled itself and there was silence. The three were enclosed in a large sphere made of some impenetrable material.

"WOW!" This was the coolest thing Travon had seen so far.

"Your safety is above all else," Merlin explained. "Do not worry. You are protected, for now."

Neither Annora nor Honor wanted further clarification. Memories of the circle of smoke were still fresh. They watched the men disappear.

"We rode all that way for yet another chauvinistic display," Annora said.

"We held our own at Narconess," Honor recalled.

"*Because of Loathel. Y'all are salty af.*" Jalen had the nerve to laugh in their heads. "*They offered to teach you how to fight way back at the beginning, but y'all salty.*"

"*Get out of my head, Jalen! Or Loathel is going to have hell to pay.*"

"*Trill too.*"

In the immediate silence, Honor added to her list of grievances. "Not even a kiss goodbye." She put her hand on her hip.

"At least you got to see him." Annora put her hand on her hip.

Travon made a face. Sometimes, girls were the stupidest things ever. Here they were inside a magic bubble, *magic,* in the middle of an important battle, and all they could think about was kissing. *Yuck.*

Maldonus turned to his companion with feigned interest.

CHAPTER XLI

The dungeon was huge, with several doors. But the gloom pressing in from every direction made it claustrophobic. Torturing devices lined the walls. Chains, whips, knives—several rusted over with dried blood and dead flesh. Scattered about were the remains of unfortunate victims. The odd mixture of dust and use and the odor of death, filled every crevice.

Maldonus turned to the woman at his side. "What do you think, my sweet? Is he dead enough or should we kill him a little more?"

She leaned over, sneering, "Christif darling, are you dead enough?"

Christif moaned. Four of Maldonus' henchmen beat him, after which Maldonus shredded his skin with a spiked metal whip. He was stretched across a rack while the Grand Lephan's companion poured hot oil into his wounds. Christif's face was disfigured: his eyes swollen shut, one oozing blood. A few cracked, chipped teeth remained, the others knocked away. Also, the bite of the whip had torn part of his lip away from his mouth. They fractured his right shoulder, broke his left arm and several ribs, and crippled his legs. His death was near. "Whhh?" Blood dribbled down his chin as he tried to talk.

"Whhh?" Maldonus turned to his companion with feigned interest.

"Whhh," she repeated in toddler tones. "Does him mean, why?"

Christif nodded once, unable to do more.

"Why? You ask why?" Maldonus sneered. "We wanted to make it fair for little Travon. You cannot expect him to defeat a fully able Jodian, do you?"

The woman grabbed a handful of his hair. "You vile, treacherous, worthless piece of Jodian trash. You deserve it. I've been waiting a long time for this." She slammed his head down hard, almost knocking him unconscious. When she would have banged his head again, Maldonus stopped her.

"Patience," he said. "We need him a while longer."

"You have his strength. Why burden ourselves? We've all but killed him already, let me finish it."

"No." It was a stern command. "I desire the boy. I will not have Christif's son grow up to challenge me. He will surrender his will to me now, or they will perish together. Either way, I will have no more trouble from the line of Christif. Go get the boy. It is time."

"But—"

Maldonus waved his hand, silencing her in a most humiliating way. "Do not let your thirst for revenge cloud your vision; lest you forget, it is *my* will that shall be done." The demonic glow in his eyes grew bright. The beast had no love for anyone, not even his favorite. "Retrieve the boy. Christif is dying. If I need to prolong his life to aid my cause, I shall replace it with yours."

The woman looking at him saw undiluted evil, anticipating the infliction of pain.

"It would be in your best interest to hurry."

She wanted to argue, but he held her in silence until the defiance drained from her.

"Hurry," he said, as if encouraging a child.

"Yes, my lord," she whispered when her voice returned. Beckoning two of the four henchmen to accompany her, she did his bidding.

A moan from the rack made the lord of Alpravage look down at the pitiful Jodian. "Do not worry, Christif. It will be over soon. I have you. I have your son. You'll be dead in a little while. But you'll be back. When I open the prison of Bedalamon you will return as my willing servant. I hope it does your heart good to know I will accomplish all I desire. Because of you, I am unstoppable."

"Arrogance is a dangerous thing, Maldonus. It makes reality bitter."

Maldonus swung around.

Trill stood in the opposite doorway, his sword tip touching the floor while he leaned on the hilt. How Trill got to him undetected was mind-boggling. The Jodian scared him. He hadn't felt fear since the last time Trill conquered him. For the first time, the lord of Alpravage was unsure of himself. Yet he determined not to lose again. His two remaining thugs moved toward the intruder. He stayed them. "Trill, is my wisdom deceived? Are werewolves no longer dangerous? How is it you are still alive?"

"Your wisdom is much deceived if you know not the answer. I am still alive because I am yet undead. The question of more importance is why do you again attempt the impossible?" Wordplay was not Trill's method, but he needed to delay the inevitable confrontation for as long as he could. Every second mattered.

"Impossible?" Maldonus said. "Impossible, you proclaim. Why is such a belief in existence? Nothing is impossible." He too wanted to procrastinate. The Jodian's appearance was an enigma he needed resolved. "Whatever I am about, you must realize you are too late." His conversation was mild as he reached for Trill's mind.

Trill flexed his supernatural muscle, warding off the Lephan's attempt to enter his thoughts and making Maldonus wince. "Do not toy with me." His voice carried real authority. "Even if you master the arts that are not your birthright, Christif's stolen abilities have no efficacy upon me."

"Mayhap not. But I am a god. Have a care, whelp, the abilities work where they will. Christif's life, well, you know." He shrugged. "Christif's powers are not all I possess. I have the boy. I have drained him. The scales tip in my favor. You are no longer the superior one in our game of bondage."

Trill did not comment.

Christif groaned, taking his last breaths. Trill and Maldonus were aware, and neither could afford to have him die now. They eyeballed one another, recognizing the one, all-consequential difference between them. Trill would do something about it. Maldonus would adjust to the loss.

They both knew what he would do and what it would cost him. Trill would breathe for him. He would send some of his own quintessence into the dying man, prolonging his life. However, the price would be great.

Trill was Maldonus' better by a margin so small, it was not guaranteed. Saving Christif meant lessening himself. It also meant strengthening his enemy. Christif's mind and will were under Maldonus' rule. With every breath given to him, Christif would fight his nephew.

"So what is it to be? No need to tell you, I procure a certain gratification from watching him die." Maldonus closed his eyes and sighed at Christif's strangled cough. "Ohh, it makes me warm and tingly all over."

There was no decision for Trill to make. He spared a glance for the face so like his father's, then stretched his hand out toward the rack and took a deep breath.

***

Outside the fortress, in the ball, Annora choked and everything hurt. The pain sent her to her knees, unable to breathe.

Honor and Travon came to her but could not determine the problem.

"*Shh, love, it is all right. What you feel is not actual. Your mind tells you these things. Your body feels them, but they are not there. You may trust me. Relax, it will pass.*"

Annora understood what he said, but it was difficult. She didn't know how not to believe what she felt. She was dying.

Trill did not want her to suffer, but he didn't have time to minister to her.

The solution hovered on the air, penetrating the protective globe.

Elven serenity came to Annora. Without words, Loathel lent his aid. He wrapped her in peace until she was calm. She felt Trill regulating her heartbeat. Her breathing became normal again. She fell back against the barrier, exhausted.

"*I am sorry, my love. I had not the time to warn you of what was coming. Please, forgive me.*"

"*Are you hurt?*"

"*Nay. The suffering you felt is Christif's. We are giving him strength.*"

"*You shouldn't be talking to me right now. I can tell whatever you're doing is hard. Talking to me is a burden.*"

He wanted to deny it. "*Speaking with you is a necessary pleasure.*"

"*I'm not dumb. Right now, I am a burden and I'm not allowing it, so shut up. I love you. Do whatever you're doing and be quick about it, 'cause I love you and I'm not talking to you again until you're safe.*"

Trill stood in the deepest dungeon, facing extreme evil with Christif's life dependent upon his choices. Because of Annora's sassiness, he smiled. He was reminded of sunshine, warm nights, and their reunion. For a moment, things did not appear bleak.

Maldonus was fast to rob him of his pleasure. "Tranquility, Trill? Prolonging his miserable life may seem noble, but it is hardly worth the effort, and I know there is no joy in it."

"You know nothing of my joy."

"You don't have any joy. If you did, I would have taken it long ago." Maldonus pressed his edge. "Seize him," he ordered his henchmen.

Except for raising his sword, Trill did not budge. As a unit, the fighters moved to sandwich him between them. They were strong, and Trill was weary from the fighting he had done so far. Even so, he made quick work of killing them both.

Maldonus expected the outcome, but not as fast. He made a *tsk tsk* noise. "I shall not forgive you. I was fond of the one on the left."

Trill walked forward. "If you are annoyed with me now, for certain you will be perturbed when you learn of your upper floors."

"Mischief making, were you?" He crossed his arms. "What havoc have you wreaked upon my home?" If not for the grating hum of wickedness in his voice, Maldonus' tone could have been playful.

"A good portion of your army has met with a fate like those two." Trill tilted his head towards the slain. "Also, I would venture to guess your fortress is in flames. The blaze was out of control from the start. Travon and I barely escaped. Many of your Kildar won't be back tonight."

The mentioning of Travon's name struck the nerve that snapped Maldonus' control. Trill stole Christif's son from him. He had to retaliate. Without warning, objects in the room flew at Trill from every direction.

As opposed to ducking, Trill locked his will with the Lephan's, overriding his mental command. Everything airborne hit the floor with a resounding clang. The Jodian did not release him but brought Maldonus to his knees. He grabbed his head, unable to free himself. To his dismay, Trill was stronger than ever.

Annora squeezed her eyes shut in concentration. She could feel Trill focusing his energy on one point. She did not know who or what but was compelled to do the same, giving him a stronger force of compulsion. She felt the danger the same moment he did and turned around when the sword tip touched his back.

CHAPTER XLII

By degrees, Trill lessened the pressure. Maldonus panted in the wake of
the subsiding pain. Mustering a slow dignity, he rose to his feet.

Without turning around, Trill said, "I wondered when you would
arrive, Montanae."

She circled to stand in front of him, keeping the tip of her weapon in
contact with his body as she moved. She let it rest against his heart. "Trill,
my darling." Taking in his form with lustful appreciation, she said,
"Marvelous. So virile. You have aged well." Her sultriness was practiced.

His lack of a response was an insult.

Montanae studied her captive while giving Maldonus a report. "There
is fire on the floors above. Our army is partly unaccounted for. The rest I
have set to subduing the blaze. There is no way to get to the boy."

Speaking to Trill, she said, "You have no doubt caused this trouble. It
has cursed back upon you. The boy has perished. Why now are you here?
What more can you do?"

"Lower the sword, Montanae." Not only was it not a request, Trill
issued his command in such a manner, compliance was immediate.
Montanae's sword arm fell like dead weight.

Her eyes grew at her body's response to his authority. She wondered if
she held the same power over him.

"Why, Trill, I do believe you have come into your fullness." Maldonus
smirked. "At least it explains the enhancement of your talents. I did not
think it possible for you. Tell me, am I accurate? Who is the fortunate
female? Some Elven lass with long shimmering hair? Whose beauty
surpasses her years and they both shall surpass you." Again, the tone was

light, almost playful, belying the inner workings of a corrupt mind. There was no well-wishing on the part of the Lephan.

Montanae snapped her head around to glare at Maldonus. "What do you mean, 'Who is the fortunate female?' I brought Trill into his fullness years ago." Haughtiness born of selfish pride dripped from her words and sizzled on the air. She assessed her prize, running her fingers across the warm steel of his shoulder. "Even with time between us, you have come for me because you can do no other. Am I not correct?" She was not looking for an answer but wondered how best to exploit this new power for her own purpose.

Montanae's thoughts were easily discerned, Trill with nonchalant indifference, Maldonus with bitter effrontery.

"Methinks, my dove, you are ever the harlot. Moreover, you have deceived yourself. It is not Trill, but I, who owns you. I shall be the one reprimanding you for your wayward thoughts. Besides, there is a female who carries the stench of Trill. It is not difficult to see it. She is the chosen one."

He said to Trill, "She reeks of you because she is you. Am I right, Trill? Or is she some convenient plaything? Do you suffer the same proclivities as your uncle?" The Grand Lephan delighted in Montanae's distress and what he hoped would be Trill's discomfort.

Montanae raised her sword again, pushing the tip hard against Trill. "What game do you play at?"

"Lower the sword, Montanae." This time her arm fell with such force, the weapon slipped from her fingers and crashed to the floor.

"Without a joining, how can you do that?" She pointed to her sword.

He caught her by the throat with one hand and lifted her off her feet. Deep ebon eyes grew darker. "What I do is no affair of yours." His fullness was not an issue they had a right to discuss. For such low and depraved creatures to think on his beloved was a trespass that demanded immediate retribution. The volcano living inside Trill rose, unleashing a monster he had no will to control.

Judging him occupied, Maldonus countered with a blast of power. He hurled a ball of fire at the Jodian.

Trill was waiting. He closed his eyes and concentrated, forcing Maldonus to fight against himself. His outstretched hand turned against his will, sending the blaze veering toward the stone floor, where it died in a harmless puff of smoke.

Trill did not release him. Maldonus was held captive against some unseen force. His actions mirrored those of Montanae. She clawed at the hand holding her throat. Maldonus also felt the tightening fist of strangulation, although his adversary was not physically touching him.

Trill meant to end it. He increased the pressure.

Montanae's eyes bulged out of her ashen face. Maldonus paled. He could feel himself losing consciousness, but he was not defeated. With effort, he choked out, "Christif."

It was enough.

Trill had forgotten Christif's life was intricately tied to Maldonus. He could not kill the Lephan without damning his uncle. The pressure around Maldonus' throat lessened by a fraction; enough for the Lephan to breathe. Montanae's feet touched the floor. Soon, she too could take in small amounts of life-giving air.

"Rise." Maldonus pushed his advantage, though Trill had done nothing more than allow him a little oxygen. He could feel the indecision in his foe and rejoiced. The Jodian had proven he was the stronger, but the Lephan knew it was he who would be the victor.

Christif could not move on his own; the effort alone would kill him.

Trill knew it. It had taken Annora's aid and the adrenaline rush for him to hold both Maldonus and Montanae for those few successful moments. He could not maintain the bondage and give Christif aid as well. He needed to replenish himself. Once free, Maldonus would not give him a chance to regain his momentum. To continue meant death for Christif. To let go meant death for them both.

Christif pulled against his ropes. The pain was so intense, he screamed. However, he was compelled to obey. His outcry filled the chamber as he repeatedly attempted to rise.

Without the time to decide, Trill shifted his focus. Montanae dropped to the floor unceremoniously. The hand that had been around her neck extended toward his ailing relative, sending him into a deep, comatose sleep that stilled his movements and blocked further compulsions.

Montanae's retaliation was basic. From her position on the floor, she swung her foot out, clipping Trill at the ankles, knocking his legs out from under him. He hit the floor hard, the wind knocked out of him. Montanae was on her feet and out of the door before he could stop her.

Contact with Maldonus was broken, and the evil lord seized the opportunity. He applied the same stranglehold Trill used on him. "It appears our positions have reversed. When will you learn, Trill? Christif is not worth the effort you emit on his behalf." He raised the Jodian several feet off the floor.

"I give you full merit for your endeavor, but you cannot defeat me. You have not the heart." He slammed Trill against the farthest wall. "Your precious Merlin should have taught you: without heart, skill is useless." He let him fall.

***

An arrow pierced Maldonus' outstretched hand. At the same moment, a previously nonexistent wind swirled about the room. It caught and cushioned the unconscious Jodian, lowering him to the floor.

Maldonus whirled around to see Merlin, Loathel, and a third person. It was the third person who concerned him most. It was a young Christif, personifying the Jodian's abilities. Unsure, Maldonus looked to where his hostage lay.

CHAPTER XLIII

"How come you guys are acting weird?" Travon looked from his agitated tense sister to his agitated tense aunt.

Honor sat down beside him. "Don't worry, dude. You know how girls are. We're a little nuts right now."

"You're always a little nuts. That's not it."

"Did anybody ever tell you you're too smart for your age?"

"Everybody. Now tell me what's going on."

"We don't know what's going on, honey." Annora ruffled his hair. "We're sensing some things."

"Mostly feelings," Honor added.

"We can feel some of the stuff Trill and Loathel feel."

"Way cool. Can I?"

"It doesn't work that way." Honor shook her head. "Sorry, it's kind of a boy-girl thing."

He made a face and would have commented, but his attention shifted to the castle gate. "MOM!"

She was hungry, dirty, and very, very tired, but her countenance rose and she picked up her pace when she heard her baby's call.

Honor and Annora added their shouts to Travon's.

Imani ran. She'd found them, she had finally found them. Half of her family was safe, at least.

She threw herself against the bubble, but it did not crack or break as she had hoped. She still carried her club and didn't hesitate to swing it like a baseball bat, beating the barrier with newfound strength. Imani didn't realize they were yelling at her. She heard nothing they said but continued to bang on the clear ball until her club splintered.

Unstoppable, Imani yanked off the ringblade and sliced through the bubble. She hacked away for a few seconds before realizing the blade penetrated the sphere, but it had the same effect as slicing smoke. She could touch the structure with her hands, but the knife encountered nothing.

That was more than she could accept. To have come so far, to be this close and not be able to hold her loved ones was too much. She crumbled down into a hysterical mass against the prison her family was in.

"Imani, listen to me."

"Mom, it's alright."

"Mommy..."

"Imani, honey, you're scaring Travon. Calm down and listen."

Scaring Travon...calm down...it's alright... One by one, the words reached her. Imani struggled against the despair clogging her mind. She focused on the speakers.

"Imani, it's alright." Annora kneeled close to her elder sister.

"Mom, we're fine," Honor said.

"Wh-what is...this?" Imani took a few fortifying breaths.

"Mr. Merlin put us in here."

Before Imani could get the wrong idea, Annora said, "To keep us safe." She felt around the interior of the globe, biting her bottom lip as she worked. "I don't know if there's a way in, but I'm pretty sure we can't get out."

"Merlin? Where is he? Where are the others?"

"In there." Honor pointed. "They're getting Daddy out."

"Chris? Chris is in there?" Imani's relief overrode her anxiety. Her husband had not abandoned her. She shook as the doubt left her body. For the first time in days, the hope she clung to grew. "Travon, baby, are you alright?"

"I'm okay, Mommy. Trill and Loathel and Jalen got me out first."

"Trill?" She scanned her sister's face.

Annora's broad grin confirmed Travon's implication.

"Oh, Annora." Imani wept with happiness. Despite everything, so much was good.

"Mom," Travon said. "Jalen has a sword. A big one. And I helped." It occurred to him if he still had his torch, he would get them out of this stupid ball.

His mother's love was at its fullest. She ached to touch her child. She took a few more calming breaths and let herself be content with having Travon back and knowing he was safe.

A voice brought her out of her respite, stiffening her spine with its chilling closeness. "The females I am familiar with. I assume this to be your second son."

The three inside the sphere looked up, surprised. Imani turned around, crossing her arms, exasperated. "You are on my last nerve, Dayown. Why are you here?"

Annora and Honor exchanged looks of disbelief.

Travon hid behind his aunt; he had seen enough scary men.

"Do you not recall? I have business here." They stared at one another, giving off equal amounts of defiance and annoyance.

"Why are you here?"

"Did I not tell you? One would think someone knocked *you* unconscious." His two-toned jeweled eyes glinted.

"If you have some business here, go take care of it." Imani waved him off.

"I am about it."

"Leave me alone."

"No."

"Yes."

"No."

"Yes."

"My presence here should indicate my lack of regard for your wants on this matter. However, your speech reveals a need for me to make it plain. You belong to me. Once I have punished you for your defiance, you will be happy."

"My defiance?" Both hands went to her hips as her self-control evaporated. "You have got some nerve."

"Yes, I am aware."

"You lied to me. You were taking me back to Narconess."

"I've made no secret of my goal."

"You wanted me to believe you were leading me here." The more outraged she was, the more placid he became.

"Yes."

"But you weren't."

"You have a point to make?"

"Youuuu...ughhh, why do I bother? You don't listen, and you don't care."

"I listen."

Imani closed her eyes in frustration. She prayed when she reopened them, he would disappear. She did. He didn't. "Dayown, you are driving me nuts. Please go away. Why can't you do that?" She pointed off into the distance. "Go."

"Woman, you have caused me no little embarrassment. You remain alive only because you are under my protection." He thumped himself twice in the chest to be sure she knew to whom he was referring. "I am your lord and master. If you understood the peril you have placed yourself in, you would be attached to my ankles, worshipping. Not imparting useless orders to aggravate me and provoke my clansmen."

"Your—"

"They have been close at hand these many days. It displeased me they saw me subdued. Retribution is a sure thing," Dayown growled.

Imani and her family looked in every direction for the supposed clansmen.

"You will not see them until it becomes necessary. We are being watched, as are the watchers."

CHAPTER XLIV

"I refuse to believe your timing is impeccable. I credit it to dumb luck, Merlintum."

"Call it what you will, I am here all the same."

Maldonus pulled the arrow from his palm. "Have you nothing better to do than be a pest, Bright Elve?" Although he was far stronger than any other evil in Zendelel, Maldonus also experienced difficulty in looking at the purity radiating from Loathel.

"I could let this arrow fly as well. What think you of that?" Loathel was pleasant, his tone harmonious despite the seriousness of the situation and the honesty of his intent.

Maldonus' answer was a grunt. Finally, he addressed his largest misgiving. "And who might you be, boy?"

Jalen remained silent. Tiny pinpricks of fear stabbed at him. Never had he been in the presence of corruption so complete.

"Are you a cheap illusion cast by Merlintum in an attempt to confuse me? Speak, if you can."

Jalen received Elven serenity. Merlin spoke to his mind. *"It is he who has the greater fear."*

Jalen squared his shoulders. "I am no illusion, Maldonus. I am Christif's son. You wanted me. Now I have come."

"The son of Christif is but a babe."

"'Tis a riddle you offer," Merlin said. "You were disturbed because the son of Christif came of age. I know of no babe capable of such a feat."

Maldonus' eyes glowed with red hate. It was inconceivable he would make a mistake. He shrugged. "Now that you are here, I find I have no use for you. Your father has aided me well. You are excused." He made as if he would turn his back on the trio.

"Christif will aid you no further; his abilities will not help you. At long last, your hold will be broken."

"My hold, Merlintum, will never be broken. Not even Christif's spawn can undo what I have done."

"I can undo what you have done." Merlin drew himself up to his full height. He became the wizard of the legends, a formidable foe, worthy of the fear he instilled in the hearts of lesser men.

"It comes to it at last." Maldonus flexed his palm. The wound healed. "You would face me, Merlintum?"

"Like all the others before you, Maldonus, you must be destroyed."

"Like all the others?" The Lephan sneered. "You forget, brother mine, you too are like all the others. Who will destroy you?"

"Say what?" The implication baffled Jalen; he lost his focus and studied his friend instead.

Maldonus used the lapse to his advantage. A mental blast knocked Jalen backward into a heap of rubble. Suits of old armor, broken weaponry, torn chain mail, and helmets, all with sharp edges and points, bit into him.

He hurled Loathel across the room and would have slammed him into the wall were it not for the rush of wind enveloping him. A ball of fire fell from above and engulfed Merlin in flames. The aid he gave Loathel disappeared, but the lithesome Elve somersaulted backward and landed on his feet.

Maldonus made a face, disgusted.

The floor beneath Loathel's boots burned white. Before any imprisonment could arise, he leapt with the nimbleness of a cat, several feet away from the spell. Maldonus' control gave way to impatient outrage. It had taken one fireball to destroy Merlin. He took no further chances on Loathel and sent three in rapid succession to bear down upon the Elve.

"*Now is your time, Jalen!*" Loathel reached for Jalen as the first daystar appeared. He pulled his Elven cloak about him in a grand sweep of motion.

One! Two! Three! The fire hit with the impact of explosives three times on the spot where Loathel stood.

Honor couldn't stop the heart-wrenching scream bursting from her soul. She felt the blazing heat frying her skin.

***

Jalen was dazed from the blow he received. Seeing his friends incinerated shocked him motionless and locked his mind in fear. He heard what Loathel said but couldn't make himself react. A slight movement caught his attention. He followed the path of a bee as it buzzed past his nose and landed on his shoulder. It circled his head and flew towards the rack where Christif lay unconscious.

The flight of the bee called Jalen back to reality. He assumed Medrid would want him to fight. The bee's trajectory brought his father into focus. He remembered the connection Maldonus had established with his family. If his father was less powerful than the Lephan and Trill was more powerful, he had at least a fifty percent chance of doing some damage. There had to be a reason Maldonus wanted him. Merlin said he was afraid.

The bee flew past again. Jalen jumped to his feet, absently wondering how a bee came to be flying around in this deep, dark place. He gripped his sword in the same manner he had seen his cousin do. A sereneness he could not explain filled his being. He walked forward with one purpose. Before him was an evil he had to defeat. He could do no other.

Maldonus watched him approaching and panicked. The son of Christif could destroy him. Because he hadn't known Jalen existed, he didn't know how strong the young Jodian was. There was no way to observe his capabilities without engaging him in battle. A battle that would have to be the end of one of them. From the fearless look of determination on Jalen's face, Maldonus wasn't sure it wouldn't be him.

Jalen had one thought in mind. Whatever Maldonus wanted to do, he did not wish to see it happen. He underestimated his talent. The Lephan was held to his place, unable to break the grip Jalen had on his abilities.

The young Jodian moved forward. Because Jalen was expecting to fight, when he was mere steps away, Maldonus drew his sword.

"Stand down, whelp," he barked. "You cannot conquer me." On the heels of his announcement, he attacked. Jalen sidestepped and launched an attack of his own.

Blades clanged together again and again. The fighters moved in a frenzied dance of death. Maldonus was more skilled, but Jalen was running on sheer tenacity. If the Grand Lephan defeated him, it would be no small task.

CHAPTER XLV

Honor's scream triggered a domino effect. Maldonus' army swooped down on the people in the courtyard. Assuming their king was in danger, the forward motion brought forth a like response from the dwellers of Narconess. The wolven people charged, many becoming animals as they ran. Soon the quadrant was overrun with animals and undead things crashing together in a kill or die confrontation.

A second wave of the Grand Lephan's soldiers converged onto the courtyard. Dayown's clan was outnumbered. As the battle raged, more of the enemy appeared. Latter assaults brought greater numbers of fresh fighters. Having many capable men locked in the bodies of wolves worked against them. As men, they would have been better able to defend themselves against the larger numbers. Those in wolven form fell far quicker than their human counterparts.

Dayown made his stand beside Imani, the only human not inside Merlin's protective sphere. He defended against any who dared to venture near the woman or her people. Beyond that, he did not participate. Emotionless, he witnessed his people giving up their lives for a cause unknown to them.

Imani had become a warrior. It never occurred to her not to join the fray. Full of fury, she had no qualms about killing anything that might be a threat to her family. Dayown tackled and wrestling her to the ground.

"What are you doing?" She tried to push him off.

"Keeping you from getting injured, fool."

"You moron. Get off of me."

As he dragged her to her feet, they heard an agonized moan.

"Day...own...Day...ow...n...help...meee...Day..." The labored breathing belonged to Tristole. He lay on his back, a sword protruding from his stomach and his life's blood pooling around him.

Imani's heart would not allow her to turn her back on someone in need. She pulled free of Dayown's grasp and went to the injured man. She knelt beside the victim, attempting to assess the damage.

Dayown grabbed her from behind, yanking her back.

"What are you doing? He needs help."

"No, he doesn't. He's dying."

"He's still conscious. If we can stop the bleeding—"

"I don't care. I don't want you exposed."

"Day...own...help...me..."

"Dayown!"

"I do not have the time for him, even if he is my brother—"

"Brother? This is your brother? You act like he doesn't matter." Once again, Imani knelt beside the dying man.

Once again, Dayown pulled her up. "My concern is not with him. I am keeping you unmarred."

She stood there, stunned. "Never in my life have I met a more selfish, cruel... What happened to loyalty? He's your brother."

Dayown opened his mouth to answer but nothing came out. He lurched forward, falling into Imani.

She screamed as his weight brought her down.

Someone had thrown a knife. It found its mark deep in the wolfking's back. Pained words came to her in a whisper. "I have loyalty." He stopped breathing.

Imani struggled to get from under Dayown. She heard another voice, equally pained, equally unfeeling.

"You'd...have been...delicious." And then Tristole was gone too.

Somewhere in the confusion and chaos, silence reigned, and Imani was amazed. A king was dead. A kingdom was dying. Aside from herself, no one would care.

Before she could get off the ground, the edge of a sword touched her throat. With her free hand, Montanae pulled her knife from Dayown's back. "Are you his woman? Or rather, were you his woman?" She smirked.

"No." Imani leaned back.

"Lucky for you. I liked Dayown. If I thought you were his bitch—in any definition—you'd meet a like end. But that is not to say you will not meet a like end, anyway."

"Who are you?" Imani showed more bravado than she felt.

Montanae pushed the sword closer. "The one with no reservations about ending your life. Get up. Over there with your kind."

With Dayown gone, a dozen Kildar converged on Merlin's ball. It was their reason for initiating the battle. They recognized the women as the source of their trouble and held them accountable.

Montanae held authority over Maldonus' subjects. They bowed and parted before her. She addressed the group with nothing less than absolute disdain. "What are you waiting for? Retrieve them."

"Your majesty," the nearest assailant spoke, "we are trying."

"Not hard enough."

"They have the protection of the unknown."

"Bring them to me."

"We cannot."

Her expression never changed. "Are you sure?"

"I am positive, Highness. We have been relentless in our efforts." He bowed low to show his respect.

Montanae sliced off his head with one neat sweep of her sword. The disconnected member rolled against Imani's foot and the bloodied weapon was pressed against her back before anyone could react. "Retrieve them."

The body of Kildar fell on the ball, beating at it with sword, knife, stone, and stick. The occupants inside huddled in the center, praying Merlin's magic would last.

"Enough, imbeciles. I'll do it myself. Move."

Again, they made a path for her, each bucking to be the farthest from her reach. She prodded Imani until they were next to the sphere. "Travon, sweetling, you've been naughty. Come out now and bring your friends."

Travon shook his head no. He got behind Honor, who was behind Annora.

"Do you want it to be your fault I kill her?" She pushed the sword in far enough for Imani to wince.

"NO!" was shouted three times in unison.

"It's not your fault, Travon."

"Don't worry about me, baby."

"Don't listen, Tray."

"Such concern." Montanae feigned emotion. "You may wish to stop. It makes me nauseous."

"We can't get out." Honor was done being afraid. She stood next to Annora. The women blocked Travon.

"Inconceivable. You got in there, did you not?"

"It's an enchanted ball," Honor said. "We don't know how to work it."

"Pity you," Montanae said. She prodded Imani. "Actually, pity you. You have to die."

"Killing her won't benefit you," Annora spoke with a coldness she was unaware she possessed. The woman was her personal archenemy. She didn't know why she thought it, but she was certain she was right.

Montanae noticed her and felt the same hatred. "You assume much if you deem to know what will benefit me."

"I know we are untouchable. If you harm Imani, you'll have nothing to bargain with."

"What need have I to make bargains? I hold the sword."

"Little good it will do you if you kill your hostage."

"Who are you? Which of you lay claim to Trill the Jodian?"

"Montanae." Honor's breath caught.

"Is it you?" Montanae directed her venom at Honor.

"I am Trill's fullness," Annora returned the venom dose for bitter dose.

"Come to me, pretender, and I will end your charade. I brought Trill to his fullness years ago. I own his heart and I do not share."

"You don't mind being shared." Annora sneered. "Stupidity and selfishness have blinded you to the simplest of truths. Do not whine to me, I don't care." She hunched her shoulders with an air of boredom. "Take it to Trill. But I warn you, don't go without your hostage. Otherwise, he won't bother to listen."

The Lossmans were dumbfounded and unable to conceal it.

Montanae swallowed her shock. "You dare to address me in such a fashion? You declare what you will because you believe yourself protected. If you are so confident, come out. I need to kill you. No, remain safe, 'Fullness.' We will see who owns the Jodian. I shall have *him* call you forth and send you to the next realm. It is my heart's desire." She turned away. "Bring her."

Two Kildar took hold of Imani and followed their mistress. The others remained to guard the prisoners who could not escape anyway.

Honor turned to Annora. "What the hell? Sorry, but...what the hell?"

Annora waved the cursing away. "It was the only thing I could think of. Imani has a better chance of being protected by the guys than with us. We can't help her; we can't help ourselves. As a hostage at least, she's still alive."

"Wow, Aunt Nora." Travon hugged her. "You're so smart."

She returned his embrace. "Don't put me on a pedestal. I don't know where that thought came from. I have no idea how this stuff works."

"I know, I'm baffled." Honor checked her arms for burn marks for the hundredth time.

CHAPTER XLVI

Fire raged throughout the middle floors of Alpravage. Those trapped above it could only hope it would soon spend itself. They could not get past, but huddled around the windows and openings, crying out for help from the fighters below. Little good it did them. The occupants of Alpravage had no love for one another. They did the will of their master without care for the wellbeing of their fellow servants. In the halls of Alpravage, compassion was an unheard of concept.

The fortunate few below the inferno not combating Dayown's people salvaged what belonged to them and looted what did not. There was such a mass of confusion, no one knew or cared what anyone else was about.

The fire came closer, its heat making the temperature rise far into the mountain. Because the walls were stone, the outside world remained ignorant of the spreading wildfire. Almost everything except the walls themselves burned, especially the Kildar. The holocaust was unmerciful. Flames found the pitiful creatures in every corridor. Where they ran, fire erupted, catching, cornering, consuming them. White heat traveled with them, bringing hell to each level of Alpravage.

***

Montanae, followed by the two guards toting Imani, worked her way through the disarray. People stopped short, petrified at the sight of her, fearful of rebuke. She gave no heed to the activity around her but moved with practiced skill through the twisting halls of Alpravage. Both guards halted.

Montanae looked over her shoulder. "What is it?"

"There is danger for us, Highness."

"We cannot be in here. We will die."

"So?" She faced them, not caring to understand the problem.

"Beg-begging your pardon, M-Majesty. We-we don't want to di-die," the second guard stuttered, his courage depleted.

"The reality of your dilemma is you will rest and return tonight. We should all have it so well."

"No, Milady," the first said. "Not with fire. If we burn, we cannot return."

Montanae rolled her eyes. "This does not interest me. I have matters more pressing than the two of you." The flamboyant swirl of her hair and cape as she turned away announced the conversation was ended.

The Kildar did not move but looked at one other, unsure which was the greater risk: following Montanae or not.

Sensing their hesitation, Montanae paused. "Run if you must. But I warn you, it will not do you any good. Do as I bid and you may die. Do not do my bidding and it will be certain."

Still, the Kildar hesitated.

"I grow weary of your nonsense."

Against their instincts, the guards moved. They feared nothing more than fire, except the lords of the keep.

As soon as they were within reach, the witch-woman put her sword to work. The nearest Kildar slid to the floor, dead, his heart bleeding. The other soldier drew his weapon, but he was not as quick as she. "The fire is not a decisive factor, is it?" She rammed her blade into his chest.

Then it was Imani's turn. Montanae pointed the crimson sword at her. "I am in a foul mood. Make it easy and you may continue to breathe...for now."

***

Maldonus hadn't engaged in a physical battle in almost two hundred years. The activity took its toll, but his opponent was also weakening. Jalen didn't know how much longer he could last. It had been a horrendous day. This last battle had taken everything and still, Maldonus pressed him. They were both wounded and bleeding, a symbol of Maldonus' experience and Jalen's speed. They fought on, oblivious to all except each other.

The Grand Lephan sensed, with Jalen's energy draining, the control the boy had over his will was fading. He sent a mental nudge to test his theory. Jalen stumbled backwards and Maldonus grinned. "Your time has come to its end." He moved the teen further. "Your strength has failed you."

Jalen tried to push forward. Maldonus held him fast, lifting and holding him suspended. "I am in control now. You will bend to my will, and then you will die."

Jalen dropped to his feet as Maldonus was thrown into the far wall. "It is you who will pass from this realm, Maldonus. Your vicious reign is over." An immovable force generating from Trill held Maldonus to the stone. The Jodian towered before him, restored, puissant, and more dangerous than ever. The truth reflected in the midnight pools of his eyes.

The Lephan looked at him and knew.

What happened then was almost more than Jalen could take in. Merlin was back. He stood before the rack. "Master Christif, awaken unto me."

Trill removed his sleep aid. Christif moaned, overcome with pain.

"Awake now, I say." Merlin was firm. "Your time has come."

Christif managed to open one eye.

"You must renounce your actions, seek forgiveness, and accept this holy personification of body and blood in place of the evil imitation you took into yourself." From the folds of his robes, Merlin produced the small leather pouch he procured at Harpers Ferry. It contained a single wafer and a tiny phial filled with wine.

"NO!" Maldonus struggled to break Trill's hold. Utilizing the power of hell, he held to Christif's will.

"Will you take responsibility for your misdeeds and seek forgiveness?" Merlin asked.

"Uhhh...uhhh..." Christif's confused mind reeled. He couldn't do what he wanted. He wasn't sure what he wanted. Blood pumped through his brain, hot and throbbing, intermingling the promises and threats of Maldonus, fighting his cooperation.

"Dad," Jalen urged, coming to his side.

"*We cannot aid his decision, cousin. He must freely choose. If he does, it will be well.*"

"And if he doesn't?"

"He will pass to Bedalamon." Trill concentrated on subduing Maldonus.

The hold on Christif's mind was lifted, yet indecision remained.

Montanae burst through the door, shoving Imani ahead of her. Imani fell forward, flinging her arms out to catch herself. She landed on all fours. As she steadied herself, her eyes met with the bruised half-closed lids of her husband.

"CHRIS!"

Her presence, her voice, the anguish on her face touched Christif in a way no magic could. The fog cleared. Unhindered by any force, Christif understood.

Imani jumped to her feet. Oblivious to the world around her, she went to her husband.

In Montanae's opinion, Imani had lived far too long. She raised her sword high, intent on decapitating the unsuspecting woman. In rapid succession, three arrows flew across the room. The first caught the sword in mid-swing, breaking it in two. The second embedded itself into the witch's head as the third pierced her heart. She crumpled to the floor beside her broken weapon, dead. Her unseeing eyes fixed in lifeless surprise upon the Bright Elve.

A glance over her shoulder gave Imani the entire story. She offered a smile of gratitude for her beloved son-in-law—he was beloved—before returning to her task. She was a few steps from Christif when Merlin halted her. She would have protested, but all was silent when the wounded man spoke.

It was no more than a whisper, but to the ears of the listeners, it reverberated throughout the dungeon. His words were broken, barely decipherable, yet he spoke them and was understood. "I kno' wha' I 'ave don'... 'kno' I 'ave... 'aused 'ain...grea' 'ain... 'spe cee to 'ou, 'y yove," he told his wife as best he could. Weeping, he attempted to say more and his words were precious because of his struggle. "I'm 'orry... If I cou' undo 'y 'any 'isdeeds, 'ladly I wou'... I as' 'or your 'orgiff ness... I as' 'or da 'orgiff ness... of da Grea' Triune—"

"Nooo..." Maldonus again tried to waylay Christif's confession. His denial came out weak and without effect.

"Will you receive the forgiveness you seek? Will you receive the gifts I offer you?" Merlin offered the wafer and wine to Christif. "Though it may bring about your death?"

"I 'ill."

Maldonus fought against Trill. He shouted curses in protest of Merlin's administrations. The ground shook. Bits and pieces of the ceiling fell about them. Evil pressed in from every direction. It struggled to break upon those attempting to hold it captive. An unseen force pulled at Merlin's hands, trying to dislodge the all-important objects. Trill went down upon one knee, calling all his strength to hold against the power of the Grand Lephan.

Jalen added his will to Trill's, and Annora was locked deep in concentration. Loathel flooded his mind with hope so he would not give up. He received energy from them all. The Lephan's abilities were shut down.

Merlin placed the wafer in Christif's mouth, followed by the wine. It burned as he swallowed, singeing the baneful nature dwelling within him. Twin screams of a dying beast erupted from the Lephan pinned to the wall and the Jodian on the rack. Christif strained against his fetters. His body glistened with a sheen of perspiration that turned to blood.

The blood streamed and hissed as if boiling, carrying with it the acidity stench of malfeasance. Maldonus too hissed as his life's substance spilled from his victim. Christif vomited several times, his body finally ejecting the poison that had been in him for hundreds of years. One final heave and the Jodian lay still, dead, his face serene, knowing a peace like Elven tranquility rather than the black pain of Alpravage.

Stunned horror washed over Imani and Jalen. Fear held them to their places. Christif died. It could not be disputed. He did not move. He did not breathe. Only the peace remained.

"It is complete," Merlin said. He looked from Trill to Loathel. "It will be me. Do it now."

"You're damned right it will be you—" Maldonus' adulterated speech was shut off.

Trill was suffering.

"He will not release him," Loathel spoke Trill's thoughts aloud. "He is unwilling to put any of us at risk. None more than you, Medrid."

"Trill, you must release him ere Loathel's arrow finds its mark. If you remain connected..." Merlin would not complete the sentence.

"He means to do it himself," the Elve said.

"You cannot. You are beyond your endurance as is. His Jodian ability is defeated. It is the spirit of Lephan that will retaliate. You can do no more."

"Medrid, are you sure?" Loathel readied his bow.

"I am only sure of what we must do. The hope is for the proper outcome, but the final decision is not mine."

"What? What's happening?" Jalen asked. His face paled when he heard the explanation. "Medrid?"

"There is no other way, Master Jalen," Merlin said. "All we have done will be for naught if we do not see it through. Unless you wish to give my brother the victory, we all must do our part."

Imani realized Merlin did not expect to live through whatever was going to take place. She touched his arm, mixing her sorrow with awe.

Having no time to form an alternate plan, the warriors worked in unison. Trill released Maldonus from his telepathic bondage. Loathel let fly the first of several arrows aimed to end his life.

Maldonus was hit before he could react to his freedom. He flung his arms, sending bolts of lightning haphazardly around the room. The occupants had to duck and scatter from the chaos he caused. Maldonus crashed to the floor, bleeding from multiple wounds. Sizzling, oozing plasma burned his flesh. He shrieked, enveloped in bitter agony, then he too was silent and still. Unlike the serenity given to Christif, Maldonus lay in deleterious torment. Seconds went by with no one daring to move. The threat of Maldonus was not past.

"Now is your chance," Merlin spoke into the silence.

There was hesitation in Trill, and Loathel would not abandon him.

"Fools. Think you Christif will walk out by himself? Mayhap Imani could fling him over her shoulder."

A strong wind swept through the room, chilling them to the core. Merlin eyed Maldonus' corpse. Time was closing in. Sounds of ferocious animals resonated around them, through them, climaxing in a wailing echo that hurt their ears and assaulted their beings.

Merlin struck his staff against the floor. "Your women are in danger. I withdraw my protection." He struck the floor again for effect.

Comprehension was easy, but neither Loathel nor Trill bothered to voice their opinions. Instead, they raced to the rack. Loathel sliced the ropes holding Christif's hands, while Trill attacked the ones at his feet. Together, they lifted him and made their escape. Jalen wrapped his arms about his father's middle and Imani fell in step behind the men. Only Merlin remained where he stood.

They were at the door when the defunct Lephan contorted. His body broke apart and a dismal blackness emitted from him. It curled and knotted into itself, then burst into a flame of blackfire. The demon soul of Maldonus was free and in need of a new home. It ricocheted off the walls with such a force the foundation shook and, in some places, gave way.

The moving party cleared the entrance, leaving Merlin to battle the demon alone.

CHAPTER XLVII

Carrying Christif was cumbersome, but they moved as fast as they could under the burden. Heat was everywhere, as were the screams of the dying. Heedless of the pandemonium around them, they pushed on. By now, the conflagration had reached an unchecked extreme. The walls, in some places, had begun to melt. Pools of molten lava puddled and glowed throughout the corridors.

***

"Uh oh."

Honor, Annora, and Travon sat back-to-back-to-back, resting against one another. They turned to see what Travon saw. He'd noticed a spot near his foot, where a small opening in the clear white had appeared. They watched it expand, revealing a patch of hard ground with no protection covering it.

***

A disturbance in the foundation vibrated throughout the courtyard, bringing the already dwindling battle to an abrupt end. Those still alive had to focus on keeping their footing. A tower caved in. Large stones— some blazing—crumbled and crashed to the ground, adding to the commotion.

To see the mighty fortress in such a state struck fear into the hearts of those watching. The combatants forgot the fight and fled in madness and terror.

***

The ball of protection disappeared, but no enemy remained to see. Annora, Honor, and Travon looked about, dumbstruck by the total devastation.

"Hellfire." In his awe, Travon named the sight before them. It did not occur to him that he started it.

The woman went toward the forlorn castle, summoned by the irresistible call of the age-old bond connecting them to the warriors within.

Travon dragged behind. "Hey, you guys. I don't think this is a good idea. I'm not going in there."

"*Neither are you, Milady.*"

"*At least one of Christif's offspring exercises intelligence.*"

The women halted, smiling at the air.

"So what are you saying, Lowell?"

Travon stopped, stared at Honor, and then took a step back.

"*Run.*"

"What?"

"I didn't say nothing." He backed up another step.

"*RUN!*"

On the tip of his warning, Loathel, Jalen, Trill, and Imani burst forth, cutting through the rubble lying about the castle entrance. The men carried Christif, and they ran as hard as they could under the weight. Annora, Honor, and Travon fell in step and they cleared the castle gates, racing toward the nearby forest.

No one barred their way. Nothing pursued them, but they did not halt or slow down. Even when they reached the semi-shelter of the dead trees, they kept going. Using his senses, Loathel led them through the maze of wood until at last, the shoreline came into view.

Cautiously, they lay Christif down. Ever tireless, Loathel immediately set off, running parallel to the water's edge. Trill bent low over his uncle, waving his hand and murmuring sounds of soothing in his native tongue.

Loathel's serenity aided him as he worked. It enveloped the travelers where they waited.

"Is my daddy dead?"

"No, my cousin," Trill smiled at Travon's obvious relief. "Your father is in Narlopami. A deep sleep. A healing sleep."

"Did you put him there?"

"Yea, I did, lad. That was my part."

Annora was standing near. Unruffled, she awaited an explanation for the loss of her voice.

"*We know not the circumstance of Medrid. It is best not to speak of him.*"

"What did you say, Aunt Nora?" Travon asked from within his mother's embrace.

"I was wondering what we were going to do now."

"We wait for Loathel's return. With diligence, he will procure the means of our escape," Trill said.

"Where did he go, anyway?" Honor studied the direction he had taken.

"Why don't you ask him?"

She didn't have time to respond before the answer was in her head.

"*I am searching for a water vessel.*"

"*Are you alright? I haven't talked to you or anything.*"

"*I am well, as are you. Were it not the truth, I would know it.*"

"*You are so arrogant.*"

"*I am also correct.*"

"*Why did it feel like I was on fire?*"

"*At the time, fire had been rained upon me. I stood in the midst of the blaze.*"

"*I'm sorry I asked. Feel free not to tell me anymore. It doesn't sound like something I need to know.*"

"*As you wish, Mistress. I should not like to dwell upon it yet, anyway. I would ask for your thoughts to remain with me. I desire nothing so highly as your company.*"

Trill and Jalen kept vigil. The others rested.

"*Thank you, Cousin.*"

"*Thanks for what?*" Jalen leaned on his sword.

"*You bested Maldonus.*"

"I didn't—"

"Yea, you did. You held him occupied while I recovered. You kept his stolen abilities limited."

"I..."

"You weakened him and added your strength to mine. 'Tis a gift I have only received from Yaunt."

Jalen had no words.

"That was your part. And I thank you."

"We thank you," Lothel added his gratitude.

As the first twinkling of twilight made them nervous, a boat appeared in the distance. The fairness of the Elve stood out against the evening shadows. He manned an intricately designed rowboat of Darqueon origin. It was large enough to carry the group. Beaching it, he tossed the rope to Trill. "Hurry, night approaches. We do not want to be here when the Kildar arrive."

He, Trill, and Jalen went about loading the still unconscious Christif. They laid him against the floorboards. Travon and the women settled in around him.

"Shouldn't we wait for Mr. Merlin?" Travon looked to see if the wizard was coming.

"Nay, my cousin, we cannot."

"Why not? Is he dead?"

"We do not know if Medrid has passed from this realm. We should not grieve for that which we are not yet certain. I did not wish to address it now, but the death of Medrid is not the worse fate that could befall him. A Lephan may experience many deaths before he enters the next realm."

"If the choice is his and Medrid does not accept his doom," Loathel said, "he could become a foe worse than Maldonus."

Honor noticed something under the seat. "What's this doing here?" She reached for her bag. The last she had seen it, they had left it full of food for her parents and Jalen.

"It went swimming," Jalen said. "Maybe it was floating around and somebody picked it up."

"And filled it with nuts and some plants and stuff. Is it edible?" She showed the contents to Loathel.

"Yes, Mistress, it is all edible. Placed there, no doubt, by the others."

"Others? What others?" Honor asked, but all the Lossmans were curious.

"There are other Mayadalians here. They travel with evanescent as well."

Jalen, Annora, and Imani all had similar reactions.

"Are you serious?"

"Really?"

"Here?"

Honor didn't comment. She had a thought, and there was only one way to find out. She sent her friend Kourtney a text.

"*Eyise and Balazze are here.*" Loathel shared the news with Trill.

"*Let us hope Medrid is strong and the others are fast.*"

"*Let us hope,*" the Elve said. "*I do not wish to return.*"

They didn't speak about it again. The group was somber, sailing away from the shores of Alpravage with the night closing in around them. Being fortunate enough to have the current to aid their flight, they guided the boat in shifts.

By the time the first blue-gray streaks of day broke through the darkness, the harsh sea had taken them to a steadily flowing but tranquil river. All about them, the land was lush and growing. The dead lands were far beyond the horizon.

***

Eden. To the Lossmans, this place equated every story, description, and imagery of the first garden. It was full of splendor and breathtaking magnificence.

Loathel answered the unspoken but obvious question. "We are in Zendelel still. The land of sleep contains more than Queon and Kildar. Many dreams are full of majesty."

They sailed past exotic animal life and foliage. They watched, spellbound, as here and there people-like creatures splashed and played along the banks of the river. If it puzzled them to see travelers, it did not show. A few waved as they passed, but most continued in his or her activity, uninterested in the boat or its occupants.

At length, they could feel the pull of a waterfall and needed to disembark. They beached on the far bank and marched inland with

Christif in tow. Their destination was unknown to all, save Loathel and Trill.

They had not traveled far when they halted, a sudden, grating voice making them stop. "Return to the river. The gate is open for you." Before them appeared a tall hooded figure. He was cloaked in black, covered so his features were not visible. He was commanding, frightening to look at, and out of place surrounded by such beauty. He did not seem to see them but rather through them, as if he were aware of each of their thoughts. As formidable as he was, he offered no threat but waited for their response.

"Where will the gate lead us?" Trill asked the dark figure.

"Do not question me. The gate will not lead, nor does it follow. It will offer you passage and little else."

Trill tried not to smile at the reprimand. "Will you accompany us through this passage you have provided?"

"Nay. Now is not my time. Many lost things need to be reclaimed."

"We will await your coming with anticipation," Loathel told the stranger.

"I would caution you to lend balance to your anticipation. You do not yet know for what you wait. Grief may be your reward."

"Joyful or grievous, your coming will remain an eager anticipation." The Elve did smile.

"More the fool, you." The next instant, he was gone.

"Whoa," Jalen said. "Who was that?"

"*Lackwit.*"

CHAPTER XLVIII

A bright light hovered over the water's edge. As before, Loathel leapt through to wait at the receiving end. Jalen passed through next, holding to his father, keeping Christif's weight balanced during the transfer from Trill's support to Loathel's. Trill handed Honor, Imani, and Travon through before holding his hand out to Annora.

She shook her head. Offering him a smile to rival Loathel's brightness, she jumped into his outstretched arms and kissed him soundly as they disappeared through the light.

***

Streetlights. Paved sidewalks. Storefronts. Roads. Although they'd seen it a million times, Harpers Ferry felt foreign. No more was the untouched beauty of Zendelel. Gone was the stillness they had grown accustomed to. They were back to civilization. They were home.

The predawn hours cloaked their coming. There was no one about to bear witness to their arrival. The general sentiment was relief mixed with uncertainty. What were they to do now? Was it over? It felt surreal. Did it actually happen?

The proof stood with the two imposing fighters from another realm and the comatose Christif whom they held. And more substantial was Jalen: Strong set jaw, new muscles, the sword hanging naturally at his side. The change in him, total and palpable.

"Madame, have you a guess as to your vehicle's location?" Trill brought them into focus.

"I don't know." Imani looked first in one direction, then another.

"It's up there." Honor pointed to the parking lot beside the hillside church. "Who moved it?" They didn't ponder the question but piled into the SUV—no baggage, one trip—and raced for home.

***

Five minutes into the cramped ride, both Honor and Jalen jumped, startled. Their phones made a combination of wacky noises. There was shifting and swift tapping of buttons before the silence.

"Loathel," Honor gasped.

Jalen burst out laughing.

More buttons, followed by greater gasps and deeper laughter. Jalen delighted in Honor's horror. It was not because of their psychic connection, but their joined cell phone plan.

Jalen cleared his throat. "There seems to be a bit of a problem here."

"I can read, Jalen," Honor said through gritted teeth.

"Not talking to you." He snickered. "Let me see." He scrolled through the information on his phone. "Our lack of an international data plan did not stop someone—not my line—from talking, texting, racking up roaming fees... A lot of roaming fees... Several hundred—"

"Yes, Jalen," Honor talked over him.

He wasn't discouraged. "Not only that..." he scrolled through screens of information. "Somebody—not my line—ignored the subscription and purchased in-di-vid-ually seven hundred and eighty-two songs from iTunes. We're talking anywhere from ninety-nine to two ninety-nine a pop. We're also streaming from two...no, three new services we're paying for." Jalen grinned at Honor.

"Your music is rich and full," Loathel said. "I enjoy the variety."

"I noticed." Honor glared at him. "Who were you talking to?"

"The evanescent have much to speak about."

"You didn't need to listen."

"Dad is going to kill you." Jalen snapped Honor's picture.

"Yep," Travon said. "And take her phone away, forever."

"No, he's not. He's gonna kill Loathel, 'cause I didn't do it."

Loathel and Trill exchanged curious glances.

Trill said, "Christif is not yet awake and certainly no threat to Loathel."

"Trust me." Honor clicked her phone off and handed it to Loathel. She wanted nothing to do with the incriminating evidence. "You are so dead."

***

A brief trip to Mayadal left Christif in Talazim's healing hands. A week later, he was strong enough to finish his healing at home. He was himself but no longer himself. His abilities were gone. The Jodian was purged of the corruption caused by his association with Maldonus. As a result, there was nothing left of him which was not inferior and fully human. Chris was grateful. He caused so much trouble, so much turmoil, yet he would pass into the first realm. He would live out his days as an evanescent, with one life and one family to dedicate it to. Imani never lost faith in him. He would need a lifetime to repay her for her unwavering fidelity. He was grateful to everyone for everything. For his family, for his friends, for his life.

***

Chris' healing brought the time for parting to the Lossman household. Jalen and Annora would return to Mayadal with Loathel and Trill. Jalen, because he needed formal training and continued protection. They had no way of knowing if Maldonus could return. Also, until they were positive he could withstand the enticements that ensnared his father, Jalen would be kept away from the fourth realm and its perversions.

Annora had no choice but to go with Trill. She had no desire to be anywhere without him. She would miss her family but was filled with hope and love. This was her destiny. She embraced it.

For Loathel and Honor, time ran out. Of all the things they endured, this was the absolute worst. It felt like hell, and they hated it. The end had come for them. Honor gave her goodbyes to Jalen, Annora, and Trill. Loathel said farewell to Chris, Imani, and Travon. Afterwards, he led her into the backyard, away from everyone. His last moments, his last remarks, were for her alone.

"What would you have me do? Tell me?" The voice, usually full of tranquility, was overwhelmed with anguish. "Shall I do what I want though 'twould be wrong?" He held her hands. "I would, were it not for the lessons we have learned. Should I love you less? It would be easier for me to cast down the sun than to lower my passion by even one degree."

Each word he spoke called forth a tear. Honor let them slide down her face unchecked.

"I would stand against any foe to have you, yet I cannot conquer myself." He reached up to trace the silvery wetness upon her cheek. "I cannot conquer myself." This time it was a whisper, his heart broken.

"Why can't I be with you?" She sobbed. "I know we should be together."

He pulled her close, enveloping her.

"I want to be with you."

Each word she spoke called forth a tear. Loathel's translucent blue eyes became a blue-black storm, brimming with emotion.

"It is my duty to place your needs above all else, above my desire—"

"I need you—"

"You need not what I would bring to you—"

"We don't know that. I'm willing to take a chance—"

"I am not."

"Loathel, I love you."

In answer to her declaration, he lowered his head and claimed her mouth with fierce, demanding force, consuming her spirit. He placed all he was into that kiss, into her. They passed thoughts of desire back and forth between them as they clung to one another. When they were out of words, they held on. When they were out of breath, they held on. Only when they were out of hope did he release her.

"I love you, Honor, above all else. Because I love you, I willingly damn myself." His form shimmered.

Her arms were around him and she held on tight against the feel of him dissolving beneath her fingertips. A flash of color, then he was gone, and she was alone.

"You damn us both," she whispered into the silence.

CHAPTER XLIX

The passing months brought a myriad of changes to the Lossmans. The remaining family had to relocate. Where people knew them, Jalen's disappearance raised too many questions. Imani and Chris grew more in love with life and each other. If there were any lasting effects on Travon, it was only his love for swords and fire. Encouraged by his mother, he took up archery for good measure.

Honor walked through life in a zombie-like state, part of her never fully there. She made new friends and socialized, but an important piece of herself was missing. She could still feel him, or at least she thought so. Sometimes it was as if he were right there, behind her or just ahead, close enough to touch but always out of reach. Many nights, she would awaken with the overwhelming sensation of his presence in her room. She would wait for him to appear, aching to hear him speak. She learned to harden her heart against the tears when dawn would come, but he never did. After a while, his visits ceased, and she could feel nothing but a painful void.

***

There was substantial fear in Aezilden. All of Mayadal worried. Loathel was dying. He was struck by grief so tremendous his immortality dwindled. Soon, he would be beyond recovery. He spent his days alone, with little conversation for anyone other than Trill or Jalen. Clouded over by sadness, his eyes lost their translucent quality. He seldom smiled, he never sang. His peace was gone. At first, he comforted himself by visiting Honor. Unseen, he watched her. He basked in her presence until a meeting of the

Kelmaragin Council put an end to his trespassing. They forbade him to travel to the fourth realm unless it was to collect his bride.

The council's decision drained him of his desire to exist. For him it was basic: If Honor could not be in his future, he did not want a future. He had lived over four thousand years already. Before, he didn't have emotions. But he had them now. Without his fullness, without Honor, he could not continue.

***

It was the darkest night Honor could remember. The eclipsed moon was no more than a shadow hovering above the trees. A storm was coming. The air was charged with expectation. Honor sat in her window watching, waiting. It had been a year since those bizarre events brought Loathel into and out of her life. She believed the anniversary would not pass uneventful, so she waited. All day she waited. Afternoon was chased by evening and now night had come. Honor did not waiver. She knew something was going to happen because she willed it to happen.

Overcome with daydreams, she dozed off and was unaware of his appearance. She awoke to the sound of her phone going nuts. A zillion pictures and messages were being shared. She realized she was not alone. "Hey!" One leap brought her into his outstretched arms. "I'm so glad to see you. How long have you been here?"

"Long enough to know you snore, cousin."

"I do not."

"Yea, you do. Be comforted, so does your aunt."

"I doubt she'll appreciate your overshare."

"Because it is you, all will be forgiven."

"How is Aunt Nora?"

"Perfect, save for missing you all. She wishes you could see the children."

"Children?"

"Mirror children. Boys. She is with child now." He beamed with pride. "She sends her love. Jalen conveys greetings also." He held up her brother's phone. "He said it knows what to do."

"It's doing it," she laughed. "You have to tell me everything. Come on. We've got to wake the others. They'll kill me if we don't." She took an excited step toward her bedroom door.

"Wait. What I would say is for your heart alone."

She paused. "Loathel..."

"I am here because I could do no other. If I am wrong, you must forgive my trespass. However, I believe I am right to suspect you are without knowledge and should be told."

She remained silent, her heart pounding.

"Loathel's time is short. It may already be too late."

"Too late for what?"

"He is dying."

"WHAT? How? Why?"

"Because of you."

"Excuse me?"

"In the days since our parting, you have not called to him. Because of this, his life diminishes."

"What the hel-lo? What are you talking about?"

"He will not live without you. He cannot come unless you call. Without your initiative, he is doomed."

"Umm, how come I didn't know any of this?"

"We are speaking of Loathel. You did not know because he did not wish for you to know. There is none in Mayadal with the will to oppose him."

Honor giggled, recognizing Loathel's crafty style. "Wait a minute." She sobered. "He is in trouble and everybody is so scared of him, nobody will do anything to help the fool. I don't know who's worse, you, Loathel, or the entire population of Mayadal."

"I am here."

"Barely. Oh, wait until I get my hands on that...that...pixie. I am going to wring his neck until his ears fall off." She paced around the room. "I cannot believe that...too-tall-toymaker..." She hadn't had a good rant or called him names in ages. She got into it. "He could have said something...Overgrown Leprechaun...Mr. Spock...Tooth Fairy wannabe... What?" She stopped in front of Trill feeling more like herself.

"Do you understand why he has chosen this end?"

"Because he's an idiot. A self-absorbed idiot. And...and why isn't he here?"

"He has been here many times."

"I never saw him."

"You knew he was here."

"Yeah, well, I never saw him."

Trill did not comment.

"Why did he stop coming?"

"The council forbade his trespass. They are justly fearful. This is the house of Christif. A reminder of what frequent visits to the fourth realm can do to those who do not belong."

"Sorry, but we're talking about Loathel, not Daddy."

"Before the fall of Christif, no one thought he would fall."

"Uh-uh, not the same thing at all. Not Loathel." She reached for a ponytail holder. Earlier, she had been playing with her hair, but now she was about business and needed it out of her way. "It amazes me they would consider Loathel in the same category as...anybody. Isn't his father in charge?"

"He is."

"He should know better. Hey. Why didn't the council forbid you? You're a blood relative."

"Without the blessing of Triune, we are all forbidden. Especially me."

"How did you get to come?"

"I did not seek the council's permission."

"Trill. Ooooh. Since when did you become a rebel?"

"Since we are speaking of Loathel. I do not doubt I shall be called before the council when I return."

"So what do I need to do? Call him and tell him what?"

"Your life and his are connected. Loathel has chosen his fate. Now you must choose yours. I would caution you to think it through." The shimmering light came with his last syllables. Honor got her goodbye out just before he disappeared.

She took a moment to reflect on the strangeness of his visit and then grinned. She could do strange. Strange felt good. It was nice to feel good. Honor padded down the hall to her parents' room. "Think it through," she repeated Trill's advice. "Yeah, right. Like I have time for that. Mom..."

CHAPTER L

In the time it took Imani to rouse herself enough to come downstairs, Honor made coffee, pulled out the cookies, and scrolled through her camera roll.

"What's going on sweetheart?"

"Trill was here." Honor fished through the cookie jar, seeking one with a lot of chocolate chips.

"He was? Is Jalen all right? Annora?"

"Fine, both of them said hello. Aunt Nora is pregnant and they already have twins." She held a cookie up for inspection.

"Impressive."

"Jalen sent pictures." Honor slid her phone across the table.

"Aww," Imani smiled at the babies. She set the phone aside to focus on her daughter. "Why didn't Trill stay? You should have gotten us up."

"I know." She said with her mouth full. "He wasn't supposed to be here, but he needed to talk to me."

"What's wrong with Loathel?"

"Nothing." She swallowed and searched for another cookie. "Except he's dying."

"What? Dying?"

"Yeah."

"He's an Elve. They're immortal."

"Certain things can take them out. Like fighting, heartbreak, being stubborn." A second cookie passed inspection.

"He's dying because of you?"

"He's dying because of him. He's stubborn." Honor sighed. "It's the whole joined thing. If we aren't together, he can't survive."

Imani, being less picky than Honor, helped herself to a handful of cookies, unmindful of the number of chocolate chips each one contained. "I never understood why he didn't want to be with you. It was obvious you two were in love."

"We *are* in love, Mom." Her tone was the firmest she had ever taken with her mother. "We aren't together because he loves me."

"Explanation please."

Honor released another sigh and slid the cookie jar out of her reach, her interest in snacking gone. "If Loathel and I join, formally join, I could become part Elven."

"That sounds like a good thing." Imani sipped her coffee.

"It is while I'm alive. It's when I die the problems come."

"Excuse me?"

"Elves don't get into heaven. No Empyrean for them. If I'm half-Elven, I'm screwed. Half of me won't live forever and the other half can't pass into the first realm. I could end up in Zendelel or Hell or lost in space or who knows what. The thing is, it would be for eternity and that's a long time to be...I don't know what I would be. A ghost, maybe."

"Oh, dear."

"Mmmhmm."

"You're handling it well."

"Unlike you, I've had an entire year to think about it."

"I'm going to miss you."

"I haven't told you my decision yet."

"And your decision is?"

"I'm going."

"Call me Captain Obvious."

"Don't try to be witty; you don't know how. The question is, is it the right decision?"

"It is."

"How can you be sure? You haven't thought about it."

"What's to think about? Look at you. Your hair. Your eyes. You are your father's daughter, Jodian girl. You and Loathel belong together. The whole joining thing would not have happened if you weren't made for each other. What happens after is a problem for after. You live and love in the now."

Honor's eyes glossed over. The truth was beautiful.

"I wish you would have talked to me sooner. You two are full of nonsense."

"He is."

"I note you are here instead of up there telling him what he's full of."

"Aren't you supposed to be sad? I am leaving, you know." Honor went back to her chocolate chip search.

"I'm sure I will be later. I can't be sad when I'm so happy for you. I know you're doing the right thing." She went back to looking at pictures.

"I know. I'm happier now than I've been in...in a year."

"You don't say?"

"Don't do sarcasm either. You suck at it."

"Do I?" Imani liked the idea of sucking at sarcasm.

"Yes. But I love you anyway."

"I love you, too."

***

Honor stood in the backyard, contemplating how to call her long-lost Elve. "Loathel," she whispered into the night air. It didn't feel right. She tried it again, this time a little louder. "Loathel...Loathel come here." And louder still. "Loathel, SON OF TALAZIM, COME TO ME." *Oh, where are you Lowell? I need you*, she whined. *Don't you dare die on me!*

***

Trill sat by Loathel's bedside talking with Jalen and Talazim. The sleeping Elve awakened. As a unit, they turned to see him sit upright, fully conscious. He focused intently on something they could not see or feel. A light that had not been in his eyes sparkled.

He steadied his gaze on Trill and said, "You interfered."

"Yea. I did."

The last thing they saw before the flash of color took him away was his bright Elven smile.

***

Imani and Chris peeked at Honor from their bedroom window, trying not to give themselves away. Travon had no such qualms. He called down from his own window, "Hey, Honor, you're going to wake up the whole neighborhood. He can't hear you like that. The head thing is better."

"Shut up, you freaky little gnome. You're going to wake up Mom and Dad."

"They're already awake. Who could sleep with all that racket? Ask Dad, he'll tell you how to call Loathel *quietly*. I don't know why you don't do it in your head."

"I don't know why I haven't locked you in the basement, an oversight I intend to correct."

"*He is accurate. The head thing is better.*"

Honor spun in a circle, coming to rest in Loathel's arms. Before anything could be said, any greetings exchanged, Loathel pulled Honor to himself. He locked her in a blazing, all-consuming, passion-laden, soul-bonding kiss that was filled with the agony of separation and the ecstasy of finally being together, finally becoming one. But he did not stop there. While their lips were fused, he made his pledge to her mind, to her heart. "*Honor, tTlEe uURo ztT RpEejJjpoqVqV. tTlEe xuUNo KIzo hI zo uUpL aA uUz pIQ QxIjJjo. aA qVxuUjJj fFo QaIhx tTlEe. RpIB aA uUz tTlEeBqV, aARp tTlEe QaAjJj xuUno zo.*" (*Honor, you are my fullness. You have come to me and I am now whole. I shall be with you. For I am yours, if you will have me.*) He whispered soft words into her mouth. "Say yes. Yes. I will allow you no voice. Except to say...yes."

"Yes. Yes. I love you, Lowell. Yes! Don't you ever leave me again."

Only then did he release her tenderly bruised mouth. "Never, love. Forgive me what I have done, what I will do to you. I am selfish. Selfish and glad of it. I cannot be without you, I cannot—"

"You'd better not be without me." She pulled him to her.

EPILOGUE

Loathel and Honor's joining was celebrated across Mayadal. It was a hallmark event. No Elve had waited as long to receive his fullness. It ushered in a time of lasting happiness and peace. The Jodian blood in Honor was strong and by the banks of Aezilden her life spanned many millennia. She and Loathel enjoyed numerous generations of descendants.

Honor outlived all the Lossmans and several years after the passing of Trill and Annora's great grandchildren, she too passed from the second realm. Loathel grieved for her, but with it came a sense of comfort. Without knowing how or why, he understood his time was also nearing its end. It was his hope wherever Honor's life resumed, there he would be as well.

***

The day was clear and tranquil, not too hot or cold, perfect. Loathel wandered through the woods, gazing up at the emerald green leaves that reminded him of his beloved. He climbed to the top of his favorite: The one in which he spent many hours sitting amongst the branches with Honor in his arms. There, they would talk and laugh and dream. That was back when they had a future and not merely a past. He sighed reflectively, letting his mind drift, as it often did, to Honor.

Sleep began to overtake him...

"Put me down, you disproportioned fairy!"

He was often tired these days...
"Say it with me: Personal. Space. It's not that hard."

Loathel took a deep breath...
"Go away you, you annoying little fairytale reject."

Then another...
"Loathel, I love you."

And then his last.

***

One short breath, then another, and then the deep cleansing breath of new life. Loathel inhaled and looked about him. He was standing, although he did not remember coming to his feet. A light that was bright even to him surrounded him. It also emitted from him. Loathel wondered at the purity he felt and was.

"Lowell."

All was forgotten when the heard her voice. "Honor?" No dream had ever been so real. "Honor!" They crashed into and crushed one another. "If I have fallen into a dream, I pray you, do not awaken me. Do not awaken me."

Honor led him forward to be greeted by Trill and Annora. Jalen and Travon came toward him, followed by Imani and Christif. Yaunt worked his way through the descendants of Jodian. They crowded around to welcome the Elve who had been such a big part of their existence.

Joy upon joy was heaped on him. Amid the exultation, a question came to Loathel. Honor supplied the answer as he thought of it.

"Yes, Lowell, Empyrean. We had it backwards. I didn't take on your Elven immortality. You received my mortality. The plan was to welcome you back to Triune. You, Bright Elve, are the first of your kind to be received into the first realm. Because you were not willing to risk me losing heaven, you have gained it. And not only you, but all in our line who so choose will inherit mortality."

Together with their family, friends, and the host of heaven, they delighted in the coming of the Elve and the wisdom of Triune.

ABOUT THE AUTHOR

Made entirely of rum and snacks—International Bestselling Author, Tracy A. Ball, is a native Baltimorean and veteran West Virginian, whose family is a mashup of cultures. She writes real and raw interracial romance with an intensity that burns because she has been busting stereotypes while teaching interracial/generational healing for more than a quarter of a century.

Tracy engages with folks from every twist of fate and all manner of experience. She has hung out with murderers and dined with people who have dined with the Pope, which is why she needs the rum...and a nap.

Her published works include: *Blood Like Rain*, *The Other Shore*, "*Mercury Chain Thomson*" *If By Chance: A Shorts collection*, *Welcome to BBs*, *Death's Desire*, *Big Guns & Bullsh@t*, "*Imogene's Flowers*," "*Thorns*," "*Black's Magic*" "*Truly, Madly, Kiss Me*," "*Cumberland Christmas*," *Civil*

Warriors, Dragonfly Dreams, KAYOS: The Bad & The Worse, The Tiger & The Snake, The Right Way to Be Wrong, Mail Duty, White Russian Lies, Swords & Cell Phones.

* * *

Find and Follow Tracy

https://mailchi.mp/dcc40b02b5e6/ball-books
https://www.amazon.com/Tracy-A.-
Ball/e/B00JH7R8XY/ref=ntt_dp_epwbk_0
https://www.facebook.com/groups/601509103800290/625996514684882/
? https://www.facebook.com/Tra3Ball/ tra3ball@gmail.com
https://www.bookbub.com/profile/tracy-a-ball
https://twitter.com/Tra3ballA
https://www.goodreads.com/author/show/3171920.Tracy_A_Ball
https://tracyaball.wordpress.com

NOTE FROM THE AUTHOR

Word-of-mouth is crucial for any author to succeed. If you enjoyed *Swords & Cell Phones*, please leave a review online—anywhere you are able. Even if it's just a sentence or two. It would make all the difference and would be very much appreciated.

Thanks!
Tracy A. Ball

We hope you enjoyed reading this title from:

BLACK ❀ ROSE
writing™

www.blackrosewriting.com

Subscribe to our mailing list – *The Rosevine* – and receive **FREE** books,
daily deals, and stay current with news about upcoming
releases and our hottest authors.
Scan the QR code below to sign up.

Already a subscriber? Please accept a sincere thank you for being a fan of
Black Rose Writing authors.

View other Black Rose Writing titles at
www.blackrosewriting.com/books and use promo code
PRINT to receive a **20% discount** when purchasing.